ADVANCE PRAISE FOR

The Convention of Wives

"In a story that spans centuries and crosses continents, Debra Green weaves a complex tale of family secrets, love, loss, and redemption."

—SUSAN SCHOENBERGER,
author of *The Liability of Love*

"If you love historical fiction, family sagas, women's friendships—and a juicy secret or two to tie them all together then *The Convention of Wives* is the book for you!"

—ALINA ADAMS,
author of *The Nesting Dolls*

"Debra Green's skillfully braided story of two families, several generations, love, marriage, friendship, and a medical mystery makes for a thoroughly entertaining and oh-so-satisfying read."

—DEBORAH K. SHEPHERD,
author of *So Happy Together*

"*The Convention of Wives* is a captivating story about friendship, marriage and survival, but also opens our eyes to the impact of genetic disease and emerging treatments. A delightful and timely read!"

—KAREN A. GRINZAID, MS, CGC, Assistant Professor,
Executive Director of JScreen at Emory University

"Debra Green is a wonderful storyteller, and her sweeping tale of family secrets had me turning pages from beginning to end. Green masterfully moves the narrative back and forth in time and place, weaving together the lives of Dina's Jewish ancestors and Julia's Christian heritage to remind the reader that long-hidden family trauma still lives and breathes in each of us. A gripping family saga."

—MALLY BECKER,
author of *The Turncoat's Widow*

"In her compelling debut, Debra Green explores how our emotional and physical DNA shapes who we are. This multi-generational tale braids together myriad elements including a fresh narrative about Jewish history in Barbados and an unflinching portrait of contemporary suburban life. The Convention of Wives reads like a mystery, along with the depth and heart to convey the human capacity to transcend the most devastating family traumas."

— MICHELLE BRAFMAN,
author of *Washing the Dead*

". . . compelling and enjoyable. . . . Any reader interested in the science of genetic diseases and forensic paternalism will find this book intriguing."

—BARRY ROSENBLOOM, MD, Clinical Professor
of Medicine, Cedars-Sinai Medical Center

The Convention
of Wives

Rienate
All good things
in life a love!
Debra Green

The Convention of Wives

A Novel

Debra Green

SHE WRITES PRESS

Published 2022

Printed in the United States of America

Print ISBN: 978-1-64742-241-7
E-ISBN: 978-1-64742-242-4
Library of Congress Control Number: 2022903965

For information, address:
She Writes Press
1569 Solano Ave #546
Berkeley, CA 94707

She Writes Press is a division of SparkPoint Studio, LLC.

For my beautiful family

Inspiration for women from our foremother Dinah—

the strength to break societal expectations

and the heart to befriend other women.

—SIMCHAT BAT CEREMONY,
Reconstructionist Rabbinical College

Dina and Rob's Family Tree

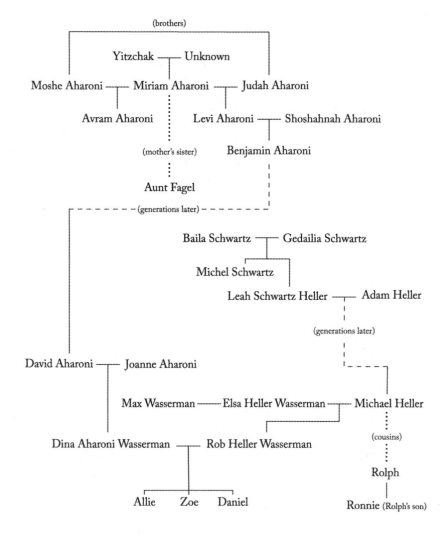

Julia and John's Family Tree

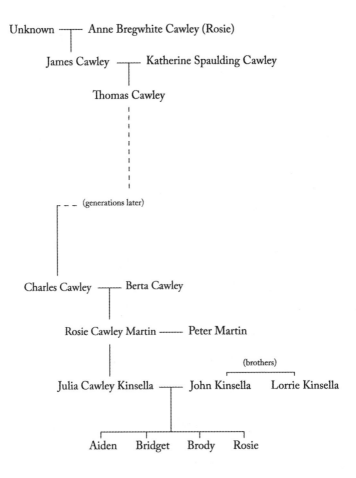

Unknown ── Anne Bregwhite Cawley (Rosie)

James Cawley ── Katherine Spaulding Cawley

Thomas Cawley

(generations later)

Charles Cawley ── Berta Cawley

Rosie Cawley Martin ──── Peter Martin

(brothers)

Julia Cawley Kinsella ── John Kinsella   Lorrie Kinsella

Aiden   Bridget   Brody   Rosie

Chapter One

Dina Aharoni Wasserman

Millburn, New Jersey, October 1978

Dina knew she should have changed out of her sweatpants, but they were the only comfortable bottoms that fit over her still swollen abdomen. The facial mask she wore—a dark sea green—complemented her auburn hair rubber-banded high up on her head. Rob's athletic socks and a sexy silk pajama top with matching circular stains, one over each nipple, completed her outfit. She reached to pick up a box of tissues and caught a glimpse of herself in the mirror. *How lucky he is to have me.*

She headed down the hallway to check on the children. Allie, four, was in the bottom of her bunk bed sleeping in her usual pose, one leg under the other poking out from the covers. Two-year-old Zoe lay on the other side of the room in a small daybed that had recently been converted from crib number one. She sucked her thumb contentedly, snuggled in with the ten or so stuffed animals she refused to sleep without. Dina sighed, feeling truly blessed.

Daniel, two months, lay peacefully next door. She was tempted to pick him up, physically drawn to this little drooling being by an invisible thread. Instead, figuring she had at least an hour before his crying summoned her, she headed back to her room and the Halloween catalogs on her bed. Allie wanted to be a superhero and Zoe, a ballerina. A funky bib would do for Daniel. Maybe some colorful socks.

Dina walked into the bedroom where she tripped over a paint can. "Shit!" she yelled, limping by the half-finished wall, the stepladder, and brushes corralled on a drop cloth in the corner of the room. She had abandoned the project when her water broke. It remained abandoned because Dina couldn't seem to meet everyone's needs. At least not fast enough. What crazy person moved to a new town, knowing no one, a month before she was scheduled to give birth? New house. New preschools. New pediatrician. New baby.

Rob couldn't stand disorder, but Dina took pleasure watching the expression on his face each time he saw the mess. Perhaps she left it like this to annoy him. She *probably* left it like this to annoy him. Everything about the last month or so confirmed it. She'd barely made him a meal and would forget to give him his phone messages. She kept putting his undershirts in the dryer and they kept shrinking. He noticed. She still did it.

On her bed next to the Halloween catalogs sat the unfinished letter she'd written in response to an article in the local paper about the joys of motherhood. She was annoyed by the piece, a fluffy take on maternal fulfilment and marital bliss. The response she'd drafted, knee-deep in diapers and postpartum haze, attempted to keep sarcasm to a minimum while defining "joy" in more realistic terms. But the jokes fell flat, and the tone seemed downright resentful. Was this the impression she wished to make in her new community?

Dina had wanted to write stories for as long as she could remember. Her first efforts were in grade school when she described the magic of her family's Shabbos candlesticks. She knew the objects were special because she and her brothers weren't allowed near them. On Friday nights, the light from the candles reflected off their silver-and-lapis holders, making the ceiling dance. She'd questioned her father more than once about where they had come from.

"Someone had to make them. Who, Daddy?" Dina had asked, fighting off sleep in her pink Dr. Denton's.

"I don't know; they've been in the family for a long time, since before anyone can remember."

One night, when Dina asked about the candlesticks yet again, her father shook his head. "Sweetie," he said, "why don't you tell me where you think they came from?"

And so began Dina's nightly account of the origin of the candlesticks. Her father's *oohs* and *ahs* encouraged her to come up with more and more outrageous stories. Sometimes the tales stretched on for a few nights as she added detail after detail.

"The candlesticks were the magic lights of a witch who lived in a forest made of silver trees."

"The candlesticks were stolen from the Spanish king and queen and brought by Columbus when he sailed to America." When her father laughed at this explanation, Dina admonished him. "We learned in Hebrew school that Columbus was Jewish. It makes sense." She remembered how he had smiled.

Dina's father hugged her tightly when she showed him the A she had received for her illustrated collection of candlestick stories. Those third-grade papers, held together with brass fasteners, now lay next to her moth-eaten baby blanket in a box in the attic.

Over time, her father's interest in her writing waned, as did his interest in his daughter. At least that's how it seemed. It was around Dina's tenth birthday when the focus shifted to her older brothers. She'd come home with a new tale about how the candlesticks were made from metal and stone mined in a mountain in the Alps, but her father barely looked up from the table. Helping the boys with their homework had become the thing; that and discussing their sports teams.

The Convention of Wives

That was a lifetime ago.

The letter to the newspaper was a mistake, a waste of time. She crumpled the draft of the article she'd written and headed to the kitchen. The sample of formula she'd squirreled away on the day she'd come home from the hospital peeked out from behind a jar of peanut butter. Formula—the ultimate sin of motherhood. One of many, it seemed.

She grabbed a few sugar snap peas and some Nestlé chocolate chips for good measure. Back in her bedroom, she pulled out the latest *Cosmopolitan* from her secret stash in the bottom drawer. Tugging the basket of laundry toward her, she picked up the TV remote and put on *Three's Company*. She alternated between watching the show and skimming the magazine, all the while folding laundry. No need to look to know which garment she had picked up.

Dina glanced over at Rob's empty side of the bed and the "Best Doctor" figurine on his nightstand, a Father's Day gift from her parents. The body was exaggeratedly tall and lean and held a golf club in its left hand. It closely resembled Rob. A sudden warmth and aching in her chest drew her gaze downward to her swollen and sagging breasts. She medicated herself with a few chocolate chips, slid across the bed, placed the statue faceup on Rob's pillow, and gave it a kiss. *Date night.*

What happened to that couple who couldn't take their hands off each other? She still wanted him, but for what? To be held by him or simply for him to pick up one of the kids when they cried?

Julia would so get this.

Dina thought back to the conversation they'd had on the beach in Barbados, the one where they'd discussed whether they were Chrissys or Janets. They were both Janets. They didn't know any Chrissys. Dina reached for the phone to call Julia, even though it was long distance, then stopped herself. She didn't know what had gone wrong on the island, but Dina's subsequent calls to Julia had gone unanswered. At some point, she'd just stopped trying.

Dina was settling into tonight's episode—the one where Chrissy falls under the spell of a shady guru—when the phone rang, startling her. She was hopeful for a second that it *was* Julia. "Hello," Dina answered. The phone was silent. "Hello!" she shouted.

"I'll be right back, just make sure you don't overhydrate her . . . Dina—sorry, sorry. It's me, just finishing up here," Rob answered.

"Oh, I thought you were my nightly caller again. Must be some drug dealer with a beeper number close to ours and—"

"Listen, I'm sorry I'm so late again. Are the kids in bed?" Rob interrupted.

"I'm watching Jack, Chrissy, and Janet. Does that give you a clue?"

"Look, my intentions were good. I was leaving and Boche called me to the OR; he had a bleeder who wasn't . . . well, anyway . . . I wouldn't have gone if I wasn't so new to the practice and—"

"What do you want me to say? It's okay that you haven't seen the kids in three days, or me for that matter? We have a newborn!" When he didn't reply, she took a deep breath and started again. "Somehow, I'm sure you spoke to your mother today at least once."

"Dina, that's not fair—"

"Are you waiting for Allie to ask me if you died again? The kids don't know where you are. They wake up in the morning and you've already left. I put them to sleep and you're still not home."

Tears streamed down Dina's face. She grabbed a tissue and blew her nose.

"Dina, what do you want from me?"

"I've barely met anyone here. I spend more time speaking to Bill than you. It's amazing he wasn't the one with me in the delivery room. Wasn't it enough that he drove me to the hospital?" She reached for another tissue, wiped her eyes, and popped another piece of chocolate in her mouth.

"Bill, huh? Should I be nervous?" Rob replied. "Maybe finishing a basement isn't keeping him busy enough?"

She didn't reply.

"Look, I don't know how to be any other kind of doctor. You think I'm having a party here? The nurses are screaming at me, and the food in this cafeteria is disgusting. I'm coming home as soon as I dictate this chart. I'll stop and pick up some Ben and Jerry's. Chunky Monkey? Maybe you're just feeling premenstrual?"

"Nice. Every time I get upset you think it's physiological. Premenstrual? God, I hope so!" She thought of Daniel, safe and peaceful in the next room, and immediately felt ungrateful. "I know this isn't your fault. I just don't know who to be angry at anymore."

"Chunky Monkey, that's what we need. We'll talk when I get home. Okay?"

"Okay."

Dina hung up. The whole conversation had left her feeling patronized, even though she was looking forward to the ice cream. Maybe he really was trying to make things up to her. Some men came home with flowers, others came home with sugar. Wasn't it chocolate that had brought them together in the first place? She thought of the long-ago day when, frustrated by the Hershey bar hanging by a thread in one of the hospital's vending machines, she had kicked the damn thing and injured her ankle. Rob had come to her rescue.

"Hey, can I help?" he asked, as he offered an arm to steady her.

"Not unless you can perform miracles." She had let her injured foot touch the ground gently to see if she could support her weight. "I'm okay, really. Thanks," she said from her perch a foot below him. "I shouldn't be eating this stuff anyway."

"Come on. You're perfect," he had said. Then he turned to the machine, hit it twice with his fist, and the chocolate bar dropped down.

"Wow, neat trick," she said, retrieving the spoils. "Thanks."

"My pleasure," he said. "Who am I to stand between a pretty nurse and her candy bar?"

Why did guys think that sort of line would work? "Thanks again," she said, as she turned to walk away.

"Hey," Rob said, a bit too loudly. "Rob Wasserman." He reached out his hand.

"Dina Aharoni," she replied, shaking and disengaging quickly.

"Aha-what?"

"Aharoni."

"Like Macaroni? What is that, Italian?"

"No, it's Sephardic. Jewish. You know? Well, maybe you don't? Wasserman? Is that two *n*'s or one? German or . . . ?" she asked, leaving her question unfinished.

"Certified member of the tribe," he replied.

"I'm not really sure how we got the name Aharoni. And we're not really sure we're Sephardic, actually. It's a long story."

Meeting Rob seemed forever ago as her breasts leaked in response to Daniel. The holding, touching, feeding; her arms, her hands, her breasts, every part of her demanded by the children, her husband, every minute of the day. She was losing the constant struggle to maintain sovereignty over her own body.

After a quick visit to the kitchen, she settled on the rocker with Daniel on her lap. He fussed and struggled momentarily and then, shockingly, began sucking on the bottle of formula.

"Thank you," she whispered, looking at the small tufts of hair forming on the crown of his head, smelling his delicious baby scent. She sang Joni Mitchell's "Both Sides Now" to him softly, calming them both. He stopped eating and looked up at her. She was in love. Perhaps a bigger love than even she and Rob had. Then Daniel's face scrunched into that of the old man he would someday become, as she felt the heat expand in his diaper. *Thank you, Joni.* She changed him quickly.

The nursery clock read 2:00 a.m. when she realized that some of this *was* within her control. Not much, but some. She turned the bottle, eyeing the ingredients label. *Lactose, maltodextrin. Ultimate sin of motherhood, my ass.* She'd managed to take a small part of her life back.

Chapter Two

Julia Cawley Kinsella

Boston, Massachusetts, March 1973

Julia preferred to keep to herself, but when the woman next to her extended her hand—Dana? Dina?—it seemed she had no choice. She gave a quick "Hi," along with her own name, hoping that would be enough. This was Julia's first time at a spa and all she really wanted was to enjoy the blissful calm of the posh waiting area. She picked up a magazine of her own in hopes of cutting short any possible conversation. Then she noticed the woman's well-shaped legs protruding from her robe and wondered if John was at that very moment being pursued by sexy drug reps.

The women sat in amiable quiet for a few moments, when suddenly the silence was pierced by a thick Boston brogue.

"*Fawk*, Julia, that can't be you? It simply can't!" yelped a chubby woman with long dark hair teased high on her head.

It was Jeannie Mancussi from the old neighborhood. Julia rose and gave her a perfunctory embrace.

"I would never have recognized you in that white robe," Julia said with a saccharine sweetness she hoped would disguise her revulsion. She couldn't stand this girl with her thick Southie accent. Julia had made sure to lose hers. She'd even practiced listening to movies of Audrey Hepburn to break her habits. "How have you been? What is it, almost three years since . . . ?" She went on without finishing the question. "What are you doing here?"

"Conference. I work for the Aluminum Association. We refer to it as 'AA' in the trade, but, you know, people really get confused."

Julia froze. *What was she talking about?*

Jeannie continued, "You know, Alcoholics Anonymous? The no-more-brewskies folks."

"Oh, right." Brewsky.

Out of one corner of her eye, Julia noticed the other woman listening to the conversation, while doing a bad job of pretending to read her magazine.

"Are you married yet? Kids? Why are you here?"

That was Jeannie, as relentless as ever.

"Yes, I'm married. We're in town for a medical conference. I mean my husband is here for the conference, and yes, we have a baby. A boy. Aiden." *Please, God, make this woman go away.* "And what about you, Jeannie? Besides aluminum, I mean. Are you married? Any kids?" Julia asked, inhaling deeply. This was not how she wanted to spend her morning.

"Do you remember at school how my parents used to order me a pizza from Pat's on Shawmut Street every week to make sure I had some good food to eat—as if there was no food in the cafeteria? Anyway, you know the really cute delivery guy?" Jeannie asked.

Julia nodded. The closest thing Jeannie got to a steady date was the pimply, greasy-haired delivery guy.

"Johnny, right?" Julia guessed. She had no clue.

"Close. Tony. Well, besides my aluminum work, Tony and I own a pizzeria. Two of them, on Mass Ave." Jeannie's right hand shot forward. Fingers outstretched, palm down, she showed off her diamond ring. "Tony's parents actually own them, but we're running them. My business major is coming in handy. Here, I

10

know we weren't supposed to bring anything with us, but you just can't trust anybody in a place like this." Jeannie reached into the pocket of her robe and pulled out her wallet and, from it, a few pictures. "This is us at the Cape," Jeannie explained, as she pointed her long, glittered fingernail at the baby girl in the photo, a small replica of her stocky, moonfaced father.

"Antoinette. Gorgeous, right? And Julia, are you enjoying being a . . . what was it you left school to do again? Radiology tech?" Jeannie asked, as she smiled broadly.

The question caught Julia off guard. It had been a horrible time back then. Her dad's business had taken a dive. In the middle of freshman year, her parents had given her a choice: take out loans to finish school or come home and go to community college. The thought of telling John, who was attending BU on a scholarship, was mortifying. But the thought of taking out loans terrified her. In the end, even tech school had been a bad investment. She was no longer working. What did she actually do these days? Her life had become an endless loop of feeding, bathing, burping, cooking, and cleaning. This was the first break she'd had in months.

"Well, you know, when I graduated from tech school, I worked in the city for a while," Julia answered, hoping her inquisitor would be satisfied.

"Right, I know. But where do you work now?" Jeannie asked, head tilting.

"So, I was working for a private radiology group, but I'm home with a baby now. I've thought about going back, but my husband is in medical school and he's doing clinical rotations and not around much and . . ." Julia knew this sounded lame.

She was momentarily distracted from Jeannie, as she noticed the woman—*what was her name? Dina?*—shaking her head up and down supportively. Their eyes locked. That was enough to turn Jeannie's attention.

The Convention of Wives

"You know," Jeannie said, rudely appraising the other woman, "it's amazing what a baby can do to you if you're not careful."

There it was. The reason Julia couldn't stand Jeannie. That's when Julia caught this Dina rolling her eyes and mouthing "bitch" in sisterly support.

Activities were limited for conference wives, so Julia wasn't that surprised the two women bumped into each other at aerobics class the next morning. They smiled when they saw their equipment laid out in precisely the same pattern: weights perpendicular and to the left of the step, bands to the right, and mat to the left of the weights. She wasn't sure who asked whom, but Julia found herself having coffee with Dina after class ended. Like Julia, Dina had a young baby at home and was married to a medical student who was presenting a paper at the conference. Julia laughed when she learned that Dina's husband was *also* interested in a surgical residency, as was her husband, John.

"Rob was thinking orthopedics, but I pointed out that he was simply not the type . . . you know, not a jock," Dina said, taking off her leg warmers.

"My husband, John, fits the bill, but I don't think he's headed that way. I've known him since middle school. We both ran track, and he was the quarterback of our high school team."

"A quarterback?"

"Yeah, that's partly why I fell for him. The cheerleaders were all over him. He loved the attention. But somehow," Julia explained, primping her hair in the nearby mirror, "he wound up with *me*."

"Wound up with? Look at you. You're gorgeous. *Shiksa* chic on all accounts!" Dina exclaimed, motioning up and down Julia's body. "I'd kill for that shape, especially since giving birth. My stomach looks like a subway map of New York City and my boobs will never be the same."

"You're crazy . . . and what's a *shipsa*?"

"No, sorry, my Jewish is showing. *Shiksa* with a 'k.' It's a word for a female non-Jewess. I'm assuming, of course, that you're not Jewish. Maybe I shouldn't, it's just your bod, your nose." Dina raised her hand and covered her mouth. "I'm being terrible."

"No, that's okay." Julia smiled. What the girl had said was complimentary, but somehow offensive. Still, she seemed genuine. "I'm a good Catholic girl. Irish Catholic. Well, maybe not so *good*, but definitely Catholic. And definitely Irish. Probably a bit lapsed in every way but my ability to get pregnant and drink shots. I swear, John just looked at me. Well, not quite, I guess. So much for the rhythm method." She drained her coffee. "I'm going to get another cup, and I'm starving. Want to split one of those corn muffins?"

"Sure, maybe a half is okay."

Half a muffin? Julia never had to watch what she put in her mouth. She ate when she was hungry. Whenever and whatever she wanted. John had commented on her appetite from the moment they'd met. He seemed to enjoy watching her eat. Most of the women she knew grappled with their weight. She'd observed friends attempt multiple diet fads and fail to make a change that stuck. Thank goodness that wasn't her struggle.

"So, does yours do any of the dishes or the cleaning?" Julia asked, balancing her coffee and the muffin, which she'd had cut in half.

Dina shook her head, grabbed the plates, and set them on the table. "I stopped working," she complained, "but the baby still keeps me up all night long, and Rob's just not around, so I'm exhausted most of the time. I'm not sure I could function at a job at this point, especially nursing. I wanted to go back, but by the time we paid the babysitter, we'd barely break even. And God forbid I complain. I'm 'a doctor's wife,' what else could I possibly want?"

The Convention of Wives

Julia knew too well. Her own plan to return to work had evaporated after she'd spent a few weeks at home with the baby. There was no way she could imagine leaving Aiden in the arms of a stranger. And yet, she felt isolated. And an imposter. A fraud of a woman who had no idea how to be a mother. She loved her baby in a way she had never imagined possible. But each day was a battle against fear and monotony. Once she got the food shopping and laundry done and tidied their small apartment, it was time to settle Aiden for the afternoon. Then it was time to prepare dinner—a dinner she'd usually eat alone.

Julia felt her resentment growing when her husband would sail in and regale her with his daily triumphs, his ability to meet the serious responsibilities placed upon him. She oversaw the care of just one small, healthy human who only needed food, diapering, and a nap. John was saving lives—plural. She was just doing what was supposed to come naturally. He was putting into practice years of study and growing technical skill. It wasn't supposed to be a competition, but somehow it was. At the end of the finish line each day, his job came with applause from a thankful world, hers with the silent appreciation of a human being incapable of verbalizing. Resentment, indeed.

"I know what you mean," Dina said, nibbling on the muffin. "His mother thinks I should be happy being able to stay home with the baby. It's a luxury, right? How many women can do this? But I'm angry most of the time. I feel like there's something wrong with me."

Julia placed her hand on Dina's arm.

"I'm just not sure at whom. Certainly, not at the baby." Dina continued, "I chose this, right? You chose this. It's not the guys' fault. Is it ours?"

They went back and forth while refreshing their drinks.

Dina just got it.

By the end of their two-hour talk, they had exchanged room

numbers and contact information. They met each morning for aerobics class and took walks through Little Italy each afternoon. Between eating gelato and strolling through art galleries, they chatted about the large and small details of their lives. Their parents, their in-laws, their husbands, their children. Even birth control methods. Dina treasured her Planned Parenthood diaphragm, though she admitted the contraceptive jelly was messy and gross. When Julia admitted to using the rhythm method, Dina lectured her a bit, but maybe she had a point. It was 1973, after all. The sexual revolution had been going on for the past fifteen years.

Chapter Three

Dina

San Diego, California, December 2000

Dina reached into her beach bag, pulling out the hotel pads she'd taken from her room at the Marriott Marquis. She sat, admiring the crisp vermillion logo, poised to write. *Nothing.* She doodled an impressive paisley design, pretending she was writing actual words. *Still nothing.* Expertly removing her bathing suit cover-up, while keeping her butt on the chair so that no one could catch sight of her thighs until she could sit with knees bent, she created a flattering ninety-degree angle. Cellulite be damned. Suntan lotion came next, a generous application to legs, arms, and décolletage.

The waitress approached. "Ma'am," she said, "can I get you anything?"

Ma'am. "I'll have a Bloody Mary with lots of olives, please. Room 1014."

"Anything else?"

"No, thank you."

Ten minutes later, recuperating nicely from being *Ma'amed,* Dina sipped away and turned her attention to the blank page. It should be easy. She was pretty much on her own at these conferences, except for the usual business dinners, golf outings, and romantic couplings. Truth be told, the latter was becoming less and less frequent between Rob's backaches, her waning estrogen levels, and the chance that a new episode of *ER* would pull them in. She had nothing to worry about, no one demanding her attention. So where were all those creative juices? *Juices?* She took another slug of her Bloody Mary.

The pool waitress arrived with a second drink just as Dina's straw made a sucking sound and she finished her first. Dina sipped, saddened by how easily she could be distracted from writing—from what she considered her third act, which made her think of when it had been her thwarted first.

It was 1967, the summer of love, but not in the Aharoni house. Dina was eighteen and had just graduated from high school. For the past few summers, she had worked as a junior secretary in her family's *shmata* business. While most of the clothing production was done in Georgia and South Carolina, the design and distribution end were handled in New York City. Dina's older brothers were already in college studying finance; they'd work for her father when they finished. When she told her parents about her interest in studying creative writing, her mother had laughed so loudly she had gotten the hiccups. Her father shook his head and insisted she spend at least a year working in the family business before deciding anything about college; especially, as he'd put it, "that writing nonsense."

"And you might want to consider picking a college where you can also find a decent husband," her mother added between swallows of sugar.

In protest, she had decided that after high school she would go into the office just one day a week and fill the rest of her time teaching arts and crafts at a summer camp. Surprisingly, her father said little when she announced her plans, except to tell her that it might do her some good to spend time out-of-doors.

"With a little color in your cheeks," he said as he pinched hers, "maybe you won't even need to go to college to find a mister."

"Daddy!" she had screamed as she left the room in tears.

"What, what did I say that was so terrible?"

By late August, she was nicely tanned and, despite herself, enjoying the Mondays she spent in New York. She'd even had time to prepare some dress designs for her father, to prove she was worth being taken seriously. Maybe there was something to working in the business after all. One day, she got the courage to show him her sketches.

Waiting on the leather bench outside her father's office was like being sent to the principal. Dina was relieved when, a few moments later, her father's secretary waved her in.

David Aharoni's large walnut desk was covered with messy piles of paper and a cigar resting in an ashtray, its smoke rising to join a growing circle of gray discoloration on the ceiling. Her father was looking through thick-lensed glasses at some papers, his feet resting on the desk. He smiled up at her but said nothing.

"Daddy, I wanted to show you what I've been working on. I took a few of the florals and reworked them a bit, adding more vivid colors like the ones I've seen on concert posters. You know, some lime greens, hot pinks. I changed the sleeves to bell-shaped and made a few of the dresses empire. Here," she said, holding up her sketchpad. "What do you think? Maybe these would appeal to some of the younger customers?" She stood frozen before him.

"I can't mind read," he said, cleaning off his glasses. "Bring it over here to me," he grunted and swung his legs off the desk. As she approached, Dina noticed that the papers were travel brochures. Maybe her dad was going to take her mom away somewhere romantic. He shoved the pamphlets under his blotter and grabbed Dina's sketchpad.

"Nice, nice. Interesting," he said while flipping through the designs. The phone rang and he grabbed it. "Morty, how's it hanging?" He took a suck of his cigar. "Yeah, but not more than a two-day delay or I'll miss the deadline if we have to ship further than Pennsylvania. Thanks."

Her father looked at another page of her designs and closed the pad.

"Dina, I'll pass these on to Dottie and see what she thinks. She's always had an eye for spotting new talent. Now, be a good daughter and go to the deli and get me one of those cherry Danish and a *good* coffee. The coffee in this office is *dreck*. Extra sugar and get something for yourself." He reached for his wallet and handed her a five-dollar bill.

That was it? He was going to show them to Dottie. *Dottie?* The woman had been in the business for as long as her father! She was lovely, had always been nice to Dina, but come on— Dottie was ancient, at least fifty years old. What did she know about current styles?

"Dad, I don't think you understand," she said, trying to show him another design. She had spent weeks working on the book. "No one my age buys anything we produce. How are we going to make new customers, customers of the future, if we keep just reproducing the same designs season after season?"

"And, while you're out," he said as he pulled a white ticket from his wallet, "stop at the silver shop across the street. You know, Stein's. They just called to tell me the candlesticks are ready. Be careful, come right back to the office once you've picked them up."

"But Daddy . . ."

Her father pushed himself up from his chair and took her hands in his.

"Dina, look, it is very sweet that you have an opinion about these things, having been in the business for a total of what, two months? But I think the business strategy of my father, and his before him, is still working. What do you think pays for all the miniskirts and tie-dyed shirts you love? Get out of the office for a few minutes. I really need that coffee, and make sure to get the candlesticks or your mother will kill me."

Grabbing the money and the ticket stub, Dina walked out. She threw the pad on her desk and headed toward the hallway that led to the elevators. Halfway there, she turned, went back and threw the sketchpad in the garbage. He could get his own coffee! She'd get the candlesticks, but he could get his own coffee. She was done with the family business.

Stein and Sons was an oasis on a hot summer day. The contents of the jewelry cases glowed in the subdued lighting. There were no other customers, and the quiet was disturbed only by the hum of fans shifting the damp, slightly mildewed air.

"Hi, I'm here to pick something up," Dina said, handing over the ticket to the girl behind the counter. The young woman's eyes opened wide when she looked in the large green ledger. "Oh, I'll be right back, I need to get Mr. Stein."

"No, really, that's okay. I'm sure you can help me, I'm here for some candlesticks." The last thing Dina wanted was to get into a fifteen-minute conversation with Mr. Stein.

"I'm sorry, but I really have to insist." The girl turned the ledger around to show Dina the entry. "You see that little asterisk here, next to the entry of the ticket number? It means you're a VIP. And here, do you see the word *NEIROT*, candlesticks, in capital letters? Well, Mr. Stein only does that when it's a major piece. I'll be right back."

Dina noticed two items, a necklace and earrings, listed under the candlestick notation. Both had AD written in the customer column. Under the second column, where her item had said *NEIROT*, was a *W* next to "necklace" and a *G* next to "earrings."

Mr. Stein came out of the back holding two boxes, each over

a foot long. Placing them on the counter, he buzzed the security gate open and came around to give her a hug.

"Dina, you are quite the young lady now," he said as he cupped her chin in his pinky-ringed hand.

She had never known a man to wear such elaborate finery. Or talk so much.

She placed her hands on the counter and pulled her face away.

"In a few short years you'll be charming all the young men. Maybe a *shitach* with my son is in order. He's a college boy. Thinks the family business is not for him. But with a girl like you, maybe he'd stick around. I know I would." He placed his hand over Dina's.

She squirmed, pulling her hand out from beneath his sweaty paw, and stepped back. "I should get the candlesticks to my dad before he wonders what's happened to me," she said as she reached for the boxes. If she went right home and never showed up at the office with the candlesticks, her father might think about calling the police. *Let him!*

"Wait, wait, you don't rush this process, especially not for these items. You're the customer. You must inspect the work before we sign them out in the ledger. Have a seat while I unpack them."

Sitting on the blue velvet chair, Dina swiveled back and forth like a four-year-old.

"After all, it's not every day that you get to see something that's got to be a couple hundred years old. I keep telling your father that these need to be in a museum. He's crazy to keep them in the house. What? You think I'm kidding. You know we think they're early nineteenth century. From somewhere in the Ottoman Empire."

Dina laughed. Every few years they brought the candlesticks into Mr. Stein. According to her father, their history was probably the usual Jewish saga: They tried to kill us, we survived, let's eat. She was surprised to learn a bit more and now wondered if her father's reluctance to give her detail had been a way to spur her imagination.

"Seriously, they're just not insurable. Come."

Dina watched as Mr. Stein carefully removed the layers of felt and tissue wrapping. She was always surprised when men took such care.

"Natalie, you too. I bet you've never seen anything like these in your life."

The girl came closer as he placed them upright on the counter.

Breathtaking. Dina had forgotten what they looked like when they were fully polished. The slender stalk of each was straight, with a base that broke off into multiple thinner shoots, like the roots of a tree. The top ended in a small plate holding a cup the size of a candle's width. Each stalk was wrapped by two rippling stems with multiple shoots and leaves. The leaves were made of a dark blue stone.

"And now, the magic," Mr. Stein said, rotating the candlesticks until one rested into the other, their stems and roots intertwined. He pointed. "Here, you see the new joint? This is where we had to do some work. The design is beautiful, but fragile, and the intertwining of the branches and roots, well, it causes stress over time. But, with a little help . . . they're good as new."

"They look wonderful. Thank you," Dina said.

"The bill is taken care of. It's on your family account." He showed her the ledger. "Here, see the AD, that's for Aharoni, David. Just our little double check with the ticket. I wouldn't want to give these candlesticks to the wrong family. Boy, would I be in trouble." He smiled and finished the rewrapping.

"I was wondering what the W and G stand for," Dina said, pointing to the ledger. "Near the AD?"

"Oh . . ." He hesitated. "Never mind about that, just our

internal coding. Now, initial here under the pickup column and you're all set."

Dina did as she was told.

After the debacle at her father's business—and after day camp had ended—a friend of Dina's asked her to volunteer as a candy striper at the local hospital. Dina jumped at the chance. Her parents seemed almost happy with her choice. She didn't understand until she overheard them talking over coffee after dinner one night.

"It could be worse," her mother said. "Maybe she'll meet a doctor."

A few months later, convinced she wanted to become a doctor herself, Dina went to the library to research colleges with good premed programs. Her parents were having none of it. They agreed to pay for a good school nearby, one where she could come home on the weekends. But medical school? Out of the question. "Why go through the trouble of becoming a doctor when you could just marry one?" her father asked. She was furious. She cajoled and pouted until a compromise was struck. Nursing school in New Jersey. To her parents, it might as well have been Ohio.

Now, all these years later, sitting by the pool, she wondered whether she would have abandoned her nursing career so quickly if it hadn't begun with so much angst.

She picked up her phone.

"Hi Daddy. It's me."

"Dinala, hey, hold on. Your mom made me practice my putting inside. We're in Boca, for God's sake, and she still thinks it's too windy outside for me. Ridiculous . . . I . . ."

"Daddy, I need to ask you something."

"Okay, my putter is away. Shoot!"

"Do you remember the stories I used to write when I was little about the candlesticks?"

"You mean your cartoons. Of course, I remember. Dina are you okay?"

"You do?"

"Sure, sure. The stories you made up about those things!"

"Were they any good?"

"You were a kid."

"I know. But, for a kid, were they any good?"

"You sound funny. Are you sure you're okay? They were more than good. They were great."

"Then what happened?"

"To what?"

"To them? To me?"

"Dina, are you all right? Is Rob all right? Are you and Rob okay?"

"We're fine."

"The kids?"

"We're fine. Fine. I just always wondered if you knew more than you were telling me about them. About the candlesticks."

She thought she'd lost the connection when he didn't respond. Was she on the phone with him or dreaming she was on the phone with him? She was definitely buzzed.

"Daddy, are you there?"

"Some stories should remain just that . . . stories."

"What do you mean?"

"Look, Dinala. All these years later, passed down through so many generations, who knows what's real anymore? Why would I repeat something to my child, especially when it wasn't bedtime material?"

"*Bedtime material?*"

"What do you think I mean? Do you think your ancestors fled Europe because they were kicked off the golf course?"

"Fled? You always said it was complicated, but you never, ever told me anything about fleeing; not even when you talked about them in your toast at Allie's bat mitzvah. That was a great speech Daddy, great. But wouldn't that have been the time . . ."

"Are you drinking?"

"No. Well, maybe one little Bloody Mary. I'm good. I'm just relaxing by the pool here."

"You're a lightweight. Be careful. Nothing worse than a sloppy wife."

"Daddy!"

"Sorry. Anyway, where was I? Right. Jews are always fleeing for their lives. Well, maybe not in Boca, but you never know. That's why I always have my passport handy. Dual citizenship in Israel, the only way to go. I always say—"

"Daddy, just tell me. I'm fifty-three years old, and I have time to listen."

Chapter Four

Miriam Aharoni

Odessa, Ukraine, 1821

Miriam carried the seeds in two large, deep pockets that her mother had sewn expressly for this purpose. Small muslin pouches weighing one tenth of a *funt*—carefully labeled: beetroot, five rubles; potatoes, three rubles; carrots, four rubles—wadded each pocket. She was careful not to allow her leather water sack near the seeds. She couldn't permit her wares to lose value—not now, with another mouth to feed.

Miriam's breasts ached when she thought of Avram. Though he had weaned himself in the last few weeks, her body seemed slow to catch on. She had placed small rags in her undergarment before she left the house, but now she wrapped her shawl across her chest to hide the growing stains on her shirt. She could not look like a common cow on market day.

Avram, her little calf, youngest of the Aharoni clan, with his dark curls and big brown eyes, was tenacious. The evening before, he had taken a few steps, and that was that. He may have toddled like a drunkard, but he couldn't get enough of it. He crawled back and forth to the chair by the dining table, pulling himself up over and over again; stepping, falling, and crawling back, until he had mastered four, then five, then six.

She'd been busy helping with the meal when she heard her father, Yitzchak, giving her husband some advice.

"I have known these farmers for years, Moshe. They have been good to our family." Her father stroked his beard as if contemplating a section of the Talmud.

"Who do you think buys most of my seed? I would not have a business without them. You think they don't tell me how you speak to them?"

Moshe's leg shook rhythmically under the table. His face tightened.

"Already the landowners pay you and your father to squeeze these peasants for as much rent as they can pay. You cannot bully them," her father continued. "They're caught in an impossible situation, like we are."

Moshe looked at his father-in-law, his face implacable, his jaw stern.

"We're not much different than they are. We're not allowed to own anything either in this godforsaken place. *Uch* . . . if you ask me, it's all a nasty business."

"Papa, please stop," Miriam begged, knowing what was to come.

"You see how your father bullies you, and you are his son," Yitzchak said, his voice rising, his hands pounding the table.

"Enough," Moshe shouted. "If not for this bully, your daughter would have no future, nor your grandson." Moshe rose from the table and headed for the bedroom. "You, with your seeds!"

"Really? Because with men like your father, we might not have a future!" Yitzchak shouted back.

The argument ended with the slam of a door.

What should have been a celebration of Avram's progress had quickly become a catastrophe. She loved her husband, but her father was not wrong about the effect his family's business had on all of them. She had to tolerate Moshe's moodiness, his frustration after a day at work, to say nothing of his near obsession with his violin. She was so tired. Tired of working all the time, of not having a minute to herself. When was the last time she had even taken a comb to her hair? Mostly, she was tired of being told that she had made a good match. At the butcher's, the baker's, she would hear the same thing from the women she met. "Moshe has a wonderful future with his father's company. You'll live a life of ease; have a servant to do the housework. *Uch*, what a match you've made for yourself, Miriam."

She looked out of the front window and saw the tall tree she had swung from as a child. Closing her eyes, she envisioned the tree reaching out and enfolding her in its strong limbs. She so longed to be held.

Moshe was not a devoted father. The night was an aberration. He'd given Avram a few moments of attention, but only because the child had started walking, had accomplished something. It was Moshe's younger brother, Judah, who would show up for dinner and play with the baby. Judah, who had been sent by his father to apprentice as a silversmith since there was no room in the business for both of his sons. Judah, who seemed to accept his lot in life—and everything thrown at him—with grace.

For Moshe and Miriam's wedding gift, her brother-in-law had designed a beautiful pair of Shabbos candlesticks, inseparable and strong. The craftsmanship was exquisite, like nothing Miriam had ever seen before. It must have taken Judah months of work to make them. At the wedding, he shyly came forth and made a toast to his brother and his new sister-in-law, and he presented the gift to them; a loving representation of the two families coming together in marriage. They were overcome by his generosity. Judah embraced Moshe and kissed Miriam gently on the cheek. How could she say no to an additional guest during the week and, especially on Shabbos, when the beautiful candlesticks were the glowing centerpiece of the table?

The road, rutted from recent rains, made walking treacherous. Miriam made her way to the market afraid she would damage her shoes on the stony surface. She was a consummate worrier, a trait she had inherited from her mother.

"Don't get too close to the marsh; it will be the end of you if you fall in," her mother would warn. "And don't stay on the main road to town if you can help it. Someone you don't know may recognize you as a Jew, and God forbid what could happen."

But who could really blame her mother? She had lost three children after Miriam, one while still in the womb and two boys soon after birth. Miriam understood the fear, now that she was a mother herself. Her daydreaming was disrupted by the sound of men laughing. She looked back: workmen from a local farm. Three of them. She was only minutes from town, but she knew enough to be frightened. She took off at a run, and their laughter faded. Sweat was streaming down her face when she got to the market stall she shared with her mother's sister, her armpits sodden. Aunt Fagel seemed more concerned with Miriam's appearance than with the fact that something might be wrong.

"What will the customers think of you, Miriam? You are a married woman. You should know better than to run and play like a child. And you're late again. I've already sold half of my cakes. Do you have the seeds?"

Miriam tried to explain what had happened, but she was interrupted by a customer. The rest of the morning went quickly. With only a few *funts* of seeds left, she walked over to the baker and bought two loaves of bread for a reduced price. The women were packing up their wares for the midday meal when they saw Judah running toward them.

"Quick, Miriam, come with me. We must get home. Leave everything," he whispered to them fervently.

Her aunt protested. "Judah, what is the matter with you?" she shouted but stopped when Miriam reached out to touch the blood on his shirt. "Oh, my God, what has happened?" Her eyes filled with tears and she clutched her hand to her chest.

"Miriam, come now. Tante Fagel, go home." He gripped Miriam's hand and pulled.

She looked back and saw her auntie, hands to her mouth, staring after them. She ran until she couldn't breathe, then she dropped to the ground.

"If something has happened, why did we leave my aunt at the market?"

"We can't save everyone."

"What?"

"There are choices to be made."

"I don't know what you mean. Tell me. Judah. What has happened?"

"I'm not sure. They say some priest has been killed . . . by Jews!"

Close now to home, Miriam looked ahead to get her bearings. That was when she saw them—small mounds of blankets, tinged with red. Wrapped turkeys, like those she'd seen at the butcher. Who would have been so careless to leave such precious bundles strewn about? Then she got closer. No. No. No! Children. They were children, their limbs lying at unnatural angles . . . some only babies. Some clothed, some naked, bleeding, dead. She vomited into her hair.

Judah grabbed a rag that was knotted to his belt. He wiped her face.

"Miriam, we're meeting Moshe by the river. Now."

"What do you mean? We have to get Avram. We have to get my—"

"There is no need."

"What? What are you saying?"

"They are gone. Gone—all of them."

"Gone where?" Miriam asked, refusing the obvious truth. "Judah, what do you mean?"

"Dead."

"Dead . . . ? Where is Avram, my parents, your parents?"

"Dead, all dead."

"You're lying, lying. I don't believe you! I'm going home, now!" she screamed, hitting him in the chest. He held her arms tightly to her sides with his.

"Miriam, you don't want to see; please, you don't want to see. We have to get to the river. Now. Moshe has a rowboat."

"I have to see or I'm not going."

Miriam was never sure if Judah had indulged her at that moment because her home was on the way to the river or because he knew she would not follow until she believed him.

Her knees buckled as she saw the smoldering house, the bodies strewn about the garden.

"Who would do this to us? Why?"

"The Cossacks. The farmers. Your father was right, a nasty business my father and brother were in. They are pitted against each other, and we are stuck right in the middle with our money-lending. And now they think we've sided with the Turks. What do we know of Turks?"

The last thing she remembered seeing was the body of her sweet Avram, his legs splayed on the ground, never to take another step.

She awoke feeling like she was flying—no, running—but her feet were not on the ground. She opened her eyes to a world upside down: she was being carried over someone's shoulder. It was a man, and in addition to holding Miriam, he had two canvas bags slung over his back. A sharp twig scratched her face. Her head struck something metal in one of the sacks.

"Quickly," said a familiar voice. "Let's get her in the boat." It was Moshe. Judah had been carrying her. She was passed between the brothers like chattel, followed by the bundles. Moshe set his wife down in the boat. Judah jumped in beside Miriam, while Moshe pushed the boat away from shore and jumped in. But they were caught on something. Snagged. Moshe tried to pull them closer to the mooring, but the bottom of the boat, now weighted down with the three bodies and their baggage, dragged to a halt in the shallows.

"*Gevalt.* It's not enough you have done to us? Where is your divine power when it's needed? *Got in himl!*" Moshe cried. Cursing under his breath, he jumped out into the cold water and unfastened the ropes. Attempting to jump back in, he lost his footing and fell onto the sharp edge of the stern. He cried with pain as Judah pulled him onboard. The men sat dazed for a minute. Slowly, they picked up their oars and propelled the boat forward.

Moshe grunted like a wounded animal. "I think I may have broken a rib," he said through gasps of pain. "I don't know if I can do this."

Cold, wet, and terrified, Miriam grabbed the oar. Her heart raced and pounded in her ears as she lost herself in the rhythm of the boat. Not one word was spoken as she and Judah rowed together through the menacing marsh, the only sound the dipping of the oars.

Hours later, as the sky's pinkish cast announced the sunrise, they stopped on the sandy bank of a small island to rest. It took the strength of both Judah and Miriam to lift Moshe out of the boat. They stashed the vessel behind a large bush. Once hidden from shore, they shared some bread and some water from the stream before sleeping the day away. They were back on their way before dusk. It was midnight when the port lights of Odessa became visible in the distance. Judah carried the two sacks from the boat and, with Miriam's help, supported Moshe who was limping badly. She thanked God it was nighttime.

"Where are we going exactly?" Miriam asked.

"To Ezra, the merchant. He'll know what to do, where to go, and how to get there. Your father said he's our only chance," Moshe said haltingly.

"What? You spoke to my father?" Miriam asked frantically. "What else did he say?"

"Nothing Miriam, I swear. That was all he said to me before he . . . he . . ."

Ezra arrived an hour after the three got to his house. He appeared displeased to see them, but his heart softened when he heard of their losses.

"I wish there was something I could do . . . we're leaving the city tonight ourselves by ship," Ezra said, putting his hand to his heart. "The cost of passage for my family is prohibitively high, and I need to keep something for the overland trip. I can give you our wagon and our horses, food and water. You could try to head inland and south." Miriam sensed that even Ezra didn't believe in the escape plan he was suggesting.

Moshe took out his violin case and slowly unwrapped the instrument.

"Moshe, this is not the time for music," Miriam reproached him.

Moshe flipped the violin over and gently shook the instrument. He removed a small pouch from the violin. "My mother won't be needing these anymore."

Moshe's fingers looked as if they were burning as he pulled a few shiny objects, one by one, from the bag. The necklace of amethysts and diamonds his mother wore when accompanying his father to the great synagogue. Miriam had never seen the sapphire and emerald rings that came out next, each of the stones surrounded by small diamonds. She guessed his mother had worn these to evening dinners to which she was not invited.

Ezra smiled. "A *yiddishe kop*," he said as he touched the top of Moshe's head. "I will take care of the arrangements." Ezra took the necklace, fingering it gingerly.

He reached for the rings when Judah grabbed them.

"Miriam, why don't you hold on to these for now?" Judah said as he turned to Ezra. "We'll need these for the land journey, in case we get"—and with this he stared at Ezra—"separated."

Ezra smiled, a flicker of admiration in his eyes. The merchant turned to his wife. "Rachel, get the children, we'll leave for the ship now, while it is still dark. All of us, including our"—he turned toward the newcomers—"niece and nephews."

She awoke to the smell of fish and sweat, a rough blanket lying on top of her. Moshe and Judah were talking softly.

"It is our homeland, surely we will find peace there," Miriam heard Judah whisper.

"Peace? You are naive. We will never find peace, just momentary lapses in which the world stops trying to kill us."

"Moshe, we must have faith. Remember, we are the Ch—"

"The Chosen People!" Moshe scoffed at his brother. "What are we chosen for anyway? To scratch out a living wherever we go? To be chased, killed, tortured wherever we settle?" Moshe cried out. "There will be war with Amalek in each generation! The Talmud tells us this."

Miriam felt nauseous. Trying to sit up, she hit what she thought was a tree limb. Her eyes adjusted to the light. She was inside. This feeling, this motion, this place, it was familiar.

"Moshe, I think she is awake," Judah said. "Miriam, Miriam?"

He placed his hands on her shoulders. "Do you remember what has happened?"

The images flooded back. Her aunt's terrified face as they ran from the market. Her house burning in front of her eyes. Avram, her baby, on the ground. Oh, her baby . . . She retched. Judah pushed a bucket under her mouth. She stopped only when there was nothing left but clear, yellow liquid. She sat like a limp cloth doll while Judah wiped her face, then the front of her dress. Moshe shoved his brother away.

"Enough, enough Judah! She can do that herself," Moshe yelled as he lurched and fell down, grunting in pain and grabbing his chest and stomach.

"Do that herself? Look at her. She's in shock, look at her eyes. And you shouldn't have gotten out of the hammock," Judah said as he helped Moshe back to his perch. "Moshe, she has lost a child." Judah wrapped a wet scrap of cloth around Miriam's neck.

"I learned this at the silver shop," he told her. "It will help you feel better. It is cooling," Judah said sweetly as he adjusted the makeshift scarf.

"A *schmatte* will help me?" She shook her head and smiled slightly. "Judah, nothing will help me. I have nothing."

"You don't have 'nothing,' you have me," he said. Seeming to forget himself, he placed his hand softly on her cheek.

She began to cry. He held her. *He is holding me?* She made no effort to push him away. Moshe made no move to intercede. That's when Miriam understood that the world she knew was gone.

Miriam found her footing as the floor beneath her rocked. She headed toward the light coming through a small, round window.

She began to quietly, then more loudly, hum a song she always sang for Avram when he awoke.

A hand suddenly closed across her mouth. "Miriam, be quiet," Judah whispered in her ear. "We are hidden from most of the crew.

The Convention of Wives

Ezra's family is in another compartment nearby. Only the captain and a few men he trusts know about all of us. *Shh*, be quiet."

She turned to him. "I keep thinking this is a dream, but I can't make myself wake up."

"I wish this were a dream."

"What are we going to do?"

"We are headed home."

"Home?"

"To *Eretz Yisrael*. It's been decided."

Been decided. Like so many other times in her life as a daughter, a woman, and a wife, she had heard those words. *It's been decided*. Without her input, without question. They were headed to an uninhabitable desert where she knew no one. She was merely a piece of detritus, carried along by the currents and tides. Controlled not by the moon, but by the whimsical decisions made by the men in her life; the often-foolish plans of men.

"We are heading south toward Constantinople. We'll board a larger ship there and head toward Jerusalem. It is a long journey. Here, let me show you," he said as he pulled a rudimentary map out of a book in his bag.

Aleppo, Damascus. The names were strange to her.

"How long?" she asked.

"What?"

"How long will it take?"

"Ezra said it will take us ten weeks on the ships, then a few more by land. But this is just what they've told me. I really don't know for sure. I don't know, I . . ." he faltered as his head began to shake.

He looked like a young boy trying to be strong; trying for himself but, she knew, also for her. She took his hand, thinking of the small hand that she would never hold again. "It will be all right, Judah; we will get there. Together." She looked over at Moshe who was sleeping fitfully, his brow now gleaming with sweat.

Her husband's health continued to deteriorate. She pleaded with him. "Moshe, you have to drink or eat something." But he took nothing. Instead, he lay, staring, his face gaunt, his belly swollen, his skin slightly yellow, and his hands holding tightly to his violin.

As the days went on, while the children played and read, the women sewed. Miriam and Ezra's wife took apart the empty sacks they found in the corners of their rooms and cut and pieced them together to make changes of clothing, using needles made of bone. Miriam reached for a sack on the floor. Judah lunged at her, grabbing the bag.

"Don't!" Judah shouted, shoving her hands away.

Too late. She felt the forms held within the fabric. The thin, wavy roots, the thicker trunks ending in circular cups. "The candlesticks!" she whispered. "Judah, how did you manage . . . ?"

"I don't know. I bent down to check on your father and saw them in the cabinet nearby. I just took them. Miriam, we may need these. Please don't tell anyone we have them."

"I won't," she said, touching his arm. He had given them such a generous gift for their wedding. He was still giving. Miriam looked at her brother-in-law and she saw not just Moshe's brother, but a man who cared for her in a way that was forbidden. A curtain came down over his face and his expression changed. He knew now that she knew.

Moshe no longer drank the water she offered and was delirious when he wasn't sleeping. She covered him each night with his blanket, trying not to vomit at the stench. And then he was gone, hefted overboard into the Mediterranean Sea while they softly recited Kaddish.

Chapter Five

Julia

San Diego, California, December 2000

She ran for her head and heart, rain or shine, whether the kids were in bed with colds or even now, children grown, with the house empty and no real reason to get up. Today felt different. As she skirted the San Diego Convention Center, Julia saw in the distance the bridge to Coronado and the Hotel Del, with its red-shingled rooftop, a favorite honeymoon destination. The sight brought back memories of her honeymoon thirty years ago, a weekend trip to Niagara Falls where they'd stayed in a similar large, historic hotel.

The honeymoon hadn't been particularly remarkable at first, especially their continued attempts at sex. Strict Irish Catholics that they were, she and John had vowed to save themselves from the time they met at CCD classes in middle school. Best laid plans and all that. They'd lasted until John went off to college. Julia was worried about all those female undergrads but managed to hold off until witnessing one too many classmates flirt with him at a party. That's when she sealed the deal. A six pack of beer and a few shots in, too drunk to fight when her thighs held him tightly as he came, God blessed Julia with what she felt she deserved. Three months later, John hastily proposed. The wedding was a month after that. "Romantic" her mother had said to her father, but they knew otherwise. Julia had been vomiting for weeks in the bathroom at her parents' home. She was tired, sick, and scared on her honeymoon; until the pain started and the bathroom floor was covered in blood. In all those years, they'd never spoken about that night or the baby they'd lost. Nor had they ever really taken the time to learn about pleasing each other. Life just seemed to keep coming at them.

Before she left the hotel complex, she crossed paths with a small group of young women, girls really, on their way to the conference. They were shielding their eyes and blinking in the sun, looking like three blind mice in oversized sunglasses. Jackets slung over their shoulders revealed sheer white, sleeveless blouses. Formfitting skirts displayed tanned legs. Julia shook her head. Drug reps. They looked more like models.

Thank goodness for the distraction of the view; so much better than her usual run through the burbs of Atlanta. The lack of humidity was glorious. California had clearly been designed by a kinder god than the one attending to the state of Georgia. She could see the naval base in the distance, could almost make out a submarine behind a humongous curtain of netting. She stopped to take a sip of water and wondered how a curtain that size even got made. An extra-large grandma with matching knitting needles came to mind.

Julia had started running again when she almost tripped over what looked like a large black plastic bag. When the bundle began to move, she stepped back and let out a high-pitched yelp, as if she'd been bitten. Her heart raced as the contents of the bag morphed into a person.

"Are you all right, are you hurt?" she asked the faceless, nameless soul. "I'm so sorry . . . hello in there?"

"Just leave money or dog food if you feel so bad," came the muffled response.

"Excuse me?" she asked, taken aback. *Dog food?*

The Convention of Wives

The man shifted the covering and out peeked the snout of what looked like a beagle. She'd loved animals from the time she was young. Her family had kept mutts—one after another until they died—and it had been her job to feed and walk them. She hadn't minded at all. It was with her pets that she'd felt unconditional love and connection. But John had been bitten when he was younger and wouldn't let any animals in the house. The risk of an injury to the children was too great, he'd insisted. Another part of herself gone to the compromises of marriage and motherhood.

Feeling suddenly vulnerable, Julia looked around to see if anyone was nearby. That was when she noticed them—fifteen or so dwellings, real tents and makeshift shelters created out of stained blankets strung between trees. She smelled, then saw, small, extinguished campfires letting off hazy gray smoke. Large empty water bottles littered the ground. Rusted shopping carts filled with clothing and food sat parked next to the tents. And everywhere, people were sleeping on blankets on the ground; in pairs and alone, their shirts and pants torn and faded, their feet mostly bare.

San Diego was a conference town; it made money from people like her. Shouldn't tax dollars be spent to help these poor people?

Should she just get the hell out of there or do something? But what?

Julia had on her diamond tennis bracelet, one of the many anniversary gifts she'd bought for herself. John got her a card if she was lucky. Now she questioned wearing it all the time. She never took off her wedding rings when she ran, but what else could they take? Okay . . . a few dollars in the waist belt pouch and one of her credit cards. She could put a security hold on the cards quickly. Unless they killed her. They wouldn't do that. Would they? *Doctor's Wife Murdered.* Even in death, it would be about John.

Did she dislike him that much?

Sweating profusely and frozen in place, Julia tried to remember the moves from her self-defense course. It had been a few years. John had insisted she take it because she ran alone at all hours of the day. Atlanta neighborhoods tended to blend into each other, and she had found herself in a questionable area on more than one occasion. She was the mother of his children, he'd said. Who would take care of them? As if being left alone with all their kids was his biggest fear.

Her mind was going in all directions now. Surveying her surroundings, she realized that the homeless were also parked in wheelchairs on the nearby dock, fishing. San Diego was becoming overrun. She felt guilty she could even think these people were ruining her run; but on some real level, she resented them. And she was angry at the hotel concierge, who had clearly misled her about where she could safely go for some exercise. The young woman had pointed to the very path she was now on without any mention of its current occupants. Had the girl been naive or simply stupid?

Then she felt like a complete shit.

What could possibly have happened to these people to reduce them to this? Did they, like Julia, simply lack the basic computer skills suddenly needed in the workforce? Or was it the result of either mental illness or drug abuse and an extended family who'd experienced too many years of trying unsuccessfully to intercede?

She wondered if John's oldest brother Lorrie might have ended up in an encampment like this, had he survived. The whole family avoided the topic of his death. No photographs anywhere. His name, if spoken at all, came in hushed tones. From the few stories John had shared with her, it was clear he'd worshipped Lorrie. He was convinced an undiagnosed illness had sidelined him. But their other brothers implied on more than one occasion that his death had been drug related. John would have none of it.

The Convention of Wives

The mystery surrounding Lorrie's sudden death had sparked John's interest in medicine. Julia had fallen in love with her husband in part because of this. The raw, emotional side of him she hadn't seen in a very long time.

One after the other, she lifted her feet, testing their ability to move. Satisfied she was steady enough, she turned around and headed toward the safety of the hotel. She held her breath, expecting someone or something to suddenly appear in her path, blocking her way, but she saw nothing but the trees and sky and high rises in the distance. Then she stopped and reversed course back to the sack man. Removing her credit card, she left the remaining contents of her fanny pack—the granola bar, tissues, and her emergency money—and fled back to the hotel.

The reception area was freezing cold. How did these places manage to consistently overcool their lobbies? It reminded her of winter trips to her in-laws' Sarasota apartment. It would be eighty outside, but inside it would routinely be sixty-five. She always went home with a cold. Still, she had liked those visits to Florida, not just because it was the only vacation besides Provincetown they had been able to afford, but because John's parents served as built-in babysitters, giving them badly needed moments of kid-free time.

She tolerated her in-laws better than John, until they started their usual tirade about how the Democrats were ruining the government and the Jews were running the country into the ground.

"We live on the West Coast of Florida because they've taken over the East Coast. The Jews. It's crawling with them anywhere north of Miami. Del Ray, Boca Raton, even Palm Beach," her father-in-law lectured.

Not "Jews" . . . "*The* Jews." This was usually the time that John found some excuse for them to leave. Neither of them wanted their children exposed to these diatribes.

Julia's mom wasn't that different, always asking whether the kids Julia wanted to bring home after school were, *you know, the same as us*. This meant to Julia not only white, but Catholic. Julia had shocked her mother by befriending and bringing home both Blacks and Jews in grammar school. At first she did it without thinking, but as a teenager, she did it on purpose to annoy her mother.

Dina would be mortified if she ever met Julia's in-laws. That would never happen. Dina really was no longer a friend. Funny that she still thought of her after all this time. It had to be what— ten years at least since the two had spoken. They had been so much more than convention buddies, and they'd ruined it all. She thought back to their first days as friends, laughing and crying about their frustration with being wives of doctors in training. Dina was the one person who'd known about all the boring and trying parts of her life. Someone with whom she had shared confidences—not all, but most. Time had gone by so quickly.

Shit.

Time. She had an appointment at the spa. The massage would help her shake off that upsetting walk. And afterward, maybe she'd have a pre-dinner martini. *Maybe not.* Her version of a dirty martini—Ketel One on the rocks, olives in, extra olives and olive juice on the side—was always getting screwed up. Waiters had brought her orange juice on more than one occasion. How could a bartender seriously think that she was interested in putting orange juice in her vodka with olives?

Crossing the lobby, she spied the travel ad on the wall: Barbados, Come enjoy the sand, the sun, the surf. Above the writing was a classic photograph of one of the two famous baobab trees. *The baobab*, the largest tree in Barbados. She and Dina had stood underneath one of them together, barefoot, wriggling their toes in the grass. The story was that the tree, one of few remaining on the island, had drifted in as a seed pod from Africa.

Maybe it was all fable. The tree, the trip, the friendship. All of it.

Chapter Six

James Cawley

Glasgow, Scotland, 1821

He couldn't feel his toes. Although the mossy discoloration on his green, mildewing shoes was unsightly, it worried him more to imagine what lay beneath. Held in a cell in the Glasgow jail for eight months, James had been outside only once every few weeks as part of a work detail. How had he wound up a part of the scruffy and disorganized group of men who'd gotten him there? A cause, *the* cause. What had he, a simple farmer, been thinking?

Bells tolled outside the prison, announcing the New Year: 1821. It would be his last in Scotland. He barely remembered that night the previous April when, emboldened by ale, he agreed to march for reforms. The justifications presented in the pub had seemed sound. The government of Scotland was not reacting to the economic challenges of the masses. Some were starving, others barely surviving. Why not a national strike? The adventure of it all was impossible for him to resist. And he had a wife to consider now.

He was surprised when, instead of a cloth talisman to steel him for the fight ahead, his mother had handed him a worn piece of paper. His parents' official certificate of marriage. It was her way of sending his father into battle with him, she had said. Her way of protecting him. So why was the name "Anne Bregwhite" in the spot where his mother's should be? "Rosie" was the nickname given to her by her own mother, she told him. They had shared a love of Scottish roses, yellow in particular. He'd never known.

He felt for the paper in his pocket. Finding it now brought him a bit of comfort.

For a minute he thought he smelled bread baking, but then the smell was gone. He was becoming delirious. Lack of sleep, food, and mostly water. He wanted to go home to his mother's cooking and his wife's warm bed.

He thought back to the night he'd been captured on Bonnymuir. They'd tried to march to the foundry, intent on finding weaponry to arm their cause. But the hussars had been waiting. In that dark portion of night before the blackness begins to turn to gray, he became separated from his comrades. He took his best guess at what would have been a southeasterly direction toward home, creeping along on his hands and knees. The sun was coming up in front of him. He didn't see the details of the hill so much as feel the slow rise under his feet. Then the ground began to vibrate.

At first, he wondered how ants could make such a commotion, black ants, tens of them heading down the hill toward him. But the ants were horses, men on horseback, coming straight at him. The hill was suddenly alive. He felt a sharp pain on his forehead, then blackness. The next thing he sensed was the bumpiness of the road underneath him.

"We've got another one. He's young, looks alive to me, don't shoot him."

James guessed that he was on some kind of cart. His clothes were wet and torn. The sky was filled with purples and pinks. Whether sunset or sunrise, he couldn't tell. He next awoke feeling warmer, the sun heating him. His shivering had stopped, but his head hurt like hell. He reached for his forehead and felt matted blood and hair. He was being prodded with a rifle.

"Get up now or you can choose to make this place your grave! Up to you!"

As he was shoved inside his prison cell, the sounds of moaning and screams filled his ears. He stood up and bumped his head on the low ceiling. His eyes began to adjust to the dim light and as he bent to walk forward to find a place to sit, he noticed buckets of piss and shit overflowing onto the floor. The place was filled with filthy, wounded men.

Within a few days, some of the older and more severely wounded just stopped eating the daily bread they were given. The jailors came in a few times to remove dead bodies. He found himself watching to see who seemed to be sleeping, unconscious, or worse, and was quick to take any rations held in a limp or lifeless hand.

News traveled fast from the victors to the prisoners, the jailors reveling in the revolt's outcome. They were being called seditionists. He'd heard about the execution of their leaders, Baird and Hardie. It made him sick with fear to think his life would end this way.

During the months that followed, he'd spent most of the time thinking about his wife, Katherine, when he wasn't thinking back to the choice that had changed his life.

James felt the grip of a rough, calloused hand on his arm. "Look at him, boys!" he heard. "James Cawley! Now that is the kind of specimen I want fighting next to me!" The man turned to face James. "I'm sure your mother is proud. And how is that young wife of yours?" he asked with a smirk.

James tried to extricate himself as he looked into the kind eyes of Royce Williams. The man's craggy skin flowed into his wrinkled work shirt as if cut from one piece of cloth. The knot of men standing nearby contained variations on this theme, mostly men in their thirties and forties who were shriveled from their endless labors.

Royce shook his head back and forth. "I don't understand it, boy. You would think rutting would be something a farmer would know all about. Maybe you need us to explain a few things to you so that young wife of yours bears you a son before another harvest season has come and gone?"

As the men laughed and made lewd gestures, James broke free and made his way to the other side of the room. The men meant well; they had felt a collective responsibility toward him ever since his father had died. But this was beyond the pale. It had only been a few weeks since Katherine and he had tried the latest idea she had heard from the local women at the market. After they'd lain together, he'd held her legs high above her head. They had laughed so hard it was a miracle they'd lasted as long as they did.

He grabbed a glass of ale and kept walking to the far end of the tavern. As he did, he was surprised and somewhat concerned to see that, besides Royce's group of elders, the place was filled mostly with boys, many looking as young as fourteen. How could this ragged group possibly overpower a government?

He caught his image in the tavern mirror and realized he was one of only a few men in the crowd who still had a full head of hair. Curly brown and running down his back, it was tied in a red ribbon his mother had given him for good luck. Then he mentally chastised himself for his vanity. This was not how he was raised. He knew better.

The local church had warmly embraced him and his wid-owed mother. It was here that he learned about not only the sin of pride, but also the blessing of kindness. The latter came in the form of a young playmate named Katherine, the eldest daughter of a local farmer. On one of the first days of class, when the children took out their snacks of apples and cakes brought from home, lovingly wrapped in protective cloth, Katherine noticed that James had none.

"I have plenty," she whispered as she handed him pieces of apple.

"Thank you," he replied, his face reddening.

"I'm Katherine, Katherine Spalding. Some call me Kate, though." She scrunched up her nose and mouth at this comment.

He decided then that she would always be Katherine to him. "You're very kind, Katherine. I didn't know we were to bring something." He noticed her eyes seemed to be smiling.

"Well, are you going to tell me your name or not?"

"Oh." He brought his hand holding the apple up to his face and, in the process, a piece of apple stuck to his hair.

"You're hopeless," she said, reaching up to remove the sliver.

James had begun working at Katherine's family's farm when they were both fourteen. Eighteen now, they were inseparable. Because of the long days of work during harvest season, he no longer made the trek home to his mother's house each night. Instead, he would dine with Katherine, her father, and sisters, and sleep in a corner of the Spalding's barn. It was after a special dinner to celebrate the end of the harvest that he mustered the courage to help Katherine clean up. He offered. She declined. He insisted. That's when Katherine's two younger sisters began giggling and went to sit on the rug near the hearth. They took out their favorite board game and began to play.

"You outdid yourself tonight, young lady. My belly is so full, I could sleep for days," Katherine's father said, kissing her cheek. Then he whispered in her ear, "Your mother would be so proud," and headed off to his favorite chair near the hearth to nap. "Lena, get your mangy ass off my chair!" he shouted to the dog as he did each night. Lena jumped off the chair and paced on the rug.

"The meal was delicious, Katherine. Thank you," James said,

grabbing a spoon and scraping the remains onto the wooden floor in front of Lena.

James was glad that Katherine was not in front of him, as they stood together at the washing tub, so he didn't have to look directly at her. He found it more and more difficult lately to do so without becoming lost in her green eyes. The gold-colored flecks within them reminded him of the amber they sometimes came upon while plowing the fields in the spring to prepare for planting. Looking at her eyes always led him to look at her cheeks, which invariably led him to her lips.

"You don't have to thank me. There would be something wrong with me if I didn't know what you liked to eat after all this time," Katherine playfully scolded him.

He stuck the first plate in the pail of clean water now in front of Katherine. They stood within inches of each other, and James could feel the warmth of her body near his. He avoided touching her as he handed her the next plate, but she teasingly grabbed it, sliding her fingers across the back of his soapy hands.

"You and Papa finished the last acre today. This was a celebration," she said, leaning into his shoulder so gently that he wasn't sure she realized what she had done.

He stopped scrubbing mid-wash. His hands held the dish submerged in the soapy, warm water.

She reached in, her movements slow, her fingers lingering on his. "Do you think it's been a good harvest?" she asked, looking up at him expectantly.

Her face was close, her cheek touching his. He tried to ignore the impulse to grab her tightly to him. Her eyes appeared glassy and her pink lips were opening and closing slightly. With each breath she took, he thought he could almost sense her heart beating beneath the rounded breasts that rose out of her sheath. He inhaled her scent as wisps of long hair that had escaped from her kerchief tickled his cheeks. Their lips touched.

The Convention of Wives

He was in heaven, or what he imagined heaven might be like.

Soon James loved Katherine in the way a young man loves his new wife—shy and struggling to satisfy her, unsure of exactly what he was doing, attempting in vain to interpret each soft noise she made while he found his way over the curves of a body he was unable to see in the evening's darkness. She was a mystery to him. Nothing was ever spoken aloud about their time in bed together. He'd tried to keep the candle lit a few times when they started, but she always snuffed it out. So, they groped in the darkness and awoke each morning next to each other as if two other people had been lying with each other naked in their bed a few hours before.

James was presented with about ten other men. There was a brief description of where the men had been captured and what they had been doing at the time.

"Directly challenging the life and limb of His Majesty's army . . ."

He scoffed at this. What he'd really been doing was trying to escape. Worse than a traitor, he was a coward. When his sentence was handed down, and it was not death but indentured servitude in some place called Barbados, he felt he had been given a reprieve.

He would survive. Far from home, far from those he cared about, he would be enslaved, but alive. He had never heard of the island, this *Barbados*. One of the men had heard it was like living in hell, hot and filled with sweaty, constantly laboring slaves. James was terrified, then distracted, when the man also explained that Barbados meant "bearded" because of the dense moss that hung in great clumps from the trees. What a strange new home this would be, far from everything he had ever known, from everyone he'd ever loved. He doubted that his mother could survive the loss of him. And he was leaving Katherine alone, in charge of her younger sisters and without the child he had promised her. How could he bear it? He had utterly failed her. He had failed them all.

Chapter Seven

Dina

San Diego, California, December 2000

Dina looked down at the notes she'd scrawled while listening to her father's story. He'd gone on for some time about the candlesticks but hung up abruptly when he realized he was late for a bridge game.

To think of it. Her ancestors had fled a pogrom in Odessa. How absurd that here she was, sitting in the sun, having someone bring her drinks. Her biggest complaint was that she didn't know what to do with all the time on her hands; that, and that no one seemed to have time for her anymore, especially her children. She loved them and simultaneously was angry about their growing independence. If she were totally honest, she was also jealous: Allie, a physician, was living out Dina's dreams in Manhattan; and her middle one, Zoe, gardened on a professional scale for the Brooklyn Botanical Garden. At least they lived nearby. Her baby, Daniel, an accountant in Boston, only came home for holidays. But wasn't this just the natural order of things? Isn't this what a mother was supposed to want for her children? Why did she feel so deflated?

Was this attempt at writing even real, or was it just a desperate effort to find meaning, to redefine herself, to justify her existence?

The Convention of Wives

Dina had completed a screenplay way back when the kids were young, which she distributed to the typical local folks separated by six degrees from a cousin in the biz. The editor friend of someone they knew from temple turned out to publish cozy mysteries. The guy "in development" at a film production company was, in reality, just a summer intern. Then there was Saul, an entertainment accountant they'd known for years. Dina had always thought him boorish, but she was so eager for someone to take her seriously, to see her writing as more than the hobby of a bored housewife, that she invited him to their house as part of their synagogue's "surprise guest" dinner program. What a bust that turned out to be. Despite enduring his cracks about her cooking—something about how *not even she* could ruin a kosher steak—and a few clumsy double entendres he threw her way while cornering her in the kitchen as she stirred a sauce on the stove, nothing ever came of the connection.

Dina sucked the remaining drops of Bloody Mary through the straw, a piece of errant pepper burning her tongue and bringing tears to her eyes. These tears were replaced with real ones as she placed the glass down haphazardly on the table and watched it spill onto the writing pads. Tears came easily and unpredictably between hot flashes these days. Where was Rob with his ever-present handkerchief at the ready? She could use one now. His habit of dressing seemed gentlemanly when they first met, but on one of their first dates he explained how his mother bought them for him. It was, she admitted to herself now, somewhat of a turnoff.

Early on, Dina had asserted her wifely claim and attempted to buy the handkerchiefs herself, but Elsa took one look at them and pooh-poohed the quality. "These will never do," she had said. So, her mother-in-law continued to include a package of new squares in every one of Rob's birthday and Hanukah gifts.

A horn sounded from the harbor and she squinted at her watch. Crap. It was noon and she had plans to meet Rob for lunch. Dina gathered her writing supplies and books, put her cover-up back on, and made her way toward the hotel. This was what her life had always been. Glimpses of him. And now, mere glimpses of her children. And in between, what exactly? No one had warned her that when the kids left, her "career" would walk out the door with them. Why should today be different? *Shit, which tower is her room in again? Right, north, "not our real true home,"* the mnemonic she'd made up to help with her increasing senior moments.

They had planned to meet in the room before lunch and golf. She'd been ready for fifteen minutes. *Where the hell is Rob?* Once again, she'd entered the waiting *zone*, a place doctors' wives frequent as often as patients frequent the waiting room. She wished she had scheduled her massage for today and not tomorrow. She hated wasting her time; but of course, as Rob continued to point out to her, the value of her time was somewhat questionable since she didn't work. "The wife shift," he had called it. *The hell with it* . . . she wasn't waiting any longer. She dialed the spa on the hotel phone.

"Hi, this is Mrs. Wasserman in Room 1014. I'm wondering if I can switch my massage scheduled for tomorrow for some time today, preferably within the next hour or so."

"Yes, we have an opening in about fifteen minutes, can you make that?"

"Perfect."

"Great, just head to the fifth floor on the north tower elevators, and we'll see you shortly."

"Thank you."

Screw it. He'd have to lunch and golf alone. All those lessons. For what? She was so fucking tired of waiting that she decided to forego leaving a note. Let him wonder for once where *she* was.

Dina hurried into the spa elevator. Vaguely aware of another body standing next to her, she slowed her pace of chewing on the tasteless piece of gum she had popped into her mouth to eliminate the remains of the Bloody Mary tell. The candy treat had been included in the welcome bag given out to convention participants. After years of schlepping to meetings with Rob, this was her big prize. Gum.

She was aware of her breath slowing. She'd become adept at self-calming, putting her frustrations behind her. Rob's tardiness was just another minor skirmish in the war of their marriage, a war they both needed to win. Despite everything, they were committed to each other, a team. She pulled out her phone to leave him a message, but as she stepped out of the elevator, her shoulder smacked into the other woman trying to leave. "Oh!" Dina said as her cell phone dropped out of her hand and into the woman's shopping bag. "Excuse me, I'm so sorry."

"Oh, no, I'm sorry," the other woman replied, as she reached into her bag and handed Dina her phone.

Their eyes met.

It couldn't be.

After all this time. Julia.

Her old friend's face was slightly more lined, and a few gray hairs peeked out by her temples, but this was clearly her. She wondered how she looked to Julia.

"Julia, is that you? That *is* you, right?"

"Dina?"

Reflexively, Dina grabbed Julia and hugged her. "What is it with the two of us and spas?"

"Yeah," Julia said, pulling out of her grasp.

Shock and nervousness made Dina giggle. She tried hard to stop, especially when she noticed Julia uncharacteristically not chiming in. Dina began choking on her gum. She coughed loudly. Tears streamed down her face.

"Ma'am, are you okay? Do you need a glass of water? Should I go get somebody?" the receptionist asked.

"Oh, no, no we're fine," Dina answered, having successfully swallowed the gum. She placed her hand on the young girl's shoulder.

"At least let me get you a tissue." The receptionist held up a box.

"Thanks," Dina said, wiping her face and blowing her nose.

"We just need to check in for our treatments," Julia said crisply.

"Your last names?" the receptionist asked, all business.

"Wasserman."

"Kinsella."

"Thank you. Please have a seat near our tea bar, and your technician will be with you shortly." The girl gave a royal wave with her perfectly buffed nails.

They made their way to the seating nearby and sat down.

"Well," said Dina.

Julia nodded, looking down at her feet.

Dina confirmed what she already assumed. Their husbands were at the same conference. She got up the nerve to ask Julia if they could meet up after their massages in the *relaxation den*. Julia hadn't responded when a masseuse, an attractive woman with athletic build, called out Julia's name.

"I'm not sure I'll have time, I have another appointment," Julia said. "But I'll try."

The phone calls that ended quickly. The letters without response. Dina doubted whether the fifty minutes she'd have to think on the massage table would be long enough to figure out what to say and what not to say should Julia even show up. Would she have the guts to ask what had fractured their friendship?

Chapter Eight

Julia

San Diego, California, December 2000

The massage gave Julia time to think. She'd acted too coldly toward Dina. She needed to normalize things. To keep things at a certain level. At this point, what was the harm? They were on their second cups of chamomile tea in the hotel spa's relaxation cove by the time they got through updates about colleges, internships, jobs, and romances for all the kids except their two oldest—Aiden and Allie. Julia had tried politely to end the conversation multiple times, but the longer she stayed, the more she felt herself slipping back into the old conversational patterns she'd shared with Dina. It was so easy. *It had always been easy.*

She'd missed it.

She'd missed her friend.

"So, Aiden is on his way to becoming Mr. Wall Street," Julia said, realizing how braggy it sounded as the words escaped her lips. "I can't even explain what he does, frankly. But he's excited about it. He works late most nights, and there's always some crisis. He's got a nice apartment, but it's barely furnished. He doesn't date much. Well, there was this one girl for a while, but then it ended." The words kept flowing out of her, a nervous stream, putting off the inevitable discussion of the end of their friendship.

Debra Green

"It's strange when you get to the point where your kids' lives aren't entangled with your own on a daily basis. Remember when they were clinging vines?" Dina asked, sipping her tea. "Just going alone to the bathroom was a pleasure. Now we get to watch what's happening from a distance or hear about it after the fact."

We . . . but there was no longer a "we." They were both talking around it, the state of their friendship. She should leave. She should get up and leave now. It was a big hotel. What were the odds of running into Dina again?

She pushed herself up off her seat with her hands.

"That leaves Allie," Dina continued.

Julia stopped and instead of saying good-bye as she had planned, leaned down, picked up her teacup, and put it on the counter nearby. She grabbed some nuts. Julia wanted to hear what was going on with Allie, the little girl whose hair she had braided while dreaming of the day she'd have her own daughter.

"She's doing really great in so many ways. She's had her own apartment for years; well, she's got this roommate." Dina seemed to hesitate.

"What, you don't like her?" Julia asked, sitting down.

"It's a *him*, not a *her*," Dina explained. "Can I have some of those?" Dina asked, pointing at the nuts.

"Sure." Julia offered up the napkin filled with an unsalted mix of almonds, hazelnuts, pecans, and Brazil nuts. "Are they . . . ?" Julia asked without asking.

"No. They're just friends."

"Come on, Dina. It's the year 2000, the new millennium. You were always a little blind about that stuff." *What am I saying?*

"Truthfully, I'm not sure. I don't really understand their relationship. But I think it's stopped Allie from moving on, finding someone. They've been friends since—"

Julia's cellphone rang. Bridget.

57

"Sorry, Dina. It's one of the kids. It'll just be a minute. I'll tell her I'll call back."

Dina gave Julia a "don't worry about it" nod and headed over to the counter for some more nuts.

"Hey Mom, Rosie's not feeling well. You know that flu shot she got a week ago?" Bridget began to explain as Julia walked out into the small hallway nearby to take the call.

How could Julia forget? The call from Rosie, her youngest, about the flu shot had occurred two days before they left for the conference and was, as usual, perfectly timed to coincide with Julia's hair color appointment. Dismissing her advice to call the insurance company to see if the shot was covered, Rosie had hung up quickly saying she'd call John instead.

Somehow, their youngest always had a way of making her feel incompetent.

"Mom! I'm at St. Vincent's Hospital with Rosie. She's still having side effects from the shot. She's got some bruising on her leg from a fall, I think from basketball. Now her arm hurts. I tried calling Dad, but it went to voicemail. Is he in a lecture or something at the meeting?"

"You're at a hospital!"

"Yes, St. Vin—"

"Wait! Did you say *bruising*?"

"Yes, Mom. Please listen."

Julia tried to keep the panic at bay as she digested everything Bridget repeated. She knew about strange bruising.

"Bridget, I'll find Dad and call you back really soon. Can I talk to Rosie?"

"They won't let me use the cell phone inside the ER, and I want to get back to her. Mom, she's really uncomfortable. She hasn't slept in days. And then the fall. She was trying to wait it out. How long can a flu shot affect you? Listen, Aiden is on his way, but he has some meetings he can't get out of, and he's coming from all the way downtown. Please call back when you find Dad."

Rosie and Bridget were too young to remember when John's dad had been diagnosed with AML, acute myeloid leukemia. He had lived for five months. *Bruising on her arms and legs. Oh, God. Is that what Bridget said?* Julia was thinking about how quickly she could get home. Instead, she ended the call calmly. "I'm going to bounce that by Dad as soon as I locate him," she said. "I'll call you back. Please give Rosie a big hug from me."

Dina was just setting her teacup on their shared table. "Is everything okay?" she asked.

"It's my youngest, Rosie. She's at St. Vincent's, in New York City, in the emergency room," Julia said flatly.

"Is she all right? I mean, is it serious?"

"I need to find John. Can you help me?"

"Of course. Julia, did you say St. Vincent's?"

"What? Yes, why?" she grabbed her towel and headed for the spa lobby.

Dina grabbed her arm.

"Julia, we need to go to the locker room first and get dressed, right? Come on." Dina guided Julia up and out of the cove. Once changed, they made their way into the elevator.

"I'm sure she'll be okay, Julia."

"That's what everyone says before the shit hits the fan. She's twenty-three years old and she may die."

"Die! What's wrong, what happened?" Dina shouted.

"No one is ever honest about these things," Julia said quietly, ignoring Dina's question. She tapped her foot on the floor and rubbed her left elbow repeatedly with her right hand. There was no one in the elevator to witness her strange dance except Dina, then it ended as the doors opened on the lobby level.

Julia shot out of the elevator.

"We'll find John. But I'm calling Allie. She's a resident at

St. Vincent's, in the ER," Dina explained breathlessly, trying to catch up.

"What, what did you say?" Julia asked, turning around to look at Dina while continuing to move quickly ahead.

"Allie, Allie is at St. Vincent's."

Chapter Nine

Katherine Cawley

Barbados, 1830

Katherine had struggled to keep her son safe during the seven-week journey to Barbados. She worried about his prolonged battle with motion sickness, but he recovered despite the limited food and water. Once again, Thomas had the energy of a typical nine-year-old and insisted on hoisting himself up on the ropes he found dangling on deck. She was convinced it was just a matter of time before he swung himself into the sea. And all of this—the waiting, the struggling, and this journey—to finally see James again.

Their lives had been filled with promise. Katherine still had a hard time believing that James had been uprooted and thrown halfway around the world because of one impetuous political act, leaving her to raise their son. A child she'd told him she was expecting right before he'd left. Thomas had grown up on a steady diet of stories about his brave and strong father.

James and Katherine settled into a long-distance friendship of sorts, with her letters filled with Thomas's latest adventure and the health of James's mother, Rosie, with whom Katherine and the young boy lived. James's letters were brief, businesslike; a recounting of the money he'd saved, the acres of land he'd purchased, and the crops he'd sold. Lists of numbers, little else.

Where was the James she had known? The one filled with stories? He didn't tell her how much he missed her. He didn't ask about their son.

Before Rosie died, she insisted Katherine add the money from their cheese business to the money James had sent in the last few years and book passage to Barbados. When she'd written to tell James she was coming, his response had been less than enthusiastic. She wasn't sure what to make of it. But Katherine understood her place was with her husband. A man she barely remembered.

They pulled into port at Bridgetown. At first all she could see were warehouses: large gray buildings made of weathered timber with a few windows on the upper floor. The one large gaping opening on the ground level looked like an angry, hungry mouth. Katherine guessed these warehouses were the ones James had described in his letter; filled with the sugar, tobacco, ginger, and cotton that would make their way to England.

"Mama, do you see them?" Thomas asked. "The Africans? I thought they were black, but they're brown. Not at all like in the book you showed me."

He was right. They were mostly brown, their skin tones varying from lightest toast to almost blue. But, regardless of color, most were dressed in rags, many shirtless, even the women, moving around in groups led by white men shouting and cursing at them. As they neared, she saw ropes around their feet. No, not ropes . . . not ropes at all. Chains of metal! People were emptying cargo boxes from wagons and hauling them on their backs between the ships and the warehouses . . . and they were in chains.

Desperately she scanned the horizon in search of someone of her sex and race. She found none. This was a land of men . . . and slaves. She was horrified. Where had she come? Why?

Thomas, who could barely see over the side of the ship, was

standing on tiptoe staring at the scene below. He was glued to her side, gripping her hand like a three-year-old. Patting his head to comfort him, she thought of her mother-in-law Rosie's strong hands, calloused and swollen. Hands that were always there to nurse Katherine and Thomas through fevers and nightmares. How she missed her.

The ship jerked hard as it docked. The steady breeze they had been enjoying lightened and then ceased all together. The humidity and heat settled on them like a soggy blanket. Something pricked at Katherine's ankles. Looking down, she saw a swirl of black insects feasting on her flesh. She batted them away. Perspiration dripped from her forehead, stinging her eyes. Dampness seeped through her armpits and under her dress.

Then she saw him. A bit more stooped and with less hair than she remembered, but it was James.

"James, James, we're here!" she shouted. But the sun was shining directly in his face. Could he see any more than the dark outlines of people? She watched him turn away as she grabbed her bags and gently pushed Thomas ahead of her and off the ship. Heading down the gangplank, she noticed a raised platform on the dock and a group of Black men huddled nearby. The youngest of them—a boy really, not much older than Thomas—was being pushed up on the platform.

"Seventy-five pounds for him, a bargain! Look at him, these fine white teeth," the auctioneer shouted, pulling apart the boy's lips. "Now walk, that's right, walk." The boy, chains around his ankles, took five lurching steps forward. "Now back with you," the man ordered as the boy turned and completed his dance.

"I'll give you fifty!" a man in a green waistcoat yelled.

"Fifty, my ass. He's worth double!" the auctioneer roared back.

Katherine stood, swaying, her legs shaking as her body adjusted to being on dry land. Mesmerized, she did not realize that James was next to her until he spoke.

The Convention of Wives

"Katherine, it is you. I wasn't sure," he said as he placed his large hands on her arms and pulled her around to face him. He looked at her, nodded his head, and then turned to his son. "And this must be Thomas."

James put out his hand to shake. Thomas hesitated.

"Come, quickly, let's get you and the boy out of here," James said curtly as he picked up the two larger bags, unceremoniously giving Thomas the smallest of the three to carry, and marched them out of the crowd. "We're this way, not too far."

She was disturbed by his greeting but happy to escape the scene at the port.

The three walked silently until they were a few streets away from the dock, in the cool shade of a tree, when James suddenly stopped, put down the bags and turned to face them both.

"Aye, let me get a better look at you, boy. *My* boy," James said, as he grabbed Thomas's face and tilted his chin up.

Thomas at first averted his eyes, but then he stood up very straight and saluted his father.

"Ho, ho. A formal greeting, yes?" James said, as he grabbed Thomas, hugged him, swung him around and placed him down. "Finally, you are finally here in front of me."

Katherine stood waiting for the embrace she had imagined hundreds of nights in the moments before falling asleep, cold and alone, reaching below her covers to remind herself of the passion she and James once shared.

"Katherine," James said, holding out his hand to her.

"James."

A few moments passed as they stood holding each other's hands, but for Katherine it felt like an eternity.

All this waiting, this hoping. For a handshake.

She was miserable, hot, and tired.

"Come, we're almost there," James said, picking up the bags.

He took a few steps with Thomas trailing him but then noticed that Katherine wasn't following.

"I, I don't understand. I thought you lived on a farm?" Katherine asked, hands on her hips. "We're in a village."

"This is not a village. This is a town. Bridgetown, as I told you in my letters," James explained as they all started to walk again.

"Where's the bridge?" Thomas asked.

"We'll see it soon enough," James said as he tousled his son's hair.

"The farm's a few miles from town. About twenty-five acres now that I've been able to buy a number of slaves. But you . . . we will live in town. You wouldn't be comfortable out on the farm. Come, you must be tired. We'll talk more after dinner. Here we are."

He owned slaves. A man who had been an indentured servant owned slaves.

"Don't look at me like that, woman. You have no idea what I've been through trying to survive on this godforsaken island."

"But your letters never . . ."

"You expected me to tell you everything? You never would have understood. You never would have come."

Before Katherine stood a house of two stories with yellow roses in the flower boxes below each window. At the door was a young Black woman, a light-brown-skinned child beside her. The girl was staring at Thomas. Katherine looked from one child to the other. They could have been brother and sister.

"She'll help you get settled," James said, nodding at the woman without further explanation.

Katherine smelled one of the flowers and looked up at James. *Who had he become?*

"For my mother. Pick one if you like," James said.

The Convention of Wives

"For Rosie," Katherine answered.

The woman took their larger bag.

Katherine hesitated briefly, gently removed a blossom, picked up her small satchel filled with cheese starter, yarn, and needles, and warily took a few steps toward the rest of her life.

Chapter Ten

Dina

Millburn, New Jersey, April 1986

She went over the details for the bat mitzvah one last time. The big *machers* in her synagogue would be shocked that she and Rob had decided to forgo the typical pseudo-wedding reception. She didn't care. Spring was in the air and everything was turning green. The crocuses were already in full bloom, and the rest of the flowers were peeking through the soil. An outdoor, evening celebration for the kids was just the thing for Allie, Dina's April baby who was no longer a baby.

So why was she fretting about the table linens for the indoor luncheon that would follow services, instead of enjoying the beautiful day? The tablecloths were from Rob's bar mitzvah, one of the things Dina had accepted from her mother-in-law when her in-laws downsized. They had been mildewed and moth-eaten when she got them, but the local dry cleaners had pulled off a minor miracle. After being patched, cleaned, and pressed, the Scottish, plaid table coverings were now in good enough condition for the luncheon reception. The synagogue's recreation hall—like the cloths—was somewhat tattered and patched in multiple places, but it was usable with the right lighting.

Her mind drifted back to the floral centerpieces she and Allie had spent hours designing. Her daughter loved the experience, as did she.

"Mommy, this is like painting, only with flowers," Allie had said while fingering a sun-yellow daffodil and crimson tulip.

The florist overheard Allie's comment and smiled. "Maybe you'll come work in my shop when you're a bit older, what do you think?" she asked cheerfully.

But Allie didn't answer. She was busy placing some Queen Anne's lace in a symmetrical pattern around the daffodil and tulip. Her ability to concentrate on a task was impressive, even at a young age, and had come in handy for Dina. While Dina tended to the needs of her younger children, finger painting had distracted Allie for hours at a time. Once Zoe and Dan were old enough, Allie had a new and elaborate project for her younger siblings every weekend morning, allowing Dina and Rob to sleep in.

Dina and Rob had thoroughly discussed when to have a family. There were so many cons. She had just started her nursing career. Rob had so long to go between finishing med school and residency. They had no money and wouldn't for a long time. But then, one night while looking at Rob, Dina couldn't help but think that the thing she wanted most in the world was to have his child. *Their* child, a small replica of him with his beautiful eyes and strong yet refined looking hands.

It might have been the wine they were drinking to soften the impact of the grueling day they'd both had at the hospital. They'd both lost a patient: his, a middle-aged man who'd suffered a stroke; hers, an older woman with a badly infected leg ulcer that was too far gone. Life was just unpredictable, not in their control. Why wait for anything?

They'd figure it all out, he'd said, as he nuzzled and licked her neck. She'd pushed away and gone to the bathroom to pee before they had sex, taken the rubber flesh-toned orb out of the medicine cabinet, squeezed its hard, circular outer ring together and held it tight until her fingers gave way. The thing jumped into the toilet bowel. She took it as a sign. Rob was right. Baby Allie was born nine months later, the product of love, wine, and weak fine motor skills.

The final flower selection—a huge bouquet of red roses, blue hydrangeas, lime green orchids, white lilacs, and purple irises—feminized the royal blue, red, and emerald-green plaid cloths of clan Wasserman. Allie's red dress and jacket, with dyed-to-match shoes, were the final jewel in the crown of the luncheon; until a week before the event when she decided she hated the dress.

"Mom!" Allie screamed as she entered the kitchen. "Everyone is wearing long dresses. Why did you make me pick this—this *thing*?" she asked, pushing the dress toward her mother.

Dina was in the midst of shaping salmon croquets. She held up her hands helplessly. "I didn't *make* you pick anything. You liked it in the store. You loved it."

"I never loved it, *you* loved it," Allie insisted, throwing the dress on the floor.

"Are you crazy? Pick that up right now!"

"I won't!"

"I'm not getting you another dress, if that's what you think this little performance of yours is all about," Dina shouted as she washed her hands and dried them on the nearby dish towel. "You look beautiful in that fabric, the color complements your hair and complexion," she said, picking the dress up off the floor and placing it carefully over the back of a kitchen stool. "Allie, there will always be styles that come and go, but understanding which classic fashions fit you well and are your personal style . . . well, that's a skill."

"You sound like Grandpa Dave. I thought you hated that stuff! You've become a Stepford Wife!"

"A what?"

"A Stepford Wife . . . it's a book I got at the library. It's a bestseller. You should read it. I'm never becoming you, never in a million years. I'm going to be a doctor like Daddy and work and never get married. Ever. This dress is your style, not mine. I hate it. I hate it. I hate you!" she concluded as she ran out of the room.

Allie ran upstairs and slammed her bedroom door. Dina turned back to the business of the patties, then she stopped as a few of her tears fell into the bowl. It was a little after eleven when she heard Rob come into the house.

"I don't know why your mother insists that we use two sets of candlesticks. She knows my family's are the heirlooms, a few hundred years old, at least. I know she loves hers, but they're so plain," Dina said as she watched Rob take a bite of what she knew was a somewhat dried out meal.

"A little saltier than usual. I just read an article that they've linked salt and high blood pressure. Might want to cut back on that."

"You shouldn't believe everything you read."

"Why do we have to discuss the candlesticks again anyway? What is the difference, one set or two? They represent both of our families. They're meaningful to my mother," Rob said as he dug into his wilted salad.

"I've spent hours trying to make this event special. Every detail. You have no idea. And why would you, why should you? We always agreed we were good at dividing and conquering."

"I'm not allowed to say anything?"

"Of course, you're allowed, but I find it ironic that you care so much about this one thing. Did you ask to see the flowers? Allie's dress? No. You bought your suit and tie. No, wait, I bought you a suit and tie.

"What's the matter with you? You are so uptight. It's just a bat mitzvah."

"The matter with me, *with me?* Your mother has never really—"

"Oh, come on. Not this again."

"Yes, this again, Rob. I know I'm not the child of Holocaust survivors. I know I'm not Jewish enough for her . . . but why do I have to keep placating her?" She turned away from him, placed the frying pan in the sink, and squirted it with an overly generous portion of silky, green Palmolive. "It's as if nothing ever happened to the Jews before the Holocaust." She turned to see Rob reading a medical journal as he ate. "Rob, are you even listening to me?"

"I'm listening, Dina. The Holocaust, you said that nothing ever happened to the Jews before the Holocaust."

"Oh, my God, what do I have to do to get your attention?" and with that, she took the spray hose and doused her T-shirt with water. "Here, come on, if this doesn't keep you captivated, I don't know what will." Her nipples hardened as they cooled from the water. He stared at the now see-through tee.

"You are crazy. This bat mitzvah is making you crazy. But that," as he pointed to her breasts, "is the kind of crazy I can deal with. 'Cause I am one *c-raaaazy* guy," he said with his best impersonation of Steve Martin's *Saturday Night Live* Festrunk Brothers accent.

She shook her head and let out a sigh, then she cleaned the spatula and pan with vigor, as if the food left on them was poisonous. "Why does she think I'm incapable of empathy for her? She lost her family, she was widowed young, all horrible. But she remarried, she made a life, and still . . . still she is just so miserable to me." She reached for the dish towel and froze, rubbing the terry cloth between her fingers. "And the handkerchief thing. I can't even buy you handkerchiefs. She won't allow it. *Too much synthetic blend, the stitching isn't done well.* I'm from a family that produces clothing. Could she give me a little credit? What did I ever do to her except marry you?"

The Convention of Wives

"My mother is only trying to be helpful. It's her way."

"I don't need her help or her way," Dina said as she went into the refrigerator and brought him some ketchup and applesauce to complement the croquets. "There is such history behind my candlesticks, they were made so long before hers."

"History? You're not even sure where they were made. And since when is the Holocaust *not* part of our history?" he asked as he squeezed out the ketchup and wolfed down the food.

"I'm not saying that. Of course, it's a part of our history, but her candlesticks are just so plain, so Germanic looking."

"I can't believe you just said that. They look *Germanic*? I know you don't like them. You've made a face every time we're at my mother's for Shabbat." He got up and took his plate and silverware over to the sink. "Come with me!" He grabbed her hand and dragged her to their bedroom.

"Rob, what the hell are you doing?" she whispered to him so as not to wake the children upstairs.

"Here. Look at this," he said as he opened the bat mitzvah file that lay open on the dresser and shoved a piece of paper at her. "Does this help?"

"What is this?"

"It's their pedigree, my mother's candlesticks. I did some research for my speech."

Dina read what was on the paper.

Lazarus Posen Witwe candlesticks, Berlin & Frankfurt: founded in 1869, the firm became the largest supplier of Judaica in the late nineteenth century, receiving a royal warrant in 1903. In 1938 the company was forcefully closed and looted on Kristallnacht, the Night of Broken Glass.

"Do they count now?" he asked, raising his voice.

"What are you, a doctor or a lawyer?" She couldn't believe he had presented her with this document.

Why were they fighting? Their daughter was having her bat

mitzvah. This was supposed to be the fun stuff. But they were miserable.

"I just wish your mother liked me more." That was really all she had ever wanted. For Elsa to accept her.

Rob came to her and held her. Dealing with his mother had been hard for her over the years but far worse for Rob. He lived Elsa's pain in the daily calls in which she expressed her constant fear about everything, especially the children. The dutiful son, he listened as she doled out endless advice about how he could avoid ever letting their welfare be threatened. Dina thought it was partly why Rob had become a doctor, to gain some logical control, some perspective and rationality over the fears Elsa instilled in him.

"Don't go near the stove, Rob, you'll burn yourself." That one had worked. Rob didn't know where anything was in the kitchen.

"Don't use the knife. I'll cut it for you, you'll hurt yourself." Dina remembered Elsa saying this to Rob, even after he'd become a surgeon.

Dina loved him for putting up with all of this. If she was being honest, her parents were no bargain either.

Suddenly their hug turned into an embrace, and they were kissing. They danced backward toward the bed, the quilt covered with goody bags meant for the reception. He pushed her down as if the bags weren't there, and Dina motioned angels in the snow to scatter them off the bed.

When she felt him unhook her bra and throw off the remaining bags, she pushed him up and took off her T-shirt and bra in one swift move. She lay back as he sucked hungrily on her nipples, one then the other until she groaned in pleasure. She grabbed at his back and reached for his pants, but he pushed her over on her side and lay behind her as one of his hands massaged her breasts and the other pulled her pajama pants down. She groaned in pleasure as he thrust. He reached around to touch her, but she shoved his hand away and reached between her legs and squeezed his balls. Soon he was making the sounds she knew he always made before he came. He grunted loudly and she felt herself get wet.

"Sorry," Rob said as he began playing with her hair.

"Sorry. Why are you sorry? Don't be sorry," she said as she deftly removed his fingers soaked with God-knows-what from the hair she'd washed that morning. She placed them on her breast instead.

Was he sorry about his mother or because he thought he'd come too quickly? Because she hadn't? She reached down and her hand worked quickly. Why was the best sex always after an argument? And why was some of the most expedient sex done with her own hand?

She groaned in pleasure, trying to be quiet and not wake the kids. After a moment, she exhaled deeply and turned toward him.

"All right, we'll use both sets of candlesticks," she said, giving him a tear-salted kiss.

Dina sat in the hair salon, a somewhat old-fashioned townie one, where Allie was getting the up-do she'd insisted on, although Dina was pretty sure she'd come to regret the pictures someday. Allie looked like a princess perched in the white vinyl chair. She wore one of Dina's blouses so she could easily remove it without ruining her hair. A touch of lipstick and mascara, and voila, perfecto.

Perfection never lasts long, though. That's what Dina realized when they got to the Friday night dinner only to learn that she had somehow miscounted the attendees, thirty-two not twenty-eight. Four chairs short became a nightmare as they scrambled to fit more seats into the small room. She'd chosen this setting instead of the larger, main social hall because it would be more intimate; but the spring heat wave, the unexpectedly broken air-conditioning, and a seating shortage combined into a crowd of hungry Jews ready to riot. Things calmed down once everyone was seated and a few fans were brought in. Almost. Rob was sweating on the top of his balding head like he'd eaten some spicy food.

The rest of the weekend flew by. Allie did a great job at the Saturday morning service. Her *Amidah* and *Shema* were flawless, if a bit rushed. Her *Haftorah* was shaky but gained strength by the end. By the time she reached *Aleinu*, it seemed she didn't want to leave the *bimah*. Dina stole glances at Elsa throughout, expecting to see happiness reflected in Allie's grandmother's face. Instead, the woman stared solemnly at Allie leading the congregation, alternately wiping tears from her eyes and squeezing a handkerchief tightly in her hand. Dina could only imagine the whirl of emotions Elsa was feeling.

At the luncheon, she was thrilled to hear her mother-in-law's Upper East Side friend, another Holocaust survivor, comment to her table of contemporaries that "this is what a bat mitzvah is supposed to be." After that, Dina felt able to sit back and enjoy. The kids' Saturday night party in a tent in the backyard was loud and fun and tiring. The highlight of the weekend came when Allie and her friends were let loose with magic markers on the wall between the den and living room. Why not take advantage of the fact that it was scheduled to come down the following week as part of the renovation project? Dina never thought she'd be thrilled to have kids writing on a wall in her house, but she guessed that it would be the creative moment they'd all remember.

The weather was warm for the Sunday brunch, and almost everyone was outside on the patio in the back. Dina had come inside for more plastic forks when she saw Elsa, looking younger than her sixty-eight years, standing straight and still, staring at the colorful wall. Dina wondered, as she tiptoed behind her, whether this was just another confirmation for her mother-in-law that nothing was permanent.

"It's not something we'd normally have allowed the kids to do if we weren't doing the renovation," Dina responded to Elsa's unspoken criticism.

Elsa turned to her, appearing somewhat startled. "I think it's fabulous. I'm not surprised you'd think of this. I know I never would. You've always encouraged the children to be creative. Even if it does sometimes get messy."

Dina was so surprised she didn't know what to say.

"I can't quite believe I have a thirteen-year-old granddaughter. I feel like she was just learning how to color, making me presents in preschool. And now this." She waved at the wall. "Where did the time go?"

Dina stepped closer to her. "I feel the same way." They rarely agreed. Dina tried to slow down the moment. "I think you and my father passed down the artistic gene to Allie. Rob always talks about the hats you described to him that you designed back in Berlin."

Elsa looked like she'd been slapped. "*Uch*. So long ago. Who can even remember?" she said, bringing her hand up to her chest before she turned away and walked out of the room.

How stupid to bring up Berlin.

Elsa would remain ever the wandering Jew, with a *minyan* of memories and places she called home. Dina's family had lived in the same country for over a hundred years, moving less than twenty miles away from where they'd gotten off the boat. Rob's family had barely a generation of stability. They could never protect Elsa from the dark memories that seemed to surface at the happiest of times. In that moment, Dina understood that her mother-in-law was constantly battling invisible demons.

She put the plastic ware down on the couch, went to her bedroom, and opened the top drawer of her nightstand. She took the handkerchief Elsa had purchased for Allie for the bat mitzvah, the one she'd secreted away, conveniently "forgetting" to show her daughter, and brought it over to the cardboard box that held all of the weekend's "remains," including Allie's *tallit* bag. Unzipping the bag, she put the handkerchief inside.

Chapter Eleven

Shoshana Aharoni

Safed, Judea, 1840

Shoshana sang softly to Benjamin, sleeping deeply after his feeding:

> "My little one has curly hair and eyes as dark as night,
> and when he sits upon my lap he is a pretty sight.
> Ya la la, la la la, ya la la, la la la la la."

The child was wrapped in the blue woolen cloth Shoshana's mother had woven for him. His small toes stuck out at one end like little pink pearls. She kissed each one of them. Before Shoshana's wedding, despite an increasingly painful illness, her mother had insisted on weaving the cloth in hope of a child to be. A month after the ceremony, they were sitting *shiva*. Perhaps this was why their family and friends had been so generous with the food today: cheeses, breads, dried fish, cakes, and platters of fruit.

After the *brit milah* earlier in the day, the family was resting at Shoshana's parents' house. Her in-laws had gone home. Her father, who had been so proud to serve as the *sandek*, holding the baby during the ritual circumcision, was snoring softly in his rocking chair. Levi, her husband, was lying on some blankets nearby. She stared at him unashamedly. He was handsome, his hair a flow of brown waves, his arms strong and sinewy beneath his shirt, a testament to the manual labor he did each day.

Shoshana was pleased to be at her parents' home, to enjoy its familiarities and comforts. When she and Levi were betrothed, Shoshana assumed they would live near her parents, but she soon learned otherwise. It had been not much more than a year ago when Levi's mother had asked her future daughter-in-law to help with the ritual preparation for Pesach. Miriam had recounted the family's history as the two women swept and scrubbed the food cellar in the small home.

"When my husband and I first came to Safed, twenty years ago, barely escaping Odessa with our lives, we had very little."

"Very little, not so very little," Levi's father Judah interrupted, as he came down the stairs holding a candle and grabbed a bag of grain. "We had each other—far from very little. And enough to afford this house in the Jewish Quarter. And you cannot forget to tell her about the candlesticks. Or has Levi told you already?" he asked Shoshana.

"No, he's told me many stories about your family, but not this one." She was still uncomfortable around Levi's father, a tall man with a graying beard so long that he had to roll it up under itself to stay out of the way while he worked.

"Always you upstage me. Even with my future daughter-in-law!" Miriam scolded her husband.

"My Miriam, it's a story worth telling," he said as he came over and kissed his wife.

Surprised and embarrassed at witnessing this intimate gesture, Shoshana turned away. She was not used to this type of display.

"So," he continued, "we purchased a small plot of land when we arrived. It is where we have stayed. It is where you and Levi will live. We have already purchased a small house for you a few houses away from us. There is an attached building perfect for a silver shop. Bigger than the one I now have. With Levi having a family to support, it is time to expand."

Her in-laws had already decided where she was to live! Did Levi know? Is this what her new life would be like?

She grabbed her skirt and squeezed her hands shut. "But Levi and I haven't discussed where we'll live. And you're nowhere near my parents' house." Her parents' house was in the southeastern, Muslim section of the city. Perhaps her in-laws had judged the area not good enough for their son's family.

Levi's parents exchanged looks. "It is done."

"But . . ." She sniffled.

"We can talk about it more when we're together with you and Levi next," his father said kindly. He picked up the sack and walked back up the stairs.

"Aren't you forgetting something, my husband?"

"What? *Uch*, yes." He headed down and over to a crate in the back of the cellar. He motioned for Shoshana to come over to him. As she approached, she saw the light reflecting on the cellar walls before she saw the silver objects he was unwrapping from the cloth.

"Here they are. The remnants of our family's history."

She stared at a set of candlesticks, tarnished but magnificent. "They're beautiful," Shoshana offered through tears.

She'd never seen anything like them in Judah and Levi's silver shop. He quickly rewrapped them and put them away. The wooden box banged shut.

"I only show them to family. Our past," he said seriously, then smiled at her and pinched her cheek. "You and Levi are our future!" He took her face in his hands, wiped the tears off her face with his thumbs, and headed back up the stairs. It was the first time he had smiled at her.

"Aren't you forgetting something else?" Miriam asked as she handed Judah the sack of grain.

"Woman, I'd forget my head if it wasn't for you," he said as he left.

"Let's take a rest," Miriam said to Shoshana, putting down the mop she was holding. "Come, we'll have some cake and tea. I need to get rid of some *chametz* from the pantry anyway, it's almost Pesach."

Not wanting to be disrespectful, she followed Levi's mother upstairs. They ate and drank quietly for a while, feasting on the cake they would not be allowed to eat during the festival of Passover.

"I will be the enemy here, not my son. Mothers-in-law are always the enemy anyway," Miriam said with a smile. Shoshana managed to smile back. "I'm sure Levi meant to tell you."

She and Levi fought about it for weeks before the wedding; she was tempted to cancel the betrothal. After two days of refusing to talk to him, her own mother sat her down.

"I know you don't want this, my daughter, but I need you to hear me. I don't want you to go, but you need to go. I've always been jealous of the breeze Miriam enjoys when she sits on her porch. And the new shop will mean a secure future for your family." She took Shoshana's hands in hers. "You know I haven't been well for some time."

Shoshana's eyes filled with tears. She had been denying what was happening in front of her eyes. Her mother's thin body, her yellowed skin, her hair, once shiny and full, now dull and thinning. The nights of screaming pain.

"Levi's mother is doing me a kindness. There is nothing another woman can do that is more meaningful than to let you know she will take care of your children. Someday, when you are a mother, you will understand."

Shoshana began to cry.

"Shh, shh, shh," her mother said, wiping Shoshana's tears with her apron. "She will help you make a good life with her son.

The Convention of Wives

Her wish as a mother is for her son's happiness, and *you* are that happiness."

They hugged for a long time, her mother stroking her head and kissing her.

"This is what life is. For us, and for those who came before us, and it will be the same for those who come after. Happiness and sadness with life lived in between. And people who come into your life in unexpected ways who help you endure the sadness and who celebrate the good."

The baby had been born two weeks later than expected. He was big, and his healthy head of dark hair reflected the candlelight shed by the five silver candelabras lit in the house for the special event. Despite the wine he had consumed, Benjamin emitted a robust cry of protest when Levi performed the ritual circumcision. The crowd had chatted about it while they ate and drank, joking about the baby's strong lungs and placing bets on whether he would blow shofar someday on Rosh Hashanah. Shoshana was happy that, because her husband was a silversmith, he had a steady hand. She wondered what their guests would think if they knew the baby was wearing clothing that Yalgoot, her Muslim neighbor, had sewn for him.

After the guests and her in-laws left, they lay down to rest.

Suddenly, the ground shook violently. Shoshana lost her footing with Benjamin in her arms. Levi pulled her to him and together they fell, cradling the baby. Her husband lay on top of them until the tremors stopped. Minutes passed; she wasn't sure how many. When the churning subsided and Levi pulled away, the first image Shoshana saw was the hutch, fallen over, surrounded by broken plates and glassware. Looking closer, she saw her father's legs and a pool of dark liquid coming out from underneath. Her brother, covered in red clay roof tiles, sat up nearby coughing dust and blood out of his mouth.

Though their house was still intact, it took hours to dig

through the debris blocking the front door. Levi determined that it was far too dangerous to go walking around before daybreak, even to help their family or neighbors. He and Shoshana cleaned up what debris they could, then they sat near one another as the aftershocks hit. Their sleep was interrupted by the crying all around them—for the dead and for the missing. The house shook a few more times during the night as they lay near each other on one side of the room, the body of Shoshana's father on the other, wrapped in a blanket.

He was just one among hundreds of Jews who died that day, nearly half their total population. The Muslim area of the city had suffered much less damage, as did the top level of homes in every section, cushioned as they fell on the lower levels. Her family had been spared doubly because of her parents' home's location. Her in-laws' home had slid farther down the mountain. They located the house and shop, but no bodies were ever found. All that was left of Levi's family was the candlesticks stored in the basement—now at ground level—and the silver that hadn't been looted from the new shop. Shoshana and Judah's own house, given to them as a wedding gift by Levi's parents, had been utterly destroyed, so they returned to stay in the Muslim Quarter.

It took over two weeks for survivors to be pulled from the ruins, for all the dead to be buried. It took several more for help to come and set up a temporary hospital to distribute medicine and bandages.

"Shoshana, there is no work to do. The silver I could find in the shop is secured. I'm going to help at the hospital," Levi told her.

"You are leaving us? After all of this? We are still in mourning for our parents!" Shoshana yelled. They had buried her father less than a week before.

"There is nothing we can do for the dead. But we can help

the living. This place . . ." In one motion, Levi picked up one of the remaining intact ceramic pitchers and threw it to the ground, the sound hitting her like a slap in the face. "If we are not being murdered in our beds, then we are being killed by the earth itself. It is cursed. Your brother will stay to help you."

Levi left that day after morning prayers, and each day afterward, coming home as the sun was setting. He always returned with another story of what they had found beneath the rubble: a child's doll, a ruined book, and, always, another body. She tried to pay attention to this accounting but was often too concerned with trying to feed them all with the little sustenance her brother struggled to bring home.

She knew something was going on when the silver began to disappear, but she wasn't sure until Levi bounded in the door, grabbed and twirled her around.

"The young doctor sent to us from Jerusalem is organizing a group of families to leave for America. I've sold most of our holdings. We travel next week to Haifa and then by steamship to New York in America. All of us," he said, looking at her brother stacking kindling near the fireplace.

America. New York. A big city. The trip would take almost two months. With a new baby. Without her parents. She was seventeen years old and terrified. But Levi was her husband. She would have nothing and no one left in Safed. She would follow.

Chapter Twelve

Rob Heller Wasserman

New York, New York, June 1973

The Wassermans' apartment was a small one-bedroom, but the sleeper sofa and playpen were all that were needed to accommodate Julia, John, and baby Aiden. The weekend of their visit, it was overly warm and humid for June, but that didn't seem to bother Julia, who had never been to Manhattan before.

Dina and Rob planned to stick to the routine they reserved for first-timers. After a quick dinner of pizza and cheap wine, they left their guests to settle into the sleeper sofa in the living room with Aiden in the playpen nearby. Miraculously, despite the whirring of the fans Rob had set up, they all slept until the babies stirred at around six o'clock. By ten in the morning, it was already seventy-five with an expected high in the nineties as they maneuvered strollers and diaper bags on the subway to visit the top of the Empire State Building. Even Rob was excited as he admitted to the group that he'd never been. The women chatted on and on as the men followed with the strollers, but when they got to the top and stepped out onto the viewing platform, everyone became quiet.

Rob looked out at the clear blue sky. It was so peaceful. He scanned in all directions, the beauty of the city beneath him. He was aware of the sounds of the wind and his own breathing, broken only by the soft rhythm of the infants sucking on their pacifiers and the occasional cry of a gull overhead. He looked over at Dina in her mommy uniform of jeans, sneakers, and sweatshirt, her hair in a ponytail. He looked down at Allie, who'd been born with nothing more than peach fuzz and now sported a mop of dark curls.

Rob wasn't quite sure how or when he'd become a *family man*. His rotations and residency applications had kept him so busy he often felt like an observer of his own life. Dina's pregnancy was a blur. So was Allie's birth. He looked at the baby, searching unsuccessfully for himself in her facial features. Those almond shaped eyes weren't his. Where did the cleft in her chin come from? Neither he nor Dina had one.

Rob had been relieved when he rotated out of the Neonatal Intensive Care Unit; the infants seemed so fragile, their thin veins barely able to accommodate the IV needles, their paperlike skin translucent and otherworldly. But there was no rotating out of fatherhood. This was a forever thing. As his hold on the stroller tightened, the moisture on his palms made him feel he was losing his grip. He was having trouble catching his breath.

"Rob, Rob, didn't you hear me? What's wrong with you?" Then Dina whispered, "Are you okay?"

When he didn't immediately respond, Dina placed one of her hands on the stroller and with the other, angrily pulled his hands off. Her brows knitted together like two caterpillars, her dark hair flying about her face, loosened by the breeze. He had embarrassed her in some way. He raised one of his hands in the sign language they used to indicate "I'm fine." Dina wiped her hand on the back of her jeans, groaned, and wheeled the stroller in the direction of Julia and John. He took his time rejoining the group.

"I could use a cup of coffee," Dina said as she handed the stroller back to Rob. "I've hit my morning slump. Maybe we can find a diner somewhere?"

"Sure. Let's go," he said, pulling his gaze away from Allie, who was staring intently at the toe she had wriggled out of her sock and managed to pull up to her face. Was it wrong to be jealous of his own baby's abject happiness, or, for that matter, her flexibility?

At a lunch of gyros, the conversation lagged. Dina had mentioned Julia so often since the women had met at that conference, it was as if the Kinsellas lived next door. But how well did they really know this couple? Maybe the weekend was a mistake.

After a trip to the Statue of Liberty, the group headed back home.

"Dina mentioned you have a movie theater near your apartment. Maybe we can see that comedy *Young Frankenstein*. I'd love to get into some air conditioning," John said as he wiped his forehead with Aiden's baby blanket. Rob noticed the large circles of perspiration under John's armpits and thought he probably looked the same.

The kids slept through the movie. A minor miracle. They headed back and ordered in dinner.

"I just love Gene Wilder. What a hoot!" Dina commented, passing out paper plates.

"But what about Frau Blucher," Rob added, whinnying for emphasis.

They all laughed.

"I think it was Brucher, with an *R*," John corrected.

What a jerk.

"Where's this from?" Julia asked, holding a framed photo from the bookstand.

"It's Rob and me on Fire Island. When we had a life," Dina said with a mock groan.

"I know what you mean. John, look at this. Are we ever going to get back to the Cape?" Julia asked.

"Come on. How could I keep my little *islander* away from the sand?" John joked.

"What?" Dina asked.

"John's little nickname for me. I think he's being racist."

"Bullshit," John reprimanded her halfheartedly.

"My mom was born on Barbados," Julia explained.

"Barbados? Rob, did you hear that?"

Rob put the ice he'd fetched from the kitchen down on the bar. "What about Barbados?"

"Julia's mom was born there. Small world . . . tell her!"

"There's not much to tell. My mom and I lived there for a little while. After the war, before coming to America."

"Have you ever been back?"

"No."

"Me neither. My mom was born there but had a falling out with her family and left. I always wondered—"

"Well, I don't care what island it is. As long as it has a nice beach, I'm in," John said, cutting her off.

Julia put the photo down and quietly retreated to the rocking chair, the furthest place to sit from her husband. Rob couldn't help but notice.

"We could have planned a beach day for tomorrow, but at least we'll have a pool at my parents'," Dina offered.

Did she need to mention the pool? Who was he kidding? The Kinsellas would get to see the Aharoni compound soon enough. He was happy when they retired for the night. It was exhausting being "on" for hours with people he didn't know. Between the additional body heat and Chinese food, the temperature rose quickly to a toasty eighty-something, even with the fans going full blast. No one would sleep well.

The next morning everyone was excited to get out of the city and drive to Dina's parents in Scarsdale for brunch and pool time. They parked the rental car in the circular driveway of the large colonial, white with black shutters. The entryway, with its impressive marble floor and imposing, curved staircase, was just short of intimidating. A white baby grand piano took up most of the alcove the staircase created. Rob noticed Julia staring at the crystal chandelier cascading from the second floor above.

They arrived to the smell of coffee, fresh bagels, and lox, and the sound of the phone ringing. Walking down the entryway toward the kitchen, they passed a beautiful brunch buffet set up in the dining room: three kinds of cream cheese, six kinds of bagels, scrambled eggs, regular and decaf coffee, grapefruit halves with maraschino cherries on top, Entenmanns's crumb cake, and freshly squeezed orange juice. This would all have been arranged by Adele, who had been with the family since Dina was a child.

"Mom, Dad, hello? Anybody home?" Dina yelled. No response. She asked Julia and John to wait a second and pulled Rob into the kitchen.

"Dave, Dave, where are you, it's Dottie on the phone, Dave?" Dina's mother yelled loudly as she came out of the mudroom and into the kitchen.

"I've got it, I've got it, I said!" Dina's father screamed back from his office nearby.

"Well, why didn't you answer me? I shouldn't have to run around this house trying to find you. I'm not your secretary!"

Rob cleared his throat to let his mother-in-law know they had arrived.

She turned to face them, holding a bottle of detergent like a weapon in her hand. "Rob! Dina, sweetie, I didn't hear you come in. Good, you used your key. Sorry no one answered, but Adele set everything out and then took the day off. If you can believe this, I'm actually trying to use the new washing machine. I'm having a bit of a problem. And your father is on that phone with Dottie day and night about work. It's enough already after all these years. We're getting too old for this!"

Their friends appeared near the kitchen door.

The Convention of Wives

"And you must be the famous Julia and John!" She gave hugs all around. "Please, call me Joanne."

"Okay, okay, I'm passing the cream cheese already," his father-in-law shouted. "You would think there was a world shortage the way you're all acting!"

"Your father-in-law," Dina's mom whispered to Rob, "once he starts telling a story, it's impossible to get his attention." She turned to her husband. "You hear that, Dave? I could be on the ground bleeding, and you'd ignore me. You could be talking to the milkman and . . ." She got up and grabbed the orange juice and started pouring for everyone, even John who waved her off. "There I'd be, dying on the floor, before you called 9-1-1."

"You're exaggerating. Rob, you see that. Women! Always finding something to criticize. Dina, take a lesson, and you too," he turned toward Julia, "I'm sorry, Joanie?"

"Julia, Daddy, Julia," Dina corrected.

"You see, again with the criticism. I'm sorry, Julia, my dear, take a lesson."

Rob was embarrassed as Dave unabashedly drank Julia in, from the top of her head to the bottom of her tight, red T-shirt, her breasts dangerously perched above her plate. He realized he was doing the same. Hear it comes, another pearl from his father-in-law. He looked over at John, whose mouth was wide open taking it all in.

"So, after brunch, girls," his mother-in-law interrupted, "we'll head to the pool out back with the babies. Dad wants to take the boys to the club to play golf."

"You do play golf?" Dave asked, turning to John.

"I can hit a bit, sir," John answered.

"Good, good. Now, where was I? Oh, right . . . a man works all day and comes home and what does he want? Nothing that complicated. A little respect, a little affection. Something good to eat. That shouldn't be too much to ask."

"Daddy, please, you sound like a caveman."

For some reason that he would later regret, Rob got up, grabbed Dina's long hair, flexed his bicep and said, "Woman. Listen to you father or I'll have to drag you off to our cave and . . ."

"Rob!" Dina yelled. "What is wrong with you?"

Everyone laughed as he let go of her hair. Everyone except Dina, that is.

Baby Allie started crying. Rob bent to pick her up. She stank. Clearly a poop. He would normally have handed her off to Dina. Instead, in an act of penance, he said, "I'll go change her and be right back."

He glanced around the table as he left the room. Julia offered him a broad smile; her head tilted to one side. John was one lucky dog. Was it the hair grab or the baby changing? He didn't care which. At least someone appreciated him.

"You know, this club wasn't open to Jews until about eight years ago," Dave said from behind the wheel of his Lincoln Continental. "I mean, of course we had our own club, but nothing like what the *goyim* had."

"Dad," Rob implored as he put his hand on Dave's elbow.

"*Goyim?*" John repeated from the backseat.

"Oops, my apologies," Dave continued, "*Goyim*, an outsider. In other words, not Jewish. You're a *goy*."

Rob could feel himself turning red.

"Amazing about timing. I had tried to get into the club for years with no luck. But I heard a capital campaign had been launched." Dave continued with a Tevye-like lilt, "I asked if I would be considered for membership were I to make a sizeable donation to such a capital campaign. And presto change-o . . ." Dave snapped his fingers. "The chairman of their membership committee called the next day. All you need is a little chutzpah."

The caddies took their bags to the driving range so they could practice. Dave stood behind both men, giving instruction.

"Don't move your whole body, just rotate the hips, Rob."

"John, keep your head down. You keep standing up as you hit. That's why you're mis-hitting the ball. It's fading to the right."

The first hole, a par four, went surprisingly well. It was a forgiving dog-leg to the left, so all of their drives landed on the fairway. Rob hit with a five iron and landed impressively on the green in two. It took John three more shots to land slightly to the right of the green. Dave's ball hit the flag, dropped, and rolled slightly past the hole.

"Wow. That was amazing!" John shouted.

"You know what they say, 'luck is where preparedness meets opportunity,'" Dave shouted back.

Everyone fell in love with his father-in-law, women and men. Rob had not been immune. He was drawn to the praise, hugs, and even the kisses Dave generously bestowed. But over the years, Rob began to better understand Dina's underlying resentment toward her father. He was, after all, the ultimate salesman.

"Nice putt."

"You're a ringer, for sure!"

Rob watched as John continued to bask in Dave's compliments.

John made positive comments to Rob after each stroke, regardless of outcome. His favorite phrase was, "Don't worry, you'll make it next time, buddy."

Rob felt like anything *but* John's buddy. He could barely shake hands with him at the completion of the round.

"You boys stay, have a snack, a drink, and relax. I'm going to head home to see my granddaughter and for a bit of a nap." He pulled two cigars out of his coat pocket. "Cubans. Shh," Dave pretended to whisper as he looked conspiratorially around him, as if making sure no one overheard, while speaking loudly enough to ensure that everyone did. "Sign with my account number for the drinks and include a nice tip. I'm 118. Good number, right?"

Rob steeled himself for another Dave moment; he'd heard this explanation a few times before.

"I was supposed to be number 117, but I handed someone a fifty and *voila*, 118." He winked at the guys. "Thought I'd remember it easier, you know, for luck, especially with the golf!"

Thankfully, John nodded politely without asking for a translation.

"Thanks, Dad," Rob said. Despite everything, there was a part of him that admired this clearly flawed man. He'd taken a small rag business on the Lower East Side of New York and turned it into a company that manufactured and sold nationally.

"Anything for my *boychick*," Dave said as he kissed Rob on the cheek. Rob was slightly embarrassed in front of John but loved, once again, being the golden child.

"Here, John, you hold onto these cigars, okay? See you at the house."

Rob looked over at John, pitying the newest shiny object within Dave's magnetic field.

The hostess led them to a four-top near the window overlooking the course below. They had a nice view of the eighteenth hole, with the green on an island in a small pond, accessible only by a wooden footbridge.

As they ordered, Rob noticed John staring at their waitress, Alicia, her nametag bobbing above her generous cleavage.

"So, St. Vincent's for general surgery, huh? Julia said you don't even have to move apartments . . . lucky break. We've got to head across town; Boston traffic can be a bitch. I shouldn't complain, I'm excited about being at Brigham's. Were you surprised by Vincent's?" John asked.

The Convention of Wives

"Well, I figured my chances were pretty good after finishing med school at NYU, but I actually ranked it second. I was hoping for Duke," Rob replied, taking a sip of his beer.

"Duke . . . that far? Really? I never even thought about it. I tried to stay in Boston. Julia's mom is there and everything," John replied, looking down at the two rejected French fries left on his plate.

"What about your family? I thought they were in Boston, too? Dina mentioned that you have a few brothers." Rob grabbed a cocktail napkin and golf pencil from the holder in front of him and doodled.

"I have three . . . sorry, two," John answered between bites of the last of the fries. "The oldest, Lorrie, passed away. My other brothers always picked on me, you know, I was the youngest, kind of a nerd. My dad thought it would help make me a man and just watched it happen. But they didn't touch me when Lorrie was around. They wouldn't dare."

The waitress walked toward them with the check, but Rob waived her off and motioned for two more drinks.

"You know, we're typical Irish off-the-boat types . . . thieves, laborers, then cops. Lorrie wanted better. But then he got sick."

Rob wasn't sure what to say, so he said nothing.

After taking a few sips, John continued. "Once he got into law school, he couldn't seem to focus. He couldn't sleep, started having stomach issues. Couldn't even sit through a class. My father was so angry with him. Thought he was weak. Lorrie saw a few doctors, but nobody could figure it out. And then he was just gone. The funeral was horrible. I think there was something seriously wrong with him that just got missed."

The two were silent for a moment. "That's partly why I went into medicine. I was thinking about GI, but somehow I got sidelined and wound up in surgery." John took another sip of his beer.

"Maybe you weren't sidelined; maybe you just wanted to be able to cut out a problem, not just come up with hypotheticals?" Rob said.

John nodded.

The men clinked glasses.

Rob suddenly realized he liked the guy. He had more in common with him than he thought. "I'm sorry to hear about your brother," he said. "It sounds like you were close. I had a younger cousin who died. Ronnie, on my dad's side. My biological dad. Ronnie and I were like brothers. I had two stepbrothers when my mom remarried, but they couldn't stand me. I wish I'd had your brother around to stick up for me. They were—no they *are*—assholes."

As if establishing a brotherhood, the two men clinked glasses again.

In a ritual befitting a six-year-old, Rob folded and refolded his cocktail napkin before wadding it inside his water glass.

"Julia said you had a complicated background."

"My real dad died in a DP camp after the war, soon after I was born." He noticed John's confused look.

"A DP camp?"

"Displaced persons. They were set up all over Europe. My Uncle Rolph was the one who found a sponsor to get us to the United States. My cousin Ronnie, who got sick in his early twenties, was Rolph's son. He'd always been a klutzy kid, always covered in Band-Aids, even had a few broken bones. But then he had some other weird stuff going on medically. When I was in college, and he was in high school, we'd lost touch. Then one day, I got a phone call saying he'd OD'd. I knew he'd been experimenting with drugs a bit. Who wasn't?" Rob took a sip of his beer. "I always felt like maybe if I'd stayed in touch . . . it's crazy, right?" Rob looked to John for reassurance.

John nodded.

"After that, I was kind of interested in going into research and applied to medical school. But surgery just appealed to me more once I got my hands on some patients."

"To general surgery," John toasted, raising his glass.

While Rob signed the check with Dave's lucky number, it occurred to him that John had become more than just Julia's husband.

"Let's pick up our clubs and get back to my in-laws' or our wives are going to kill us," Rob said, two fingers sliding across his throat.

They tipped the locker room assistant who had cleaned off their rented golf shoes and equipment, made their way outside to the valet stand, and ordered a cab to head back to Chez Dave.

Chapter Thirteen

Dina

Barbados, March 1978

Nothing in the greater metropolitan area could compare to the rugelach from the Swiss Bakery. They were that addictive. The nut-filled delicacies were included in the dessert spread at every Jewish holiday; except, of course, Passover. It was only a matter of time until Tom, the baker, developed a *pesadich* version. At that point, Dina thought, he could go national with a distribution plan that would put Pablo Escobar to shame. But now, she had to "transport" the tasty little cakes to someone named Sylvia.

Sylvia belonged to the same Essex County chapter of National Council of Jewish Women as Dina's mother-in-law, Elsa. When the Barbados snowbird heard that Dina and Rob would be going down to the Caribbean later in the month, she had to put in an order.

"If you don't mind, Dina, would it be possible for you to squeeze some of Tom's rugelach into your suitcase?"

"Do they travel okay?" Dina wondered how she would really accomplish this task.

"I thought you were going to Bermuda," Elsa inserted.

"I usually put them in Tupperware and freeze them in case they get warm on the plane ride. I've never had a problem," Sylvia continued, ignoring Elsa's comment. "Of course, I take as many as I can when I go down, but it's never enough to carry us through the winter."

"Of course! How many? What flavor would you like? Chocolate or mixed?" Dina asked. She'd already decided that the chocolate ones were the best.

"We're traditional, make it mixed. Four pounds should be plenty."

"Four pounds?" Dina had no idea how she would squeeze four pounds of pastries into her luggage.

For once, Dina watched her mother-in-law sit quietly without weighing in.

"I'm sorry, Elsa, did you say something?" Dina asked.

"I'll compromise. Two would be wonderful. Here, let me pay you now or I'll forget," Sylvia said, taking a twenty-dollar bill out of the small change purse affixed to the black elastic belt that hugged her waist.

Dina pushed back the twenty. "Don't worry about it. We'll settle up on the island."

"Okay, you'll come for Shabbat dinner."

"We'd love to, but we have some dinner obligations at the conference. And I have a friend and her husband meeting us down there. It's our final break before the guys both join practices."

"So, bring them to dinner."

"You should go," Elsa urged, breaking her silence. "But I thought Rob said Bermuda."

Dina imagined inviting Julia and John to Shabbat dinner.

"Ah, they're not Jewish? I can tell from the *punim* you made."

"Well, it's just that—"

"Julia's not Jewish? I don't think you ever mentioned that," Elsa said in a whisper, shaking her head disapprovingly. "Hmm."

Of course, she had never mentioned it. She knew what the reaction would be.

"All right, then how about a tour of the historic synagogue?

I'm part of a group trying to raise funds to refurbish the place. Your friends will find it interesting, Jewish or not. And, Elsa, Rob would find it interesting, no?"

Elsa didn't answer. Her mother-in-law was just weird. Rob seemed excited about seeing Barbados. After all, he'd lived there as a young child.

"I doubt the guys can get away from the conference for a tour, but I'll ask Julia. Maybe. I'll let you know. Is that okay?" Dina asked.

"Of course."

Rob was going to kill her for saying yes to the frozen rugelach. And how would she explain the tour to Julia?

The breeze kissed Dina's shoulders as she stepped outside the Fairmont Hotel. It was eight thirty, and the sky was filled with clouds that looked like inverted scoops of vanilla ice cream. Her husband had left early for the conference, so she and Julia had agreed to a morning walk followed by a leisurely breakfast. They were thrilled with the short getaway. With five kids between them, the oldest in the bunch five years old, the two friends were finally able to talk about something other than vaccination schedules and missing blankies. But first, Sylvia.

"I really appreciate you going along for the ride," Dina said to Julia as they walked. "You've always been pretty understanding about the Jewish thing."

"No biggie."

"Sylvia did mention that the larger museum in Bridgetown has a number of exhibits about early Irish and English settlements," Dina said. "Would you be into that? I mean, your mom grew up here, right?"

"Thanks, but I don't think so. My mom made it sound like this is the last place on earth she'd want me to explore. I love her, but she's a bit of a whackadoo. She insisted there was no family left to see."

"That's too bad."

"She even asked why John wouldn't take me on a real vacation, instead of to a rundown island. Does this place seem rundown to you?"

"Not really."

"Right. He finally takes me somewhere without the kids, and all my mother can do is pick apart the vacation. I just don't get her sometimes."

Dina loved not being the only one with mother issues.

"Really, it'll be fun, and this Sylvia sounds like such a hoot," Julia said with jazz hands for punctuation.

"She is. I want to be her when I grow up. She is vivacious, interested in everything, always suggesting I read the latest novel, really bubbly. Have you read *The Thorn Birds*?"

Julia shook her head.

"Me neither. Who has time or energy?"

They finished their walk and sat on the shaded veranda staring out into the turquoise ocean. Seabirds effortlessly floated on the frothy white waves.

"Anyway, I think you'll like her," Dina mumbled between bites of croissant and slurps of decaf coffee. She noticed, somewhat irritated, that Julia was sticking to fruit and black coffee. "God, this is delicious, and, mostly, no one is bothering me for a cup of juice or to help them go to the bathroom. I'm in heaven. This is the first thing I've been able to keep down for weeks."

"Dina could you be . . . ?"

"No, no. My period's just been weird since I had Zoe. My obstetrician thinks my body is readjusting, but it's been over a year. When they do come, my periods have been pretty light. I still use a diaphragm, well, most of the time. It's such a pain, the jelly, getting it in and then, oh God, getting it out. What do you use now?"

Julia just shrugged.

"What, wait, you guys still aren't using anything?"

"You know, good Catholics and all. Frankly, lately it doesn't matter that much. With John's schedule . . . well, you know . . ." Julia said, shrugging. Then she turned to the waiter. "Can I get a mimosa?"

Dina thought it a bit strange, drinking so early in the morning, but she said nothing. She was just happy to be with her friend. They hadn't talked or written letters too often since the kids were born, but whenever they got together, they just continued their conversation right where they'd left off. It had been like this ever since the guys were in medical school. They were the sisters neither of them had.

They hesitated to share too much with friends who weren't doctors' wives, the ones who thought marrying one would make life easy. The shopping, lunching, vacationing, abundant babysitters for the kids these friends imagined, all funded by an ever-growing bank account. They would never understand budgeting, having to make up for the years spent in medical school and the years that followed living on a resident's puny salary. There was Rob's beeper going off just when she'd gotten to sleep after feeding the baby. The missed family events, the holidays—even the kids' birthdays. Having to drive alone with the children to her folks. But crying poverty to her parents, complaining in general, was the last thing she would ever do. It was exhausting. It was depressing. Mostly, it was always coming in second to the demands of a sick patient. Not something anyone with half a heart could complain about.

She and Julia were the glue that made their families' lives work. Dina approached this role with masochistic gusto, grabbing the happy moments in between all the crap to keep her going. Watching Julia gulp her mimosa, she wasn't sure her friend was coping in the same way. Just the day before, Dina and Rob had been waiting for their friends to arrive, hoping to witness the hotel staff greet them with papaya cocktails. But Julia and John had been arguing when they got out of their cab.

"Shit Julia. I told you not to bring such a big piece of luggage. Seriously, what the hell! If it's so important for you to have enough clothes for a month, carry it the rest of the way yourself!"

John dropped the suitcase and headed toward the check-in desk.

"That's my husband for you," Julia shouted, spying Dina across the lobby, "knowing just how to start a romantic vacation!"

Dina and Rob reluctantly joined the couple in time to see John down both of the drinks offered by the staff. "Oh, I'm sorry, your royal highness," he said to Julia. "Did you want one of these?"

John shook Rob's hand and patted him on the back as if nothing were wrong. Julia blinked back tears. Dina hadn't noticed a moment's affection between the two for the rest of the day. Not even a handhold.

The next morning, after the men headed off to the conference, Julia and Dina sat on the porch of the hotel overlooking the beach, finishing their breakfasts. The women high-fived as they watched a few young families arrive, silently congratulating each other for not having any children with them. The waitress topped off their coffees.

"Do you think it matters that neither of us work anymore?" Dina asked.

"Matters to whom?"

"Oh. Our kids. I mean, are we sending the wrong subliminal message, especially to the girls, about women and work?"

"I don't know what message we're sending, but if we hadn't decided to stay home, our kids would have wound up being raised by nannies."

"That's true. But some of these other women I know. They figure it out. She leaves later in the day and gets them off to school. He picks them up. Or a grandparent comes over."

"Do you think that would really have worked with our husbands' schedules?"

"No." The thought of enacting such a plan, finding some kind of compromise, seemed daunting.

"No. So stop feeling guilty. We want to be home for them, right?"

"Right."

But the sight of an attractive woman in a suit and high heels, briefcase in hand, entering the restaurant for what appeared to be a breakfast meeting, ended Dina's moment of assuredness.

Sylvia rolled up to the circular driveway of the Fairmont in her white 1965 Dodge Dart that, she later explained, her husband had shipped to the island from the States. Though it was thirteen years old, it was in impeccable shape. Every Sunday, her husband spent the better part of the morning waxing and buffing the car to stave off the effects of the humid, salty climate.

"These are my two lovelies from the Far North," Sylvia gushed to the valet.

"Miss Sylvia, always lovely to see you," he nodded, his head bowing, as he opened the car doors for the two women.

"Wait, wait just a minute," Sylvia ordered, making her way out of her car and planting a dark red lipstick kiss on Dina's cheek. "Dina, darling, you look marvelous, practically glowing, love your shoes; and you must be Julia, look at that hair, you're as stunning as Dina described you, sweetie. You girls enjoy it before it all shifts from here to here," she said, pointing from her breasts to her knees. She completed a quick shake of Julia's hand before turning back to Dina.

"So, Dina, where's my special delivery?"

"Here you go!" Producing the bag she'd carefully kept guarded in her carry-on, Dina handed it gently to Sylvia.

Sylvia turned to the valet. "Would you mind keeping these someplace cool until we get back? Rugelach baking in the Barbados sun is not a good idea."

"My pleasure, Miss Sylvia," the man said, taking them away.

Dina mouthed the words *Miss Sylvia* to Julia, and they both stifled a laugh.

Sylvia must have had eyes in the back of her head. She swung back from the valet, stared at Dina for a moment, and seemed to make a tactical decision. "Julia, sit in front with me. I know all about Dina already; you I need to get to know," Sylvia said sweetly. "You don't mind, Dina?"

It was a statement more than a question. Dina felt demoted.

"Of course, Sylvia, no problem."

"There is so much I want to show you," the older woman began as they pulled out from under the portico.

They turned right onto what was labeled Highway 1, though it was, Dina noted, nothing more than a two-way street.

"I know you're not Jewish," Sylvia said, turning to Julia, "but the synagogue is quite a historic sight and so interesting." For the next twenty minutes, Sylvia made her way from the Fairmont south to Nidhe Israel Synagogue, busily pointing out restaurants and hotels along the way, when she wasn't asking Julia pointed, intrusive questions.

"How did you meet your hubby?"

"Is Dina your first Jewish friend?"

"Is that hair color really yours? Come on, it can't be. Just gorgeous!"

"Do you think you're done having kids? That's some brood you have."

A moist ocean breeze blew through the car's open windows. Dina caught most of it in the backseat, scattering her long hair. She envied Sylvia, who wore a scarf, and Julia, who had thought to bring a clip, which, with her stick straight hair, she didn't really need. Dina did her best to hold onto her ballooning tangle of frizzy curls.

"I know the Fairmont is lovely, just lovely, but if you ever get the chance to stay at Sandy Lane, it's coming up here on the right, oy, what a gorgeous place. And if you play golf, well, the Green Monkey course is known everywhere by golfers. Do you golf? What am I saying, of course your husbands golf, right? On Wednesdays, right?"

Julia and Dina looked at each other and laughed.

"Sylvia, what's a green monkey?" Dina asked, deflecting.

"Oh, the monkeys here, they have a coat that is really brownish-gray, but with specks of yellow so that, from a distance, they actually look green. They cause all kinds of mischief on the golf course. My husband's foursome once got bombarded by ugli fruits and had to leave the course. It was, well . . . ugly," Sylvia explained, laughing at her own joke.

"What's an ugli fruit?" Julia asked.

"I'll show you one later. We're here, this is it. Nidhe Israel."

Dina was shocked. Why had their tour guide brought them to such a dump?

"Let me explain . . ." Sylvia began.

With that she launched into the history of the synagogue, describing the impressive wooden ark that once held the Torahs and the raised platform at the other end of the room where the scrolls were read to the congregation below. Only remnants remained of a second story that used to be the women's section. The lighting was rudimentary, but Sylvia explained—as if she could see it all before her as it once was—there had been beautiful wrought iron chandeliers that illuminated the place.

"We're trying very hard to purchase this place," Sylvia said.

"What do you mean?" Dina asked as they found shade under one of the few remaining trees on the property.

"It's been used as a warehouse, a machine shop—you name it. But the Jewish population on the island wants to restore it."

"Won't that be expensive?" Dina asked.

"We're hopeful that we can begin in a few years, once we raise the funds. There's a history here we need to preserve. Both the Sephardic and later the Ashkenazi Jews who worshipped here. It shouldn't be lost."

"What's Sephardic and Ashke . . . did you say *Nazi*?" Julia asked, looking at Dina for explanation of this strange phrase.

"*Ashkenazi*. Different types of Jews, depending on where they are from. Absolutely nothing to do with Nazis," Dina clarified.

"I thought there were only Orthodox, Conservative, and Reform," Julia admitted.

"No, that's the religious breakout, and within that there's—" Dina began.

Sylvia seemed to finally notice her guests and interrupted. "I'm sorry, I get caught up in this place. Come on, let's walk a bit more, first the cemetery, then I want to show you Jew Street."

"Jew Street?" Dina asked. Julia looked embarrassed.

"Yes, around the corner. It's where the Jewish merchants sold their wares and lived with their families. Mostly Jewish. So, Julia, Dina said that your family has a history here, like her husband Rob's?"

"My mother doesn't like to talk about it much," Julia said.

"I know what that's like," Dina piped in. "My parents have no problem going on forever about who they met at ShopRite, but the important things never get airtime."

Julia nodded. "They came here with nothing, became wealthy landowners, but I don't think it ended well. By the time she was growing up, they were left with a tavern. That's where my mother worked before she came to the States."

"What happened to the property?" Dina asked.

"Oh, that's long gone, sold before my grandmother died."

"Your mom never came back?"

"No. She had a falling out of some kind with her father. I

never really pressed her. And her mother never came to visit the States. People didn't travel in those days. Not the way they do now," Julia explained.

"Rob and his mom ended up here because it was the only way for them to make their way to the United States after the war," Dina said. "Maybe it's time to make some better memories of this island," she said, putting her arm around her friend. Hugging Julia to her, Dina suddenly felt nauseous and lightheaded. She stopped and put her hands on her knees.

"What is wrong with me, we haven't looked at the cemetery," Sylvia said as she motioned for the girls to follow. "Dina, are you all right?"

"I think I need a bathroom. My breakfast isn't agreeing with me," Dina murmured.

"There's a temporary bathroom set up over there." Sylvia pointed to a blue plastic structure.

Dina barely made it inside before she vomited. She hoped she wasn't coming down with something. It was so easy to catch a bug while traveling. She wiped her mouth and hands on the paper towels provided and escaped what felt like an oven.

She was sweating profusely when she got back outside.

"Are you okay? We were worried?" Julia said.

Dina just nodded.

Sylvia pulled out a plastic water bottle from her backpack and handed it to Dina who sipped, then gulped.

It was stifling outside, and the thought of walking through the sun-drenched cemetery among hot stone slabs was not appealing. Dina was regretting the whole excursion. All she wanted was the cool sheets and quiet of her hotel room.

Sylvia encouraged them to move ahead. "This was a garbage dump for quite a while. Many of the headstones had been pushed over and defaced. Volunteers have spent hours to get it back to its original condition," she said with pride.

The Convention of Wives

The small pebbles crunched under their feet as they strolled among the graves. Some were ornate, others simple in design. Dina read:

SARAH RIFKIN COHEN
1820–1842
BELOVED WIFE AND MOTHER

Another smaller headstone was nearby:

TZIPORAH COHEN
B. 5.1.1842
D. 6.12.1842

"Look at this, Julia. Just a baby. Wow, the mother died the same year as the baby was born. And the baby lived for just a month. How horrible."

"The story is that the mother died in childbirth and they tried to keep the baby alive, but it didn't survive. Things were not that advanced on the island at that time medically. Very sad," Sylvia explained.

And then Dina stopped dead in her tracks.

"What is it?" Julia asked.

Julia hurried back to Dina, followed more slowly by Sylvia.

"There," was all that Dina said, pointing to a plain, gray headstone.

MICHAEL (MICHEL) HELLER
BORN, BRESLAU, GERMANY, 1917
DIED, BARBADOS, 1946
BELOVED HUSBAND OF ELSA AND FATHER OF ROBERTO

"I don't understand. Elsa said Rob's dad died in a DP camp in Italy."

"I'm confused, Dina. I thought Rob's father was Max, right?" Julia asked. "Max, who passed away last year? And your last name is Wasserman?"

"Max was Rob's stepfather. Michael Heller was Elsa's first husband," Dina explained, stooping and touching the lettering on the headstone.

The women walked away from the synagogue and turned right on Swan Street, passing a barber shop, a candy store, and a few places stuffed to the brim with fabrics and hardware. The cloth was piled in bins and stacked on racks like abandoned rainbows. The hardware store windows were covered in grime, but Dina could make out a table of what looked like antique saws and pliers and some larger farm implements. The place looked abandoned, as if the midday heat had sent all the shopkeepers home and wilted the contents of the stores. She turned to see Julia retrieve her suntan lotion from her bag and apply it to her pink shoulders.

"This was where the Jewish merchants had their businesses, near the synagogue. It's labeled Swan Street but, as I said, it's really known as Jew Street. Most lived nearby," Sylvia commented. They walked half a block more. "Here we are," Sylvia said.

The three-story, red brick building had yellow shutters and a black door. Beautifully kept, it stood out among the bright pink and aqua buildings on either side. And, on the door, was a heavy brass knocker in the shape of a rose.

Chapter Fourteen

Leah Schwartz

Breslau, Germany, 1855

The *esrogs* were piled in the chopping bowl, looking like small balls of sunshine in a wooden boat. Leah picked one up and inhaled its fresh citrus smell, careful not to disturb Felicia, who was chopping vegetables in the sweltering kitchen. The squat woman, her graying hair tied in a netted bun, had served as the family's cook and substitute nanny since Leah was born.

Approaching from behind, marveling at how a woman of Felicia's girth could move about with such energy, Leah stretched her arms as far as they could reach around the starched white apron. She hugged the woman fiercely.

"What are you doing? Please, I'm holding a knife," Felicia scolded, nevertheless enjoying the embrace. "You are too old for such foolishness."

Leah slumped back to the kitchen table, rolled up the sleeves of her blouse, and gently unwrapped the remainder of the *esrogs* from their straw packing. She filled the wooden bowl. The cook hummed a tune while the two women toiled companionably. Opening the dining room window, Leah marveled at St. Elizabeth's Church. The red brick building, with its tall tower, overpowered the colorful marketplace and could be seen for miles outside of Breslau. Years ago, her older brother Michel had snuck into the tower at night with a few friends and climbed to the top. Now eighteen, Leah thought herself too dignified for such nonsense.

The sky was overcast and gray, the street below wet. Leah looked back at the bright yellow balls and smiled. Maybe they were God's way of changing the weather in her tiny corner of the world. She sat down again and continued unwrapping, still thinking about the tower. Michel had told her that being up on top had made him feel like a bird. To him the city had looked like a living cell. It wasn't just the way boats in the Oder River snaked around the city's twelve islands. It was the people, too, rushing around conducting their business, crossing the various bridges. It was life. Sweet life. Leah wanted to be part of it.

The young girl's education, provided at first by her mother and then by tutors, had been limited to language study and a smattering of geography and math—no science. Girls were not expected to learn about the natural world. Her skill at drawing led to the hiring of a painting tutor, though, and while the old man had stopped coming to guide her work, Leah continued to enjoy putting brush to canvas. Her father had also encouraged Leah's mathematical skills. She was not surprised when, at sixteen, at the completion of her studies, he had asked her to help with the bookkeeping for the family's produce business. But the work, soon mastered, grew tedious. Anything was more entertaining than adding up rows of numbers—even unpacking *esrogs*.

Leah had read in the newspaper about women being educated to be teachers in Sweden, and about a university in a place called Iowa in the United States that was now admitting women. She wondered briefly what it would take for her to travel across the world, but her parents' expectation was that she would soon marry and have a family. How did her father envision her continuing in her role in the family business? She wasn't sure. Perhaps she would find the fruit trade more stimulating if her father involved her in dealing with the suppliers and other merchants. Leah had never seen a woman in this role and, from her father's recounting of these transactions at the dinner table each night, the work seemed far from fascinating. At least it would be more interesting than what she was doing now.

Leah picked up another *esrog* and noticed that the *pitom*, the remains of the site of pollination, was intact. She imagined her counterpart in Palestine carefully placing the fruit in the crate. An *esrog* with a complete *pitom* would fetch the highest price, but her father's inspection and opinion were the only ways to be sure the one she held was kosher enough.

She went to the cabinet and grabbed the blue ceramic bowl her mother used to bake *mandelbrot* for Shabbos luncheon and was about to place it next to the wooden one on the table when Felicia grabbed it out of her hand.

"Not that one! You know better. It's *milchik*. The *esrogs* must remain *pareve*. Your mother will be angry," Felicia said. She put the bowl away and, grabbing a metal market basket instead, placed a clean white cloth inside of it. "Much better. I'm going to empty the scrap bucket. I'll be back shortly," she said.

Leah placed a few of the *esrogs* in the basket. The arrangement of the shiny silver-colored carrier with its leather handle and brass fastenings, the starched white cloth, and the globes of yellow with their green *pitoms* drew her attention. *What wonderful subject matter for a still-life painting.* She would take just a few minutes away from her work and sketch a small outline. Leah tore off a sheet of butcher's paper, ran to the oven—now cooled somewhat from the morning baking—and found a remnant of charred, black coal.

Bending to close the crate by her chair, she saw the imprint BEN DAVID, burned into the top in Hebrew, a cluster of grapes below. Her father, Gedalia, had explained that this family in Palestine, who also made wine, had set aside orchards in previous generations for the fragrant yellow citrus used to celebrate the holiday of Sukkot. The Fruit of the Goodly Tree Association, the source of her father's supply, tried their best to ensure quality, but you never knew exactly what you were going to get. Gedalia always put in a special request for the Ben David *esrog*s. To increase the odds that they received a shipment from Ben David, her father made sure the wives of the men who headed the association received only the nicest produce in their Shabbos orders year-round.

Leah rested her feet on top of the crate and sat at the table sketching. She doubted that the daughter of the owner of the Ben David vineyard would be responsible for wrapping or unwrapping fruit. Leah really wasn't sure what life was like for girls in Palestine, but in the end, what did it matter. They would share a similar fate, married off to someone their father chose for them. Half a world away, her counterpart was also limited.

"All right, my girl, what do you think?" her father asked as he came up from behind and kissed the top of her head.

"Papa, you'll ruin my drawing, stop," she said, playfully pushing him away.

"I'm sorry, I forgot that you're not a baby anymore. All grown up. So, miss," he bowed to her. "The *esrogs*? Your professional opinion?"

"The color is bright, I don't see any green so far, and they are firm, but I'm still inspecting. I would say about a third have the *pitoms* intact."

Felicia walked back into the kitchen and began cracking and peeling some hard-boiled eggs over the sink.

Her father picked up one of the fruits from the basket in front of her and his expression changed as quickly as the sun retreating on a cloudy day. "Oy, what did you do? What is on them? What is this?" he asked as he showed her the black smudges on the fruit.

"Oh, Papa, I've been sketching." Her fingers were covered in soot. "I'm sorry, I'll clean them right away." She began rubbing one of the *esrogs* on her apron, but the smudge didn't budge. Her heart raced. Her eyes filled with tears.

"All right, all right, I'll get your mother," her father said. "Do you think you're the first person to dirty an *esrog*? Your mother can remove a stain from anything, she'll know what to do . . . it's her specialty." He moved toward the stairs and shouted, "Baila, Baila!"

"What? I'm just finishing dressing. Can it wait?" Her mother yelled down.

"Can it wait? I don't know. You tell me. Can being able to buy meat at the butcher wait? Can buying flour wait, to say nothing of the new dress you bought last week? Tell me, wife, can they wait? Because if *they* cannot, then, no, this cannot wait!" her father yelled.

While the shouting continued, Felicia soaped the citrus, rubbing them gently in the sink, to no avail.

Her mother descended the stairs wearing her new dress, a green satin skirt with a wide hoop and several layers of ruching toward the hem. A matching jacket covered her chemise. Her brown hair was pulled back in a chignon, and she held a bonnet in her hand.

"What could make you so angry, Dal, on a beautiful day like today?" she asked as she twirled in front of Leah's father, showing off her new dress.

Dal, the pet name her mother called her father Gedalia when he was upset. Leah always found it embarrassing.

"Do not think for one moment that this dance has any power over me," he admonished.

But it did. Her mother Baila, aptly named "beautiful," had just that effect. Leah doubted she would ever have this power. Although she had her mother's curvy physique, her hair was a mousier brown. Unlike her mother's refined features, she had inherited her father's large nose and square jaw. Glancing at her own white blouse and simple gray skirt, Leah admitted to herself that she put more effort into picking the colors for her paintings than her clothing.

"Your daughter, you know, the oldest," he said as he looked over at Leah who was smiling at her parents, happy to get even this negative attention. "You know . . . the unmarried one," he continued as the smile quickly faded from Leah's face, "has decided to use her artistic talents to decorate the *esrogs*. Somehow, I do not think my buyers will be enthusiastic about her work. Perhaps you have a solution?"

"Mama, it was an accident, and I only got a few of them dirty. I was sketching them. But I can't seem to get the soot off the skin," Leah explained.

Her mother came over to her daughter and grabbed her hands and the *esrog* within them.

"My Leahla," she said comfortingly, "I'll be right back. Felicia, the soap won't work, you can stop. And, Dal, enough with the 'unmarried one' already. Certainly, she has a few good years left!" Her mother removed her jacket, put on an apron, and went down into the basement. She returned a minute later with a bottle of white wine, which she opened. Wetting a fresh rag with the alcohol, she gently rubbed the fruit, and the soot came off like magic.

"You see, Leah, this is why I married your mother. She has an answer for every problem; and, frankly, a few answers for questions I haven't even asked yet."

Without missing a beat, her mother handed Felicia the wine and rag. "Leah, you and Felicia finish cleaning them."

"Thank you, Mama," Leah said, giving her mother a hug. She always smelled like vanilla. Hugging her was like eating a cookie.

"A *thank you*?" her mother said to her father.

"What?" he answered.

"Thank you! Where is my *thank you*? You are always stingy with the thank yous. That behavior is not something I want to teach our daughter to accept in a husband."

"First, you need to find her a husband, then we'll teach her about thank yous. Which reminds me, Leah, you'll be coming to the fair with me. You can help me at the booth."

"Dal, I'm not sure that is a good idea," her mother said.

"But, Mama, I want to go," Leah pleaded.

"Baila, we'll talk about this later."

"But, Dal, I don't think . . ."

"Mrs. Schwartz . . ." Her father always addressed her mother formally when he was serious. "I said later. Felicia, my morning paper?"

"On the counter, sir," Felicia said, pointing.

But apparently her mother wasn't finished arguing.

"Dal, she is not a piece of fruit to be bargained for. Next, you'll be allowing them to give her a squeeze to see if she's ripe."

"Woman!"

"I don't think the market is the place to introduce her to the other merchants or their sons. We can have a dinner or attend something at the synagogue and—"

"You'll pick out something for her to wear, and she'll come with me. I've decided. The future of the family is my responsibility." Her father grabbed the newspaper and placed it under his arm.

As he strode from the kitchen, Leah thought she saw him pat her mother on the rear end. Her mother's face reddened and her mouth made the strangest expression; then, as quickly as it had happened, the moment was gone. Marriage was such a mystery.

"Come upstairs when you're finished, Leahla. We need to brush your hair and decide what dress you will wear tomorrow to the fair. I've heard there are lots of things a girl can get at market these days, including," she looked out of the kitchen door in the direction of her husband's exit, "a husband more reasonable than the one with which I wound up," her mother said, winking at her.

Felicia started humming loudly.

"But Mama, dress or no dress, I need to unwrap the rest of the supply for Papa," Leah said as she used the wine-soaked rag to clean her fingers.

Her mother smiled at her. "Oy, my little *esrog*. Finish and then come upstairs, but quickly, I need to get to the synagogue or my tardiness will become the topic of conversation among the other volunteers. Women!" her mother said, shaking her head, as if that word were enough explanation to describe their entire sex.

It seemed to be the nature of women to quickly pounce upon the reputation of a missing member of the group. Leah's own friends did this on occasion, but they were girls. Her mother and her friends were grownups. Did this kind of behavior never end?

Leah was glad she lived in the old part of town, not far from the White Stork Synagogue where her mother spent most of her time busy with the Ladies' Auxiliary. It was comforting to know where her parents were while she worked on the books. But now Leah wondered what the next years of her own life would be like, and if she could withstand the disappointments that no doubt awaited her.

She was excited at the prospect of attending the fair. This might be her first and last year doing so. There had been a few years that the *parnasei ha-yarid*, the treasurers, had raised the rates so high for the tradesman that her father refused to attend out of principle. He had sold his merchandise to other dealers at a loss, rather than give in to their demands. But this year he hadn't even discussed the fee. There seemed to be no question that they would attend. Now she knew why. She was to be paraded in front of her father's customers, just another commodity.

An outside noise alerted her to the back courtyard. It was her brother Michel, kicking a ball with his friends. Michel had wanted to be a physician, but their father had persuaded him there were enough Jewish doctors in the world. But a rabbi? A rabbi would be a coup and bring *yicchis*, pride, to the family.

Michel and his friends from the seminary were dressed identically in white shirts and black pants. Each had a scraggly beard and *payos*, side whiskers, which made it hard for Leah to tell one from the other. But she recognized David Katz and Adam Heller.

She returned to the table to unpack the rest of the fruit. The *esrogs* usually all looked the same to her, like yellow oversized eggs created by mating a chicken and an ostrich. But as she picked up one and then another, she began to notice slight differences. Some had much richer hues. Others were more fragrant. While some had smooth skins, others looked like the wrinkled faces of old women.

She heard shouting outside in the courtyard and returned to the window. Michel, trying to catch his prized possession—the ball made of a cow's bladder covered in leather, had fallen over a storage barrel. Leah watched as Michel's friend Adam ran over to him. Adam bent down and reached for his friend's hand, his shirt sleeve rolled high, his arm pale and muscled. He quickly helped pick up Michel, cuffing him affectionately and yelling, "Klutz!" When she laughed at their antics, Adam looked up, saluted her, and smiled. When had he become so tall? And when had he grown that bushy beard? Her cheeks warmed. She was about to pull the curtain in front of herself to hide when she felt one of the *esrogs* fall from her hand. Leah smiled down at Adam, who caught it easily. She pulled back from the window and looked at the remaining *esrog* in her hand. How had she never noticed each one was so unique before? She realized she had never looked.

Chapter Fifteen

David Aharoni

Millburn, New Jersey, April 1986

Dave sat alone in Dina's den, surrounded by floral centerpieces, when most of the company had departed after the hoopla of the bat mitzvah. What a milestone. He wasn't sure he'd make it after the angina he'd been dealing with for the past year, a diagnosis he toyed with revealing but, in true Dave fashion, preferred to keep close to the vest, even from his wife.

There were two people who he would have liked to share the day with who weren't present. His father would have been proud. Proud of the company he'd built from his father's rag business that allowed Dave to pay for half the celebration. Even prouder of the family he'd made. But then, family had always been the important thing. The topic had been the keystone of the speech he'd given at the service on Saturday, the style reminding him of the many his father had given when he was a boy.

It was 1940, the hundred-year anniversary of his family's arrival in the United States from Palestine; a place which, ironically, many European Jews were now trying desperately to reach. His parents held a special Shabbos dinner at their apartment to celebrate. The mahogany table—laden with steaming dishes, polished silverware, and Rosenthal china—was crowded with family and friends. Mustachioed Uncle Marty held his diminutive wife, Phyllis, by the shoulders in an attempt to stop her Carmen Miranda hat from tipping onto the table. Dave and his cousins, all of them barely twenty, took bets as to which adult would dare interrupt his father during what they knew would be an intolerably long speech, all the while sneaking wine from pre-poured shot glasses. Finally, the adults came to order. His father finished saying *Kiddush*, the blessing over wine, and then regaled them with stories about his forebearers.

"These fine people, who came to this place with nothing, neither funds nor connections, lived in conditions no one should live in, not in a country like the United States of America. My great-great-grandfather Levi, a skilled silversmith, could no longer pursue his craft and was forced to become what so many became . . . a humble rag picker. Eventually, his tenacity and his wife's sewing skills allowed them to sell custom clothes out of their house." Dave had heard it all before. A great many times before. But these folks seemed enthralled. His father was nothing if not a good storyteller. When he had learned about the time of King David in Hebrew school—the Davidian Era—he thought more than once that they were entering the next eon of the same name.

He could feel the chicken soup, brisket, potatoes, and *kreplach*, beef-filled dumplings, lying in his stomach like dead weight, while his father droned on. "From the ancient land of Palestine, across a sea and ocean . . ."

Dave pictured himself sinking to the bottom of that ocean, weighted down by *kreplach* ever expanding inside him.

"The only remnants of their life in the Holy Land were these silver candlesticks that they bundled in cloth and brought with them."

Dave stared at the candles' glow as his father concluded his speech and everyone toasted.

"To the Aharoni family, l'chaim!" Uncle Marty shouted.

"To our family who cannot be here with us. To those suffering in Europe and in Palestine." The crowd became subdued.

"We've told them for years, our fancy cousins in Berlin. Thinking they're Germans. Idiots, all of them. Jews will be Jews to the *goyim* no matter where, no matter when. I pity them, but they brought this upon themselves!" one of the guests added.

Uncle Gene, a boxer in his youth, got up from his chair, hand drawn into a fist.

Dave's father was faster. "Enough, enough. We have enough problems with other people who hate us. We can't be fighting amongst ourselves. This is a time to come together."

Dave turned to face his mother who stood holding a Frank Sinatra album cover as the singer's voice suddenly poured from the Victrola. His parents made a good team. His father, brash and loud, ever the producer; his mother quietly controlling, ever the stage manager.

The discussion soon turned to rumors they were hearing about the Jews in Poland.

"There's no food or medicine left in Warsaw," their neighbor Gussie shared.

"I read that the trains are emptying all of the major cities of any Jews and transporting them to concentration camps. All of them. And Roosevelt won't bomb the tracks. It's a *shanda*."

"I volunteered to sponsor my brother's family, but they can't get papers. I keep sending money, but he tells me they don't need money, they need papers. The last letter I had was over six months ago. I'm not sure what we can do." Sympathetic nods abounded.

Dave looked around at the bedroom apartment, their women's and girls' clothing shop located directly below, and thought how lucky they were to be safe in New York City. Life was good. He had food to eat, clothes on his back, and parents who loved him.

The Convention of Wives

But then, his father pointed out, none of them should ever feel completely sure of their future.

"The State of Israel is our future. Jews will never be safe until we're living in our own free state carrying guns to protect ourselves," Dave's father implored.

"Ourselves? I don't see you moving so fast to the Promised Land," his Uncle Marty countered. The rivalry between them was legendary.

"You're right," his father answered in a hushed tone. "Wars are fought by young men. Old men like me stay back, raise money, and strategize. So—" he reached into his pocket and pulled out a few bills. "One hundred dollars, one hundred dollars for The State of Israel," his father said, dropping the money on the table. "Anyone care to join me? Come on, you *mamzers*."

One by one, the men added to the growing pile of notes.

"On that we can all agree. Usually two Jews, three opinions. Imagine, a crowd of Jews agreeing. To Israel!" his father toasted, scooping up the loot. Every glass in the room was raised.

Dave was proud of his father's ability to control the crowd, but he was confused about why his father thought anyone should return to a place from which his ancestors had run. A desert in which they only spoke Hebrew. More than that, he simply could not imagine a modern-day army of Jews. Jews with guns? With tanks? It was absurd. Weren't they supposed to be the People of the Book?

Watching the milkman making early morning deliveries, a chunk of bread spread with *schmaltz* in his pocket, Dave left his house for the twenty-minute walk across the Brooklyn Bridge. He was the first member of his family to attend college. Cooper Union, between Third and Fourth Avenues, was larger than any building around it for a few blocks. Each time he passed through the

Great Hall on his way to class, Dave marveled at its noble design, its spires seemingly reaching the sky.

"Aron!" a classmate shouted the nickname given him because he was one of four Davids in his class. Too many first- and second-generation Jewish boys sent off to get an education. "Wait up!"

"Horowitz, how's it hangin'?" he yelled back to David number two. The joke never got old. Horowitz was short, with a mop of unruly ringlets and a perpetual smile on his face. Dave couldn't help but like the guy.

"Did you finish the calculus? I got stuck. Derivation, integration . . . *uch*, my head is spinning. I just need to know how to best cut fabric; who are we kidding?" He punched David playfully.

"Come on, mate, we have a few minutes before class. Let's take a look at the assignment." The two sat down in a corner on the floor and spread their papers in front of them. It was not the first time Dave would be helping his buddy out, nor, he thought, would it be the last.

Both flat-footed and 4F, the two boys had bonded quickly. Horowitz's family, like Dave's, was also in the *schmatte* business. But Horowitz Private Apparel had been founded a generation earlier than Aharoni Dresses. Unlike himself, Horowitz was the son of a wealthy maker of ladies' undergarments and could easily afford full-time tuition. Not for the first time, it occurred to Dave that his life had been determined simply by what year his ancestors had decided they'd had enough of being abused and paid passage to the United States.

At lunchtime, textbooks in hand, he walked over by himself to McGinn's on Seventh Avenue to eat and study. His friends would have been mortified by the non-kosher food, but with what was going on in Europe, he wasn't sure what being Jewish brought him, except grief. It was Dave's first act of defiance.

The place was dark though it was midday. The rowdy lunchtime crew of construction workers headed in.

The Convention of Wives

"Pass that bottle over here!" yelled a man wearing suspenders over his grimy shirt. "I'm dyin' of thirst. And I'd like the lunch special with a side of bacon, pronto."

"Yes, sir, right away," Dorothy answered.

Dave's eyes locked with hers.

"You got a problem, Jew boy?" the man shouted at Dave.

"No. No sir." He headed away from the bar, finding a table in the back.

"Fighting to save a few Jews. What a waste," the man mumbled at him as he left.

"I'm sorry about that," Dorothy said, bringing him a water. Daughter of the owner who'd recently died, the girl served him regularly. She made sure his plate was generously filled and his glass was never empty. They didn't talk much. He was too busy reading. "What can I get you?"

"The usual." His usual was a roast beef sandwich, pickles on the side.

Later, while he was sketching out a new idea for his father's fabric cutters, a way of patterning both a woman's and a girl's dress from the same yardage, Dorothy came over and watched as he moved around the pieces.

She was wearing a conservative but stylish dress, a blue-green that complemented her blond hair and light eyes. Dave wondered if she'd made it herself. The tailoring was beautifully done. The bodice fit snuggly but not too tightly across her ample breasts. He felt himself getting hard and was afraid she might notice the bulge in his pants. But when he dared to look up, she was bending over his work, gazing intently.

"What is that? A puzzle? I thought you were here to read and eat?" Dorothy asked playfully as she placed a piece of cake on the table.

"I didn't order that." He barely had enough in his pocket for lunch.

124

"On the house. We don't like our customers leaving here thinking they've had anything but a good time."

"Thanks."

She looked expectantly back at his drawing.

"I'm working on something for my family business. We were studying efficient design at school for use in building materials manufacturing, and I thought that the concepts had some application to my job," he replied. He interpreted her expression to mean that she didn't understand and began to explain more. "What I mean is, we were learning how to best position patterns on material in order use the least amount of fabric—" but she cut him off.

"What kind of business?" she asked, genuinely interested.

He was a bit taken aback by her reaction. Most girls found his work boring. "Well, we make women's and girls' dresses. We've been knocking off the European designs, but now, with the war, we're having to rely on ourselves a bit more."

She stared at the piece of paper for a while and then pointed at the sleeve of the girl's dress. "What if you moved this over here?" she asked, pulling up a chair.

"That could work," Dave said, realizing that what she'd proposed was helpful. He also noticed how close her left arm was now sitting to his right.

"But I really don't like that collar. It's not particularly stylish. Wait, I saw something in *Vogue*," she said.

She went behind the bar, retrieved the magazine, and placed it on the table, showing him the page that she remembered.

"*Hmmm*, I like that," Dave offered. She was so close that he smelled the parsley on her breath.

"I like to sketch. I have a design book that I keep. What if I show them to you and you'll let me know what you think?" she asked tentatively.

"Are you sure?" Dave asked.

The Convention of Wives

"Are you kidding? Do I look like pouring beer is something I intend to do my entire life!" she said, squeezing his shoulder for emphasis.

"Thanks, Dorothy," he said. He'd known her name for a while; the customers shouted it constantly, demanding her attention.

"It's Dottie, to you. Dottie McGuinn," she said. Then, blushing, she backed away from the table toward the kitchen, almost colliding with another customer.

Chapter Sixteen

Julia

Atlanta, Georgia, July 1986

Fourteen, twelve, twelve, and eight. No, almost fourteen, twelve, twelve, and eight. The ages of her children. Birthdates, *oh crap*, how was she expected to fill in medical forms for all four of them while keeping them quiet and seated? She considered increasing the donation she secretly sent to Planned Parenthood each year, her surreptitious attempt at supporting her sisters in the revolution. Father Brennan would be appalled.

And whose bright idea was it to bring all four at the same time to start at the new pediatrician? *John's*. It was more efficient, he had said. Besides, everyone now fit comfortably in the new station wagon, the Taurus, with the two extra seats in the way back, he had said. So why not?

This morning was why not.

She had to stop depending on Aiden so much to play second mother, especially to the twins. He was embarrassed to still be going to a pediatrician's office, but there was nothing she could do about that. He sat quietly reading his book and trying to look invisible. Brody, bored as usual, was scattering blocks meant for children half his age. Bridget was attacking the small library of books, removing them from the shelves, and using them to build a structure of some kind. Maybe she would be an architect one day?

The Convention of Wives

Julia looked over at Rosie, who was soft-spoken and cerebral. She was sitting next to Aiden with a book of her own, her dark olive complexion a contrast to Aiden's reddish hair and freckles. Maybe the whole thing about the "Black Irish gene" was true, the one that transferred brunette hair and a sensitive personality. Although Rosie's eyes were hazel, they drifted to brown when an emotional storm was about to brew.

Her fourth was the only one who had to be encouraged to eat. She'd refused to have breakfast that morning. It was an issue Julia intended to chat with the doctor about. Clairvoyantly sensing her concern, Aiden went into his backpack and pulled out a bag of pretzels, handing them to Rosie, who began eating them willingly. *Anything for Aiden.*

She glanced across the room at a woman with dark hair, calmly leafing through a *Good Housekeeping* magazine. Next to her sat an older woman, infant on lap, reading to a two-year-old sitting on the floor nearby. The mom didn't look up once, while her nanny carried on. *A different life.* The woman had a different life. Julia wasn't sure it would have been her choice. John considered such women spoiled. Most of her friends from the Y didn't have a nanny. The mom glanced up as if sensing Julia's stare. She resembled her old . . . no, her *former* friend Dina. Julia smiled and looked away. Did Dina have a nanny now? They never should have been friends. She'd been kidding herself all along.

There was something about that day at Dina's parents' house that set the tone for everything that came after. Could so much have shifted in just a few short hours?

Aiden and Allie were just babies. The women had settled by the pool with the kids. Aiden was napping in a playpen that matched the one Dina had let him sleep in at her and Rob's apartment; his arm was draped around Allie's stuffed pink teddy bear, the one that matched the toy she'd been playing with in

Manhattan. Apparently, Dina's mother had insisted on having duplicate baby equipment at the house—to make things easier, her friend had explained.

"Dina, do you mind watching Aiden for a minute? That pool is so inviting," Julia said, taking off her cover-up.

"No problem."

"I don't understand how you do it, really, especially with the boys so unavailable to you and so little help. I always insisted on having a girl living with us. Adele was a godsend," Dina's mother said.

"Mom, come on. You can't call her a *girl* anymore. Besides, Julia and I are a different generation. We're doing okay. And I've told you! Rob's salary won't cover something like that. Not yet anyway."

"And I've told *you*, it would be our pleasure to pay for some help. Even a babysitter once in a while. A girl, a woman, whatever you want to call her. I've always maintained that a Saturday night date with your husband is paramount. Reminds them why they come home after a long week at work. Your father wasn't completely wrong at brunch. Men will always be men, after all. They think with their—"

Julia, standing nearby in the water, started laughing.

"Mom, please!" Dina yelled, cutting her off. "Julia, I'm so sorry."

"Really, I think your mom is just trying to be helpful."

"I knew I liked your friend. Dina, all I did was tell the truth. You girls are a little naive. The world of men is filled with more than just men. It's not as if . . ." Julia detected a hint of something—resentment?—in Mrs. Aharoni's comment. A shadow closed over the older woman's face, but only for a moment before she corrected herself and resumed her motherly authority. "Think of all those conventions your husbands will be attending over the years. I've heard plenty from my friends who are doctors' wives.

The Convention of Wives

Professional education? *Pu-lease!* Those exhibition halls are filled with nothing but one blonde, buxom *shiksa* after another!"

Dina covered her face.

"Really, Mrs. Aharoni," Julia said, laughing. "John has his own buxom *shiksa* to come home to. I'm not terribly concerned." Julia did a few laps of the pool. The cool water was exhilarating, and she was glad to have a moment to herself. She appreciated the weekend and knew that Dina had gone to a lot of trouble arranging things. Nevertheless, Julia had to admit that being a good guest was tiring. Being engaged all the time, asking the right questions, showing appreciation, trying to appear grateful. It was nice just to feel the sun and water on her skin. She was able to tune out Dina and her mother for another few minutes, but to stay in the water any longer would feel rude, so she got out and wrapped a towel around her, rejoining the conversation on the patio.

"Mommy, really, do you need to talk like that?"

"What, what did I say that was so bad?"

"Are you kidding me—"

"No, I am not kidding you. It's time you realized that women's lib or no, some things never change. I mean, in my day—"

The women were cut off by the sight of Dave and John.

"Where's Rob?" Dina asked.

"He's meeting us out front by the car. He needed to put on suntan lotion. I told him a little sunshine never hurt anybody, but he insisted." John jumped as Dave patted him hard on the back.

"We're heading over to the club to play nine. So the boys get a real break. Not that the pleasure of your company isn't utterly charming, ladies." Dave smiled, the benevolent patriarch.

Dina turned to her mother as the men left. "How is it okay that they get to go off like that? When do we get our break? This is 1973, for God's sake! Gloria Steinem would be screaming about this."

"Gloria who?" Dina's mother asked. "Oh, you mean the jeans lady. Vanderbilt . . . the millionairess. I think she's coming out with a jewelry line."

Dina just shook her head. "I give up."

"You know, I'd rather not sit in this wet bathing suit," Julia said. "I think I'll change back into my shorts. I'll be a minute." She headed up the stone path and entered the house.

Cool air blew onto her neck as she wandered down the hallway looking for a bathroom.

Central air conditioning. Was there no end to the wealth these people enjoyed?

Four steps more and she reached the bathroom.

Wow.

Gold-plated faucets and black velvet wallpaper embossed with gold herons. The mirror above the sink was enclosed in an opulent frame. Julia stripped off the towel and bathing suit. If not for the prominence of her ribs and shoulder blades, she could pass for a Botticelli painting. Her nipples were hard from the cold and the flesh on her arms was covered with goosebumps. She pulled her long hair off her shoulders and held it high on her head. Her reverie was broken by the sound of the door opening. It was Rob. She froze.

He stood there taking her in.

She let him.

"Mrs. Kinsella, you can finish those forms during the visit. The doctor is ready to see you now."

Julia almost dropped all the paperwork. Were they all going to fit in one exam room? Exactly how was this going to work? Especially with both boys and girls.

And then *he* walked in.

Handsome was simply not the right word. Stunning. No, that was too effeminate a phrase. His hair was a remarkable blue-black, his nose Roman, his body . . . seriously, was she really looking at his body? *Get a grip, shake his hand, and make eye contact*, anything to stop the whirring sound that was blocking her ability to hear what he was saying.

"Mrs. Kinsella, so nice to meet you and your crew."

"Thank you, Doctor . . . Doctor . . ." She had absolutely no idea what his name was.

"Dr. Panzano," he replied warmly. "But the kids all call me Dr. Bob."

She detected the start of a laugh coming from deep inside of herself, which she quickly covered with a cough.

One by one, from the youngest to the oldest, the doctor sped through the physicals, expertly shielding the kids from each other when they were being examined, especially Bridget, who was shy about her developing body. He was simply the most perfect pediatrician she had ever met. The kids loved him. Hell, she loved him. And what was he wearing? Some Italian knit sweater, impeccable trousers, not khakis, actual trousers. *Is he talking to me?*

"So, we'll see everyone back in a year, unless of course something eventful pops up."

"Pops up?" She touched her hair, played with her necklace, and smiled.

"Excuse me?"

"I'm sorry doctor, what were you saying?"

"The twins are almost due for their meningitis vaccine. You can see the scheduler on your way out. Any questions?"

Questions? About a million.

Did he not wear a ring because he was single?

Did he prefer Sauvignon Blanc to a nice, rich Cabernet?

Blondes to brunettes?

Julia was hoping for strawberry blondes.

Okay, questions, seriously, questions.

"None right now, thanks," she answered as she got up, shook his hand, and tried to look as attractive as she could with dirty hair tied back in a scrunchie and the remnants of yesterday's mascara smeared below her eyes.

On the way home, once everyone was belted in safely, she realized she'd forgotten to ask about Rosie's lack of interest in food, but the thought passed. The twins powered up their Game Boys, Aiden read a book he'd been assigned for school, and Rosie softly snored. Eddie Murphy and Rick James sang "Party All the Time" on the radio. *Some party*, Julia thought as the blue skies darkened and the wind whipped up.

What did they call it? Swooning. Yes, she was quite sure she had swooned in the pediatrician's office. What the hell was the matter with her? There was something seriously wrong. She hadn't had any sexual energy or interest in her own husband for the past few years. She hadn't looked at a man like that in . . . she couldn't remember how long. Maybe something was seriously right.

The rain pounded the windshield as she struggled to turn on the wipers in the new car.

Then again, here was a man who was taking care of her children, talking to her, asking her questions, smiling at her, and all the while looking like a modern-day Greek god. She needed to gain control of herself. She knew the drastic consequences of losing it, and she'd sworn that was never going to happen again.

Chapter Seventeen

Berta Cawley

Barbados, October 1930

"Rosie, get inside here right now! Charles, send her in. These winds are getting out of hand." Berta struggled to hold the front door open. Her hair whipped around her face so hard it hurt. The dust and anything else not held down were flying everywhere—papers from the newsstand down the street and dried flower wreaths that had decorated the door of the fabric store nearby. And this was supposed to just be a storm, not another hurricane.

Lake Okeechobee Hurricane had raced through on its way to Florida just over two years before, something the people of Barbados would not easily forget. Winds had reached 150 miles per hour, decimating the houses, killing the crops. The British Bank, subsidized by American investors, was not loaning to farmers. Charles had done his best to get financing to tide them over until the next year, but any additional funding was out of the question. A few months later, the bank had recalled his original loan. With no way to pay his debts, he had been forced to sell the remaining acreage of the farm. The home in Bridgetown was all that was left of the family's fortune. She and Charles had converted the three-story structure into a boarding house and pub to help bring in additional income. And now they were in danger of losing their only asset to another storm.

Ten-year-old Rosie ran into the house, pigtails flying.

"Mama, I fed and watered Coconut. I tied her loosely like you told me. But if she runs, will she come back?" Rosie asked.

"She'll only run if she needs to, and if she needs to, then we won't be able to help her, so best if she can," Berta answered, worrying what they would do if they lost the horse too. "Now, come sit by me and clean off these beans. Your father will be hungry."

Rosie plopped herself down beside her mother. The girl snapped the ends off the beans, breaking them in two. She put the beans in the wooden bowl and the leavings on the table.

Berta couldn't believe how the house had changed in two short years. The main level, previously their parlor and kitchen, was now a pub. Their bedrooms remained on the second floor, but the third floor now had five bedrooms for rent, and only two of them occupied. There was one bathroom on each floor with a sink, a claw tub, and a commode, a luxury that Charles had installed soon after Rosie was born.

Berta looked back at the bar that Charles had made of woman's tongue, a Bajan ebony. The same kind of tree was planted in the backyard. She heard the tree chattering now as the wind whipped through its papery pods. Men at the bar often joked that they went out at night to escape from their wives' incessant talking only to wind up sitting at a bar made of woman's tongue.

"Let's light at least one of the kerosene lamps," Berta instructed. "The electric lines might go, and then we'll be sitting here in the dark." Rosie retrieved a lamp and some matches for her mother. Berta lit the flame. Together they watched it flicker from the wind that came through the cracks in the building, but the flame steadied as if getting used to its new home. And then, as if God knew that they had lit the lamp, the electric lights sputtered and went out.

"We're in for a good one," her husband said as he came inside and bolted the heavy wooden door. He took his wet jacket off and smacked his arms with his hands to warm himself.

"Let me get you some tea, Charles," Berta offered. She could hear her husband talking to her daughter as she busied herself in the kitchen.

"You know, Rosie, we need to take good care of this house, this pub. It's all that we have left," Charles said sadly. He must have taken a few of the beans Rosie had cleaned off and popped them in his mouth because Berta could hear him chewing while he talked. "But some people have a lot less than we have. We're making a go of the boarding house and pub. It's not what any of us are used to, but we'll make do. These islands are a blessing and a curse. They kept our family fed for a hundred years before the wind and sea decided to take back some of what it had given us. Then the bank took the rest."

The timbers of the house groaned as the wind gained strength. Charles continued talking as Berta came out of the kitchen and put tea and cake in front of him. She braced for the story she'd heard ten times before; but its telling seemed to comfort him, so she sat still and put her arm around Rosie.

"The wind that day was ten times as bad as this one. You and your mother were in the house. Here," he laughed softly, as he pointed about them, "in the parlor. I was out at the farm trying to tie down what we could. Only half of the sugar cane had been harvested, some on carts, some in the harvest barn. But then it hit us, and we ran for cover in the barn. And then the barn started to collapse." Charles seemed transported. "The doors ripped off, and then the roof started to go. We opened the storm door to the shelter and fit everyone inside. Everyone, except for George. I saw him heading up from the field. I told the men inside with me to wait, but it was getting so bad and they . . . they needed to close the door. It was like a bomb going off outside. The noise was horrible, the sounds of breaking and tearing, things hitting above us. We lay there, the five of us, like children lying down together for a nap. It lasted a few hours. Toward the end, we couldn't breathe. Then it was quiet. Still. We opened the shelter up and there was nothing. No barn, no cane, no horses, nothing. We walked about looking for George for the better part of two hours and then the wind was picking up. By the time we got back to the shelter, the rains began again, and the winds strengthened. We were on the other side of the eye of the hurricane."

Rosie gripped her mother's hand.

Charles stared off into the distance.

"We found George face down about a half a mile away. Never forget having to tell his wife and kids."

"I know, Charles, I know," Berta said as she rubbed his arm.

Her husband's eyes shifted slightly, but he was looking through her.

"And the cane. The cane was just gone. Either blown away or soaking in mud. Just gone . . ."

"I tried, I tried to save it. I tried. But then, the bank . . . ," he said to no one as his eyes filled with tears, his head shook back and forth as he sipped his tea.

"Charles," Berta said, "you're scaring Rosie. Please. Stop."

He was quiet for a while and then picked up the cake and took a bite.

But Rosie wasn't frightened. She'd heard the story many times before and was used to staying quiet until her father stopped talking.

"We really did try to wait for George. We tried," Charles said, looking into the kerosene lamp.

"Dad, Dad," Rosie whispered to him, her small hand reaching past Berta and touching his face. "It'll be all right. I like my new room. We're having fish with mango for dinner, your favorite."

He seemed to come out of his trance, smiled, and sighed.

The Convention of Wives

"I'm sorry, both of you. It's just this weather, it brings it all back. We're safe here. We'll be all right. But if it gets worse, we go into the storm cellar, everyone knows what to do, yes? Rosie? Lanterns out, grab the water and food, and down we go. No delay."

Berta knew they would survive the storm, here, in their well-constructed home. Funny to think of it as just a home anymore when they sat in the middle of a pub. She looked at Rosie and saw a slight tear in the sleeve of her dress. She'd already mended it twice and Rosie was wearing an old pair of Berta's shoes. Her daughter was growing so fast. It wasn't possible that God would take anything else away from them, was it? They had lost their land and her husband's inheritance, but they had each other. It would have to be enough.

Chapter Eighteen

Allie Wasserman

New York, New York, December 2000

Allie was big picture. Raj was all detail. They were great together, attending family events and holiday dinners as each other's plus ones. No one believed they were just friends. Allie was beginning to doubt it herself. There was nothing she liked better than curling up on the couch with him on a Saturday night, watching a movie and eating Chinese food. It was comfortable. Maybe too comfortable? Could be time to rethink the unshaven legs and torn sweats. She went on the occasional date, had brief serially monogamous relationships that fit in with her crazy study and on-call schedules, but Raj was always there at the end of the day.

She looked at her cell phone: four unanswered calls from her mother. That was nothing new. Allie was used to ignoring them.

"It's Mom. I was out yesterday at Target and I found these cute T-shirts. Do you want green, blue, or both?"

"Hey, sweetie, I called a little while ago and you didn't answer, so I got you the blue and green. I'll bring them in next Wednesday when we're having dinner. You have that on your calendar, right? Wednesday at I Trulli. I love that place, especially the outside garden, probably way too cold for that though, maybe they have heaters. Oh, okay, right, you're not answering, of course you're not answering. I'm leaving a message. Oh, it's Mom. Right, you knew that. Okay, bye."

"Allie, I haven't heard back from you, it's been a day and a half. I'm wondering if you're dead. Just kidding. Not really. I'm worried. Just wait until you have children. You'll know what this feels like. Call me. We're leaving for San Diego. Please. Call me. Oh. It's Mom. Did I say that?"

"Oh, it's Mom." That could be the title of a book. A little volume with a collection of her mother's voice mails—and cocktails to match. The *mom*osa! The cos*mom*politan! Oh God, now she was acting just like her mom, thinking of writing a book she would never write. Grandpa Dave always said, "Ideas are a dime a dozen, it's the execution that's key."

Allie and Raj reviewed the first chart of the day in the ED. The handoff at change of shift had only given them a general sense of the case. As they entered the patient's cubicle, they were pounced on by a young woman standing next to the patient's stretcher.

"We've been here for six hours, this is ridiculous. And who are you two? More doctors? Ugh! She seems to be a bit better. Can we go home? We'll get her to a specialist. My dad is a doctor, he's away at a conference, but when he comes home, really, we'll know where to take her," the woman said in one long, breathless rant.

"I'm Dr. Wasserman. And you are?" Allie asked politely.

"Bridget, I'm Bridget, Rosie's sister. My brother is on the way, too. My family strongly feels that my sister would be better off at home until my father can . . . ." the sister offered, but all Allie heard was "blah, blah, blah, blah, blah."

Just what they needed, doctor's kids. Fantastic! Medical families were the biggest pains in the ass of them all. She'd watched this in action whenever her mother accompanied her to pediatric appointments or her father to the occasional emergency room visit when they were growing up. Zoe's broken arm. Daniel's appendicitis. It was embarrassing. The second guessing of the doctors, the production of recent articles about best practice. At these times, instead of feeling comforted by her parents' knowledge, she was mortified. Allie glanced over at Raj, whose mother was also a physician. They exchanged pained looks.

"If you wouldn't mind, Bridget, my colleague here, Dr. Khan, would like to examine your sister," Allie said.

The patient nodded a weak but compliant yes. Her sister seemed furious and loomed like a guard on watch, eyeing Raj suspiciously. "She's already been examined. You people!"

Allie was annoyed as she wondered if the sister was thinking what some of the older patients didn't hesitate to verbalize to Allie in whispered confidences. *Is he Indian, Pakistani, or what? Did he even go to medical school in this country?* But no, she probably was angry with doctors in general.

"Look Bridget," Allie said, "removing your sister from an ER is a dangerous thing to do until we have determined—"

Raj interrupted tersely. "I'm sorry, Rosie, I don't believe we've met. I'm Dr. Khan."

Raj walked over to Rosie, took her hand in his, shook it, and laid it down as gently as a child's in her lap.

"Dr. Wasserman and I are here to take care of you."

Walking around the bed, he shook Bridget's hand.

"Rosie is lucky to have you here. There's nothing like family to act as an advocate, especially in an emergency room. But I'm sure you know that, since you're from a medical family."

The tension in the room parted like the Red Sea. Allie watched as Raj continued to perform a miracle.

"Now please, Bridget, would you mind standing over here, so that I can face you both?" Bridget moved as Raj instructed, taking Rosie's left hand protectively in hers. Raj then took each of their outside hands in his, forming a circle.

Allie looked on, chastened.

The Convention of Wives

"We're all here because we're concerned about Rosie. Our problem is that she has a complicated presentation, um, list of complaints. It's taking us some time to figure out what's going on." Gently, he let go of their hands and walked over and stood next to Allie. "Rosie, I am really very sorry that you've been here for so long. But we are trying to be comprehensive in our approach. We, Dr. Wasserman and I, are getting close to ruling some things out. Would you mind terribly staying just a little longer?"

It was like watching good theater. The focus of the energy had turned from sister to patient. *How does he do that?* Allie wondered.

"Rosie, really, I think—" Bridget began. But Rosie, who—Allie noticed—brushed the bangs off her face, smoothed her hair down, and straightened her patient gown before replying, cut her sister off.

"Bridget. I'm old enough to decide here. It is my body, after all. And Doctor . . . ." Rosie looked at Raj questioningly, smiling broadly.

"Khan," Raj supplied.

"Yes, Dr. Khan, oh, and Dr. Wasserman," Rosie jutted her chin in Allie's direction, "they think they're getting somewhere. Bridget, I need answers."

Allie was impressed and jealous at the same time; and mildly thankful that the patient had even remembered she was in the room, let alone her name. Her phone started vibrating and she saw that it was her mother.

"Raj, I need to answer this; my folks are in California. I'll be right back," Allie said, holding her phone out in Raj's direction, mouthing the words "my mother" and rolling her eyes. She turned to leave and nearly collided with a tall, red-headed man barreling through the side curtain. He was slightly out of breath and his forehead gleamed. He rushed past Allie to Rosie's bedside.

"Hey, are you all right?" Allie heard him say as he sat on the bed.

"Aiden, I'm so glad you came, I . . ." A sobbing Rosie collapsed in his arms.

Allie headed to the small room behind the nurses' station. She'd seen it so many times before. Patients would be completely stoic with one family member but totally lose it when another walked in. Family relationships were so strange.

She tried her mother's phone but got her voice mail. Now *Allie* was concerned. She retrieved her recent voice mail messages and played them one by one.

"Allie, it's Mom. Call me. Please."

"Allie, it's Mom. I'm with a friend in San Diego and her daughter is at St. Vincent's in the ER. Call me."

"Allie, it's Mom. Can you stop putting me in voice mail, please. I really need to speak with you. I'm calling Zoe."

She never got to listen to the fourth call. She was interrupted by the sight of her sister Zoe walking toward her in her work shirt, torn jeans, and leftover city ranger parka, ever the environmentalist.

"What are you doing here? And how did you get into the ER?"

"I flashed my New York City ID at the security guard and voila!"

"Oh my God, Zoe, has something happened to Dad? Mom's been calling and I . . ." Allie said as her legs shook.

"Mom and Dad are both fine," Zoe said as she put her arms on Allie's. "Mom couldn't reach you. There's someone in the ER. A friend's daughter. Remember that family, the one we ran into in Maui years ago? Well, the daughter is pretty sick, and Mom was hoping . . ."

Allie didn't need to hear the rest of the story. She remembered Maui. All of it. Mostly, she remembered *him*.

Chapter Nineteen

Julia

Maui, Hawaii, March 1987

Hana was a "can't miss" destination on Maui according to her Fodor's guidebook. But the road! Julia hadn't realized how large the pineapple yellow van would feel on the narrow motorway and single lane overpasses, or that she'd spend most of the white-knuckle drive imagining her family plummeting hundreds of feet to the ground below. By eleven o'clock, she was craving a glass of wine.

"Are we there yet?" Brody asked for the tenth time.

"Almost," John answered, barely containing his frustration.

"Mom, he took my banana. He's always taking my stuff. You're a pig, Brody," Bridget shouted from the middle seat. Aiden and Rosie watched quietly from the back.

Julia turned in time to see Bridget smack Brody. He shoved her right back.

"Mom!" Bridget shouted.

"All right, that's it!" John pulled the van onto the shoulder of the road.

"Jesus, John!" Julia yelled.

"Twins! Out! Now!" John screamed. The two scampered out of the middle seat, staying out of the way of their father as best they could.

"Okay, Brody, get in with Rosie and don't even think about bothering her. Is that understood?" John threatened.

None of the kids said a word for the next twenty minutes, except for Rosie who quietly asked Julia for a tissue to blow her nose.

"Okay, everybody out, and take all of the garbage with you. Check around for any empty bottles or wrappers. I don't want to have to clean out this car before I turn it in."

"Sure Dad," Aiden responded.

"You too," John said to Julia.

"I know the drill." She breathed deeply, trying to prepare herself for the sunscreen, bathing suits, hydration, and locating lunch part of the outing. They were all hot, sweaty, and irritated. *Where is the fun and when is it starting?*

They left the car in the visitors' lot and hiked down a narrow cliffside path indicated by arrows.

"John, I don't know if this is safe for the kids; maybe we should turn back. It's really steep."

"Kids, what do you think? We come all this way and don't even try?"

"Dad, maybe it is a little steep, especially for Rosie," Aiden half pleaded.

"I'm okay, Dad. I think I can do it," Rosie piped up.

"Let's go then."

"John?" Julia begged.

"It'll be fine."

He was always pushing them. She was always protecting them. Maybe it was bravado on John's part or just the difference between fathering and mothering. She was nervous the whole time they hiked, but they made it down to the beach without incident.

The kids and John were already in the water and Julia was setting up their towels when she saw a large Hawaiian man approach with a cooler strapped across his protruding belly. *Perfect*. She purchased cut up coconut and Cokes, shielding them from the sun as best she could under one of the towels.

Sitting on the red sand, looking out of the blue lagoon, Julia did her best to regain some composure. She recalled reading somewhere that the colored sand was the result of the breakdown of the cliffs by the rise and fall of the tides. She thought of the history, of the thousands of years it would take to erode a precipice of this magnitude. And the result, a breathtaking lagoon shielded by large rock outcroppings that broke the incoming waves. It was spectacular. The loud drive out faded from her memory. Her breathing slowed.

"Excuse me."

Suddenly there was a hairy leg next to her. She jumped.

"I'm sorry, I didn't mean to scare you. Just wondered where you got the Cokes."

She looked up, shielding her eyes from the sun. "There's a guy with a cooler selling them. I think he went that way." She looked down the beach. "Yeah, there he is, see him. The blue cooler."

"Shit! Julia?"

"Excuse me."

"Is that you?"

"Hey man, that's my wife you're hitting on." Suddenly John was next to them.

"John? It's me, Rob, Dina's husband."

"What the fuck are you doing here?"

"John, language, the kids," she chastised.

Julia stood up and threw on her cover-up as the kids gathered round grabbing towels and Cokes.

"Hey kids, this is Rob, your mom's friend's husband."

"Whoa! All yours?" Rob asked, pointing at the kids.

"Yeah, quite a crew," John answered, patting Julia's behind. "Are you here alone?"

"Oh, uh, no. Dina and the kids are right over there."

Julia and Rob's eyes locked. Ten years later and they were all back on a beach together.

"**R**ob said they'll just finish their snack and be over to say hello and meet the kids," John explained to Julia.

"Seriously, you had to suggest we all get together. We're what, five thousand miles from home? How is this even possible?"

"Come on, she was your friend. I don't know what happened between you two." He took her face in his sandy hands and kissed her on the nose. "Women!"

Julia looked at Bridget, who was collecting shells nearby. Aiden was bouncing a ball on his Kadima paddle. Rosie was watching a stranded starfish squirm in the sand and pouring water over it from a yellow, plastic pail. Maybe it would be okay.

"**H**ey, small world," Julia said tentatively as she gave Dina a loose hug.

"Very," Dina responded.

Dina barely returned the embrace.

They introduced the kids to each other and within minutes the younger ones bounded off to build what would be, according to Dina's younger daughter, Zoe, a "mega sandcastle." *Zoe. Who picked a name like Zoe?*

"Aiden, go keep an eye on them; we're right by the water," John asked.

"Sure, Dad." Aiden trotted off.

"Allie, there are too many of them for him to watch alone. Don't you think?" Rob asked their older girl.

She was sweet looking, with Dina's big blue eyes and dark hair.

"Dad . . . I'm not the babysitter," she whined.

"Today you are," he answered.

"I can go if she doesn't want to," Dina suggested.

"That's ridiculous. Allie, come on," Rob insisted.

It was surreal peeking into the life of a friend she thought, and had hoped, she'd never see again.

"Fine!" Allie picked up her shells and stalked off.

"Teenagers!" John laughed.

The conversation seemed easy for the men as they talked about their work. She and Dina discovered both families were staying at the Marriott, both scheduled to attend the luau that night.

At that bit of information, Dina stood up suddenly.

"I'm uncomfortable leaving them all over there. I'm just going to get a bit closer."

"I'm coming with you," Julia said, getting up.

"No, I can watch them all, really."

"That's okay." The two plodded over to the kids, stopping halfway when a group of young boys with a football ran in front of them.

"I don't know if we'll make it to the luau. That spit thing, the pig with the apple in its mouth. Not sure that's really our style," Dina said.

Maybe she was trying to politely get out of seeing them. "Turns out not mine either. At least half of me."

"What are you talking about?"

"After we saw you last . . ." *Oh, what the hell, why not tell her?* "My mom told me I'm half Jewish."

"Jewish? That makes no sense."

The look on Dina's face. Eyebrows furrowed; chin pulled into her neck. Was Julia not good enough to be Jewish? *Christ!* "You're telling me. Turns out my dad was not my dad." Why was she telling her? It was something she hadn't even shared with John.

"Wow."

"I've never told John."

"Wow."

Wow. Julia waited. *Just wow.* No follow-up questions. Silence. The information simply didn't seem to fit into Dina's paradigm of the universe. Who cared anymore what she thought? Confiding in her had been a mistake. "I don't like to talk about it," Julia said, taking back control of the conversation. As if to be polite, Dina changed the subject.

"How are you doing with all four?" Dina asked. "Do you have any help; I mean did you?"

"I didn't really. No. John had this thing about other people watching the kids. More than once he reminded me that his mother had four rambunctious boys and did it all herself. You?"

"On and off. More off than on. Sometimes I wish I'd been able to deal better with a stranger living with us in our house."

The women discussed the pros and cons of hiring a live-in babysitter, wishing they'd had more choices. Could there ever really be more of a balance in their lives between home and work. Could they even go back to work at this point with nothing on their resumes in the last fifteen years?

They talked about how women judged each other's choices, often and harshly, always trying to justify the decisions they'd made. Never feeling adequate. Placing everyone in silos. She works, she doesn't, she's a professional, a volunteer, a professional volunteer. She lunches and shops. She doesn't. She's always the classroom mom, she's never the classroom mom. She's setting an example for her daughters by working, but they really love the nanny. Everyone with an opinion and none understanding the vagaries of each other's actual lives. How could they expect the world to take women seriously until the men stopped dismissing this squabbling as one humongous cat fight?

They'd missed each other, these conversations about life they always had, but neither said.

Later, when John asked what the two women had talked about, Julia told him she couldn't remember.

Chapter Twenty

Allie

New York, New York, December 2000

Aiden was on the phone, drumming his fingers nervously as he spoke. He was taller and leaner than Allie had remembered, but otherwise he looked the same. Reddish wavy hair, browner than she remembered. The shadow of a beard darkening his complexion.

"Yes, she's stable. No, she's looked better. Bridget? She's upset, but, you know, she's been handling everything. I'm sorry, I was in a meeting at first and couldn't get out and then . . . anyway, I'll stay. Really, we'll see you when you get in. No, who again? Maui? That doctor family. Oh right, think I remember. Braids, dark hair, hula girl. Yeah." He laughed. "Wasserman, right."

Hula girl?

Allie waved in his direction, pointed to the ID hanging on the breast pocket of her white coat, and made hula hand motions.

"Mom, Dad, I have to go. I think Allie, uh, Dr. Wasserman, just walked in," Aiden said, putting his hand over his face. "Of course, I'll say hello." He hung up the phone. "Hello," he said, revealing a wide-toothed grin. "How much of that did you hear?"

"Nope, didn't hear a thing," Allie replied to the apparent leader of the opposing team. She held out her hand, planning on showing him that she had the shake of a trucker. It was the handshake Grandpa Dave had taught her, something that would impress and put off a man at the same time.

But the touch of his hand melted her anger, her embarrassment. "Aiden. It's been a while." She remembered soft sand and warm sun. She remembered being teased about her obsession with grass skirts. Mostly she remembered puka necklaces and a delicious kiss.

She dropped Aiden's hand as the attending physician leaned inside the curtain.

"Doctors, can I speak with you both outside?"

"You can stop with the detective act, Dr. Khan. You spend more time on that damn computer than with the patient. Both of you, stick with the basics, like finishing the physical and paying closer attention to the bloodwork." He waved a lab report in their faces. "She needs to be followed up by a hematologist. You'd know that if you'd only checked to see if the latest labs were in the chart yet. I'm guessing non-Hodgkin's lymphoma, but it could be something else entirely." He shook his head and walked toward Rosie's cubicle, mumbling. "I'll handle this; come in and watch how it's done."

Allie had seen some horrible things since starting her residency in the ER. The worst was a young couple in a motor vehicle accident on the Henry Hudson Parkway—an MVA. The father survived, but the mother . . . she was splayed on a gurney, her chest split open while they tried and failed direct heart massage to resuscitate her. A nurse was trying to console the couple's crying baby.

Allie would never forget it.

But this . . . this really hit home.

Someone her age who was family, not *family* . . . but family. She tried to freeze her face in preparation for what was coming. But wasn't it too early to share a potential diagnosis? They didn't have all the tests back yet. How important was it to clear the cubicle? Allie was just getting familiar with the idea of the "throughput" imperative—an upfront limitation on the amount of time given to each patient regardless of condition that oftentimes felt like it was modeled after the drive-thru window of McDonald's.

"Rosie, I'm Dr. Carmichael, the attending physician overseeing your case."

Aiden moved closer to Rosie and took her hand. Allie could see her trembling as if the temperature in the room had suddenly dropped.

"We've got some of your tests back. We're still waiting for a few. But, preliminarily, you've got something going on with your bloodwork that we can't completely explain. It may or may not be contributing to some of your other conditions. The leg fracture, for example."

She watched Bridget sit down on the bed close to her sister, her face white.

"The ER is not really the best place to follow up on the details of your case. We'll be giving you something to take home for pain and should be discharging you soon. You'll need to see a specialist, a hem-onc, in particular. We can make a recommendation if you like."

"I'm sorry, a what?" Bridget asked, flailing inside her pocketbook and bringing out a pen and paper.

"Sorry, a physician who specializes in diseases of the blood system."

"What's the onc?" Aiden asked.

Allie knew what was coming. She watched for what she knew would be the predictable collapse.

"Onc? Sorry. Cancer. He treats blood and cancer disorders."

"Cancer? I have cancer!" Rosie screamed.

"No, dear, I did not say you had cancer. What I said was, you have something going on with your blood system and we need to find out more. It could be a whole host of things. There is no reason to worry about something you don't know is the situation."

Aiden held Rosie while she cried.

"I'm going to get you the names of a few specialists. Dr. Wasserman will come back to see you with that information." He gave Allie an embarrassed glance and backed out.

So much for seeing how it was done.

Allie wondered why she'd been nominated to bring the specialist list back to them when she noticed Raj was no longer in the room. She didn't remember seeing him leave.

"Rosie, I'm sorry. I know he frightened you. But we don't really know what this is yet. It could be something benign. You shouldn't worry until you . . . ." Allie said, trying to be comforting.

"She shouldn't worry?" Aiden blasted her. "Are you kidding? It's easy for you, isn't it? You must do this all day long. You're numb. It's not even about you, so why the hell would you care?"

"We can get our own specialists. Don't bother coming back," Bridget shouted.

Allie stood outside the curtain gathering herself and listened as Aiden left a voice mail for his parents, no doubt somewhere over the Pacific by now.

"Hey guys. Good news. Rosie's being discharged. She'll need some follow-up. Bridget and I will take her home and stay until you get there. We'll talk more when you get in." He hesitated and then added, "Hey, we love you both."

Allie felt stung but was impressed not only by the way Aiden was able to keep the concern out of his voice, but with the way he told his parents he loved them. As a doctor, she knew how important it was to say things to the people you love before it's too late. It was a hard-earned lesson, and she felt for Aiden. Allie held her tears until she made it to the small room behind the nurses' station. She opened the door and there was Raj, sitting alone in the corner, his head in his hands.

Chapter Twenty-One

Allie

Maui, Hawaii, March 1987

Allie was mortified. Who were these people anyway? This was supposed to be their family vacation, but it felt like every other time when her parents would go out and leave her in charge.

For as long as she could remember, Mom and Dad had a regular Saturday night babysitter. They called it "date night," and the thought of it made her nauseous. After her bat mitzvah, Allie had become the in-house sitter—until recently when she insisted she had the right to have her own Saturday night plans. Granted those plans mostly consisted of getting together with a couple of friends from her honors classes. Good girls that they were, they usually wandered over to the parking lot in the back of the coffee shop in town to watch the cool kids flirt and smoke cigarettes and pot.

Now, here she was in a bathing suit on a beach in Hawaii with some random boy.

"What's in the bag?" he asked as they stood facing the waves.

"Puka shells."

"What?"

Allie pulled the strings on the bag and took out a small, white object. "Puka shells. I'm making a necklace."

"Oh, cool."

She handed him one of the shells, carefully dropping it in his outstretched palm. She stole a glimpse at his chest and noticed that it was smooth and hairless.

"What kind of name is Allie, anyway?" he said, rolling the shell between his fingers.

"Excuse me?" She shut the bag and hung it back on her shoulder.

"I mean, it's short for something, right?"

"No."

He threw the shell in the sand. *What a jerk.*

"Oh," he said.

"What kind of name is Aiden? Talk about weird." She knew she was being mean.

He looked over at her. His eyes were squinting as he looked her up and down before answering.

"It's Irish. We're Irish. It's a family name."

"Does it mean anything?" She sat down, dropped her bag, and started gathering sand into a mound.

"Huh?" He sat down next to her and began adding sand to her pile.

"Like, I have an English name, but my Hebrew name is Ayelet. I'm named for my Grandpa David's mother. Her Hebrew name was Ayelet too. It means a deer, you know, like Bambi."

"And you think my name is weird."

"Nice. So, what does Aiden mean?"

"Mean? I have no idea." He flattened the top of the mound.

"Oh."

They turned to watch Daniel and Brody playing Kadima. Bridget, Zoe, and Rosie were building a sandcastle. Suddenly a large wave sent the girls sprawling. Bridget and Zoe popped up coughing, but Rosie was nowhere to be seen. Aiden sprinted to the water calling "Rosie! Rosie!" when Allie saw the knot of her pink bathing suit pop to the surface. Aiden lifted his little sister out of the water, hurling her over his back and awkwardly making his way toward them.

Allie was exhausted from dragging Zoe and Bridget up out of the waves. She sat with one arm around each girl watching Aiden and Rosie. The girl threw up water, then stopped and coughed and cried simultaneously.

Daniel and Brody ran over to them and stood nearby silently.

"Hey, you're going to be okay, Rosie. Really, you'll be fine," Aiden said, rubbing his hands on her back.

Suddenly, Rosie went quiet. She sat as still as a statue.

"Rosie, Rosie! Come on, breathe. Just breathe. Shit, please, oh God!"

Allie turned to shout for her parents but saw they were already running toward them.

A strange noise emanated from Rosie's throat. She coughed loudly and began sobbing. She grabbed her big brother and held him tight.

"I couldn't breathe, Aiden, I couldn't breathe," she yelled.

"It's okay, you're okay, we're okay. We're okay."

Allie saw tears running down Aiden's cheeks.

"I know that was scary. You have to watch the waves. Sometimes a really big one comes out of nowhere." He wiped his face dry as Rosie jumped into his lap.

Allie tightened her arms around the girls and whispered to them, "You see, she's fine. Rosie's going to be okay."

The other family was already seated when they arrived at the luau, except for Aiden. She wondered where he was. "Volunteers, we need volunteers!" a large Hawaiian dancer in a hula skirt shouted.

"Come on, Allie," her dad shouted at her. "All those ballet lessons, you'll be great."

"Dad! Stop."

"Rob, you're embarrassing her," her mom shouted at her dad.

"I am not." Her dad got up and came around to her chair. "Just because she gets A's in chemistry doesn't mean my little girl can't dance."

What was wrong with her father? She wanted to sink under the table. But the look on his face. Wasn't it enough that she got A's in chemistry?

The dancer hovered by their table. She wanted the ground to swallow her up, but everyone was staring in her direction, so off she went toward the small, raised stage where someone tied a hula skirt around her waist. Allie's brow furrowed as she followed the instructions of the female instructor. Her hips swaying, she mimicked the graceful hand movements and brought them up above her head, then out to the side, her hips and hands moving in sync. Allie almost forgot the crowd as she lost herself in the music, the gentle lapping of the shore, and the blue Hawaiian sky above. Then the music ended, and she bounded off the stage. There, at the table, was Aiden.

"That's our girl. Always the good student," her father said proudly.

Allie was mortified.

"You're a good dancer."

"Yup. When she's not in her books, she's at dance class," her father went on.

"Daddy, please!" She slunk back to her chair.

Aiden sat next to her.

"I wouldn't have thought you were such a good dancer." He was staring at her.

"You don't know anything about me." She sliced up the pineapple on the plate in front of her.

"Hey. There's a disco later for kids our age. I don't want to go alone. You wanna go?"

The Convention of Wives

They had two hours all to themselves, that is, besides the fifty or so other teens at the "disco" the hotel had arranged. They tried talking but couldn't hear above the music. Aiden motioned toward the path that led to the beach. She wasn't sure she should go with him but rationalized that he was a family friend. Where was the harm in that?

"Man, you'd think they could do better at controlling that bass. You can still feel the vibration."

He was right. She somehow felt it in her jaw. They took off their shoes and walked onto the sand. The moon was full and the lights from the hotel behind them together made it seem like either sunrise or dusk.

"You don't think it's funny we've never met before?"

"No, why?"

"Just that our parents seem to know each other pretty well is all."

Allie hadn't thought about it much. Her parents were a mystery to her. Her mom's oversharing of what Allie considered her mom's personal business. Her dad's quiet resolve to always make sure that the time they spent together as a family would become a "fun" memory.

"Do you like your family?" she asked.

"As opposed to what, another family? I only have one."

She laughed. "I mean you and your little sister seem close, but the twins are a nightmare. Your mom and dad seem okay."

"Why would you think you know anything about who we are?"

"Why would you think you know anything about who *we* are?"

"Touché."

She thought he was going to suggest they walk back. Instead, he asked, "What about your dad? He seems like a cool guy. He kind of lets you do what you want. My dad is full of opinions."

"I think that's pretty normal for a dad."

"How would we know what's normal? We're only fourteen."

She didn't want to tell him she wouldn't be fourteen for another month. He was right, but her dad did have opinions. He just wasn't around that often to give them.

"You still have that bag of shells with you?" He pointed to her waist where the bag was looped on her belt.

"Yeah, I'm almost done making that necklace."

"Cool. Can I see?"

She sat down on a log and carefully took out the puka shells strung on waxed twine.

He sat next to her and turned over the necklace as she held it.

"Here, I'll show you how to add a shell."

They sat for a while, her teaching, him watching, until the necklace was finished.

"Now what?"

"Now it needs a neck." She smiled up at him. "Here, like this." She placed the necklace on him, tied a knot and twirled it around. She leaned back a little to take a look. "Perfect."

He looked down and pulled off the headband that was holding her hair back. "Perfect."

His lips were soft and warm, his tongue wet and searching. She'd never French kissed before. It felt good. He felt good.

Chapter Twenty-Two

Rosie Kinsella

New York, New York, January 2001

Rosie squinted at the afternoon sun coming through her apartment's windows. She shifted on the couch, feeling the muscles in her butt cry out for attention. It had been weeks since her fall. Weeks while she coped with physical pain and unbearable uncertainty. Not to mention her parents, who stayed after she came home from the hospital. At first it was all happy family as her mom and dad watched over her. Then, two nights in, she heard them arguing through the thin apartment wall.

"Tomorrow? You're leaving tomorrow? You can't be serious. You're being selfish. Your patients can go on without you for a few days. This is a family emergency, for God's sake! Rosie needs you," her mom pleaded.

"I have a practice to run," her dad yelled. "What do you think pays for the lifestyle you've gotten used to? When was the last time *you* made a car payment on that Mercedes?"

"This isn't about money, and you know it. This is about time. You're never around when we need you. Especially when we need you. When I need you."

"Enough!"

Her dad left for Atlanta the following day. Her mom became Rosie's personal combination caterer and drug dealer, alternatively running to the corner bodega for food and weaning Rosie off the Percocet by giving her Tylenol with codeine instead.

"Mom! Mom!" she yelled over the soap opera blaring from the TV.

No answer.

Right, she'd gone to do some errands.

She eyed the crutches resting on the white shag carpet nearby. She was thirsty but had to pee too. How was that possible?

Shit.

Rosie painstakingly made her way to the bathroom. She was exhausted by the time she got back to the couch but impressed with her newly found talent at balancing herself between the two crutches. The phone rang.

"Hello. John?"

"I think you have the wrong number."

"Is this Dr. Kinsella's line?"

"Oh, my dad. No, this is his daughter Rosie." She thought she recognized the voice.

She heard a muffled exclamation. "Goddamn it, I told you to get me the father's number, not the patient. Can't anyone do anything right around here! Sorry, Rosie, this is Dr. Katz, we met a few weeks ago."

"Yes, Dr. Katz, I know who you are."

"Your bloodwork came back. First, I want you to know that I have some good news for you. You do not have lymphoma or any other blood cancer."

Rosie started to cry.

"Rosie, are you there? Can you hear me?"

"Yes, I'm sorry, Dr. Katz. It's just that that is such a relief."

"Yes, well, I do have something else to tell you."

Rosie held her breath.

"You have been diagnosed with something called Gaucher's disease. It could be contributing to the symptoms you've been experiencing. It is treatable, but I'll need you to come back into the office so that we can go over more information. My scheduler will call you back early tomorrow morning with a date and time."

"I have what? Wait, I have to write this down to tell my folks." Rosie grabbed a nearby pad and pen.

"Gaucher's disease. G-a-u-c-h-e-r," the doctor said slowly, then he was silent for a few seconds before continuing. "It is, and this is the interesting part . . . it is usually an Ashkenazi Jewish genetic disease. But we've seen some cases that don't fit the pattern, so let's not focus on that right now, shall we? The main thing is that you're lucky, in a sense, as it wasn't treatable a short time ago, but now it is. So, we'll talk all about that as soon as I see you, okay?"

No response.

"Rosie, are you there?"

"Wait. Did you say Jewish? I think there's been a mistake. And what was that other word."

"Ashkenazi. Jews mainly from Eastern Europe. Let's discuss that more when I see you. We'll need to talk about a treatment plan."

"A treatment plan? Okay. Thank you, Dr. Katz."

"I'll see you soon."

"Thank you."

Rosie hung up the phone as her mother opened the door to the apartment, bags hanging from her arms. She ripped the piece of paper from the pad and stuck it in the magazine she was pretending to read.

"I got you some avocados. I know you like those, and I read that they're a complete food, so healthy for you. They said they're the next big thing. I don't think so, they're kind of strange looking. Anyway, I'm going to make a salad with them tonight, before the steak," her mother explained. "Who was that on the phone?"

"Wrong number."

"What? I heard you talking as I came in."

"Not wrong number. I meant a solicitation, you know, fund-raising. I think it was the American Heart Society; right, that's what it was. They were asking for money."

"You mean the American Heart Association?"

"Right, Association. Stop already. I wasn't paying attention. I just wanted to get off the phone. Mom, I'm going to go to bed, I'm really not up to eating dinner," Rosie said, grabbing her crutches and rising slowly.

"What? Here, let me help you," her mother said. "You have to eat something. I went to all this trouble buying everything. You're going to waste away if you keep this up."

"I said I'm tired! Is this about me or you? God, I wish you'd gone back to Atlanta with Dad!" She stalked off to her room and slammed the door.

Her mother was chopping vegetables by the kitchen sink. Rosie came up from behind and gave her a one-handed hug, tenuously balanced by her crutches.

"Hey, careful, I have a knife here!" Her mom put it down and turned to face her.

"I'm sorry. I'm just so frustrated being cooped up in here. I know you're trying to be a good mom."

"That's my job."

"I know." *Her job.* Rosie had never thought of it that way. "Don't bother cooking, we can order in Chinese and watch a movie."

"Are you sure?"

"Yeah. Why don't you take a long run? The sun won't set for a few hours."

"That would be great. I am going a little stir crazy myself. I'll take you out for a spin in the wheelchair tomorrow. Take a break from those crutches. It's supposed to be a nice day. We can get hot dogs and watch the kids on the carousel and . . ."

"Mom that would be great, really."

She had about two hours, maybe less. Bridget was the wrong person to call. She'd been a great advocate in the emergency room, but this . . . she wouldn't know what to do with this information. She called Aiden and asked him to meet her at Felice, a bar they both liked in the Financial District. But she had to act fast.

Aiden arrived fifteen minutes late, all apologies and hugs. They ordered Chardonnays and some nuts, two waters on the side. Dinner of a sort.

"Rosie, where's Mom? How did you even get here?"

"Fuck, Aiden, don't you think I know how to hail a cab? I live here too."

"Hey, language. Come on. On crutches? I just thought Mom would come with—"

"I'm not a cripple!"

"Relax. I just thought you were both meeting me."

"Relax? Easy for you to say. You try having Mom live with you. She's driving me nuts. All schedules and plans, even when I can't go anywhere. Her runs in Central Park are my only break."

He nodded knowingly. "She means well."

"I know," Rosie admitted. "My apartment has never looked this organized."

He smiled at her. "So, what's going on?"

She took a deep breath, her lip started to quiver. She tried hard not to cry, but her left eye started twitching. Her cheeks felt wet. She reached for her napkin.

"Rosie, what's wrong?"

"I'm sorry I snapped at you. I don't know how to even ask you this. You're going to think I'm crazy." She blew her nose in the napkin.

"Take a sip of water, it always helps you calm down."

"I don't need to calm down!" she shouted. Nearby diners

glanced their way. Water splattered as she grabbed the glass and sipped. Whispering, she said, "I have a disease. I didn't just break my leg. I'm sick." The tears started flowing again.

"What do you mean 'a disease'? Oh, my God, is it cancer?"

"No, no, it's not that. It's something rare but treatable. That's what the doctor said."

"Thank God."

She wiped her cheeks with her fingers. They were gray from her running mascara. She rubbed them on her napkin. "That's not the problem."

"I don't understand."

"Aiden, is it at all possible, in any way that you can think of, that we're Jewish?" Rosie asked, placing her napkin back on her lap.

"What? What the hell are you talking about? What does that have to do with this?"

"Could we be Jewish?"

"Rosie, I don't know what you mean, why would you ask me that?"

"Because I think I might be Jewish. I mean, the doctor said this illness, it's called . . . wait"—she pulled a piece of paper from her pocket—"Gaucher, and it's a Jewish genetic disorder. Maybe that's why I broke my leg, why I have arthritis. Well, I mean, maybe I don't really have arthritis, but I have, I have . . ." She started to cry, then hiccup.

"Rosie, Rosie," Aiden said, taking out his handkerchief and handing it to her. He was old-fashioned that way. "I really don't get what you're saying."

She took a long drink of water. The hiccups continued. "Dad's friend Dr. Katz called. *Hic.* My blood tests came back positive for this problem, and you have to be Jewish to have this problem, this disease; and how could I have this problem if I'm not Jewish. *Hic.* But I must be Jewish. We must be Jewish, but how are we Jewish? How could Mom and Dad lie about that? We know their brothers and sisters, our cousins, and our grandparents. I mean, Mom and Dad met in CCD, right? You can't get more Catholic than that. It doesn't make any sense. Unless, unless . . . I've thought this all through."

"Unless what?"

"Unless I'm adopted."

"You're not adopted. I was six when Mom was pregnant with you. I was there when you came home from the hospital."

"Then they brought the wrong baby home. Aiden," she said soulfully, "I'm not your sister. *Hic.*" She nodded her head from side to side and started eating the nuts.

"The tests have to be wrong," Aiden said emphatically. "Hey, can I get two more Chardonnays over here? Right away, please? And some more water," he shouted at the waitress.

"They're not wrong," Rosie answered.

"What is this disease? Is there a cure?"

"It causes all the things I have going on with me. There is a treatment. I don't even know what it is yet. I don't know if there's a cure. God, I didn't ask the doctor that; I didn't ask him much of anything. He would have told me if there was one, right?"

"Wait. You haven't told Mom and Dad yet?"

She nodded.

"How could you not call Dad?"

"What am I supposed to tell our parents? That they took the wrong baby home from the nursery? I don't know what to do. I don't know what to do!" she shouted, punctuated by a loud hiccup. She sat limply like a rag doll, looking at him for an answer.

He'd always provided them for her. He'd found her missing teddy bear; and, when her first boyfriend broke up with her at the sixth-grade dance, he told her he was a jerk. But for this? She could tell from his silence and the expression on his face that— for this—he had no answers. The waitress placed the wine on the table. She and Aiden sipped.

"Does Mom even know you're here?"

Rosie nodded.

"I'm getting you back to the apartment. We'll call Dad on the phone and talk to them both, together. There has to be an explanation." He took her hand and held it tight in his. He would always be her big brother, no matter what.

Chapter Twenty-Three

Elsa

Millburn, New Jersey, January 2001

Elsa was shocked to see Rob's face at her apartment door in the middle of a workday. He looked pale.

"What's happened? Come in, I'll get some tea. Sit."

He half-shouted at his mom as he heard her fussing in the kitchen. "Mom, I've done something. I made a mistake. Years ago. With a woman. I think Dina will leave me. That stupid island."

"What?" Her face peeked out from the kitchen doorway.

"Barbados."

She sat next to him at the table.

"Do you remember Dina's friend Julia? Julia and I, she and I, we . . ."

She grabbed him to her. "Pshaw. Pshaw. Rob. There is nothing, nothing you could have done, nothing we can't get through." She held him tight. That beautiful _shiksa_. Her beautiful boy. Elsa had lost everything twice over. These young people with their marriage troubles. They should only know how lucky they were to have them.

Elsa's stockings were torn and her shoes, her good black ones, the ones she wore to work, were badly scratched. One of the heels was loose. Under her coat, her flowered dress was soiled and smelled of sweat, something that disgusted her. Her shoulder hurt from the straps of the bag she was holding, its metal contents hitting her in the ribs as she walked. She had thought the early part of the journey was difficult. That had been by rail. Now they were on foot, somewhere between Germany and Austria in a place called the Brenner Pass.

In some strange way, she was lucky. She looked at the two young sisters next to her. They were almost skeletal, their hair strangely short, with coats that were not their own and men's boots on their feet. She remembered them as the girls who, earlier in the trip, had to be dragged onto the train.

"I'm Elsa," she offered.

"Liesel," the older of the two replied. The other girl said nothing.

"Where are you from?" Elsa asked.

"Auschwitz."

Elsa was sure that was where her family had been taken, but she was afraid to ask if the girl had seen them. She had no need to learn the truth. Not now. Not yet.

"I'm so sorry. But I mean where before . . . before that place?"

"There is no before. There is no place before and no one left for us, only this . . . this after."

It must be true, what she had heard. Of course, they would resist the trains.

"This is my sister, Anna."

"Hello, Anna," Elsa said politely. Still no response. Not even the nod of a head. Elsa noticed that the girl was pressing the fingers of each hand against her thumbs in rapid sequence, repeatedly. She stared.

"She doesn't speak anymore. This helps her," Liesel responded, her eyes tearing up.

Elsa reached for the lace handkerchief in her pocket, the one that had been her mother's. She kissed it, then handed it solemnly to Liesel. "Here. It was my mother's. Keep this, please."

Liesel stared for a moment at the handkerchief, then wiped it slowly over her face and lips, blew her nose. "But . . . but . . . it was your mother's."

"Yes," Elsa replied as she reached out and touched the girl's shoulder. "It will be your *before*." The girl smiled through new tears.

Elsa could not believe that this pass through the Alps, the Brenner, was the easiest. She was not used to such hiking. And she hadn't eaten much but bread and some chocolate in days. It had been a week since the scraggly group had left Berlin, a conglomeration of survivors from the camps and others, like herself, who didn't trust that the Germans wouldn't murder any of the remaining Jews.

"Keep going, not much farther. Who needs water?" Yitzi asked. He was kind and encouraging. As a member of the Bricha, the Jewish underground helping survivors of the war reach Palestine, he would need to be.

Elsa was thirsty, but she didn't want to stop for the bathroom again, so she shook her head. It was a crisp fall day; and she was freezing. But she kept walking.

"About one more hour to go. How about another song?" Yitzi cheered them on.

The group began to sing in Hebrew: "Ilu hotzi, hotzianu, hotzianu mimitzrayim, hotzianu mimitzrayim, dayeinu!"

If He had brought us out from Egypt, it would have been enough for us!

Elsa wondered why they were singing a Passover song—then, with sudden revelation, realized it was one of the few songs common to all, religious or not. Everyone celebrated this holiday. Even the least observant gathered. And what could be more comforting than a song about escaping the slavery of Egypt.

The perfect song to sing for these war survivors trying to reach Palestine.

She could do this. Elsa knew she had to be strong for everyone she had lost. Her parents, her brother and sister, her cousins. Her grandparents. Saying good-bye to her *bubbe* and *zeide* had been horrible; the desperation with which her grandmother had thrust the candlesticks at her.

"Here, Elsala, take them. You'll make Shabbos. We'll come and have Shabbos with you when this is over."

Shabbos? They were enlightened Berliners. Her parents barely made Shabbos anymore. Only when her grandmother insisted. She knew now, hiking through the forest, that her grandparents understood they would never see her again. But at the time she had been naive and smiled at them, kissed them both, and taken the candlesticks.

"Of course, Bubbe. They are beautiful. I'll keep them for you, just for now."

Now had turned into forever.

She never saw her grandparents again. Soon her parents, brother, and sister were gone too. She alone had survived because her parents had chosen to save her.

She would never forget the evening when her mother took her by the hand to the mirror in the dining room. "Look at you, my beautiful *goyisha*-looking daughter, with those Slavic features. You resemble my mother more than I do, with that upturned nose and those blue eyes. A bit of luck for us."

That was how Elsa had learned of the plan that she was to be sent to live with business associates of her father's.

"Mr. and Mrs. Weis have a lovely family and a good haberdashery business. They have been our hat suppliers for over twenty years, and you know them. They will be good to you, and you will help them in the shop. People will think you are their visiting cousin."

The Convention of Wives

Elsa looked down at the fake documents with her new name, Elsa Weis. The papers had been expensive. She knew that her family should have all left when they had a chance. But they had hesitated to close their clothing store until it was taken from them. They had waited too long.

As time went on, she received word that they had been taken away to a work camp called Auschwitz. And later she knew that the rumors were true. It was not a work camp but a death camp. She was alone, but she was alive, her feet burning from blisters. She had not wanted to leave them all, but her parents had insisted.

And now they were all gone.

Thinking about them distracted her, and she stumbled over a rock. She would have fallen if not for a strong hand that grabbed her arm and pulled her upright.

"Are you all right?" the young man asked. "Here, let me hold that for you." He reached for the bag that had been hanging over her shoulder. Elsa held on tight.

She kept her eyes down to avoid the gaze of this stranger keeping step beside her. Though the sunlight was fading, she could still see well enough to make out the tiny edelweiss flowers popping like white twinkling starlight on either side of the path, seemingly put there on purpose to guide their way.

"I said, are you all right?" he repeated.

Elsa was not used to speaking. She was used to keeping quiet, to pretending she was invisible in the showroom unless customers approached her directly with a question about the origin of the plumage or the colors featured each new season. She had barely spoken to anyone during the last week that they had been walking, except for those two young girls.

"Do you have a name?" he persisted.

"Elsa."

"That's a lovely name." He hesitated, waiting for her to respond. "Don't you want to know mine?"

Who was this man who wanted to chat as if this were any other day? As if this were some kind of social outing. As if she weren't already struggling to breathe from the exertion and the high altitude.

"Michael. Well, really Michel, after some famous rabbi in the family. But I'm Michael. Michael Heller," he said as he tipped his hat. The hat came into Elsa's view before he did. It was then that she finally looked up at him and noticed that he was tall and slim with dark curly hair and broad shoulders. Or maybe that was just the padding in the jacket.

It was the tipping of the hat. A green felt Homburg with a ribbon and small quail feather, a smart crease in the crown. Hats, always hats. She laughed softly. The situation was simply absurd. She shuddered again from the sudden cool breeze. He was staring at her.

"I'm going to give you my scarf and gloves. You look cold."

He didn't ask, he just took them off and gave them to her. The gloves were big on her hands, but she was grateful.

"I think you need to complete the look," he said. And with that, he took off his hat and plunked it on her head. Too tired to resist, she let him. She imagined how she must look. She took off the glove on her right hand, reached up and touched the soft feather, the felt that was still warm from the heat of his head.

"I need water. I think I need water," she said as she looked up at him, tears falling from her eyes. *Someone is taking care of me.* It had been so long.

"Yitzi, over here, we need some water," Michael shouted.

She began to slow down.

"Don't stop walking, Elsa, just drink this," Michael said as he handed her the canteen.

She sipped the water, her crying subsiding as she walked.

"Thank you . . . Michel," she whispered.

"*Gornisht*, it's nothing . . . and it's Michael, not Michel," he said, grinning and looking down at her.

She smiled upon noting his comfortable use of Yiddish while insisting on his non-Yiddish name. It exemplified who they all were, trying to forget their past while being inextricably tied to it. She looked at him more closely, taking in his warm brown eyes and his slightly uneven mouth. Again, she stumbled slightly and felt the warmth of his hand through the thin glove as he took hers in his to steady her. He didn't let go until they were through the pass.

They registered as displaced persons at the United Nations Relief and Rehabilitation Agency offices, completing paperwork and being given something to eat before embarking by bus for the Bari-Lecce Displaced Persons Camp on the southeastern coastline of Italy.

Three months later, they were married. Nine months after that, they had a son. Another six months and it was becoming clear that the British would allow very few Jews into Palestine.

Elsa and Michael were getting ready to go to work in the camp one morning. They had diapered Roberto and packed his supplies for the women in the nursery to watch over him when someone shouted through their tent.

"Excuse me, I'm looking for a Michael Heller."

Excited to hear his name, Michael opened the flap, shouted with delight, and grabbed the man tightly.

"Ah, Rolph!" Michael said as he broke the embrace "This is my wife, Elsa."

"Your wife!" the man exclaimed, hugged her, and twirled her around. "You do move quickly, cousin!"

"Cousin?"

"Elsa, this is my cousin, Rolph." Michael went over to the crib and picked up the sleeping baby. "And Rolph, this is my son, Roberto."

"Michael, Michael, put him back down, why wake him?" Elsa admonished.

"Pshaw, Elsa, I want Rolph to meet my family."

"Please, Rolph, can I get you some water?" Elsa asked.

"She is beautiful and gracious, Michael. What a lucky man you are."

Later that evening they sat huddled together, talking for hours about how they had escaped Germany, had survived. Rolph had been making a life for himself in America before the war and had come back now to find what he could of the family.

"We must start again," he told Michael. "We have each other. And you, you already have a wife and child. I am heading back to America, to New York. And you?"

"Palestine."

"Palestine? How long have you been waiting?"

"A few months," Michael responded.

"Michael, tell him the truth. It's been over a year. We are in limbo here," Elsa explained.

"Elsa, we will wait. There is nowhere else that is safe."

"Safe?" Rolph asked. "Have you heard what the conditions are like in Palestine? Desert, tents, not enough food or water. Surrounded by Arabs who want us dead. And you with a young baby. You should come to America."

"I've already tried that too, Rolph. I've had no luck," Michael answered, his hand covering his mouth as he shook his head.

"I may have a way, Michael. There is an island nation called Barbados, I don't know if you've heard of it. But they are taking people. And from there you can get to the United States. I can sponsor you once I've returned."

"Michael, please, let's try this," Elsa pleaded. "We can start there on this island and then try again for Palestine or the United States. I want to get far away from this place. Please."

Her husband seemed afraid to make the decision.

175

The Convention of Wives

"Rolph, there is no way we are going to some island in the middle of nowhere just to get out of this place," Michael answered, pounding the table with his fist.

"It's not in the middle of nowhere. It is much closer to the United States than here; five thousand kilometers, not eight. And from there they are taking immigrants to the United States as long as they are sponsored. How do you think I got in? You have to trust me."

"But Rolph, we have a son, an infant. This is risky, and our plan was to go to Palestine."

"You have a plan? Let's be honest here. This," he said as he waved his hands at the sorry looking camp around them. "None of this was anyone's plan. Who are you kidding? I'm giving you a way out. Take it."

It took some convincing, but Michael finally agreed. She could make a home anywhere. All she needed was Michael, Roberto, and her grandmother's candlesticks. They may have a strange new life, but they would live.

Living. It was everything. She made Rob a cup of tea and listened to him speak about what had happened years ago. He wasn't wrong, his news would change everything. But no one was dying, what the girl had was treatable. No one was being murdered in a concentration camp.

She was being harsh. Life had hardened her. It would harden them too.

Chapter Twenty-Four

Julia

New York, New York, January 2001

Julia had come back from her run to find her children waiting for her. They had news.

"A Jewish genetic disorder?" she repeated, terrified at what she might hear.

"It's called Gaucher." Aiden answered. "I looked it up. Rosie's body is missing an enzyme that breaks down fat. And that fat deposits in bones and other places and causes damage. But they can give her something to take the place of the enzyme. It's treatable."

"Treatable? Treatable! Oh, Rosie . . . I have so many questions . . . but treatable! I am so relieved." *Relieved?* The word couldn't come close to what Julia was feeling. For the first time in days, she felt she could breathe. She wanted to cry. She wanted to laugh . . . to sing! Her Rosie would be okay.

"It's great that it's treatable, Mom. But you missed the main point, you never listen. I'm not yours and Dad's. I'm someone else's child! I'm Jewish! How is that possible?" Rosie cried.

How is that possible?

Rosie's words cut through Julia's happiness like a knife.

She had no other choice but to divulge her mother's secret. Something even John didn't know.

The Convention of Wives

"I need a drink," Julia said, grabbing a glass and pouring herself some wine. It was old and bad, and she spit it in the sink. "Rosie, do you have something stronger?"

"I think there's some vodka and whiskey on the bookshelf over there."

She found some Scotch and poured it into the wine glass. Julia sat on the couch and thought about what her mother had told her. A confession of sorts. How Catholic. How ironic.

She and John had just returned from Barbados. Their flight had landed late in the evening, and they had driven directly to pick up the kids, who were all in their pj's, bathed, and ready for bed. Her mom looked haggard when she answered the door. Julia wasn't surprised. Aiden was five and the twins were three. That was more than enough for anyone, let alone a woman in her mid-fifties. She'd thanked her mother and said goodnight, adding that she'd stop by after she took the kids to school in the morning. She had something from the trip she wanted to share.

The next day, it took Julia's mother two rings to answer her door. Unusual for the woman who walked in the park each afternoon and played bridge till nine every Monday, Wednesday, and Friday evening. Taking care of the kids had probably wiped her out and she was trying to sleep in. But no, there she was, indomitable and smiling in her yellow apron with the Brookline Gardening Club logo, gloved hands, and hair pulled back in a ponytail. Her mother was never particularly interested in her appearance, but her joie de vivre always shone through. And what was that smell? Cinnamon? Nutmeg? Her mom wore it like perfume.

Julia wished she could be more like this side of her mother, finding happiness in the simple daily routine of gardening, soap operas, and canasta she'd adopted soon after her father had died. In some ways, her mother had never seemed happier. But Julia worried that she had inherited the other side of her mom. The side that prevented her mother from displaying the exchanges of affection she routinely witnessed at the homes of friends. The anxiety that made her worry constantly. The lack of self-esteem that prevented her mother from ever challenging her father, a man who paid the bills but spent most of his free time at the corner bar. He'd never been particularly warm toward her mom. By the time Julia became a teenager, the only words they exchanged had been in anger over the limitations he placed on her social life. While her brothers were free to stay out until all hours, her curfew was early and strictly enforced. It was only when she and her father began having words, when he became more physically violent with her that her mother finally interceded. She couldn't wait to get out of her house.

"Mom, I really have to thank you again for babysitting. They're a handful, I get it. I don't know how you got them to preschool on time in the morning."

"You don't have to thank me. Who says they were on time? And, stop with the Mom thing already. It's Rosie from now on. I've told you; I'm reclaiming my name."

"Okay, already with the name thing. But, were they really late?" Julia asked.

"Oh, I'm just kidding. Anyway, they're *my* grandchildren and I love them. They are a pleasure. An exhausting pleasure, but still."

Julia was enjoying this new, evolved relationship with her mother. Perhaps it was true what people said; that your relationship with your parents changes when you have your own kids.

"Sit down. Oh wait, try one of these. I took them out of the oven before my gardening." Rosie put a blueberry whole wheat muffin on a paper towel and handed it to her. "Now, let me get this in water."

Julia stared at the rose her mother had just clipped.

"I started these in my bonus room. That place gets so much sun. They budded ridiculously early and this one just opened. Nothing like a yellow rose." The garden outside was full of them in season.

Julia took a bite of the muffin while her mom steeped some tea. She remembered the mornings when it was just the two of them, her younger brothers still happily playing in their cribs and her father gone to work. Her mom would take a break from the cleaning she started each day at the break of dawn, and they would have a tea party. Her mom would let Julia pick out two teacups from the collection in the glass-fronted case. She tried to pick something different each time, hoping to get a chance to touch each of the cups and saucers that meant so much to her mother. There were aqua-colored cups with gold rims, flowered cups, and royal blue polka-dotted cups with matching striped saucers. It was the only time Julia had her mother all to herself.

Julia placed her napkin on her lap and poured some tea into each of their cups. Then she took out the small gift bag she'd brought and put it on the table in front of them.

"So, did you bring me some ginger candy from Barbados?" Rosie asked.

"Of course, I did. It's what you asked for, isn't it? The only thing you said was redeemable about the island. I'm still not sure what you mean by that. It's a beautiful place." She handed her mother the white paper bag filled with candies.

Her mother took one out and popped it into her mouth. "Nothing like these."

A switch seemed to go off in her mother's head.

"I've been thinking about some things while you were gone, Julia. There are things it's time you knew."

"Mom, if this is the Talk, I think it's a little too late." Julia laughed.

"Take that bottle of Scotch from the counter and bring two glasses. We're going to need it."

"It's not even noon."

"Just get the glasses."

Julia brought them back to the table and poured them both a drink. Her mother was sitting bent over with her right hand on her forehead as if supporting her body from toppling over onto the table. Rosie took a sip before speaking.

"It's a simple story, really. I was in my late twenties when I met a young man in Barbados. He was tall, with dark hair. I fell in love. He left the island before I was sure I was pregnant."

"What!"

"It wouldn't have mattered. We could never have married. I moved to Boston. I met your father. His family was told that my husband had died in Barbados. He married me even though I think he always knew the truth."

Julia took a swig of whiskey. "You're joking. Mom, this has got to be a joke. What are you talking about?"

"Just a minute," her mother said, then got up and went into her bedroom. Julia could hear drawers opening and shutting. It seemed like ages before her mom came back and handed Julia two pieces of paper.

Julia quickly glanced at them. "Okay, sure. Copies of my birth certificate. I've seen this, Mom."

"Look at them both again, Julia. Look closely."

Julia scanned the first one and then looked at the second. She noted her mom's maiden name, Rosie Cawley on both. The information was almost identical to the first with two differences: the year of birth indicated was 1948, then 1949. And there was something else that was odd. Under religion, someone had indicated "Protestant" on the first form and "Catholic" on the second.

"Mom, I don't understand. I was born in 1949."

"No, Julia, you were born in 1948."

"That's just not true, that's ridiculous. You're telling me I'm thirty-four, not thirty-three?"

"Julia, stop," her mom said, putting her hand up in front of Julia's face.

The Convention of Wives

"Mom, I wasn't born in 1948; you and Dad got married then. And I'm certainly not Protestant. We're Catholic."

"Both these birth certificates are yours. Pete, your father, knew someone at the hospital and got a blank document. We filed it at City Hall explaining that there were errors on the original. Adoption was complicated. No one discussed things like this. We—your father and I—thought this was easier. You just became his child. And you and I became Catholic. No one ever questioned it . . . there was no need to explain to anyone."

Julia looked at the papers again and saw that her dad's name was not listed on the first document. "But we're Protestant, not Catholic? I mean you are. And I'm older than I think I am?" Julia asked. "And Dad is not my dad? This is crazy!"

She looked down at the certificate. Cawley, her mother's maiden name. The middle name Julia had been taunted about by school friends. So many things made sense now. The tentativeness of her relationship with her father and his zealous control in her teenage years. Her mother's protectiveness of the man. And then it hit her. She had a real father out there.

"But, Mom, who was he, this man who you loved? My father. My biological father?"

"I'm not sure at this point it matters."

"It matters to me. Where is he now?"

"I haven't got a clue."

"Tell me all that you remember."

She told Julia that he had an accent. He was German, and he made her laugh. He was visiting the family that she worked for. He was handsome and a little bit vain.

"He liked to have his shoes shined. But, after what he'd seen in Europe after the war, I think he was just overly concerned about cleanliness. Maybe that's why he liked me," at this her mother smiled again. "I was the maid, after all."

"Mom, I don't get it. You're describing a perfectly sweet romance. Why didn't you get married?" Julia asked, and then it struck her. "He was already married! Oh, Mom."

"No, nothing like that," Rosie answered. "It simply wasn't possible. He was a Jew."

Julia thought back to that morning with her mother. How difficult it had been to hear her mother's story—her story, too, she supposed—how the rush of blood to her ears had been so loud she barely heard the words. But secrets are funny things. They can be so big at the time of their reveal that you think your life has been split open. Then the wounds mend and they don't seem so big after all. So unimportant that you forget all about them. Time really is the great healer. Or so she hoped.

Julia told the story as best she could. Rosie and Aiden were incredulous. Like most children, they couldn't dare picture the love lives of their parents, let alone their grandparents.

"Grandma Rosie? A single mother? But Grandpa Pete was your dad." Julia detected a note of judgment in Aiden's voice, and she didn't like it.

"Grandpa Pete adopted me when I was a baby. It was a different time. It's hard to make you understand how people felt in those days. People didn't mix."

"Mix?" Rosie cried, screwing up her face. "Mom, that's a terrible thing to say."

"Things were different then. People married within their own faith. "Their own kind" is what they used to say. My mother couldn't marry the father of her baby because he was Jewish. She tried to shield me from the truth all those years, pretending that Grandpa Pete was my real father, pretending that we were Catholic."

"Wait, what? We're not Catholic?" Rosie asked.

"No, we are Catholic; well, *now* we're Catholic. When my mom married Pete, she joined the Church. She and her parents were Anglican," Julia explained.

"Anglican?" Aiden asked.

"The Church of England. My ancestors were from Scotland, not Ireland. I never got the chance to ask Grandma Rosie too many other questions. She died soon after that trip." All the questions she'd had for her mother about herself, who she really was, went unanswered.

"Mom, I get that you are partly Jewish, but I did some reading," Aiden began, "and I still don't think you understand—"

Suddenly, Julia was exhausted. Emotionally. Physically. She was empty.

"Aiden, that's plenty for today. Really, I'm sure Rosie has heard enough. Let's get some dinner and get to bed," Julia said. "I'll call the doctor back in the morning to find out when we can get in to see him."

"Shouldn't Dad be here for that?" Aiden asked.

"I'll take care of Dad," Julia answered.

Chapter Twenty-Five

Aiden Kinsella

New York, New York, February 2001

Aiden and Rosie had always been close. Of course, he would attend this appointment with her. "Here's the information desk," he said.

"I have a follow-up appointment with Dr. Katz," Rosie said to the woman behind the counter.

"Oh, just sign in here," the sixtyish receptionist replied. She was impeccably dressed in a dark blue suit with pearls and a broach, her graying hair in a chignon.

"We're a little nervous coming here. I'm sure you can imagine," her mother added.

The woman smiled at them all and in the sweetest voice said to Rosie, "Young lady, I hope you know how lucky you are to have a mother who clearly cares about you and a boyfriend who is a real gentleman. Dr. Katz is on the twentieth floor."

"He's my brother," Rosie shot back.

Nonplussed, the woman said, "Well, that's even nicer. Not every family rallies around someone at times like this. You'll be heading to the twentieth floor. The elevators are down the hall, take any one of them on the left. Good luck and have a blessed day."

Aiden couldn't help but think this day was far from blessed. The inside of the elevator was mirrored. He tried not to make eye contact with his mother or sister and saw they were attempting to do the same. They exited and found the registration desk easily. His mother started to write Rosie's name on the clipboard.

"Mom!" Rosie exploded.

"What is the matter with me? I'm sorry, I just go into mommy mode," Julia said apologetically.

"It's okay, Mom, really. Rosie, just sign in and you two have a seat. I'll get us some coffee," Aiden offered, having noticed a refreshment area when they walked in.

They were barely seated when a small young woman in large black glasses and red hair bounded out of the inside office and came over. She shook Rosie and Julia's hands. Aiden put his hand out to shake, but the woman merely shook her head back and forth indicating no.

"I'm Mrs. Kirchner, the genetics counselor, but you can call me Ellen."

Aiden gave her a perplexed look.

"I'm sorry, I'm Orthodox . . . Jewish, and I don't shake hands with men for modesty reasons," she said. Aiden had never heard of this before, but he was even more shocked that someone who looked fifteen years old at most was a married woman. Would his sister embrace her new identity and wind up looking like this woman, now that Rosie was Jewish? Was his sister Jewish, really? Were any of them? He wasn't sure.

"Rosie, before we go in, I just want to confirm that you're comfortable with everyone joining us, your mom and your brother."

"Of course," Rosie solemnly answered. "It's not like I have an STD."

"All right then. And, Mrs. Kinsella, you're comfortable as well."

"Yes, I spoke with the children last night and explained a few things."

"Good, that's good to hear," Ellen said. "Then please follow me to my office, and we'll start the intake. When we're done, Dr. Katz will join us to discuss treatment."

Rosie and Julia were seated across from Ellen at a small, modern-looking desk. Aiden had taken the only remaining chair, the one in the corner. He felt like he was being punished, in a time out, but he wasn't sure what he'd done.

"Now, we have a series of questions that we need to ask to get a little bit of background from each of you. Well, I mean Rosie, you, your mom, and your father. Your father is joining us?"

"No, he couldn't make it. He's in Atlanta, where we live," his mother answered. "He couldn't get time off from work. He's a doctor, you know. A busy practice. But I can call him later if you need information from him."

Aiden had heard all this before. His father was a successful doctor. His patients needed him. What about his family—didn't they need him?

"We usually like to ask these questions directly, Mrs. Kinsella. Perhaps you have a phone number where I can reach Dr. Kinsella?" Ellen asked.

"Uh, I don't have it with me, his office number, I mean . . . I'm sorry, I don't know it by heart," Julia stumbled.

"Mom, I have it right here," Aiden took out his phone and read Ellen the number. What was wrong with his mother?

His mom looked pained but said, "Thanks, Aiden."

Ellen began with some routine questions. Where was Rosie born? What about Julia and John? Where were their grandparents born? What were her parents' ethnicities, their religions?

"Well, my mom is Scottish. We're not sure where her biological dad is from, but he was Jewish. My dad is Irish Catholic," Rosie answered.

"And Rosie's biological father?" Ellen asked.

"Excuse me?" Julia asked.

The Convention of Wives

"Mom, I was trying to tell you last night. I was reading about Gaucher online and it said that both parents have to be Jewish," Aiden said, waiting for the explanation his mother had refused to provide.

"Well, yes, that is correct. I'm confused, I thought you said you had spoken to your children," Ellen answered.

"I'm sorry, what did you say?" Julia asked.

"Both the mother and father have to be carriers," Ellen answered.

Their mother said nothing and began to stare at the floor.

"Mom, that's the problem. Now, we know about you being half-Jewish, but Dad; come on, he's as Irish Catholic as they come, right?" Aiden looked over at his mother expectantly. She was quickly turning a pale shade of green.

Just then, Dr. Katz entered the office.

"Dr. Katz, I'm glad you joined us. I was just explaining to the Kinsellas that Rosie has Gaucher's disease, which is a treatable Jewish . . . a genetic disorder that is treatable."

"I was just so glad it was treatable . . . I didn't think about . . . oh Christ!" Julia stammered as she began to gasp for air. Aiden caught her before she hit the ground.

Chapter Twenty-Six

Rob

Millburn, New Jersey, February 2001

He'd swum an extra thousand yards to try and clear his head, but he emerged from the pool with no answers. The visit to his mother hadn't been helpful. She'd started lecturing him about how inconsequential marital issues were compared to the horrors of the Holocaust; told him he needed to get some perspective. When she launched into an attack on Dina—"She was spoiled and, of course, Rob couldn't make her happy. Who could?"—he left. But any doubts about whether Dina would eventually find out about Julia were obliterated after his call from John in the middle of office hours.

"Dr. Wasserman, you have a call on line two from a Dr. Kinsella."

He thought about not taking the call. How different it was sure to be from the first conversation they'd shared after playing golf together years back. He braced himself for what he knew was to come.

"So, imagine my surprise when my med school buddy calls to let me know that my daughter's biological father has to be Jewish. He wondered if I'd neglected to tell him I'd been adopted."

Rob remained silent. He could hear himself breathing hard into the receiver.

The Convention of Wives

"So, yes or no. You and Julia."

"Listen, John—"

"No. I don't need to listen to this. You no good son of a bitch!"

Rob had spent his life trying to be one of the good guys. A good doctor, a good father, a good husband. One misstep. One mistake, and it had all come undone. What was it his mother had said all those years back? "Your name, may it only bring you good things in life."

Life could get lonely with just his mom at home, but tonight Roberto was so excited he barely noticed his scratchy wool dress pants or the tie that his mother had carefully clipped to his shirt collar. But the bobby-pin that held his yarmulke on tight was giving him a headache.

He loved how the Wassermans had set up the Seder in their living room, how the folding tables were arranged in the shape of the letter *E*. At each place setting, a small, folded card hand-written with a guest's name sat perched atop a Maxwell House Haggadah, which contained the story of Passover interspersed with advertisements for coffee and other products. Each year, these free books popped up at the local ShopRite, where his mother bought special foods for the holiday.

They went to the den where the adults were having drinks and a chopped liver and matzo cracker appetizer. His mother stopped to say hello to his Uncle Rolph, who was a cousin of Rob's father and a friend of the Wassermans. Rob was encouraged to head to Ellen Wasserman's room, which had been set up with games and puzzles. When he entered, he saw two older boys fighting with his younger cousin Ronnie, who was cowering in the corner and crying, while the boys laughed.

"Stop it!" Roberto yelled. His cousin got hurt easily. He'd broken the same arm twice.

The boys stopped and turned to face him.

"Oh, you want some of this?" the bigger boy shouted as the two headed over.

"No, just stop doing that to my cousin," he answered, backing up. But it was too late.

The bigger boy let go of Ronnie, grabbed Roberto, and held him down while the other one pressed a Mr. Potato Head ear into Roberto's head. Ronnie ran out of the room. Ellen and another girl stood frozen in the corner by the doll house. He wasn't sure what to do except yell for help. He squirmed as best he could to fight them off.

The two boys were dripping sweat on him when the adults burst into the room. Mr. Potato Head's ear had been pushed so hard into his earlobe that the point had pierced his skin.

"Oh, my God! Let go of him! He's bleeding!" The boys ignored his mother's cries. It was a booming male voice that put an end to the ruckus.

"I said, let go of him, now!"

His mother dropped to her knees. "It's all right. Ronnie came to get us. Roberto, you'll be okay," she said as she took out the handkerchief she always kept in her bra. He sniffled quietly as she wiped his cheek.

"Roberto, figures, some stupid I-talian name," the older boy said.

"Harvey, that's enough. Now apologize!" the man shouted.

The smile on the boy's face vanished.

"Both of you," the man continued.

The boys came over to Roberto and his mother and mumbled, "I'm sorry."

"Now, if I ever catch you torturing a child half your age again, or any age for that matter—either of you—my hand will be on your *tuchus* so fast, you'll regret it. Your mother, may she rest in peace, would be ashamed. Go sit down at the Seder table and don't move until we start. Is that understood?"

The Convention of Wives

"Yes, Papa," the boys said in unison. The older boy smacked the younger one in the arm as they walked out of the room.

"Not the best impression of my sons, I'm afraid. They have been running wild like that for the last two years . . . since their mother died," the man explained in Yiddish, a language Rob understood. "I'm Max, Max Wasserman. A cousin of Henry's."

"Elsa. Elsa Heller," his mother said, shaking the man's hand. "Henry is the uncle of my husband's cousin, Rolph. Henry sponsored my son and me when we came here from . . . ," she hesitated.

"Henry is a special person. Please, again, I'm so sorry about my sons. I'd like to apologize to your husband, as well."

"My husband is no longer with us. But this is my son. Roberto. Roberto, please shake Mr. Wasserman's hand."

He did as he was told.

The man muttered something to his mother in Yiddish then looked Roberto in the eye, switching to English. "Son, I am truly sorry that my boys mistreated you." He hesitated a beat. "I have a secret I want to share." And, with that, he knelt to Roberto's height and whispered in his ear, "I get to hide the *afikomen*, and I'm going to tell you where it is!"

"But that's cheating," Roberto admonished.

His mom smiled.

The man shook his head. "You're right. So, I won't tell you exactly where it'll be, but I'll give you a hint. You'll need to figure it out from there. Is that okay?"

Finding the *afikomen*, the piece of middle matzo broken off during the service and hidden from the children, was the biggest deal of the night. Roberto was going to find it and get the prize . . . it was all his. He looked up at his mom for her approval. She nodded.

They walked back to the living room together as he overheard Mr. Wasserman whisper to his mom.

"I came up with a reason for your son to remember me. I'm hoping the same with you."

His mom smiled back at the man before Roberto ran ahead to find his seat.

The eldest males always sat at the head of the table and on the outside legs of the *E*, surrounding the women and children, as if protectively circling the wagons. His mother found his name at the kids' table next to his cousin Ronnie. He could smell his mother's perfume as she leaned down.

"Are you all right, Roberto?" she asked, picking up one of the crayons that had been left at each place setting at the kids' table. Drawing a face on the page, she said, *"Punkt, punkt, komma, strich, fertig ist das Mondgesicht."* (Period, period, comma, slash, finished is the moon face.)

It was their secret code, the thing she drew for him whenever he'd been upset, as her mother had drawn for her. It always helped. "Yes, Mama. But call me Rob, not Roberto," he declared.

"Rob? Are you sure?" she asked.

He'd never been surer of anything in his seven short years.

"All right, my little man." She kissed the top of his head. *"Deyn nomen zol nor der bringen gute zachen."*

"What does that mean, Mama?"

"Your new name, Rob. It should bring you only good things."

Good things. Good things. And what had he done? He'd screwed it all up. One stupid, stupid night. Everything would change. He'd blown up his life. Their lives.

Chapter Twenty-Seven

Allie

New York, New York, February 2001

The entire living room smelled of chicken tikka masala. The neighbors wouldn't be happy, but it was worth their wrath to indulge in their favorite takeout. "I have a weird question," Raj asked as he took some naan out of the delivery bag.

"What?"

"Just how close were your parents to the Kinsellas?"

It had been weeks since Aiden's sister had been in the ER.

"More questions about Rosie? She seems to be your new favorite topic. Look, I think they had a lot in common when they met, especially our moms. You know the whole 'suffering through residency as a spouse' thing." She and Raj simultaneously rubbed their eyes and pretended to cry. It was a shtick they had picked up at a party one night. "They thought of themselves as some kind of mini support group."

"That's really not what I'm asking," he said, sitting down, placing his hands on his thighs, and looking up at her. "I got a call from Aiden, the brother."

"He called you? Why would he call you and not me?" She sat down next to him, taking containers out of the bag.

"Sorry, would you have preferred if he'd called you? Anything I should know?"

"What? No. It's just that I'm the family friend. He barely knows you."

"You knew him, what? Twenty years ago? The lady doth protest too much, methinks."

"Isn't it, 'Methinks thou doth protest too much'?"

"No. Shakespeare, Act Three, Scene Two. I believe Queen Gertrude. Did we ever compare SAT results?"

"Are you kidding me? Seriously, after all these years, you want to do this?"

"Eight hundred. Verbal and math."

"Are you serious? Well, that explains our Scrabble games."

He looked at her expectantly.

"Fine. Seven forty, math. Seven sixty, verbal."

"Not bad. And, about Scrabble, that's not exactly true. You never strategize, Allie. You're always going for the interesting words. If you would just pay attention to the triple word scores and double letters. I always tell you that."

It was true, he did. But word-making was far more interesting than strategizing. And she could give a rat's ass about winning.

"So, it was the seventies, right?" he continued.

She opened two Dos Equis beers and handed him one. What was he talking about again? No wonder he'd done better on the SATs. She had the concentration of a gnat.

"Your parents and the Kinsellas? You know, people were still exploring sexual freedoms. Is it possible that, well . . . maybe they all got to know each other really, *really* well?"

"Yuck. What are you talking about?" Allie asked. She could not believe what Raj was implying. As far as she was concerned, her parents had had sex only the three times that resulted in her birth and that of her siblings. Anything else was too gross to imagine.

"I'm not thinking orgy or anything," Raj said.

"This is a ridiculous conversation." She folded a paper napkin for each of them and handed out the plastic silverware.

"I'm attempting to have a scientific discussion with you. We have them all the time. It's exactly the kind of conversation, in fact, that we usually have."

"These are my parents we're talking about."

"Try not to think of them that way. This is as simple as a combination of sperm and egg. We're just trying to figure out the possibilities."

"How would you feel if these were your parents we were talking about?"

"My parents would never have . . ." He stopped talking.

"Wow. Look who's Mr. Self-Righteous suddenly?"

"Please, I just know who my parents are."

"And I don't?"

"That's not what I meant."

"What did you mean?"

"Allie, this is crazy. Why are you getting so upset?"

He looked at her with the look of every man she'd ever known who insisted that men were all logic, women all emotion. It infuriated her. "You're implying that my father had sex with a woman other than my mother."

"Yes, I am."

"My father!"

He just stared at her, saying nothing. He caught her hand as she attempted to slap him across the face.

"Raj, I'm sorry. I don't know what's wrong with me."

"It's my fault. I insulted you in some way."

"You seemed so judgmental. Like your parents would never think to . . . but my father . . ."

"My parents were raised in strict Indian households. There was no display of love or sexuality between them in front of me. No affection for each other in public. Ever. As if it were a business arrangement."

She thought about her own parents. The hugs and kisses she'd witnessed between them. The way her father brought her mom coffee in bed.

"This is a bizarre conversation, Raj. I'm sorry I tried to hit you."

"At least it's a conversation. We never talk, Allie. Not about anything real. Sure, we like the same movies. Even the same food. And we talk about work all the time. But have you ever asked me how I felt about anything personal since medical school?"

Of course, they had talked. She tried to recall the subjects of their last conversations. They seemed pretty functional in hindsight. It was her turn, not his, to pick up the dry cleaning on the way home from work. Three bananas were about the maximum they should buy to ensure they'd use them up before they'd go brown. Until they could decide between a cat or a dog, a pet was not something they should discuss anymore, especially with their schedules. Maybe he had a point. But there was barely enough time in the day since they'd become residents to grab a meal and take a crap. She thought they were getting along just fine. She didn't know what to say. She wasn't sure what he wanted. He blessedly changed the subject.

"Rosie. She's been diagnosed. The good news is that it's not lymphoma. But the diagnosis doesn't really fit her Irish Catholic background. It's a Jewish genetic disease called Gaucher. Is it possible, could your dad maybe have been overly friendly with Mrs. Kinsella, or maybe she knew a different nice Jewish guy in Boston?"

So, they never talked, and this is what he chose to talk about: her father's possible infidelity? He was clearly unable to get off the topic. But she realized he was right, she was most comfortable chatting about banalities and medicine with him, or the banalities of medicine. The food was getting cold. Allie intently opened the box of masala and bag of chapati, stopping only to guzzle her beer.

The Convention of Wives

"First of all, Raj, I don't know why you think we don't talk. We talk all the time. About lots of things. But what you're suggesting about my father is ridiculous." She put some food on her paper plate and passed the box to Raj. "And, even if Rosie is not Dr. Kinsella's daughter," she mumbled, her mouth full, "who's to say this had anything to do with my family, with my father? Besides, Rosie's mother is Catholic. The whole family is. So that doesn't make any sense. You need two carrier pigeons . . . er, parents for these things."

Raj nodded, putting down the cold towel and biting into a piece of bread. He seemed to retreat at her comment. "That's the part I haven't figured out. Not yet anyway. I like my mom's naan so much better than this stuff." He passed more chapati to her. "Look, Allie, all that I'm saying, about us . . ."

"Us?" Was there an "us"?

"I like you. You're like a sister to me. You always have been."

A sister. She looked at his soulful eyes, the way they were pleading without words for her to say that everything was okay between them. But her world had shifted. Not knowing how he felt, not defining it, had been easier, served a purpose. Not knowing had meant that maybe someday he would be more to her than her roommate. Not knowing had made her feel okay every time she'd dated someone and it hadn't worked out; or had not dated anyone for months at a time and never felt lonely because there was always Raj to come home to at the end of the day, and the promise of something yet to come. Not knowing had meant not worrying that she'd never find someone and would be alone for the rest of her life. And all this time she'd only wanted a relationship like her parents had. Hah! Maybe even that was a joke.

Nothing had gone right since that day in the ER with Rosie. Everything had begun to shift. To unravel. She'd felt it the moment she'd seen Raj so upset behind the nurse's station. He wasn't who she thought he was. And now she knew they weren't who she thought they were to each other; or, rather, who she thought they might become.

"Raj, you've always been family to me, too," she whispered. "I'll try harder to ask more questions. I promise." She hugged him. "Now, can you pass the naan?"

He smirked at her.

"It's a question, isn't it? That's what you wanted. Questions."

He shook his head at her.

"Okay. How does thinking about your mother's bread make you feel?"

He smacked her gently.

As she tore into the bread, she remembered a trip her parents had taken to Barbados years before when she was really young, maybe in kindergarten. She'd gotten to stay with her grandparents in Scarsdale. Her grandmother's maid had fed her ice cream for breakfast. She remembered because this woman told her that she used to do the same for Allie's mother when her grandparents traveled. And when her parents had come home, her mother had a pen pal for her.

"You forgot the rogan josh!" Raj shouted, rifling through the brown paper bag. "Allie?"

"Sorry, I was just thinking about what you said. Pass me some." How easily her mind had shifted from the end of all those possibilities with Raj to her parents on that island. She poured the lamb dish on her plate, took a bite, and burned her tongue. "Oh, shit!" Allie screamed, spitting the food onto the cream-colored couch. Raj ran and came back with paper towels and stain remover. Brother and sister. Nothing more.

Allie cleaned up the mess wondering what had happened on that vacation in Barbados. Maybe the timing was right.

Chapter Twenty-Eight

Julia

Boston, Massachusetts, February 1975

Julia stood over the sink filled with soaking baby bottles. The moisture from the hot water wafted upward and beaded on her upper lip. She picked up the last of the apples on the counter, washed it off, and placed it in the dish drain.

"What in God's name did you do to your hair?" John shouted, coming up behind her and twirling her around. He'd gotten in late the night before and woken her for sex, but, apparently, hadn't noticed. "I liked it the way it was." He pushed the bangs off her face.

She pushed them down. "I needed a change. Besides, it's stylish."

He looked at her questioningly. "A bowl cut is stylish? That was my haircut for years. My brothers, too. Mom used to line us up and trim around one of the cereal bowls. You know, the one you got with Frosted Flakes?"

"It's not a bowl cut. You know the skater, Dorothy Hamill . . . the Olympics."

"Yeah, right."

"You have no idea what I'm talking about."

He nodded.

"Maybe it's a bit extreme, but I feel better, lighter." She held her wet hands in front of her chest like a set of paws.

He kissed her neck, fumbled with her shirt buttons, and began kneading her breasts.

"My hands are all wet, what are you doing?" She slapped him away playfully. "I'm cooking."

"Apples, you're cooking apples as the sun comes up?"

"Yes, applesauce. For the twins."

"A regular Betty Crocker, huh? Sorry, no . . . Dorothy Crocker, maybe?"

"Not funny," she said as he walked toward the hallway. "Just don't be late for dinner. We're meeting Rob at seven."

"I know, I know. The sitter's coming at six." But he was already gone.

Julia had loved Legal Seafood in Chestnut Hill, even before it became fancy-schmancy, as John liked to say. She enjoyed sitting at the bar between the college students and professors, the other couples, and singles. And she was glad they were having dinner with Dina's husband. Too bad Dina was too pregnant to travel.

"Rob, over here!" she cried and waved.

"Hey buddy, you made it!" John grabbed him hard around the shoulders and brought him in for a bear hug. "This weather is really something, huh?"

"Rob, Rob, really great to see you." Julia bent toward him for a quick kiss on the cheek.

"Sit, sit, what can we get you? Some storm, huh? Not used to this down south?"

"Down south?" he asked, placing his coat on the back of his chair.

"You know, New York!"

They laughed. He took his seat and placed the napkin on his lap.

"So, how is she doing?" Julia asked.

"She's exhausted, uncomfortable, really wishes she could

have made the trip. But there was just no way between Allie and the weather."

"Well, you'll have to tell her how much we wished she was here," Julia said.

"Absolutely," John added.

"Hey, you cut your hair, right? No?" Rob asked.

John put his hand on her thigh.

Julia twirled the hair closest to her chin and then tucked it behind her ear. "Yup, thanks for noticing."

The moment ended with the arrival of their waiter with three waters.

"You have got to get a lobster," John encouraged.

"I think you're right. But I'd love to start with soup. Is lobster bisque too much lobster?" Rob asked.

"You can never have too much lobster!" John and Julia said in unison.

"Three two-pounders then," John told the waiter. "We have to celebrate when we can. This on-call schedule is killing me."

"I'd like a drink, John," Julia said, touching his arm.

"Of course. Rob, you too? I would but I'm on call."

"I think I'm good."

Julia wondered if Rob was watching his money. She and John exchanged looks.

"Listen," John said. "This is on us. You were such great hosts when we visited. Man, could that have really been two years ago?"

By the time they finished their appetizers, Julia and Rob had made a good dent in the bottle of Chardonnay. They were waiting for their main courses when John's beeper went off.

"Oh, crap. I knew this was too good to be true. I've got to call in. Sorry."

"Don't worry about it. How could I not understand?" Rob said.

John headed to the phone booth near the front of the restaurant.

"So, how's my friend?" Julia asked.

"Good. She's good." Julia wondered if Rob knew how much the two women had shared. Meaning, almost everything. Julia knew that Dina was exhausted most of the time. She also knew that her friend had refused financial help from her parents or even babysitting offers from Rob's mother. Most of all, Julia knew that Dina resented her husband every time he walked out the door to go to work.

"Really," Julia said, pouring another glass of wine. "That's interesting, 'cause *our* lives are pretty much a shit show."

Just then, John reappeared and grabbed his coat off the unoccupied seat at their table. "I've got to go in, Rob," he said, shaking Rob's hand. "Sorry to do this. Can you make sure Julia gets in a cab when you're done?" He turned as he walked away, "Oh, and I gave the maître d' my credit card, next one's on you! Next conference meet-up somewhere warm for sure!"

"So," Julia said, emptying the wine bottle into Rob's glass.

"So," Rob replied.

The sudden lapse in conversation was interrupted by the arrival of their waiter balancing three plates of lobster, corn on the cob, and potatoes. The waiter looked confused before setting one plate in front of each of them and the third in the middle of the table.

"We're pretty hungry." Julia smiled up at the waiter. "And thirsty. We'll take another bottle of wine, too. Thanks."

The waiter nodded and left.

"Julia, I'm not sure the two of us can finish off a bottle. Maybe we order by the glass?"

"Oh, come on, Rob. I'm on vacation here. Do you know the last time I've been out? It's okay, really. Neither of us is driving."

The Convention of Wives

She knew he couldn't argue with that. At first the situation was a bit awkward, cracking claws and eating in front of a man who felt like a stranger. But a glass of wine later and she was aware of how Rob watched her closely as she dipped her lobster into the white paper cup of glistening butter, let it drip twice, quickly moved the meat into her mouth, and left the inevitable trail of butter dripping down her chin. Maybe she shouldn't have worn such a low-cut dress.

They finished their meal and the wine and were laughing about something her twins had done when she reached onto his lap, grabbed his napkin, and wiped his chin.

"Sorry, I just couldn't keep staring at you with that shell on your face. I mean, if anyone can look handsome with a lobster goatee, it's you, but still . . ."

He took the napkin out of her hand and placed it back on his lap to cover up his obvious arousal. "I think we need some coffee."

"Ooh, look who's Mr. Serious all of a sudden. Dina always said that about you. Mr. Responsible, Mr. Rule Guy. Do you think we're breaking the rules?"

They both knew they were breaking the rules. They were having too much fun.

Chapter Twenty-Nine

Dina

Millburn, New Jersey, March 2001

Dina took a sip of Syrah. She could taste the currant and pepper, but it wasn't really to her liking.

"I'm not loving this," she said. "How's the Pinot?"

"Not bad. Want to swap?"

"Ooh, yes, please. Thanks."

They each took a sip of the newly exchanged wine. Rob tore off a piece of warm roll and poured a puddle of olive oil on his side plate. Dina was tempted but stopped herself. She was trying to stave off the pounds that found her no matter how hard she tried.

"I'll share a salad with you. How about the tricolore?" she asked.

"Fine."

"The fish?" she asked.

"Yeah."

"Veggies, not pasta on the side. Are you okay with that?"

"Yeah."

Rob hailed the waiter and ordered for the two of them.

"You know, sometimes you could let me order," Dina remarked.

"I thought I was being gallant." Rob picked up his napkin

like a bullfighter's cape and flicked it toward her before lowering it to his lap.

"Okay, okay. I'm just saying. I'm perfectly capable of ordering in a restaurant, especially this one."

"I thought you liked it here."

"I do like it here, it's our place. That's not my point."

"What is your point? Can't I do anything right?"

Dina took a roll, tore it in half, and took a bite. What was going on with Rob? He was so changeable lately. So touchy. He seemed agitated and moody, loving one moment and distant the very next. Even the sex was off.

"Interesting way to end a conversation," he said. "I thought you were avoiding carbs."

She swallowed the bread and took a deep gulp of air. Maybe they needed something to look forward to.

"Hey—you know, let's not wait to travel a bit more. Not another conference, I mean real traveling. Maybe northern Italy next year? And what about renting in Florida in January?"

"Totally changing the subject, huh? What's gotten into you? We just finished paying off the kids' college expenses and graduate school."

"I don't know. We shouldn't wait to do things. You really don't know what the future holds. I keep thinking about Julia's daughter getting sick. Life is so unpredictable." She took a sip of wine. "I can't believe she hasn't called me back. I've left more than a few messages. I mean, I was there with her when she first found out."

"You're overthinking things. You always do. The two of you haven't been friends for years." Rob shifted awkwardly in his seat.

"You're probably right. I thought I knew Julia, but . . . I don't know. Just when I feel close to her again, she withdraws. Maybe I'm being self-centered; she's dealing with Rosie's illness. It's not about me. I'll just wait a few weeks and try her then," she said as she refilled her wine glass. He was so quiet. "What do you think?"

He didn't answer.

"Rob?"

"I thought you were speaking rhetorically. I didn't think you needed a response."

"We're sitting together at dinner. Why wouldn't I want a response? Or are we already one of those older couples who sit silently and eat their food?"

The people at neighboring tables stared at them as Rob raised his voice, spewing out a litany of complaints:

She was being overly dramatic.

Everything became about her, even Julia's daughter's illness.

They didn't need to go to Florida for a month.

He didn't like Florida.

He was tired of giving in to her needs.

He still had to earn a living.

The owner came over to ask if everything was all right. Rob assured him it was.

She reminded Rob she did work, she wrote, even if it was at home. Okay, so she didn't get paid for her writing, she was a volunteer. He chuckled so hard he started choking before he cleared his throat.

He finished his glass of wine and poured himself another, wiping tears from his eyes.

Was he supposed to just fly down to Florida for the weekends? How exactly was that going to work?

They didn't speak the entire way home. He stormed up to their bedroom and she raced after him. He disappeared into their shared closet, came out with his swim bag, Dopp kit, and a hanging bag.

"I need a break, Dina."

She stared at him incredulously. "A break? A break?" It was all she could do just to repeat what he said.

"Everything's okay. I just need some alone time—okay?"

The Convention of Wives

"You just need some time alone. Are you kidding me? What the hell is wrong with you?"

"I don't know."

"You don't know? You need to talk to me. You can't just leave."

"That's where you're wrong. I can just leave. I need to. Dina, it's not you." He haphazardly threw underwear, socks, and a few shirts into his bags.

Her mind started to spin. Isn't that what men said when they were about to end a marriage—it's not you? She was right, he was sick or gay, or both.

"I tell you I think we should start traveling more and you decide to pack a bag? Does that make any sense?"

"None of this makes any sense." He headed for the bedroom door.

"The holidays are coming."

He turned and stared at her.

She was shaking as she asked, "Is there someone else?"

"There . . . is . . . no one else."

Then he left. Just like that.

Dina always liked reading on the chaise in Rob's office. It was ten o'clock on a Sunday morning, and she had slept in since she really had nowhere to go, nowhere she was needed. That wasn't true exactly. She could have gone to work out at the JCC, but who was she kidding? She'd had too much wine the night before. Amazing, the quantity you can drink by yourself. Then there had been the weed she'd found stashed in Daniel's room.

The sun shone into Rob's office like a beacon homing in on a struggling ship. Dina lay curled up like a cat, the Sunday *New York Times* scattered over her like a collection of small tents. The cracking sound of a piece of ice falling from the gutter made her look up and out through the window at the cloudless blue sky. The sunlight was so bright that the walnut desk and matching shelves across the room appeared as if a shadow, a black hole, an entry to someplace else. If only.

Suddenly, there was the smell of coffee tempting her, holding her back. She could hear the beeping of the drip machine, reminding her that she had a *raison d'être*. The newspaper crinkled all around her as she gently pushed herself off the chaise and hurried to the kitchen. The room seemed ten degrees colder than Rob's office. *Shit!* Her bare feet were ice on the cold floor.

Her back muscles tightened as she grabbed her favorite mug, the red one she'd brought back from London during the summer the kids were at camp: *Keep Calm and Carry On*. Right. The tearing of the tiny, pink packets of Sweet'N Low seemed to echo in the too-quiet house. She realized with a certain sadness that the brew was one of the few predictable daily sources of happiness in her life. Decaf, that form of sanitized coffee standard at all Jewish events, whether *shivas* or celebrations, because one could never be too careful of litigious attendees with a caffeine sensitivity. She added the prerequisite skim milk (why waste calories on coffee?) and two Sweet'N Lows (not one, not three, but exactly two), whose composition a chemist father of a childhood friend had sworn was not metabolized in any way that affected the human body. She'd always wondered.

Weeks had gone by, and Rob hadn't moved back in. Some of his clothes were missing, so, clearly, he'd come home to replenish when he knew she wouldn't be there. She wasn't even sure where he was living.

Dina picked up the *New York Times* and turned to her favorite section, the Diagnosis Column. She was distracted by movement out the window across the way at her crazy neighbor's house. The seventy-five-year-old woman was bent over by the driveway, wearing only her pajamas and curlers, rearranging the pile of ugly white rocks that she was always attempting to fashion into some type of flower bed. They looked ridiculous.

The Convention of Wives

He had to be having an affair. He certainly worked with enough young, attractive nurses. What did they call it? Propinquity?

She opened to the financial section by mistake. The graph comparing rates of return of stocks and bonds morphed into a representation of their sex life. Up, down, nonexistent, then rallying. Ever since she'd started going through menopause, it had been all over the place. Lately she'd thought they were in a slight recovery phase. Clearly, wrong.

She was indicated in purple, he in light blue. The lines overlapped occasionally. A few spikes on her line designated her feeble attempts at masturbating before she had another hot flash, gave up, and took an Ambien. Rob's line contained lots of spikes for the more frequent times he was successful on his own. Suddenly, a third line appeared in pink and overlapped with Rob's spikes. She rattled the paper, and the graph disappeared.

They loved each other. After all these years, they still loved each other. She knew that. *Did she know that?* She took a sip of coffee. It was already cold. She went to the kitchen to warm it but stopped in front of the freezer and took out a frozen rugelach instead.

These little cakes were delicious freshly baked or frozen. The chocolate, the nuts, the raisins. Who cared anymore? Thin or fat, what's the difference, he's gone. Maybe it *did* matter? Maybe she'd need to meet someone else. She got a paper towel and spit it out. She put the rest in the freezer with a bite missing *(why waste?)* and zapped the coffee for a few seconds in the microwave.

She went back to Rob's office and opened the paper to the Diagnosis section:

"Were all of the twenty-three-year-old's symptoms related, or were they just a convergence of problems within a really bad week?" by Raj Khan, MD, Emergency Medicine Resident, Saint Vincent's Medical Center, New York, NY.

Raj Khan! Allie's roommate. She remembered when Allie called to tell her that she'd found an apartment with some Indian student at med school. Dina couldn't figure out if she thought it was stranger that Allie was going to live with a guy, a guy she'd just met, or an Indian guy. She knew she was being racist, but the whole thing was just *so Allie* that she tried not to react. Allie was always shocking them, baiting them into drama. Drama that seemed to calm down very quickly after their wild child got the reaction she was going for.

Rob hadn't been so accepting of a male roommate for his daughter. When Dina tried to placate him with, "How bad could he be? He got into your alma mater," Rob responded with, "I knew plenty of perverts there in my day."

Why hadn't Allie mentioned that Raj was going to be in the *Times*? Dina was annoyed, but also insulted. She called her daughter immediately. The call went right to voice mail. She thought Allie might be blocking her in some way but didn't have the technical savvy to attempt to figure this out. She hadn't spoken to Allie since the call in which she'd wanted to know the whole story of their friendship with the Kinsellas. Maybe she was interested in Aiden. That would be awkward. She left a message.

"It's me. How could you forget to tell me that Raj is in the *New York Times*? Call me when you get a break. Oh, it's Mommy. Also, I got that dress you liked at Bloomie's. It was on sale. Oh, and I'm trying to decide between brisket and chicken or just chicken for Passover. I need your input. Everyone's eating less red meat. And it's so late this year—I mean Passover, not the meat. Anyway, thought I'd get an opinion from the doctor in the family. Well, you know, the *young* doctor in the family."

She neglected to mention that she couldn't get Rob's opinion because he didn't live with her anymore.

She picked up her coffee and read on:

211

The Convention of Wives

The twenty-three-year-old young woman presented in the Emergency Department (ED) complaining of shortness of breath, with obvious bruising on her upper left thigh.

She remembered falling while playing basketball two days earlier, but now had pain in her right elbow as well. She also complained of exhaustion, which she attributed to the flu shot she had gotten one week earlier.

The patient told the triage nurse that she had gone to the gym that morning and started running on the treadmill when she collapsed from pain in her leg. She couldn't seem to catch her breath after the incident. The club manager had called an ambulance. The ambulance team provided intravenous hydration and oxygen. The patient's breathing returned to normal, and she was able to bear weight. She was sent home from the sports club with instructions for bedrest, icing on the sore leg, and continued extra fluids.

But when the young woman got home to her apartment, she could barely make it from the cab to the lobby. She sat down in a chair and called her sister, who lived nearby. The sister put the patient in a cab and took her to the ED at St. Vincent's Hospital.

Dina put her coffee down. Wait, was this about Rosie?

The triage nurse noted that the woman's blood pressure and heart rate were slightly elevated, but within normal range. Her respiration rate, however, was somewhat high, and she looked like she was in distress, so the patient was taken inside quickly for further examination by a physician. The patient's sister accompanied her to the curtained cubicle.

The emergency medicine resident made note of the bruising and shortness of breath. She listened to the woman's heart and lungs, which sounded normal, and checked her neurologic reflexes, which also appeared normal. Aside from the pain and bruising on the left thigh, she noted pain in the left knee. The patient's breathing was still slightly exaggerated and somewhat concerning.

The only medication indicated on the patient's intake form was Yasmin, a birth control pill. The resident ordered blood tests: a CBC—complete blood count—to test for anemia, and a CMP—complete metabolic panel—to check the woman's electrolyte levels. The woman was given oxygen, and an IV was started to provide hydration.

The resident asked and noted that the patient had just completed her last menstrual cycle, abbreviated because of the birth control pills, but still potentially a contributing factor to an anemia problem, which could account for the shortness of breath. The bruising was attributed to the basketball incident. But the pain in the left leg closer to the knee, a distance from the bruising, was strange.

This sounded familiar. Julia's daughter had similar issues, but maybe this was a more common presentation than Dina realized.

Was it possible that the woman was having a deep vein thrombosis, DVT, a blood clot, as a side effect of her birth control pill? Could she already be experiencing a pulmonary embolism affecting her breathing? It seemed unlikely but possible.

Chapter Thirty

Rob

Millburn, New Jersey, April 2001

Some bachelor pad. The small, one-bedroom apartment in an old grouping of brick buildings near his office was a dump. He sat on a folding chair, looking at the unmade bed, quickly delivered from a nearby mattress store, and the snack table on which he'd been eating bad take-out. It was depressing. The clothes he'd grabbed from the house were hanging in the closet, but they were too warm to wear in the spring. Would he be here in the summer? He'd need to go back and get a few more things.

He was living in between. Not knowing what would happen next, not knowing if his marriage was over. Mostly not knowing how to talk to Dina. How had he gotten here? He glanced over at the unmade bed and the phone on the floor nearby. How had one night in Barbados over twenty years ago changed everything?

Rob had taken the phone into the hotel bathroom to call his mother. He could barely close the door with the cord sticking underneath. It was already way past ten o'clock, but he knew that his mother stayed up late these days, mostly watching old movies. He held the phone tightly between his ear and shoulder and began unbuttoning his shirt.

"I've done so many things wrong in my life," Elsa said. "Here you are having a wonderful holiday away, and all I could do before you left was tell you not to go. You were so young when we left Barbados, barely four years old. It was such a terrible time for us, having to leave the way we did, so soon after your father died, finally getting to America, but without him."

"But why did you tell me he died in the DP camp? It doesn't make any sense."

"After all we'd been through, after he died, every time I put you to sleep in Barbados you'd shout for your papa. But then when we got to America, you stopped. At school, one of the children asked where your father had died. You came home and asked me, you couldn't remember. I was happy that you had forgotten his illness and his death. I think I told you he died in Italy, in the DP camp, not on the island. It was as if that way everything that was horrible for us had happened far away, on the other side of the ocean, all part of one big nightmare."

"But you had years to tell me the truth."

"It never occurred to me that you would go back to Barbados. You never asked me much about what had happened to me or my family or your father when you were growing up. Even when you studied the Holocaust in Hebrew school. I didn't volunteer any information either. I'm still uncomfortable talking about it. And we never talked about Barbados, the house we lived in, your father's cousin coming to bring us to America. It wasn't something I wanted to talk about, never thought the details mattered anymore."

It was quiet on the phone for a while, except for the sound of her breathing.

"Mom, I'm sorry I never asked more questions. I think I was uncomfortable too. When I get home, we'll talk. You'll tell me more, if you want to."

"I'm not sure you'll want to hear it all."

"I'll listen to whatever you want to share."

The Convention of Wives

"Okay, but Rob, first, can you go back to the cemetery before you leave and put a stone on your father's grave for me? Please."

"We leave first thing in the morning; I'll make sure we'll have time before we get to the airport. I'll figure it out."

"Thank you. And, Rob, I have a bill here from the electric company and it says that my payment is overdue," she said, somewhat frantically.

Rob couldn't believe the speed with which his mother could shift gears. Pragmatism and narcissism combined. Maybe that's what had kept her alive. No matter what they were discussing, the conversation always came back to her immediate needs. But maybe it was something else, maybe she was just afraid of the authorities. He was tired of trying to figure out what made her tick. "Mom, calm down; no one is going to turn off your lights. I'm sure that you have enough in the bank to cover it. I'll check your balance for you as soon as I come home."

"I must sound like an idiot to you. I have never felt so alone. I still can't believe Max is gone. I'm sorry to interrupt your vacation."

"Mom, remember, I called you. Look, we'll be home soon. I'll stop by and bring you lunch. The usual: an everything bagel, Nova, no cream cheese. And a decaf coffee, extra milk. And we'll talk," Rob assured her before hanging up.

Max, his stepfather, had died from a sudden heart attack a year ago, and his mother, a perfectly competent woman from all outward appearance, was becoming more and more dependent upon him. But it was understandable. Max had handled all their finances and the maintenance on the house, sometimes supervising a few workers from his construction company or doing the repairs himself.

Elsa's phone calls came to Rob every day, sometimes twice a day. Her bills, the curtain rod that needed installation, her minor ailments, her doctor appointments. It wasn't enough that they had helped her downsize from the house to an apartment five minutes from where they lived. Nothing was enough for her. It was her history, the loss of her whole family in the war, that made Rob transition quickly from feeling annoyed to feeling pity, and then guilt, for not doing enough. He felt like she wanted to live with them. Well, now that he thought about it, maybe she did. Maybe she should. They did have a guest room that was unused. She had been through so much.

"I need to talk to you about my mom," Rob said to Dina, who was already sprawled on the bed, her shoes off and her feet sticking off the edge.

"Okay, but first, can you get me a drink?"

"Sure." He started to unscrew the bottle of rum that he'd brought back to the room. He grabbed the plastic cups the hotel maid had left in the bathroom.

"I think I got too much sun today," Dina mumbled.

Rob had noticed that Dina hadn't been drinking any alcohol at dinner, unlike the rest of them. Maybe she had a bit of heat-stroke. He closed the bottle, put it on the dresser, and headed back into the bathroom to get some water.

The wine had arrived quickly that night, long before their appe-tizers. They had ordered and finished two more bottles with the main course, then ordered a fourth. The bottle of rum they'd bought from the costumed girl prancing table to table had remained unopened. The conversation flowed and, after Dina and Julia had rehashed what they'd discovered on their tour with the famous Sylvia, they soon turned to other familiar topics: kids, medicine, and Soviet involvement in the space race. Rob was feeling wobbly when they got up to leave and was impressed that Dina's friend Julia was able to stand at all when they left the restaurant; she'd drunk almost as much as the men. Rob leaned on Dina as they walked back to their room.

The Convention of Wives

There was a lot about Julia that had impressed Rob that night. She looked unbelievable for a woman who had three-year-old twins. He knew she ran each morning on the beach; he'd passed her on his way back from the gym, her hair pulled tight in a ponytail. At dinner, her strawberry blond hair was loose and swirled over her breasts, breasts of a teenager in her tight-fitting, flowered, strapless dress. Rob had a hard time keeping his eyes to himself.

Dina was still attractive but had never quite rebounded from her pregnancies in the same way. Of course, he probably didn't help the situation by bringing her ice cream every time he sensed that she was feeling isolated and a bit depressed stuck at home with the kids. And the kids were definitely his doing; well, one in particular.

They had been surprised when Dina found herself pregnant with Zoe, their second. It was not something they had planned for so soon. But he remembered exactly when and why their second child came about.

It was their anniversary, and he had missed it. He'd been on call, and there was another patient with a post-op emergency that he needed to attend to all night. When he got home the next morning, after she'd canceled their dinner plans and the babysitter, he'd tripped on the dress she'd planned to wear, left crumpled in a pile on the bedroom floor. She was sleeping, her makeup smeared on the pillowcase, her body surrounded by tissues.

But he'd made up for it. Orchestra seats the following weekend for a new Broadway show aptly called *I Love My Wife*. He booked the restaurant and even arranged a babysitter. She had been impressed. The night was wonderful. A little too wonderful. It was only in the morning that Dina started to panic about not using any birth control. They had agreed to wait a bit longer. That was the plan. She was still fifteen pounds over her wedding weight from her pregnancy with Allie and exhausted all the time. Despite his protests, she refused to take the money her parents kept offering to hire someone to help, and their own budget based on his residency salary was still too tight to do so. Her martyrdom took a toll. She was not happy when she saw the pink positive sign on the pregnancy test a few weeks later. Not happy at all.

He looked at her now, lying on the hotel room bed, her feet slightly swollen and wondered. Again?

She pushed herself up on her elbows. "Rob, please, I have a headache, that water would be great. Your mom, is she all right? What is it this time, a hangnail?" Dina chortled.

He kicked off his shoes and handed her the water.

"Dina, come on, I called and started telling her about the tour of the island you took. She just told me you were right, my dad did die in Barbados, not in Italy."

"Hmm."

"Yeah, and she wants me to put a stone on his grave before we leave. She just told me my dad had died in Europe to simplify the explanation because I was a kid."

"And there's the drama! She couldn't have told us this before we came here? Maybe we could have stayed one more day and you would have gotten to see more of the place. How are we going to have time to get back to the cemetery before we leave? There's always some way for her to make our lives more complicated."

"You don't have to pick on her. Shit, she's alone in that apartment. My stepbrothers barely call her. I mean, how far is it from New York to New Jersey that they couldn't come and take her to dinner every once in a while? Would it kill them?" Rob asked, waiting for an answer he knew wouldn't be forthcoming.

She sipped the water. "She's not even sixty years old yet. I know she's been through a lot, but she's had a nice life. She could still have a nice life. She could meet somebody else. Third time's the charm, right? It's not like your stepfather left her destitute.

And we're nearby, she sees the kids all the time," Dina answered, burping for punctuation. "Sorry."

Rob took off his shirt, his arms as white as his undershirt. He glanced down and couldn't believe he'd gotten no color since they'd arrived. He'd spent almost all of his time indoors at the conference. "She's alone, and that, to her, is the worst thing that could happen. She has abandonment issues, you know that. Look, I think it might be better if, for a while, she was to come and live with us. We have the spare room and . . ."

Dina sat up quickly and slammed the water glass on the nightstand next to her, spilling part of its contents. "Are you out of your fucking mind? I can't believe you are asking me this. I've tried to be nice to her since I met her. She's never liked me; I've never been good enough for her. I'm not educated enough for you. My family, what are they just rag men to her, *shmata* sellers? And I'm not Jewish enough for you, my family never suffered like yours. In her eyes we've always lived in Scarsdale. I can't cook or clean the way she does. She can't stand me. She only puts up with me because of you and the kids. I'm a vessel, spawning your progeny. And you think I want this woman to come and live in my house? Watch, she'll make me put away my Shabbat candlesticks, and she'll use hers. She's crazy. I can't believe you are asking me this after all I've been through with you. Medical school, residency," she added sarcastically. "What a joke. Do you think this one little vacation makes up for everything? Vacation? We're at a convention. When have we ever really just taken a vacation? Will we ever? I never see you; the kids never see you. And you want to have your mother, this woman who can't stand me, come and live with us? It's time you decided who is important to you."

He knew his mother had been tough on her. But Dina was far from Elsa's only target. And he'd worked his ass off for so many years in a row that he couldn't count them. He was exhausted most of the time and he'd done well, almost well enough to feel at times that his in-laws were beginning to think that Dina was living the life she deserved. How could she not understand how responsible he felt for his mother?

"Are you giving me an ultimatum?" Rob asked, standing over her as she glared at him.

"Are you giving me one?" Dina yelled back.

"I need some air!" he shouted as he grabbed the bottle of rum he'd left on the bureau, walked out, and slammed the door.

Rob was walking so fast that he knocked the bottle of rum he was carrying into the cement divider that separated the hotel rooms from the beach. Somehow, it bounced off, rolled in the grass, and didn't break. He picked it up and kept walking.

He needed to think. The two strong women in his life, both of whom he loved deeply, were suffocating him. His mother was not responsible for who she'd become, but she was difficult at best. Dina seemed to be drowning in motherhood and constantly playing the victim.

He couldn't make either of them happy. But why should he feel responsible for their happiness? No one seemed that concerned with his own. As if medical school and residency had not been demanding enough. And why did their family histories always interfere with his and Dina's relationship, things that happened years ago, even on a beautiful island like Barbados? If they couldn't be happy with each other here, would they ever really be happy anywhere? His feet hit the soft, cool sand, and he looked down the beach.

He saw the shape of a woman sitting about twenty feet to his right and was tempted to walk the other way, until he heard her muffled crying. He couldn't just leave her. Then he moved closer and recognized the dress.

"Julia! What are you doing here?" Rob asked as he crouched down to talk to her.

She pulled back, startled. Tears and mascara were running down her face. This was far from the pretty picture he'd seen earlier in the evening. He pulled out the handkerchief from his pants pocket, the one he always carried.

"Here," he said, handing it to her.

"I'm slow, I mean, *so* embarrassed. Thanks," Julia said.

He sat down and tried not to laugh.

They sat there for a while together, wordlessly, looking at the Barbados sky, darkened except for a full moon in the distance, its light reflecting off the clouds like a photo-negative of daytime. He unscrewed the bottle of rum, took a slug, and offered it to her. She took a gulp but when he reached for the bottle, she pulled it back toward herself.

"No. I think I need a little bit more of this," she said and swallowed a few more times. "This is better with some juice from—you know—crap, what is that thing? You know, yellow, sweet, with prickles on the outside?"

"Oh, pineapple?"

"That's right."

They sat in silence, listening to the rhythm of the waves.

"Trouble in paradise?" he asked tentatively.

"Ha. Paradise. That's a laugh," she said. "Do you want to know what else is a laugh? My husband. He's so damn possessive."

"You're a beautiful woman," he said. He meant it to be a complement, but it felt more like a come-on.

"You better not say that to me, mister," she said, throwing her head back and laughing. "My husband might just punch you in the nose." Julia was laughing hard now. If she was anything like Dina, she'd be crying in a minute.

"What do you mean punch *me* in the nose?"

"I told you. He's jealous. He didn't like the way you were looking at me," she said. "Isn't that a kicker? *Looking at me. Ha!*"

Rob should have been embarrassed. He *had* been looking at

Julia, and her husband had noticed. "Julia, I'm sorry," he said. "I didn't mean to—"

"He went on and on about it. Told me how much I loved it, that Dina was supposed to be my friend, and that I was acting like a slut."

Rob cringed at the word. To think that he could have prompted John to say such a thing . . . he felt like a heel. "Oh, Julia. That's not true, he knows that. What did you say to him?"

"I told him that if he gave me half a minute of his time, maybe I wouldn't be enjoying a little attention from someone else. He's never home. I can never reach him when I need him. We have an army of kids, and not once has he ever even suggested that I get some help."

"Oh, Julia . . ."

"I want more from my marriage, you know?"

"I do know," he said. He started talking about his problem with his mother, and that devolved into talking about his stepfather and stepbrothers and how screwy things had been growing up. How he'd never felt like they were one family. It was always him and his mother or his mother and stepfather. And then she told him that she'd had a weird relationship with her own father. Her mother even took his side when she wanted to go to college. Her father refused to pay for it, though her brothers were sent a few years later. It always felt like there was a part of her mother she'd never understood. A part of her life she'd never shared.

All the while they talked, they passed the rum between them.

At some point, maybe twelve ounces in, Julia pushed her butt through the sand and sat closer to him. He pretended he didn't notice. They continued chatting, and a few minutes later she put her head on his shoulder. It was the first time in a while that someone seemed to care about what he was feeling, what he had to say.

Her hair fell onto his chest. As he reached to touch it, he

looked down and saw her dress pooling at the top of her thighs. Her legs were muscular, and he made out her rectus femoris muscle. He touched it, and she didn't stop him. Her thighs were as hard as he had thought they'd be, but her skin was so soft. His hand began gliding up and down aimlessly. He watched this motion as if his hand belonged to someone else. And then he reached down and moved her dress aside. She moaned softly. He turned his face to hers and their mouths met, their tongues melting into each other's. They stayed like that for a while, him touching her while they kissed, as he felt himself getting hard.

He pulled away. "Julia, we shouldn't . . ."

But she fell back on the sand and lowered the top of her strapless dress to reveal her breasts. He remembered that day at Dina's parents' house and the dinner they'd shared in Boston. She pulled his hand to them, and he let out a groan. He lowered himself and began kissing her again. She tasted like mango. And her breasts, he couldn't stop touching them, her chest rising and falling quickly as her breathing rate increased. She grabbed him tightly and when he entered her, her legs, those thighs, held him as if she would never let go.

He came quickly. He and Dina hadn't had sex in a while. The release he felt was so intense that he thought he heard himself scream. He wondered if someone passing by might think he was killing her. He pulled away from her slightly and glanced around but saw no one. When he looked back at her face, she was smiling at him. He leaned down and kissed her quickly, lay next to her, and looked at the stars.

A minute later he heard a soft, rhythmic sound that reminded him of seventh-grade woodshop. He turned and realized she was snoring. Was this the effect he had on all women? Other women? What was he thinking? Other women! He had to get back to Dina.

He waited a bit, thinking Julia would wake up on her own, but she didn't. So, he shook her gently.

"Julia, Julia, we need to go back. I'm so sorry about what happened."

Her eyes opened and she turned to him and pushed the hair off her face. "Don't be sorry. Don't ever be sorry," she said as she sat up awkwardly. "I think I'm going to puke."

As she turned away from him and began retching, he grabbed her hair. When she finished, he found his handkerchief in the sand near them.

"I'll be right back, stay here," he said as he headed toward the water. He dunked the cloth, wrung it out, came back, and handed it to her. She wiped her face and put it on her neck.

"Thanks."

"Come on, we should get to the rooms. I'll walk you back to make sure you're all right."

"Rob, Dina is one lucky woman," Julia said as she handed him back the cloth and pulled on her underwear.

"What?" he asked, thinking that maybe he hadn't come as fast as he thought.

"You're a gentleman."

"Oh. Thanks."

She got up on all fours, grabbed her shoes, and he helped her up.

When he got back to his room, Dina was fast asleep. The book she was reading lay on her belly and her glasses were still on her face. He gently took the glasses off and placed them carefully on her nightstand. He went into the bathroom to wash up. She didn't even move when he got into bed.

The next morning, they rushed to pack and make an early flight. The only words Rob and Dina exchanged were about whether they had time to go to his father's grave (they did), which suitcase to put the dirty laundry in (his), and whether they had emptied the safe and gotten their passports (they'd both forgotten). The Kinsellas were leaving after breakfast. They had said their good-byes at dinner the night before.

They stopped at the cemetery on the way and silently placed stones on his father's grave.

Rob read his journals and Dina her novel until they were somewhere over Bermuda. The stewardess brought them their lunch.

"Do you want my cookies?" Rob asked.

"Do I look like I need your cookies?" Dina answered.

"Dina, come on, I'm trying here," Rob said.

"I'm sorry. Last night was horrible. What is wrong with us?" Dina asked as she took his cookies.

He smiled. "Nothing is wrong with us. I was wrong to ask you about my mom. It's too much. You have enough on your hands with the kids. I know I'm not around enough."

"That's not your fault," she said as she moved the seat divider up and took his hand in hers. She leaned her head onto his shoulder.

He felt like a total shit. He'd never tell her. She'd never understand. He wasn't quite sure he did.

Chapter Thirty-One

Dina

Millburn, New Jersey, March 2001

Rob was gone, but his damn packages kept coming. His protein shakes, his wine, his dry cleaning . . . constant reminders that he wasn't there but parts of his life still were. She was so sick of being in limbo. She picked up the packages and carefully locked the front door. Living alone in the house sucked. It was too damn quiet.

Retrieving a vintage Châteauneuf-du-Pape from one of the shipping boxes, she took some pleasure imagining the moment Rob would notice the bottle was missing. Carefully taking the remaining weed out of the pouch she'd found in Daniel's room, she struggled to roll her second ever joint. She forced herself back to Rob's office, put the "Diagnosis" piece aside and read the rest of the paper, start to finish while enjoying the buzz.

What was it called? Self-medicating? If the kids only knew.

She considered phoning Allie to ask about Raj's article but thought better of it. Allie was serious about HIPAA regulations. The only thing she had mentioned to Dina about that day in the Emergency Room was that she'd seen Aiden.

Dina picked up the paper and continued reading:

More questions, few answers
  The doctor explained that a radiology tech would be by

within a few minutes to sonogram her leg to rule out a blood clot.

Upon hearing the doctor's suspicions, the patient's sister became concerned that something very serious was going on and contacted their parents who were vacationing across the country. The resident spoke with the patient's father, a physician, and updated him on the status of the assessment.

The patient became visibly upset and stated that the leg had been hurting since before she got a flu shot a week ago. In fact, she related, the knee area had been bothering her for some time and, now that she thought about it, was what had caused her to fall at the basketball game. She was sure that the more serious issues the doctor was describing were simply not possible and refused the sonogram. The patient begrudgingly relented when her sister intervened and insisted that she take the test.

Lastly, the resident called for an orthopedic consult to rule out the possibility of a leg fracture. The ED resident was becoming increasingly concerned about the multiple, seemingly unrelated symptoms. Shortness of breath, leg pain, and bruising. Could they be merely a confluence of individual issues or something else?

The orthopedic resident examined the patient. He noted that although the left thigh and knee were the major complaints, the right elbow joint was swollen and red. Upon further examination, he saw that the left elbow was slightly red and swollen as well. He ordered an X-ray and MRI of all areas. This resident voiced the opinion that the discomfort on each side of the body was unlikely to be from the same fall. In the chart he noted "potential chronic joint issue."

The sonography technician completed the ultrasound of the left leg, which was negative for a DVT.

As the young woman was wheeled out of the cubicle, the

ED attending, who had reviewed the patient intake in the electronic chart, approached the resident wondering why "bruising and shortness of breath" was still taking up space in his department.

The resident responded that the patient had been given fluid and her bloodwork had been sent off. He also explained that a sonogram of her left leg, ordered because she was on birth control pills, had resulted in a negative finding for a DVT. Ortho had just finished their consult and ordered additional X-rays and an MRI because of a concern that some type of joint issue had precipitated the initial fall.

The attending retreated and the patient was taken by wheelchair to the Radiology Department for further X-rays and MRIs.

It was now evening, and the patient and her sister were both asking to leave the ED. The patient was feeling slightly better. Her breathing had improved, and the ice packs on the leg were easing the pain. They mentioned that their parents were on a flight back to New York, and their father was insisting that she be assessed by a colleague of his at another institution the following day. But the resident politely insisted that they stay to get the rest of the results of the blood tests to make sure nothing more serious was going on.

More wine. More thinking about calling Allie, but it would only go to voicemail again. *You can only change your reactions to things*, Dina thought in a haze. *You cannot change the behavior of others*, especially your adult children. *Or your husband.* She kept reading:

Collaboration and teamwork
The residents were confused by the number of problems and wondered if they might be missing something. The results of the X-rays and MRIs came back. The lungs were clear, but

the patient had a hairline fracture of the femur of the left leg. There was slight arthritis indicated in the joints of the left knee and both elbows. The patient was anemic, but her electrolytes were normal. Her platelet level was somewhat low.

The fracture in the femur explained the pain in the left leg. But why was there arthritis in the knee and elbow joints? And was the anemia related in any way? And was the low platelet count significant?

They asked the attending to see the patient. He looked over the entire chart and then asked if there was any enlargement of either lymph nodes, spleen, or liver. The residents realized that in their haste, they had not completed the physical exam. The attending suggested they look at the platelet count results. They were abnormal.

The attending and one of the residents reexamined the patient. The patient's coloring had improved since receiving additional fluids and oxygen. The residents asked her to lie back, and they palpated her stomach. The liver and spleen were both enlarged. They were concerned about a potential ruptured or damaged spleen, but there was no pain upon palpation. And then they began checking the nodes on her neck.

She took another sip of wine and put the paper down. Reaching for what was left of the joint, she wondered. *This couldn't be about Rosie. It sounded too serious. She would have heard, wouldn't she?*

Chapter Thirty-Two

Rosie Cawley

Barbados, 1947

The bakery was buzzing when Rosie joined the line of women waiting inside to pick up their Sabbath orders. She felt their eyes upon her, each curious pair settling on her straw-colored hair, proof that she was an outsider. She'd passed the bakery often but had never been inside. It looked almost identical to the one in her own neighborhood. Large loaves of bread were stacked in woven straw baskets. A glass-fronted case featured cakes and pies. The floor and walls were tiled for easy cleaning but coated everywhere with a thin layer of flour.

When she got to the head of the line and said she was there for the Hellers' order, the woman behind the counter simply ignored her. According to Cook, who delighted in sharing her opinion about their mistress, Mrs. Heller had been banned from the bakery after complaining too loudly and too often about the quality of the goods. Just three weeks into her new job, Rosie understood the unofficial club of merchants wary of her mistress's sharp tongue.

She stood politely waiting for the line to diminish and, in the end, perhaps out of pity, the shopkeeper added a tiny, sweet cake along with the Hellers' standard weekly order of two challahs. The cake was full of nuts and cinnamon. Rosie thought of saving it for later but hadn't eaten anything since the morning.

The Convention of Wives

"This is heaven, what is it?" Rosie asked between bites.

The woman smiled. "It's called rugelach."

Another Jewish word Rosie would have to remember. This job was full of surprises. As she walked outside, she felt the first rain drops begin to fall, popped the rest of the cake in her mouth, and put the challahs under her jacket.

It was November in Barbados, the end of the rainy season. Within minutes the lanes of Swan Street were full of cement-like mud. The teeming water had done damage to whatever gravel had been spread over the soft limestone and sand that covered the island. Rosie tried, but failed, to hold up her skirt, and it quickly became tinged with the muck that splattered everywhere as she walked. Finding temporary shelter under the faded overhang of the dry goods store, she glanced at her reflection in the window. Her sun bonnet hung down her back, her hair stuck to her face, and her dress was streaked with mud. She couldn't wait until the new shorter style dresses caught on locally. The United States were always a few years behind Europe when it came to fashion, and the West Indies a few years behind that. She'd seen pictures featured in the Bridgetown Gazette and would send away for a new dress as soon as she could save up enough money.

The rain had barely let up when she hurriedly left her perch. She had less than an hour to reach the Hellers' house before the Sabbath would begin.

Twenty minutes later, shivering in her wet clothes, she entered the servants' door around back. She smelled, before she saw, Cook's day-long efforts. Plumes of moisture spilled from the kitchen into the mudroom. Fish with manioc and chicken soup. The aromas were familiar, but the spices were slightly different than those used in her own home. So many things she'd have to learn.

Baby Roberto, sitting in his wooden highchair, was doing battle with his mother. The smiling toddler, his face covered with mashed carrots, kept trying to grab the feeding spoon. Each time his mother let him have the spoon so that he might try to feed himself, he laughed and threw it on the floor.

"Rosie, thank God you're back, I couldn't imagine what had happened to you. Quick, put the challahs on the table and finish up with Roberto so I can go get dressed," Mrs. Heller said as she stood and removed her apron.

"Ro, come!" Roberto implored with outstretched arms. The boy had quickly taken to her. Rosie was tempted to pick him up but knew that Mrs. Heller would not approve of indulging the child.

"Yes, Ma'am. I'll be right back, Roberto."

But as Rosie passed Mrs. Heller, the woman roughly grabbed Rosie by the arm.

"*Vas iz das?*" Mrs. Heller said with disgust. "Do not even think about stepping farther into this house before you clean yourself off. *Uch*, what kind of mother raised you? This is not a barn; this is a house!"

"I'm so sorry!"

As Rosie headed back to the rear entranceway to clean off, she heard Roberto wail and his mother shout, "This place, this place, Michael, why did you bring us here?"

Rosie removed her shoes, grabbed a cloth from the rag pile, and did her best to wipe the mud from her clothing. In the end, she rolled her skirt up and tied it with some twine to keep the mud-covered fabric from showing. She bypassed the kitchen and hurried to the dining room, placing the challahs under the lace cover as Cook had instructed earlier in the day.

The house was beautiful, not at all like the boarding house in which Rosie had been raised. The dining room was lit by an electric chandelier, the crystals hung from carved mahogany arms shaped like palm leaves. Matching wooden wainscoting paneled the bottom half of the walls with palm-leaved wallpaper above. Linen draperies framed the windows. The china and silverware on the table were simple but elegant. Cook had explained that morning that the candlesticks were a family heirloom brought all the way from Europe.

This is why people talked about these Jews. They had been on the island less than a year and had already established a standard of living Rosie's family had taken a hundred years to attain—and barely a decade to lose.

It was intolerable; and yet, on some level, she admired what they had done. She knew the Jews needed to escape Germany because of political persecution. She had read in the papers about the concentration camps. She should pity them. But looking around the room, she couldn't help but resent these new immigrants.

Mrs. Heller was overly structured, demanding, and short tempered. But she cared tirelessly for her ill husband, bathing, feeding, and reading to him for hours. During that time, Rosie was not allowed to go inside his bedroom, even to clean. Mrs. Heller had seen personally to all of his needs. Rosie left the meal trays, as instructed, outside the door in the hallway on a small table and came to pick them up a few hours later. The food was barely touched. In the late afternoon, when Mr. Heller napped, Rosie had seen her mistress sitting outside in the shade pretending to read but, instead, crying quietly. She and Mrs. Heller, Elsa, were about the same age. In another world, they might be friends.

Rosie's trance was broken by quick footsteps behind her on the stairs and Roberto's shouts of "Ro, Ro!" from the kitchen. She saw the swish of Mrs. Heller's skirt on the second-floor landing before heading back through the pantry. Cook held the child with one arm while stirring the pot on the stove. He reached for Rosie as she grabbed him, carrying him to the front parlor where the ocean breezes entered the house. The wood burning in the fireplace crackled. She stood for a while warming herself and rocking Roberto on her hip, humming to him. Moving to the window to breathe in the honeysuckle-scented evening air, she swayed and held the baby boy tight. Roberto struggled to keep his eyes open, his breathing steadied, his head on her shoulder. She sang a lullaby that her mother had sung to her:

"Lullaby and good night, with roses bedight
With lilies o'er spread is baby's wee bed
Lay thee down now and rest, may thy slumber be blessed
Lay thee down now and rest, may thy slumber be blessed
Lullaby and goodnight, thy mother's delight
Bright angels beside my darling abide
They will guard thee at rest, thou shalt wake on my breast
They will guard thee at rest, thou shalt wake on my
    breast"

A noise startled her. Turning, she saw a tall gentleman wearing suspenders over a shirt so wet it was as if he were standing naked before her. She was mortified, realizing what she must look like to him, until she realized that he too had been wilted by the rain.

His eyes were dark with thick brows above them. His hair wavy. He held his hands strangely in front of himself.

"Excuse me, *you* are?" he asked.

She didn't answer.

"I assume that you are employed in this household? You will answer me, please."

"I'm so sorry, sir. I'm Rosie, the new housemaid."

"Rosie," he repeated as if she were an object belonging to the house, like a table or chair. She could see perspiration on his face as he strode toward her—or maybe it was raindrops. His face was so close to hers she flinched as he bent and kissed the head of the child she was holding. He took a step backward, nodded, spotted the staircase, and left without a word.

The Convention of Wives

She assumed he was Mr. Heller, her employer. She was happy he was up and about, but his manner was offensive. How rude he'd been not to introduce himself. Her grandmother, her namesake, had taught her many things. Her alphabet, lullabies, but, most importantly, manners. And this man, as handsome as he was, clearly was lacking.

The man she thought was Mr. Heller was, in fact, his visiting cousin, Rolph. Slowly, over the next weeks, she came to know a different side of him. He was indulgent with Roberto, taking the boy to play in the nearby stream and teaching him to toss a ball in the side yard. The blocks Julia had brought from her own home and had used as a child herself became a favorite on rainy days. The stacking inevitably ended by Roberto smashing whatever structure had been concocted, his giggling filling the house. After visiting with his cousin Michael in the mornings and luncheon with Elsa, Rolph accompanied Rosie on her walks into town for supplies.

Sophisticated and gentlemanly, he was like no man she'd ever met. And when he talked with her now, unlike the night they'd first met, he looked directly at her as if every word she spoke had import. His dark brown eyes would fix on her light ones as she spoke, and she'd feel the heat rise up her neck into her face. He told her about what his life had been like before the war, how he'd been attending university and studying physics before the Nazis had kicked all the Jewish students out. How lucky he had been to be sent ahead to America, and how his cousin Michael had not shared his fate.

She talked about her frustration about halting her schooling to help out at the boarding house, her love of reading, and her hope that she would be a teacher someday. And as they talked and walked, Roberto in the stroller or held between them, swinging in the air, they became as comfortable with conversation as the silences in between.

It took less than a week before their walks became routine. By the second week, Rosie thought of excuses for running errands. Rolph seemed more than pleased to escape his cousin's room. On days when Rosie was not heading to town, she would find herself going upstairs past Mr. Heller's room for no reason other than the hope that she would run into Rolph in the hallway. She noticed him coming downstairs frequently on the pretext of having forgotten his pipe in the parlor, only to find it in his pocket. Each time their paths crossed, she felt a humming sensation between them.

A month after Rolph's arrival, Rosie made a lunch to eat on the way to market. Roberto was sick with a fever and Elsa insisted that he stay home. Elsa suggested Rolph accompany Rosie because the harbor was full of ships and the port full of sailors. It would be safer.

When they were almost in town, they picnicked next to the base of a large baobab, its multi-trunked mass creating a nice piece of shade. They sat on the blanket enjoying sandwiches of egg and leftover chicken. Rosie was careful to prepare them as Cook had instructed, making sure not to include cheese with the chicken, something she would have done at home.

They sat and talked until they realized that they'd been gone far too long. As Rolph helped Rosie up, she tripped on the blanket and fell toward him. He caught her in his arms and they stood frozen. She felt the muscles of his upper arms beneath her hands and his warm breath on the side of her cheek. He moved one of his hands around her waist and, with the other, tilted her face up and kissed her. They didn't stop until they heard the sound of an approaching truck.

Chapter Thirty-Three

Dina

Millburn, New Jersey to Scarsdale, New York, March 2001

Dina stopped to go Passover shopping on her way home from Zumba. She retrieved the *Times* article from her workout bag as she waited in the checkout line and began to read while balancing a bottle of Manischewitz grape juice that would not fit in her overflowing basket.

The residents returned to the patient's cubicle. The medical attending explained that the patient needed follow-up by several different specialists, in particular a hematologist. It was possible she had a blood disease but would need to be tested further. The discharge instructions indicated that she should also be seen by an orthopedist and rheumatologist for follow-up and, preliminarily, she should be non-weight-bearing and on crutches for two to three weeks. She was given prescriptions for Percocet and Tylenol with codeine to manage her pain. The patient was scared, but her siblings seemed more upset than she as they helped her leave the ED.

Follow-up:

The young woman felt slightly better. The bruising on her left leg turned from plum purple to yellow, and her knee and elbow benefitted from the routine icing and anti-inflammatories.

A visit to the hematologist later that week led to additional bloodwork. A few days later the results came in. The patient was diagnosed with Gaucher disease, a condition in which the body is unable to produce glucocerebrosidase (GCase), an enzyme that breaks down glucocerebroside—a fatty material produced by the body that can accumulate in bones and organs causing damage. The disease is a genetic disorder predominantly found in Ashkenazi Jews. The young woman was from an Irish Catholic family, and she questioned how it was possible for her to have this disease.

Dina's hands slipped from around the bottle of grape juice and it crashed to the floor. Could it be possible? No, surely not. But Julia was half Jewish. Dina was the only one who knew, not even John. She couldn't imagine keeping something like this from Rob. She hadn't thought about this conversation in years.

No. It couldn't be.

But Rosie's illness, Julia not returning her calls, Rob's leaving her with no apparent explanation. All those years ago, in Barbados. Oh, my God, was it even possible? Dina ran from the store, leaving her cart full of groceries and the purple puddle behind her.

She wasn't sure how she'd gotten from the supermarket to the New Jersey Turnpike, but somehow, she found herself at the toll-booth in Newark. Grabbing another peppermint from her stash, she got on 95 North and headed for the GW Bridge. She bit the candy hard, the shards exploding in her mouth. She reached for another, struggling with the wrapper, then ripped it open with her teeth. There was nothing on the radio worth listening to as she stabbed at the buttons, frantically changing stations. The news was bad all over, and the music was contemporary strangeness or elevator banality. Nothing helped. She shut the heat off and cracked the windows, the cold air making her tongue burn and eyes water from the peppermint in her mouth.

It was midday when Dina arrived at her parents' house, the usual two-hour holiday drive having taken a little over one. She barely had time to put the car into park when rage and loss took over. Convulsing over the steering wheel with loud, ugly sobs, she questioned every decision she had made in her life, every person she had known. She stayed put for the length of three songs—all of which were about love gone wrong—before composing herself enough to approach the house.

When was the last time she arrived here without some sort of offering—a bottle of wine or some rugelach, maybe some fresh bagels from the city? It felt strange to be coming empty-handed. She took in the oversized columns and immaculate landscape. It was a beautiful home, the sagging gutter on the left front corner the only hint of neglect. This was her parents' oasis, the scene of a happy childhood. *But was it?* Running through sprinklers on the front lawn, her brothers teaming up and pulling down her bottoms. Her senior prom send-off and the God-awful hot pink dress her mother had picked out for her. Once inside, using the key she'd never removed from her chain, the memories turned even darker. Screaming fights with her parents. The day she packed her bags for nursing school. Introducing her family to the woman she had thought was her friend. How had it all gone to shit?

"Hello! Mommy, Daddy, it's me," she yelled. "I'm home."

Home. Now there was a loaded word. She no longer shared one with Rob. The kids were grown and gone. She'd wind up living with her parents, an aging spinster, playing the nurse she'd actually been.

"Dina, is that you?" her father shouted as he came into the foyer. "Of course, it's you. Who else has a key?"

"Hi, Daddy," she said, eyeing the bubble wrap under his arm and the large cardboard boxes scattered on the floor. Of course. The new apartment in Boca. She'd completely forgotten.

"Did I know you were coming? Your mom says I'm getting forgetful. Can you imagine? Me. King of the P&L, forgetful. I love her, but she makes me crazy sometimes."

She stood silently.

"Dina. What's wrong? Why are you here?"

Good question.

"I'm not sure. I didn't know where else to go."

He took her hand and led her to the kitchen.

"Sit down. I'm making coffee."

Her dad? Making coffee?

"I didn't know you knew how to use the machine. Where's Mom?"

"Amazing, right? I just learned. It's not so hard. Except I can't set the timer yet."

"Daddy, where's Mom?"

"Boca. I'm sure she told you. She's getting a head start with the decorator on the new place and left me here to finish packing. It's amazing how independent you can get in the kitchen when you've laid off the help and there's no woman in sight."

Why did she think coming here was a good idea?

"Let me just find a couple of mugs. I left a few things out to use while she's gone." He rummaged in a cabinet where the Passover china was usually stored. "Here we go. Okay, sugar, milk. Voila!" And then, as if remembering why they were sitting there in the first place, he turned to her. "So, tell me. What happened?"

Where to begin? Rob had cheated on her. Rob had cheated on her with her best friend. Her ex-best friend. Rob had a child. Another child. That child was sick. Oh, my God, their children could be sick. Could they be sick? That hadn't even occurred to her yet.

The Convention of Wives

"Dina, you never had a problem telling stories. Just tell me."

She couldn't remember the last time she'd been alone with her father.

She began slowly, starting with the *New York Times* article, the conventions, the friendship. She even made a *shiksa* joke. And then it all tumbled out. All of it.

Her dad was holding her when she'd finished. He let go of her only when her sobs died down.

"Come into the living room. I'm getting you a drink."

"It's too early."

"I think it's too late." He poured a vodka from the small rolling cart nearby.

She sipped, choked, and finished it quickly. He poured her another.

She awoke with a start, scattering the blanket her father must have placed upon her. The afternoon had disappeared. Outside, the sky was pink, the sun setting. Her mouth was dry. Her head ached. She headed into the kitchen and noticed her stockinged feet. She glanced back toward the couch and saw her shoes neatly lined up nearby.

"Dina, good, you're awake." He put down the glass figurine he was struggling to bubble wrap, then got them both glasses of water. "This must all be very upsetting to you."

"Uh-huh," she managed.

He sat, putting his arm around her. "You've always been a good daughter. You know Mommy and I love you."

"I know."

He pulled back, looking at her intently. "It's going to all be okay. Things will work out."

"I don't know, Daddy. I'm not sure. This is not a skinned knee."

He smiled his ever-charming smile. "You remember when I told you the story of the Band-Aid army."

How could she forget? Band-Aids, standing upright marching toward a legion of children learning to ride a bicycle. It had made her momentarily forget her tumble and resultant scraped knee and elbow. She nodded.

"You're going to have to trust me. It's always the darkest before the dawn, right?"

"Actually," she said, sipping the water, "it's darkest at midnight, not right before dawn."

"You always were more naturally inquisitive and well-read than your brothers. I'm not sure why I didn't bring you into the business."

Seriously, now? After all these years?

Taking her hands in his, and with the seemingly combined talents of a forensic accountant and lawyer, he verbally recounted, point by point, the history of Rob's indiscretion. Hearing aloud what she'd only heard inside her head made it real.

At the end, he paused, then asked her just one question.

"This is going to hurt maybe, but I'm going to rip the Band-Aid off." He paused before continuing. "What was your role in all this, Dinala?"

"My role?" She lost her breath for a moment. Maybe even her mind. "*My role*? How dare you?"

"I know you're angry at Rob and your friend Julia right now."

"Of course, I'm mad. I have a right to be mad. And she's not my friend."

"You do have a right to be mad. And surprised. All of it. But—" he refilled their glasses, "maybe you're not ready for this question. You must know this didn't happen in a vacuum. What was *your* role?"

She tipped over her glass, the water spilling onto the wooden table. Instinct kicked in and she ran for the paper towels. Grabbing a piece, she turned and screamed at him, "You, you of all people are asking me this question. What *chutzpah*! Do you think we've all been blind? All these years with Dottie. Please! Does Mommy even know?"

He stared at her silently. She took her coat off the chair, picked up her sunglasses off the table, and headed for the door. Her dad rushed after her and grabbed her arm.

"Don't go."

"Don't go, don't go! I come here for, *uch*, I don't know what I came here for! This was a mistake. Another mistake. That's all I seem to do lately, make mistakes."

"Please, please don't go. Not like this. You're too upset to drive."

"Too upset to drive. Well, whose fault is that? I tell you my marriage is falling apart, that my husband's had a child with another woman. Hell, all of you—even my children—must think I'm an idiot. They must all know. For weeks—no, months. Leaving me in the dark. There's no one. I have no one. And I come here and, what? You tell me this is somehow my fault? You, of all people. Was Dottie Mommy's fault? What kind of father are you?"

"The kind that doesn't want to see you kill yourself in a car accident." He took both her arms and held tightly. "Don't drive now, please. I love you. Don't drive now. Don't hurt yourself. You've been hurt enough. There's something I want to show you, come on. And something I need to explain."

He walked her to the study. His home office. A place where she hadn't been allowed to go except when her father was home and working at his desk. They sat together on the small, corduroy couch, before a coffee table filled with photobooks.

"I've been going through these before I pack them up. Take a look."

She picked up a vinyl-bound album. A black-and-white photograph of her parents and brothers in New York City at the Rockettes. Another of them all in Miami. They were smiling, they looked happy.

"I don't know what you want me to say."

"We have a nice family, your mother and I."

She didn't have the energy to challenge him. Besides, the emotion in the pictures looked real, palpable. "We do, but . . ."

"Not perfect. Far from perfect . . . but nice. More than nice. There's love there. And history. Shared history. Your mother and I, and you kids."

"I know, Daddy."

He nodded. "You think I don't know you remember more than that day at the Rockettes? This was a loud house. Yelling, screaming. Arguments. Show me a house that doesn't have them. Show me a kid who doesn't hate his parents growing up. Show me a parent who doesn't feel like a failure."

She started to say something soothing about her father and mother doing the best they could—but stopped herself. That was the consolation people used all the time. Why was she, all of a sudden, trying to console her father? She was the one who needed sympathy and compassion. A fury took over her. She thought about the lack of attention. The fights about her education. Her eyes filled with tears. But this. Rob. Rob had brought havoc. And her father, of all people, was lecturing her about fidelity.

"Maybe from where you sit, it doesn't seem like it, but what Rob has done is unforgiveable. And the kids, oh my God, how do we explain to the kids! Daddy, I hate him! He's ruined everything!" Her tears began again.

Her father hugged her tightly as she cried. "Show me a husband or wife who's been perfect in their marriage," he pushed her wet, matted hair off her forehead. "Dina, it doesn't exist. Anywhere."

He pulled back from her, handed her another tissue, and closed the photo album on the table.

"You're right. You're right about Dottie. It started before I met your mother. It's complicated." He rubbed the hair he had left on the top of his head, his hands falling to his sides. "I don't think it will be helpful for me to talk to you about this. Are you hungry? I know I could use a piece of Entenmann's. Let's head back to the kitchen."

Starving. She was starving. Not that Entenmann's was a nutritious choice. But they had to get rid of the *chametz* anyway before Passover. There was something comfortingly curative about this mainstay of her childhood, even better than chicken soup.

Her father ate his cake slowly. She'd never known him to linger over anything sweet. Was he hoping she would forget about what he'd promised to explain?

"You said it was my fault too, Daddy. You're supposed to be on my side. Especially in this." She dove into the chocolate frosting, pulling it from the bed of moist cake below.

"I am always on your side. You may not think so. But, in my own way, and your mother too, as best as we can, we're always on your side. That doesn't mean telling you to throw Rob out for this one indiscretion."

"Excuse me? I should just forgive him. Just go on from here. As if nothing has happened. Has Mommy forgiven you?"

"I look at you and see the same face as your mother asking the same question. You don't think I know who I am? David Aharoni, professional bullshitter. Something I inherited from my father. Even I wouldn't trust me. Still, I have limits."

He was right. He knew who he was. And she knew her father. In this she knew he was telling her the truth. Because underneath all the many layers of David Aharoni was a man who'd managed, in his own damaged way, to put his family first.

"Your Rob is the opposite of me. Maybe that's why you chose him. Mr. Self-Righteous."

She was about to protest when she realized who it was she was defending.

"This thing with Rob, it happened over twenty years ago. I know him. He's been a good husband and father. I like the guy, and you know me, I have high standards. Look at what he had to live up to here." He pointed at his chest.

Even now, he had slid back into a sales pitch. He couldn't help himself. She gave him a withering look.

"Okay, maybe not the best choice of words."

Her father wasn't wrong about Rob, but did that make him right?

"Dad, I know you're trying to help, but you have to admit, you may not be the right person to be giving me advice in this department."

He seemed to choose his words carefully. "You're probably right. All I'm saying is that marriage is a strange thing. You have to decide in the end if it's worth staying after you realize the person you've chosen turns out to be more, less, or different than what you expected. It's not like in the romance novels. There's no happily ever after. There's just after."

Chapter Thirty-Four

Rolph Heller

Barbados, 1947

Rolph could not believe his eyes. His cousin, who he had last seen in the DP camp in Italy, had aged twenty years. He was frail, his face gaunt, his stomach bloated. His body was bruised all over.

"Michael, I'm so glad to see you," he said, sitting down next to his cousin and taking his hand.

His cousin just nodded.

"Here, let me bring you some water so you can speak." Elsa took the pitcher and poured a glass, handing it carefully to her husband.

Michael sipped slowly and then motioned for someone to take the glass. He cleared his throat and in a weak voice greeted his cousin. "Rolph, it is good of you to make the journey. I'm sorry I can't stand and greet you properly, please forgive me."

"Michael, don't be silly. Elsa mentioned that you were sick in her letters. But I had no idea . . ."

"Shocking, yes, I know. Elsa, more of a warning might have been in order. Rolph, I know I don't have much time left. You must promise me that you'll get Elsa and Roberto to the United States."

"Michael, Michael, stop talking this nonsense. The doctor says that you just need to rest and build yourself back up. The trauma of the war, the journey here, it was too much for any of us."

But Rolph could tell, even as Elsa said these comforting words, she knew better.

"I'm going to get Rolph settled, and then we'll make Shabbos downstairs and be back with some soup for you." She kissed Michael's head and his eyes started to close.

She quickly pulled her hair back with a few pins and took Rolph's arm. They stopped outside the doorway.

"Elsa, why didn't you tell me how bad he was?" Rolph whispered.

"How could I explain this in a letter? The doctor doesn't really know what is wrong with him. Too many things at once. It started right before we left Italy, but these last few months have been horrible. I'm so sorry I couldn't greet you downstairs and warn you. I've spent almost all of the money that you've sent me on getting some help. I couldn't take care of Roberto and Michael. But these women. I've been through at least five of them. Useless. Your Uncle Henry has been more than generous. But I don't know how much longer we can wait for you to get us papers to leave. I wish we had more family left. Sometimes, I simply can't bear it."

"Elsa," he said. "Dear, sweet Elsa." He tried to comfort her, but just as her eyes got glassy, she seemed to stop herself, as if turning a switch in her head.

"Come, you must be hungry. Let me show you your room and then we'll go downstairs and have dinner. It's past time to light candles and Roberto's bedtime. I've had Cook make chicken soup, my momma's recipe. It's just the thing on a rainy night like tonight. Come, come and tell me everything."

He hugged her, holding her a bit too long, until he could compose himself. As they turned and headed toward the room, they almost collided with the maid he'd met downstairs. She was struggling, carrying his bag. He noticed that her hair had been brushed and was tied high on her head with a ribbon. Her stained skirt was hanging down, and she now wore a pair of slippers.

The Convention of Wives

"Ma'am, I put Roberto to bed. Cook asked me to bring up this luggage. She explained about your visitor." Rosie placed the luggage on the floor, looked up at Rolph and then down at the floor.

"Oh, thank you, Rosie." Elsa said. "I don't know if you were properly introduced. This is Mr. Heller, my husband's cousin. He'll be staying in the guest room. Rolph, this is Miss Cawley, Roberto's nanny and our maid."

Rolph made a slight bow as Rosie curtsied. He'd behaved abysmally when he met her downstairs. Maid or not, she deserved to know who he was.

"Please bring up some extra towels for him as well. And, Rosie, I must have an extra dress for you to wear somewhere. You'll catch your death. We'll get Rolph . . . Mr. Heller settled, and then I'll take a look."

Rosie curtseyed in response. She reached to pick up the luggage, but Rolph reached for it at the same time. His hand encased hers. She was soft and warm to the touch. He looked up and noticed her cheeks had turned scarlet.

"Begging your pardon, sir," Rosie said, her eyes downcast.

"My apologies," he responded as he untangled his hand from hers. "The bag is too heavy for you. I'll put this in the room if you show me where it is, miss. And Elsa, you should go and find that dress for her. I know if I don't change out of these wet clothes soon, I believe I'll start to mildew."

Elsa laughed, and Rosie covered her mouth.

"Of course, you're right, Rolph. I won't be a minute. Rosie, please show him the way."

Rosie stopped in front of an open door and hesitated. Rolph pointed to indicate that she should enter first. He could tell she was uncomfortable. Somehow, he was enjoying that. He followed her in as she turned on the light switch. She walked over to a canvas contraption and opened it.

"You can put your luggage on here while you unpack. There are more towels in the bottom drawer, oh, and a robe."

He could see her blushing again.

"There are toiletries in the guest bathroom. It's shared between this room and the one on the other side, Roberto's room. He's usually up by about six thirty, but I come fetch him and take him down for some breakfast, so you can sleep in if you like. Breakfast is at eight, lunch at noon, and tea at four. Dinner is usually around seven, after Roberto has been put to bed."

He smiled, listening to her prattle on. She must have seen his expression, because she clenched her fists and asked, "Is there anything else, sir?"

"Not that I can think of right now, thank you."

Elsa walked in the room.

"Rosie, here you go. This should work for you. Please go upstairs and change and then come down to help with dinner."

"Yes, ma'am."

When he could hear Rosie padding up the back staircase, he turned to Elsa.

"Do you let her sleep?" he asked.

"Rolph, please. As if you didn't grow up with help in your house. She's my age. She's wonderful with Roberto, I think he truly prefers her. I don't have much time with Michael the way he is."

"Of course. I'm sorry, Elsa, I was just kidding."

She came over and took his hands in hers. "You don't know what it means to have you come all this way."

He kissed her cheek and she left the room, tears in her eyes.

Rolph knew his relationship with Rosie was wrong from the start. But he'd felt dead before he saw her. His Uncle Henry had sent him on a trip back to Europe after the armistice in order to locate and gather any surviving relatives. He'd been to four countries before finding Michael and Elsa in Italy. At every other

The Convention of Wives

Red Cross office, he'd only found records that indicated the work camps or concentration camps where family had been sent. The survivors of these camps were few, if any, and the lists were often incomplete. So, he'd left after spending too much money with almost nothing to show for it.

Returning to New York had been almost as surreal. His Uncle Henry, with whom he'd been staying, was supportive, but even he couldn't fathom what Rolph had seen in Europe. No one understood except some of the GIs he'd met in the bars he frequented at night. At first, they wouldn't speak with him, his German accent attenuated but still discernable. Eventually they talked about the survivors they'd met, the mass graves, and the wounded and dead soldiers; and about the women who'd welcomed them back home in the United States, who were comforting but with whom they feared sharing too much. It was after such a night at the bar that his uncle Henry greeted him.

"I've got good news to share with you. Their papers have arrived," Uncle Henry said, shoving Elsa and Michael's documents into Rolph's hand. "I've booked a train ticket for you to Miami and then a boat to Barbados."

And here he was, six weeks since he'd left New York and five weeks on the island, helping to nurse his sick cousin and falling in love with a stranger.

Rolph and Rosie met when they could, careful at first, and then crazily careless; he coming up to her room on the third floor in the attic in the middle of the night. The household was too consumed with Michael's illness for anyone to hear their groaning or the headboard knocking against the wall. Their need for each other only increased, and they were both the better for satisfying it, until they were not.

Rolph had waited to tell Elsa that the immigration papers had been accepted. At first Elsa resisted, but knowing that her husband's death was imminent, there was little to do but give in. Rolph had gone with her to the synagogue later that day to make arrangements for a plot in the cemetery and a headstone to be placed a year later, with prayers to be said by the remaining members of the congregation. They would not be coming back to the island for the unveiling. It was afternoon when they returned. Elsa went upstairs to see Michael. Roberto was napping.

Rosie stood before him dusting in the parlor, in the same room in which they'd first met.

"Rosie, I need to speak with you. Are you going to market today?"

"Of course, I am," she said, smiling at him.

"I'll be in the study. Let me know when you're leaving," he said, sighing and turning to leave.

"Is everything all right, Rolph?"

He hadn't disguised the tone in his voice well enough. "Yes, yes, we just need to talk," he said, his voice softening. Rosie looked at him blankly.

But as he was leaving the parlor, Elsa ran down the stairs.

"Rolph, Rolph come quickly. It's Michael—he's stopped breathing!" Elsa screamed.

Michael was gone.

Cook and Rosie helped pack up the house. Rolph knew that Rosie was waiting for him to say something to her, but what? A life for the two of them was impossible back in the United States. His family would never accept them being together. He tried to blame his behavior on the circumstances, the stress of the situation, dealing with Michael's illness, another loss in a string of losses. But he could not. He had behaved badly. What was he thinking? He wasn't thinking, he had simply fallen in love. But they were from two different worlds that had collided on a small island in the middle of the sea.

Chapter Thirty-Five

Julia

New York, New York, July 2001

"What the—?" Julia was swiping frantically at a bug on her neck. Then she realized it was just a piece of her hair, which she hadn't cut since moving to New York when Rosie first got sick. Ironically, since she and John were now separated, she'd let her hair grow back to the way he'd always liked it. She regathered her hair through the hole in the back of her baseball cap, the one from the hospital gift shop. She'd liked the color and felt like she was making a small donation.

The Gaucher treatments had been more arduous than expected. It was a good four hours each time. Following the intake, Rosie was gowned and connected.

Connected. She'd never really thought about the word, but her connection to Rosie, always strong, now seemed tenuous. Adult children were always talking about their need to *cut the cord*, but mothers? Mothers were forever pulling back on that cord, attempting to tighten it, to hold on with all their might; willing to continue to feel any pain their child experienced for the pleasure of the continued connection.

The two would sit for the hours-long infusion of a medication called Ceradase, which took the place of the enzyme not produced naturally in Rosie's body. The enzyme that prevented the accumulation of fatty acids in her organs and bones causing damage. After the infusion they waited an hour to make sure Rosie didn't have any adverse reaction, which could be as benign as temporarily losing her sense of smell to weakness or diarrhea. Luckily, Rosie never experienced anything.

Back in April, two weeks into Rosie's treatments, Bridget had taken some time off from work to enable Julia to go back to Atlanta to get some clothes and talk to John. But he'd had the locks changed and wouldn't take her calls. She checked into the Sheridan, hoping he'd change his mind and agree to a meeting. No such luck, so she spent two days alternately emptying the minibar and running in the park nearby. Julia's running was becoming more intense, more frequent. It was the only thing that seemed to help her deal with the realization that Rosie's condition—a condition Julia felt responsible for—would not magically disappear.

At first Julia and her daughter had tried to chat their way through the sessions, but they soon ran out of things to say. They attempted a few soap operas, but the problems of the characters seemed ridiculous compared to their real-life issues. Julia was desperate to come up with a distraction.

She'd just finished a few laps around the Central Park reservoir and was walking down Broadway when she spotted a bright blue sign: NEW YORK CITY ANIMAL SHELTER—COME IN AND SEE HOW WE MAKE A DIFFERENCE. She had planned on stopping to pick up some fresh produce but was drawn inside the shelter instead. The building looked like it had once housed a gymnasium and, if you looked closely at the wood planked floor, you could plainly see the faded basketball court lines.

"You want to see the adoptable animals, right?"

A man she guessed to be approximately her age with tan khakis, a red polo shirt, and white beard stood staring at her.

"Or maybe you need the water fountain?" Santa Claus said, looking down at her sneakers.

The Convention of Wives

She stared back, feeling sweat on her brow.

"Probably the animals, right? Everyone wants to take a look at the puppies and kittens, in particular. I get it. It's what brought me in here in the first place, too. They're that away." He pointed.

Who says "that away" anymore? "Do I need to check in anywhere?" Julia asked.

"No, not unless you're thinking of adopting today or," his eyes twinkled, "volunteering."

"Oh, no thanks. Not today."

"Let me know if there's anything else I can help you with." He bowed slightly and walked away, his gray ponytail swaying.

Julia never had understood the look, a ponytail on an adult. She'd always preferred a clean-shaven man with cropped hair like John's. But then, she'd always preferred John. Look how that had turned out.

The cages were lined up in four rows that ran the length of the large, high-ceilinged room. Fans turned creakingly overhead. She shivered as she cooled off from her run. It had been years since she'd been around so many animals. Years of sameness, followed by recent months of unpredictability and change. But, somehow, standing in front of these small creatures, she felt calm, more centered.

John had developed a phobia after being bitten by a dog as a young child. Despite her pleading over the years, he'd refused to allow a dog in the house. What other things had he not "let" her do? Looking into the cages, then stopping to squat down before a black miniature poodle, it dawned on Julia that what Rosie and she needed in their lives was a puppy. Something to distract them both, something to love and to give them love unconditionally in return. But Julia wasn't going to just pick one out impulsively. She'd make this a project. A project she and Rosie could work on together.

On her way out, Julia stopped at the information counter. She picked out a few books to guide them in their decision making:

You and Your First Dog, Puppies Aren't Babies, and *What Breed Fits Your Need?* Adding a decorative NYCAS Foundation doggie bookmark from the counter to her pile, she handed her charge card to her new friend who looked more and more like a hippie version of St. Nick.

"Thought you were just browsing," he remarked.

"I found something I can use. My daughter . . . ," she thought better of explaining. "My daughter will enjoy these. And then we'll be back sometime to adopt."

"Great." He put her credit card through the machine. "Sorry, ma'am, the card has been declined."

"Ma'am?" Her anger was apparent.

"Excuse me. I was raised that way. Just habit." He looked down at the card machine and back at Julia, one eyebrow cocked. "Do you have another card or cash perhaps?"

"Please try it again; there must be some mistake." *How annoying.* Thank God no one else was nearby.

"Would you like me to hold these for you, and you can come back and . . ."

"Don't be silly."

And then it occurred to her. During their recent phone conference with the mediator that she and John had agreed to use instead of lawyers, they'd discussed the need to separate their expenses. They hadn't come up with a plan yet, she'd thought. But it seemed John had. That bastard! Seriously? Her cheeks got hot as she blushed from embarrassment. She took out a twenty-dollar bill and shoved it toward the guy. He seemed as embarrassed as she was.

"That's $21.75 with tax."

He pulled back the bookmark on the counter. She reached into her bag, took out a five, and handed it to him. Without waiting for change, she grabbed the bookmark and her other purchases and fled.

The Convention of Wives

- - -

At the next infusion session, Julia took out one of the books. She and Rosie read together and discussed what breeds made sense and how they would work out having a puppy in the small apartment. Her daughter took notes and made a spreadsheet comparing different dogs. A few weeks into the process, she and Rosie experienced a minor hiccup realizing they'd have to get the landlord's permission to have a pet since it had not been negotiated in the original lease. But a phone call later, after Julia explained what Rosie was going through, the man became more than sympathetic, even offering to dog sit if needed.

Two months afterward, upon entering the shelter with Rosie to pick out a puppy, Santa Claus—whose name was Gary—gave Julia a friendly wave.

"New friend, Mom?" Rosie asked.

Julia introduced the two. She'd been volunteering at the shelter for the past few weeks. In the beginning, she'd filed papers while completing training to enable her to interact with visitors and man the gift shop. When she mentioned to Gary, who, it turned out, was the executive director, that she preferred the work the younger volunteers were assigned to do—cleaning cages and interacting with the animals—he smiled knowingly.

"I had a feeling about you," he said.

She'd dress in jeans and T-shirts—leaving dirty, smelly, and happy; but, lately, her back had been bothering her by the end of her shift. The gift shop register began to look tempting. Maybe there was a way to do a little of both.

Today, Gary offered to take her and Rosie personally to see the latest additions to the puppy section.

Most of the dogs were older, collected from apartments on the Upper West Side from tenants who'd been moved to nursing homes, or, more often than one would hope, found by landlords having been left behind after a sudden death. Many of these dogs would never be adopted. Julia always gave them extra attention during her shifts. But today was about Rosie and a younger dog was in order. There were two puppies. One a terrier mix, the other a small bichon frise, simply perfect for a New York City apartment. Julia had wondered during her shift earlier in the week how it had wound up at a shelter, since it was a breed in high demand. Then she'd seen the splint on its leg. She checked its chart. A bad femoral break, unlikely to perfectly heal.

"Mom, they're both adorable. But what's with this one?" she asked, holding the frise to her chest. It lay calmly in her embrace.

"It's got a complicated leg break. They're not sure if it will heal correctly."

Rosie put down the dog slowly and went over to the terrier mix. It licked her hands as she picked it up, then squirmed to get out of her grasp. She plopped it back in its cage and shut the door. She went back to the bichon. He got up slowly as Rosie stuck her hand in the cage, limped toward her, sat down, and lay his head on her hand.

"Mom," she said, looking up at Julia. "He's just like me. Not perfect, but look how he handles it." That was all Rosie said. That was all she had to say.

Julia asked her daughter if she was sure, even though she knew the answer. "Besides, I think I'm in love. I'm naming him Tucker."

"Tucker. I like that," Julia said, reaching to scratch him behind his ears. "Tucker, you are my first grand-puppy!"

As they walked out, thanking Gary for his help, Julia noticed a "Help Wanted" sign taped to the information desk: ASSISTANT MANAGER NEEDED. LOOKING FOR AN ORGANIZED SELF-STARTER WITH BASIC ACCOUNTING SKILLS AND LOVE OF ANIMALS.

"Have you found anyone yet?" she asked Gary.

"That's a broad question, but I've kind of been waiting for you to ask." His robin's-egg blue sweater drew Julia to his eyes.

"Excuse me?"

"Well, I was dating someone a few years back, but lately no one's come my way."

"You're impossible. I mean for the assistant manager position." She pointed back toward the desk.

"Ah."

"Yes."

"Thought you were just here for the puppies."

"Mom, these supplies are getting heavy," Rosie pleaded.

"Take this application home and fill it out. Bring it back on your next shift. As you know, I happen to have an in with the director."

"I don't know. I don't think I have the experience you're looking for."

What was she doing? She loved the animals but didn't need the job. Everything in her being was pulling her toward the door.

"Ah. You're trying to underwhelm me with your enthusiasm." He smiled. "Very cool tactic."

One job interview and three days later, she left the shelter with a new photo ID and a schedule of her hours. Scooping her long hair off her neck, she pulled it through the back of her baseball cap. It was humid outside. Summer in New York was not so different from Atlanta. The pay was less than what she'd made when she'd stopped working over twenty years before, and there were no health benefits. She was thrilled.

Chapter Thirty-Six

Dina

Scarsdale, New York, August 2001

Dina glanced at the mirror in her parents' walk-in closet. Her mother's hands looked bony and spotted. Dark circles were visible under her mother's eyes, despite the attempted camouflage. Her poor mother—she looked careworn. Both women did.

"Before I get rid of it all, I just want to know if you want anything for Rob. It's a shame. Your father had such beautiful sweaters."

Bringing a sweater or anything else over to wherever Rob was staying was the last thing she would do. "Dad and Rob are not even close to the same size. I mean, Daddy wasn't . . ." Her voice trailed off with a choke to punctuate. Dina was still reeling from her dad's death from a heart attack mere months after her parents left to spend time in their new apartment in Florida.

"So, I didn't want it to come as a shock to you, but I'm selling the house and moving to Boca full-time."

"What!"

"What is the point of it anymore? You and your brothers never come; you have houses and lives of your own. My friends have all moved to Florida already. I hate the cold. The only people I see on a regular basis are the women from the cleaning service. I've given them bag-loads of stuff already, but now I need to get rid of the golf clubs, and his cigars, and his Scotch."

The Convention of Wives

Dina was surprised. The house was more than a house. It represented the life her parents had built together. Her childhood. Hadn't they already had enough loss for one year? And Boca was a plane flight, not an hour's drive away.

"Please be sure."

"Dina, I'm sure. I've got a real estate agent already. She's asked me to take down the wallpaper in the bathrooms and pack away my *tchotchkes*. She says getting the house to look less like anyone in particular is important. I've already started. Besides, none of what we have here works in Boca."

"How can you have decided this already? We just stopped sitting *shiva*."

"It's done. I've already talked to your brothers. I need to make a life for myself. Besides, you'll all come and visit."

"Do you want me to stay a few more days and help you pack?"

"No, it's okay. I have some time on my hands."

Dina was loath to admit to her mother she had plenty as well.

Passover had been intolerable. After leaving a message at Rob's office telling him not to bother coming home, she had thrown an abbreviated Seder at her parents', telling the kids their dad was home sick with something he didn't want them to catch. Her father's funeral had been awkward, but they got through it somehow.

Dina didn't know where to start, so she just dove in, giving her mother a summary of Rob's indiscretion all those years ago with Julia and the fact of Rosie's parentage.

The momentary silence was ended by her mother's pronouncement. "I have another grandchild."

"Even this is about you! And she's not your grandchild. She's Rob's, Mom, not mine."

"About me? I sacrificed for all of you, you have no idea. I held this family together when I could have let it explode."

"This house, your life doesn't look like much of a sacrifice."

Her mother stared, unmoving. "Never mind. It doesn't matter now."

"It's not as if Daddy had a child with another woman," Dina said.

Her mother drew a sharp intake of breath. "So, nothing's a problem unless it's *your problem*?"

"That's not what I was saying, but you don't seem to understand—"

"Dina, I've had quite enough of this. Even now, with your father dead, you're always the ultimate victim, aren't you? Nothing anyone else has been through could possibly be as difficult as what you're going through."

"That's so unfair." Dina's face was wet with tears. "All those years, you think I didn't know about Daddy and Dottie?"

She met her mother's narrowing eyes, noticing the crow's feet and gray hair around the crown of her head, before her mother walked out of the closet, sat on the bed, and stared out the window. Dina followed and sat on the bedroom chair facing her. "Mom, I'm sorry. I shouldn't have said that."

"I was everything your father was supposed to have in a wife. Smart . . ." She looked at Dina and cocked her head. "Yes, smart, pretty . . ."

"Mom."

"Oh, please, Dina, at this point in my life, I know who I am and who I'm not. Besides, you look like me. Don't tell me you don't think you've got it in the looks department."

The emotional map of their conversation had always given Dina whiplash. Why would this talk be any different? But her mother was attractive despite the facial lines and creping at her neck. And Dina had always felt pretty, sexy.

"In the end, none of that mattered. Dottie and your father worked side by side to build the business. He was never home. Always with that woman. Few women had careers then. It just wasn't done. We just went on like that, your father and me, for a long time. People didn't divorce like they do now. Daddy stayed away for a few weeks while I decided if we should stay married. Do you remember the pancake breakfast he made when he got home? I think you were about five years old."

A picture of her father in an apron, standing over the griddle, came back to her. "That trip to Canada."

"That trip to Canada."

They'd sat having a pancake breakfast, her brothers in Mountie hats too big for their heads and Dina pouring maple syrup from the small set of bottles her father had given her.

"Your father and I found our way through it, a way to be with each other again. Not right away, but over time. It was never the same. But it became our new normal."

"But, Mommy, how could you live like that?"

"Your father was a good man. Far from perfect, but a good man. I never had all of him, but there was so much to love that I had enough."

"How long did you know?" Dina asked.

"You remember the jeweler? Mr. Klein. He and his wife sat behind us in shul. His hugs on the holidays were always a little too long. One day in his shop, I was eyeing a pair of earrings. He asked if I wanted to have dinner sometime, you know, seeing as Daddy was traveling so much for work with his secretary. Secretary? Dottie was never his secretary, but there was no term then for what she was. If she'd been a man, she would have been his partner. Anyway, that was beside the point."

Dottie had been the acting CEO since her father's death.

"I knew what Mr. Klein meant, the way he said 'secretary,' the way he looked at me. At first, I was shocked; then I began to see how it really was. All those business trips Daddy took with Dottie, the late-night meetings when he chose to get a hotel room rather than schlep home. I'm not an idiot. But Klein—there was a piece of work. This is what the man did to Daddy in return for years of giving him business, supplying his wife and girlfriend with jewelry. He wanted me to know about Dottie so that I'd fall into his arms. No thanks."

A memory flickered in Dina's mind of a time she'd gone to retrieve the Shabbat candlesticks. Something about abbreviations in a book. "Mommy, I could never stay with a husband who did that to me. All those years and you stayed."

"That's easy for you to say. My options weren't great. Where was I going . . . a divorced woman with three children? I couldn't support myself in any real way. And Daddy never, ever put the relationship in my face. I never asked your father about Dottie again. And every Christmas I even bought that woman a Hermes scarf. Can you believe that? I knew that she knew that I knew, but I kept buying those stupid scarves."

"But how can I go back to Rob as if nothing's happened? How do I know it didn't happen again? I don't even know if he wants me."

"Have you asked yourself lately if you really still want him?"

She hadn't. Their life together was a given, like the tooth-paste they both preferred. It was just there. How shitty a way to think about a marriage was that?

"You're asking yourself the wrong question. He did some-thing foolish, what, twenty-five years ago? And then had to live with it all these years. You two were basically still children at that point. You've grown up together since then, shared a life. Is it worth destroying your marriage?"

"It's a matter of trust. How can I ever trust him again?"

"Trust? You think a man has sex with a woman who is not his wife without there being a reason? Have you never been so unhappy with Rob that you haven't thought about being with someone else? In all these years? Do you think only the man's sexual appetite remains when they get married? A woman doesn't look anymore? You never looked?"

"Mommy! Looking is not tasting. That's not exactly what I meant. But . . . cheating, lying." Dina had never, ever spoken to her mother like this. But there'd never been a day before when her mother was widowed and she separated and possibly heading toward divorce.

"You're kidding yourself. Women fantasize. Plenty. They may not act on it as much, but I think it's just that they're too exhausted with kids and life. Maybe that's not even true anymore. Especially from what I see on the cover of *Cosmo*."

What a bizarre topic to be discussing with her mother. But the last few months had been anything but normal for both of them. There'd been Phil the carpenter. The butcher with the sexy South African accent. One of Rob's partners. How many times had she been unable to fall asleep and masturbated thinking of another man's face or body with Rob lying next to her snoring after she'd told him she was too tired for sex? Who knows what would have happened if she'd found the opportunity when Rob went to one of his conventions?

"Did your father know about Rob?" her mother asked.

"I should have told you too . . . I was embarrassed. And you weren't home that day when I found out and went to tell you and Daddy."

"It's okay. I'm glad you told one of us. Was your father helpful?"

"Yes. But I've been wrestling with what to do since that conversation, and then everything happened with Daddy, and I didn't have the energy to figure it out."

"I wondered about you and Rob at the funeral. A mother's intuition. Look, Dina. Sometimes a man is just a dog. Rob's not a dog. Neither was your daddy. But we all bring our own *chazeray* into marriage. Our own imperfections. You and Rob don't have any? Come on, Dina, I'm your mother. I know more about how you grew up than anyone. You think Daddy and I didn't do a number on you like my parents did to me and their parents to them before that?"

Who was this woman? She couldn't remember the last time they'd really talked like this. Had they ever talked like this?

"I needed your dad's sense of humor, his love of life, his success. He needed my admiration. Okay, maybe he thought I was attractive, who are we kidding?"

And her mother was back.

"We fit each other's dysfunction. It's the best you can hope for."

Dina had hoped for more.

But her mother was right again. She'd been better with Rob. He'd been better with her. They bolstered each other. They laughed at the world together.

"How much of your relationship is defined by sex these days?"

"Excuse me?" Dina hadn't seen that question coming. "I don't know what you've been reading lately, but . . ."

"Okay, I don't need to know that. I'm just saying. I have something called the Jackie O theory."

"The what?"

"You might call it the Hillary theory, too. They stayed."

"Of course, Jackie stayed. She wanted to be married to a president. A divorce wouldn't have played well. But Hillary?

"More than what their husbands did with someone else in bed, they wanted to come home at night to a man who was just as interested in talking politics, world affairs, as they were. That's what drew them together in the first place. That was their passion. Do you two still have that? You and Rob. Do you have things to talk about? Do you laugh together? I always thought you two did. It's something Daddy and I ran out of. Lots of people do. It's what he had with Dottie."

The Convention of Wives

Did she and Rob still share anything? She wasn't sure. The life they led had left her with little to talk about at dinner besides her volunteering and the occasional article she was trying to get published. But his career wasn't a page-turner either at this point. Wasn't that both their faults? And now, with the kids really out of the house, that subject was no longer front and center. They were like the proverbial lobsters placed in the pot of water slowly coming to a boil. She had no recollection of how they'd gotten here. But most of the couples they knew were in similar boats. So, their life wasn't so exciting. Had it ever been? They were both stuck. But at least they were stuck together. Was that enough?

"But, Mommy, you're talking about now. What it's like now with Rob. That's not what it was like then."

"Then when?"

"In Barbados. All those years ago."

"You're right. I wasn't there. You were. So, what happened besides the obvious?"

They were just starting then. They were too young to realize the banality of the life they would face. It had to have been something else.

She'd needed Rob's allegiance from the beginning. Against her parents, then against his mother. She needed to be first. But that night in Barbados, she was tired and cranky, unknowingly pregnant. The way Rob stared at Julia at dinner ratcheted things up . . . then Elsa called. Fireworks—and not the good kind. She needed him to choose. And he didn't choose her. How could she have wanted to make him choose between her and his mother? Maybe it was her fault. Partly.

Would she leave him over this?

Could she?

Dina had judged her own mother. Dismissed her as a narcissistic suburban princess. Put her in a box and barely tolerated her.

Now she was teaching Dina that life wasn't black and white but always, always gray.

"Dina, are you all right? You stopped talking."

In the end, it came down to one relationship. Yours. And then you didn't truly have control because there were two parties involved. And that presumed you even had control of yourself.

"Dina. Do you love him?" her mother asked.

"I hate him, but I love him."

"Exactly."

Chapter Thirty-Seven

Dina

Millburn, New Jersey, August 2001

Shivas, almost weekly. The Jewish tradition of "sitting" or staying housebound for a week after the funeral of an immediate relative, while friends bring obscene quantities of cookies, fruit, and deli to your house to prevent you from, God forbid, starving (wait for it) _to death_. She was headed to the Kleinmans' _shiva_, which reminded her of her father's two short months before.

Dina had placed the leftover _pareve_ cookies from her father's _shiva_ next to the brisket from Passover, a frozen collection of Jewish seminal events. Struggling with repurposing them for company or another _shiva_ months later, she knew she'd take a nibble, adjudge them to taste like cardboard, and throw them out. An ongoing dance. No matter how hard she tried to save herself the trouble, she couldn't bring herself to throw leftovers out when they were fresh.

Her mother, dressed in the perfect black Chanel suit with pearls, hair impeccably colored and coiffed, had remained completely silent throughout the funeral. She sat quietly solemn on the limousine ride back to the house, despite the kids laughing loudly as they retold the bawdy jokes her father had taught them. Rob stared out the window as if floating in the empty fields they passed.

Four hours later, after most of the funeral attendees had departed, Dina and her mom stood in the kitchen staring at the table laden with desserts.

"What the hell am I supposed to do with all this food?" her mother asked, dumping half-empty plates of cookies one atop the other.

"Mom, we'll just trash them, don't worry about it."

"Waste it? Just waste it?" She stooped and took Tupperware out of a drawer. "Your father and I didn't get where we are in life by wasting food. Your father and I . . ." Squeezing her hands together, she turned to Dina with tears in her eyes.

Dina held her mother while she cried, witnessing a crack in the protective armor of her Chanel. She was relieved for her mother and, glancing at the Tupperware, amused by the revelation that in some small way, despite the great lengths she'd gone to be anything but, she'd become her mother.

It happens to us all, Dina thought as she parked the car in front of the Kleinmans' and checked her lipstick. Just as, when you reached your fifties, *shivas* occurred so frequently that they popped up in daily conversation.

"I got my new plumber at the Friedmans' *shiva*, you know from Sherry, Bill's sister. Quality work, but a fortune."

Or, overheard at a West Village Italian restaurant:

"I heard about this place at the Cohens' *shiva*. Much better than the sloppy joes they served that day. The *bracciole* here is to die for. Oy, no pun intended," followed by much laughter.

All the merriment, the laughing, the hugging, the kissing— you almost forgot someone had died. This is the way Jews fend off the march of time, the harsh recognition of their own mortality.

Dina always made *mandelbrot* to bring to *shiva*. Jewish biscotti. It was a Passover recipe in which she swapped regular flour for matzo cake meal and potato starch; and pecans for walnuts. It was a hit. She was known for her *mandelbrot* community-wide, her signature dish, always wrapped appropriately for the occasion. No elaborate bows, just a tasteful black ribbon tying the cellophane over a white plastic plate. Her pantry was stocked with supplies to make up these packages, always ready for the next *event*.

It was around three o'clock when she walked in without ringing the doorbell, as was custom, and was greeted by Celia Kleinman, wife of the bereft.

"Oh, thank God, Dina is here with the *mandelbrot*," Celia announced to those within earshot. There were murmurs all around (as if the dining table was not stacked with mounds of cookies already). Word spread quickly, like when the mini hot dogs start coming out during the cocktail hour at a bar mitzvah; Jews swarming near the entrance from the kitchen like moths drawn to a flame.

"I'm freshening up my coffee and getting ready to dunk one of those. Thanks, they're my favorite," Morty exclaimed while kissing Dina with a mouth and hands decorated with crumbs. "Mmmm, yum. Oh, what's wrong with me? I'm sorry for your loss, too. Still sorry." She nodded to Morty, her dentist, as she grabbed a napkin from the dining room table, rubbed off her face, and brushed off her shirt. For a dentist, he sure ate a lot of sweets.

Dina headed into the kitchen and placed the cake on the table. She pushed on the garbage container's foot pedal, but the lid didn't budge, so she raised it gingerly with her hand to avoid the yuck and tossed in her napkin. Glancing out of the kitchen through the door to the dining room, she saw him.

Rob was standing with Matthew, Celia's husband and son of Gene, the deceased. They were deep in conversation, Rob's hand on Matthew's shoulder, mostly Matthew speaking and Rob nodding sympathetically. Rob raised his glass of soda and looked toward the kitchen counter right behind her, stocked with cold drinks and coffee. She and Rob had not seen or talked to each other since her father's death. Their eyes locked.

She was about to turn and walk out the back door when Rob mouthed her name and raised his hand signaling her to wait. He was smart not to speak aloud. Most people nearby were aware that Rob had moved out.

News traveled fast in this community. All it took was Rob using their friend Jill the realtor to find an apartment. What was he thinking? It had taken less than twenty-four hours for someone to come up to her in the supermarket and ask how she was doing.

Leave it to Shari Schwartz.

"Dina, are you okay?"

"Okay?" she answered tentatively, her sunglasses hiding her puffy eyes and her raincoat doing a poor job of covering her pajamas stuffed inside her Uggs.

"Yes, you know. Since the separation," Shari said sympathetically.

"I really don't know what you're talking about. But thanks for your concern." Suburbia. This is why people lived in New York City. How nice to be surrounded by people who couldn't care less if you lived or—there it was again—*died*.

Why had she not thought about the possibility of seeing Rob at the *shiva*? This *shiva*. They should have agreed to come different days, different times. If they were talking, that is. But here they were.

Rob headed over. She stared at him silently as he refilled two empty cups with Diet Coke. Dina put an ice cube in a cup to keep herself busy. She reached for the soda, but then thought better of it, and pivoted toward the alcohol. Funny, you were more likely to see the hard liquor at a *shiva* than a party. She was a vodka girl, but somehow decided a Scotch was in order. Filling half the cup, she sipped, pursing her lips at the taste, but took another.

"Dina, I need to bring this over to Matthew, but please, we need to talk. I'll be right back."

The Convention of Wives

Well, this was just so like him. Making her wait while he completed an act of kindness, of service to another. Nothing changed. She felt stuck to the tiles in the kitchen and took two large gulps of the Scotch, hoping they would magically provide the lubricant needed to lift her feet and exit. Her throat burned as she sipped and tears rolled down her cheeks.

"Dina, really, I didn't mean to upset you," Rob said as he returned and misinterpreted the tears.

"Rob, this is just not about you. About us. I drank some Scotch too quickly. I'm not upset."

"Great. I mean not great. But, okay, I misperceived. I apparently do that a lot where you are concerned. I'm not really aware of what you're thinking. I just project my reactions to things onto you. I've been doing it for a long time. I . . ."

"Rob," Dina asked as she placed her hand on his arm, "are you in therapy?"

"You can tell, right? I'm trying here. Really."

She nodded at him, letting only half the smile coming from her brain show on her lips as she took another sip of Scotch. This time it went down smoothly, warming her.

"Look, I want to talk. The past few months have been horrible," he said sweetly.

"Horrible. Oh. I'm so sorry for you," she said sarcastically.

"Horrible for both of us. I'm so sorry. We need to talk. But obviously not here. Can we go for coffee somewhere? Please. Dina, we have three kids, a family, for God's sake. A life together."

"A family, a life together, really? You've had months to call me, and you choose to speak to me here, in front of the world. Were you afraid to talk to me privately? Well, you should be!" Dina shouted.

He placed his hand on her shoulder. "Dina."

"Don't touch me!" she yelled, shoving his hand away and spilling her drink.

The kitchen fell silent. Even the two women helping out by the sink turned around to stare. Celia and Matthew, both now in the kitchen, came over to Dina and Rob.

"Look, maybe you two could take this somewhere else?" Matthew implored. People were moving out of the kitchen as if someone had yelled fire.

"Really, really sorry, guys. Dina, we need to leave," Rob said.

"I am so sorry. So sorry," Dina said to Celia and Matt as she took her cocktail napkin, bent, and tried to wipe up the spill. She watched as the writing on the napkins, *I've Always Been a Winer*, faded away. One of the women helping in the kitchen took the napkins out of her hand and waved her off.

"I need a ride home, Dina, to my place. I'm renting at the apartments on Hillside. I got a ride here. My car battery died yesterday."

It was the first good piece of news she'd heard in a long time, and she was happy her face was turned toward the floor. She was smiling. Maybe things weren't so perfect for him either.

"Yup, with everything else going on. Come on, let's go," Rob said as he grabbed her arm and helped her up.

Does he really think I'm supposed to feel sympathy for him? Dina turned to leave and then hesitated. She headed back to the counter filled with drinks, and took two cups and the almost empty bottle of Scotch.

"Dina, don't take that one." Celia, the hostess, grabbed a full bottle and put it in a plastic bag with the two cups. "*Merts Hashem*. Hopefully," she said. Celia, Celia the convert, speaking Yiddish. Caring whether she and Rob could save their marriage.

"What's with the booze?" Rob asked.

She didn't answer, and he seemed to let it go.

"The car needs to be washed. Don't you think?" Rob asked as if this was any other day.

What bullshit! He was lucky she was showering. She shot him a look and didn't respond.

The Convention of Wives

They'd driven a few minutes in silence when she made the turn into South Mountain Reservation, the place where they used to come on Sundays to take hikes with the kids.

"Dina, what are you doing? I thought you knew where the apartment was."

"I do."

The park was almost empty. She pulled into a spot and reached into the back seat for the Scotch. She could feel his eyes watching her as she filled the first cup and handed it to him. She filled the second and handed it to him as well, then closed the bottle and set it by her feet. Dina took back her cup.

They sipped and alternatively stole glances at each other and stared out the front of the car.

"This is not particularly responsible of us," Rob said.

"None of what's happened in the past few months has been particularly responsible of us. No, let me rephrase that. Nothing in the past twenty years has been particularly responsible of *you*." Dina could already feel the warm glow of the Scotch spreading to her legs. Her tongue felt thick as she continued. "You *shtupped* my best friend! I don't even remember when you and she could have had the time to spend alone together. I don't want to know. What were you thinking?"

"I wasn't thinking, Dina. I'm so sorry. I wasn't thinking." He reached over and put his hand on her thigh. She shook it off.

"Men. Always thinking with your dicks! I don't know what's worse. That you were with her or that you've lied to me all these years." She turned to look at him. "Wait, I'm probably an idiot. It wasn't just in Barbados, was it? How long did it go on? Oh, my God, all those times we got together over the years. Even later, on Maui? There too? After everything?"

"No, Dina no, it wasn't like that."

"Then what was it like? Maybe you've been together all these years and I just didn't know. All those conferences. That time in

Boston. I'm an idiot . . . I hate you!" She reached over and began smacking him wherever she could connect. His hands went up to block her but not before her engagement ring made hard contact with his left eye.

He screamed and she stopped. His right hand was covering his eye and his left was outstretched motioning for her to stop. "Shit, Dina! I think you might have scratched my cornea! Christ! I can see, but it's killing me."

Why the hell was she still wearing her rings? It hadn't occurred to her until that moment. "Do you think I give a shit about your eye!"

She started in again hitting him in the arm. It felt good.

"Stop. It was only that one time. I swear to you. That one stupid, stupid night. We were drunk, you and I had been fighting. Julia and I, we—"

"Julia and I! We! I can't even listen to you. You liar. Liar! We have children, a life. It's a lie. It's all a lie. I don't know who you are . . . I don't know any—"

"You know who I am. You know who I am, who we are," he beseeched her. "I love you. I made a mistake, a horrible mistake, but I love you. I've always loved you. Please, what can I do, what can I . . ."

"If you love me, why did you leave me? Why didn't you tell me what was going on? All those years. You had all those years to tell me. Why didn't you come to me?"

"At first I was ashamed of what I'd done. Then, there never seemed like the right time. You were pregnant with Daniel. There was never a good time. Life was busy, crazy."

"Never a good time? You had years to tell me. And you've had months to call me."

"You're right, you're right. But with every year that passed, it just seemed less important. They were out of our lives . . . the Kinsellas. And then Maui happened, and I almost told you. It brought everything back. But then we got home, and life went on. What good would it have done?"

"I'm the last one to know. The kids all know, they must know; well, Allie certainly knows. I'm an idiot. An idiot. The way you used to look at Julia. You think I didn't notice. I'm not blind. You probably always wanted her . . . all those times we were together. Oh, my God. That's why . . . you're why . . . why she stopped talking to me all those years ago. I thought she was my friend! I thought you were my . . . my . . . my everything. And none of it's real!" She started laughing, then sobbing, then hiccupping. Snot was running into her mouth.

"The only thing that is real is us. Dina, *we* are real. That one night was an aberration. We were young, I think we were drunk. It meant nothing."

He took out his handkerchief and handed it to her. She blew her nose and wiped her face.

"It didn't mean *nothing*. You must have been unhappy with me. On some level."

"I was unhappy that you were unhappy. My mother was unhappy. I felt like I had to make you both happy all the time and keep the peace between you. I was frustrated at work and felt like I was failing at home. It was all exhausting."

"We were both exhausted. It was hard. But I could have been better about things. About your mother."

"It *was* hard."

He took her hands in his. His were warm. She'd missed them. She'd missed him.

"But now there's a child. A sick child. Shit, Rob. You and Julia have a daughter together. It's why you walked out on me."

"I didn't know what to say."

"It all makes sense now. All of it."

He shook his head, picked up the bottle, and refilled their

glasses. His left eye was shut and swollen. It looked like he was winking at her. *Some joke.* They both sipped.

"When did you first know?" she asked.

"About Rosie? Allie called me after Rosie had some diagnostic and genetic tests run. Aiden had called Allie and started asking some questions about all of us. I mean you and me, and Julia and John. The kids put it together."

"I feel so stupid. I don't even know what to feel. I'm angry at you and Julia. Why couldn't you and I help each other through that time more instead of being so angry with each other?"

"I don't think we had the skills then."

"You're right."

"The question is, do we have them now?"

"I don't know; I feel so stupid. I'm still angry and, I guess, embarrassed by it all. And I'm upset about Rosie. She's yours, Rob. And Julia's. I can't believe those words are coming out of my mouth."

"I know." He put his head in his hands and looked down.

"Let me look at your eye."

He sat up and reluctantly opened his eye to show her but grunted and closed it quickly.

She reached up and put her hand on his cheek. "We'll have to take you somewhere to get that looked at. I'm sorry I wounded you."

"No, I'm sorry I wounded you."

He was right. He had. Deeply. But it had been so long ago. They'd been kids. They had shared twenty more years of life between then and now.

He took her hand in his and gently kissed each finger. Still winking ridiculously at her, he came closer and softly kissed her cheek, then lips. Her response was hesitant at first and then more urgent. He unbuttoned her blouse and she reached for his belt buckle. They moved like klutzy teenagers, all knees and elbows. But eventually she felt him inside her as her head banged rhythmically against the door window.

"Wait, stop—stop, this is crazy. Rob, stop!"

It took him awhile, like a Ferris wheel that keeps on spinning after the operator has pulled the lever.

"Sorry, I'm sorry." He got off her and pulled her to sitting. "I guess we got a little carried away." He buttoned her shirt.

She kissed the top of his head.

"Let's go home," she suggested.

"Home? Are you sure?"

She nodded.

"I'd like that."

The next morning, Dina turned over in bed to see a familiar sight, Rob snoring gently next to her. She turned around and backed her hips into Rob. Without waking, he turned over and put his arm around her and nuzzled her neck. The bandage they'd placed over his eye at the Urgi Center made him look like a pirate. But he was her pirate. They were spooning. *Could it be this easy?*

They decided to meet with Julia and John together, if the other couple would agree. To make amends, to move forward. To help Rosie, if they could. But first, she needed to talk to Julia alone.

Chapter Thirty-Eight

Allie

New York, New York, August 2001

The line outside the Bitter End reached from Bleecker to Thompson. Mostly people Allie's age and younger dressed flimsily for the August warmth. Allie didn't see their group at first, but then Aiden waved her over. Everyone was there. Everyone, except Rosie. All the folks she'd met over eight months ago in the emergency room. The moment she had witnessed the beginning of the unraveling that changed all their lives. She had thought of that moment in terms of "before" and "after."

After the diagnosis, first Mrs. Kinsella and then Bridget and Aiden had taken Rosie for her biweekly infusions. In time, Allie and Zoe had also rallied around their new half-sister. Bridget seemed to be having the hardest time accepting the situation. She had barely made eye contact with Allie the few times they'd run into each other at the hospital. But as Rosie improved, her symptoms abating and her energy level almost back to normal, even Bridget seemed to become more accepting of their strange, new, merged family.

Raj arrived, and Allie watched him shake hands with Aiden. The two seemed locked in a titanic grip until she interceded. For several months after the publication of the *Times* piece, Aiden had wanted nothing to do with her roommate. Frankly, neither did she. But she and Raj had found their way back to each other.

"Hey, let go of my roomie," she said, giving them both hugs. "Come on, we should head in. It looks like rain."

The line started moving. Outside the door, the event poster read:

LEAVE A LASTING MARK CONCERTS PRESENTS
OUR VOLUNTEER SINGERS AND MUSICIANS IN
SONGS OF MADONNA
$10 DONATION TO
THE NATIONAL GAUCHER FOUNDATION

Rosie had met someone from Leave a Lasting Mark through work and made a play to have them hold one of their fundraisers for the Gaucher Foundation, the nonprofit now so close to all of their hearts. Rosie had sung frequently in school productions when she was younger, but it had taken an illness to get her back on stage.

As they moved farther into the dark club, Allie shoved Aiden by accident. Aiden turned around and Allie raised her hands, offering an apology. Aiden misunderstood, high-fived her, turned around, and headed to the seating area. The sign on their table said RESERVED KINSELLA/WASSERMAN FAMILY. That was weird.

Raj, Aiden, and Allie sat together. Next to the sign with their families' names was another that said there was a three-drink minimum. She almost laughed out loud when Raj asked the waiter for a Tom Collins, something he'd undoubtedly heard ordered in one of the old movies that they had spent years watching on Sunday afternoons, zoning out between studying. He rarely drank anything.

"Beer or wine?" the waiter asked, looking at Raj like he was nuts.

"He'll have a Miller Lite," Allie interjected, rescuing him.

"Hey, I see the usual cast of characters here," Raj whispered. "Are Rosie's parents—I mean, you know—the Kinsellas, coming?"

"No, still a little tense there. We decided since my folks couldn't be here anyway, we'd keep it just us younger members of the family."

"And me?" Raj asked.

"Including you," Allie said, warmly patting his chest. "I said family."

The place filled rapidly, and the noise level was soon ridiculously high. She wished she'd brought earplugs. The Kinsellas and Wassermans were chatting away amiably. She was conscious of Aiden sitting closely to her left, could almost feel his body heat.

"So, without this new water project being approved, the current infrastructure will just continue to erode, and by let's say 2040, maybe 2050 at the latest, we'll turn on the tap one day and nothing. Just drip, drip, then nothing! And these politicians . . ." Zoe was talking and Allie was trying to follow, but the background noise combined with her lack of interest made her miss every other word. She kept nodding and quickly finished her beer.

Two girls emerged from backstage holding hands and she momentarily wondered where the night was going. After all, this was 2001 and they were in the Village. She wasn't exactly surprised by the whole thing anymore and, upon closer inspection, she could understand the attraction. One of the girls was hot!

She was wearing a black V-neck blouse with short sleeves tucked into a matching straight skirt. The outfit was so tight, she wasn't sure why the buttons on the blouse weren't popping off. Her long, curly hair was struggling to be contained inside a blond wig cut in a short edgy tomboy style. She looked gorgeous. The other girl headed for the bar, but the sex bomb headed directly over to them.

The Convention of Wives

She quickly said hello to everyone at the other end of their table, but Allie couldn't hear what she was saying. Then she seemed to make a beeline toward Allie, Aiden, and Raj. It was . . . Rosie!

Allie couldn't believe this was the same pale girl from months before in the patient gown hooked up to the IV. She looked so alive and healthy that she finally understood the term *medical miracle*. How lucky Rosie was to have been diagnosed in the decade she was, when treatment for Gaucher was available. Medicine, Allie thought, was a lot about timing. Like the pneumonia Elsa, her grandmother, was currently battling, diseases that years ago had been death sentences were now simply treated with antibiotics.

Rosie gave Allie a big hug, but then all her attention seemed to be riveted on Raj. Allie strained to hear their conversation as she stared at the two.

"Raj, I'm really glad you could make it. Allie wasn't sure you'd be here," she said as she bent down close to him—Allie assumed—because of the noise.

Allie could tell that Raj was uncomfortable. He was staring at Rosie's face, but his eyes kept drifting south where they seemed to be pulled by some outside force.

"Yes, I'm sorry I haven't stopped by to see you lately at the hospital. I've just been a little busy with applications and interviews. But I'm really glad to be here," he said, picking up his glass and toasting her. He laughed nervously and reached for his beer bottle, but it was empty.

"You might want to get another one, especially after you've heard me sing," Rosie laughed, giving him a big smile. "I was wondering what happened to you, I missed seeing you."

Missed seeing him? Allie saw drops of perspiration making their way down Raj's forehead. What was wrong with him? He was acting like an adolescent.

Rosie pulled something out of the black lacy bra that peeked out of her shirt and handed it to Raj. It was a white handkerchief trimmed in lace.

"Here, you look like you could use this. But, hold onto that. Dr. Wasserman's . . . I mean Rob's mother . . . my grandmother, Elsa, sent it to me for good luck because she couldn't be here tonight."

Elsa had given Rosie a handkerchief?

"Are you sure you want me to keep it?" he asked, blotting his brow, then offering it back, not sure what to do.

"Yes. Just hold onto it and look up at me when I'm on stage. Look at me like you did in the hospital, and I'll know everything will be all right."

The way he looked at her? She remembered the way he looked at her!

"Okay, sure," Raj said, smiling from ear to ear.

Allie took a gulp of her wine and tried not to look at Raj.

There were six singers before Rosie got up on stage. Four were pretty horrible. Two, not so bad. And then a backdrop of a beach scene unfurled, and there was Rosie, singing Madonna's "Cherish." The size of the stage limited the amount of horizontal writhing on the beach she could manage, as did her favoring of her left leg, still healing from the break after all these months. But her other movements more than made up for both.

Rosie engaged the audience but mainly kept looking back at Raj. And Allie saw that Raj didn't take his eyes off Rosie, just as he had promised. *What the hell? Am I jealous?*

After wild applause and a standing ovation, Aiden nudged her. "Hey, Doctor Girl? How about an update on your exciting life in medicine?" Aiden asked. She turned around to face him. He was a welcome distraction.

Chapter Thirty-Nine

Dina

New York, New York, September 2001

The Museum of Natural History was near Julia's new apartment and an easy subway ride from Penn Station. The museum had a café that served an acceptable sandwich and deplorable coffee. Dina doubted whether either one of them would have much of an appetite.

It was hot and humid when she climbed out of the subway and headed toward the entrance on Central Park West. Memories flooded her mind of Allie and Zoe's insistence that they return yearly, Allie team fauna, Zoe team flora, and Daniel unable to decide between the mineral exhibit and the dinosaurs. A hot dog or soft pretzel on the way home always made for a peaceful return to suburbia.

And there was Julia standing beneath the T. rex in the main lobby. Was it unkind for Dina to think it an appropriate pairing? What had her own mother said about her own responsibility? She was right. Dina had been culpable. But, taking a look at Julia, she suddenly wasn't so sure.

Julia was looking at the dinosaur, her back to Dina. It wasn't nice to be staring unseen, but Dina couldn't help it. She performed a dissection of Julia's outfit, a mix of GAP and designer knockoffs. Julia's hair, pulled back in a ponytail, was longer than

Dina remembered. She had the ass of a twenty-year-old. All that running she did. No, it had to be genetic.

As if hearing her unspoken thought, Julia turned to face Dina and headed over.

Dina's face was warm, embarrassment filling her pores.

"Hi," Julia said.

"Hey," Dina responded.

Awkward hug.

"Where do you want to go?"

"Oh, do you have a ticket already?"

"We're members," Dina explained. "We joined when the kids were young and just kept sending in our annual donation."

"Oh. We have a great museum now in Atlanta."

Were they seriously going to go down the path of comparing New York and Atlanta? Especially when Julia was now a New Yorker.

"I took one of the maps. It shows you where to go. Oh, you probably already know that," Julia said.

"Wherever you like. I've seen it all. Well, maybe there's a new temporary exhibit."

She handed Julia her pamphlet. They looked together.

"Spiders. There is something new about spiders. Is that too gross or . . ."

"No. Spiders are fine," Julia answered.

Of course, they were.

"How is Rosie feeling?" Dina asked as they headed inside and she showed her membership and guest passes.

"She's doing much better, but the treatments aren't easy. I can barely watch when they hook her up to the infusions."

Dina couldn't see into Julia's eyes—they were walking side by side—but she watched her pinch the bridge of her nose. How could she be so angry, so disappointed in this friend of hers, and still feel so deeply sorry for her.

The Convention of Wives

"I feel terrible for what she's going through. What *you're* going through," Dina offered.

"What we're all going through."

"We? What *we* are you referring to? You and Rob? You think you can so easily make this right? Suddenly, we're all on the same team? What did I ever do but be your friend? Be his wife?"

Julia stopped and turned to Dina in front of a glass case of colorful ceramics. "I'm so sorry for everything." Her words ended in a sob as she grabbed Dina in a hug.

Dina was surprised at how quickly Julia had gotten to the apology. Even more surprised that her friend, who wasn't the hugging kind, had grabbed her. Dina's stiffness gave way, and she hugged Julia back. They stayed connected that way for a while.

"Is everything all right?" a young, female security guard asked.

The two women parted.

"Not really. But we're okay. Thanks," Dina answered. She linked arms with Julia. "Come on, let's get out of here. We need a drink."

"I'm not drinking anymore. Not since Rosie's diagnosis."

"Oh."

"Yeah. Chardonnay had become one of my major food groups over the last few years, even before . . ." She shook her head.

"Okay, then. Let's go get some really shitty coffee. You're still drinking coffee, right?"

Julia nodded.

"Come on." Dina led the way past the butterfly exhibit and the plains of Africa to the basement museum cafeteria.

She was about to put her usual condiments in her coffee when she saw Julia taking it black. She put the milk pitcher down. They headed over to a table in a corner away from the registers.

They both took a sip and made equally disappointed faces.

"*Uch.* You called that one," Julia said.

"Some things don't change." Dina regretted the phrase as soon as it slipped from her mouth. She wondered what Julia thought she meant by it.

"And some things do. We've both moved on. Some of it by choice, some of it not. I wasn't sure about Rosie for years. I thought it was possible, her being Rob's, but I shut it out of my mind. Then so much time had passed."

Julia looked at her searchingly. Waiting.

"I'm not sure what you want me to say," Dina said.

"What I *want* you to say? God, Dina, something compassionate, maybe. I don't know how many times I need to apologize. This didn't just happen to you. It happened to all of us, mostly to Rosie."

"Of course, I know that. But, Julia, you were my friend. How could you do that to me? To your husband?"

"I didn't do it to you. I did it to myself."

"What the fuck is that supposed to mean. You slept with my husband."

"And he slept with me. Slept. If you think a drunken coupling on a beach has anything to do with sleeping—"

"Shut up. Just shut up."

"I didn't mean that." She sipped her coffee.

"I don't know what you mean. Why would you agree to meet with me if not to apologize?"

"I said I was sorry. But it's not enough. We're all supposed to line up to give you an apology for what we did to you?"

"I can't believe you're talking to me like this. I was your friend. We—Rob and I—were your friends. Weren't we? How could you do that to John?"

"Do you think we really knew each other?"

"What? Who?"

"Back then. You and me. Do you think we really knew each other?"

Dina took a sip of her bad coffee. "I thought we did. The phone calls, the letters, all the things we talked about."

"Well, you thought wrong. I mean yeah, we shared a lot of discussions about our lives, our husbands, our kids. But neither of us ever revealed too much about who we really were. What about all the days in between our letters. Our phone calls. What about all the crap we'd gone through with our own families. It never, ever came up."

"Maybe I didn't have the crap to share with you that you had to share with me. I don't remember."

"Well, I do. I remember because mostly I wouldn't have been able to share some of what I felt about my parents, my brothers with you. I hadn't dealt with it myself then. It was embarrassing what I was feeling."

"But you told me about your father. The drinking. You shared some things with me."

"I did. That's true. But did you ever share anything about yourself with me. Not Rob, not the kids, but *you*. You always presented this pretty picture of yourself. Your family. You still do. Always in control. Your parents, the house you grew up in. It all seemed too perfect."

"It was far from perfect." *She should only know.*

"Well, how the hell would I have known that? You never opened up to me really. I think our relationship was kind of shallow."

Shallow?

Was Julia being serious, or was she just being defensive? Dina couldn't really tell. And she'd thought of their friendship as the closest she'd ever come to a soul mate besides Rob. She'd measured all her subsequent girlfriends against Julia, and they'd all come up wanting. She was totally confused by what Julia was saying. But had she ever spoken to Julia about her dysfunctional family? Or had she been too proud to share that bit of information.

"That night. Rob wanted me. It's as simple as that. I wanted him too. I wanted him to want me more than you. That night. I needed him to. It had nothing to do with you."

"What do you mean nothing to do with me?"

"I mean, you weren't who he needed that night. I was. And he was what I needed. I'm not talking about the sex. That was almost inconsequential. We both had screwed up childhoods. I just remember him being really sweet and caring, I was thinking how lucky you were—"

Dina stood up. "Enough. I don't need to hear any more. I thought we were going to get to a different place today. To move on. I thought you were just going to apologize."

"Then you thought wrong."

Dina considered walking out. This was a mistake. But, instead, she sat back down. "Did you always hate me like this?"

"I wanted a little of what I thought you had. I didn't hate you. It's taken me a long time to understand. This had nothing to do with you. I hated myself. I'm done with that."

"What am I to you, just collateral damage? Our friendship meant nothing to you?"

"I don't think I was really capable of being a friend back then. I think we both served a purpose for each other. We deflected a lot of the resentment we felt toward our husbands, toward their careers. Toward the limitations placed on our lives. But I'm not sure about us. I don't know if we'd have been friends without all that."

"Are you saying that women only become friends based on their circumstances at the time? It's not about who they are as people, but about what they're going through?"

"I guess. Something like that."

"That's sad. I'd like to think it was more."

"Yeah. Me too. I'm just not sure anymore."

Dina's foot was shaking under the table. She hesitantly took Julia's hand in hers.

"Well, right now we both are going through something together. We share Rosie. All of us. I don't agree with your take on what we were to each other. Maybe it feels better to you to look back and think that way, but I don't believe it. Regardless, we need to be friends now or at least to get along. For Rosie. We need to agree to that. To something."

Julia looked at Dina with an air of resignation. "I'll agree that this coffee sucks. Can we start with that?"

Chapter Forty

Julia

New York, New York, November 2001

Julia wondered why Dina had picked this Midtown restaurant. The orange linoleum floor was stained and graying. The aqua upholstered seating in the booths and on the metal stools by the counter made it look like a poorly overhauled Howard Johnson's. Even the holiday decorations didn't help. Maybe it was a fitting choice after the horror of September. Who cared anymore about restaurant choices, especially for this meeting?

"I'm only here because of Rosie," John said. "She is my daughter; she will always be my daughter."

"I want to thank you for agreeing to meet like this, I'm sure it's awkward," Dina said.

"Awkward . . . what are you, the queen of understatement?" John asked with a bite in his voice.

"Look, there's really no need for you to talk to her like that; this is uncomfortable for all of us," Rob said.

"Oh, really. Coming to the ladies' rescue once again. Let me get this straight, you're sitting here with your wife and my wife, at the same table, and you've fucked them both," John shouted. He subdued his voice as the other diners looked their way. "You feel uncomfortable. Well, isn't that just too damn bad?"

The Convention of Wives

"Please, John. There is no need for this. It was over twenty years ago. It was meaningless. We're here for Rosie. Try to control yourself. We have a sick child. We all have a sick child," Julia pleaded. Now she understood why Dina had picked this place. Anonymity. She must have known the conversation would go south.

John covered his mouth and closed his eyes as the foursome sat in thick silence.

The waitress came over and placed a plate of fresh donuts on the table between them.

"I think you've got the wrong table," Rob said politely.

"I have exactly the right table," she said. "You all are clearly in need of some donuts. On me. Just give me a big tip. Enjoy." The waitress had to be in her seventies, with a gravelly voice that shouted two packs of cigarettes a day and an attitude. "Anybody need more coffee?" she asked sweetly.

"Sure, fill me up," John said, pushing his cup toward the waitress.

"I guess the main thing is that we need to present some kind of united front to Rosie. With everything she's going through, it would be so much healthier psychologically if we four came to terms of some kind," Dina said.

The waitress finished pouring coffee, then came back and filled their glasses one by one. Julia watched the water pour from the aqua blue pitcher. *The four of us, coming to terms.* What was the saying, *you can start over as many times as you like?*

"Julia, you're really quiet. Nothing left to say, huh? No other secrets lurking that I should know about?" John prodded, shoving the plate of donuts her way.

"John, please, we've been through all this. No more secrets." She shoved the donuts back. "Dina and Rob don't need to witness us going at each other."

John grabbed a Boston creme and took a big, gooey bite. "Okay. Let's say we can find a way for Rosie to think that we've come to some adult, sophisticated way of forgetting what actually happened that resulted in her birth and illness," he mumbled, his mouth full of donut. "What are we talking about here, shared custody? Because if you think—"

"She's twenty-three, there's no need for anything like that," Dina interjected.

"What we are trying to say is that we want to share in any medical expenses that you might incur and—" Rob began.

"I don't need your fucking money!" John shouted. "You people, you think money solves everything, don't you?" He swallowed the remaining donut, wiped his mouth, and breathed in deeply. "I'm sorry I said that. I don't know where that came from."

"You have a right to be angry, John. Mostly at me, though. I lied to you. Once to protect you from knowing who I really was, and then because I was ashamed of what I'd done," Julia pleaded. "But please, please don't take this out on them."

"There's more than enough blame to go around. We made a mistake. A big mistake. We were so young. But we're not kids, anymore, any of us; and if we can't figure out how to move forward for Rosie's sake, then I don't think we're worth much as adults or as parents," Rob said.

John sighed heavily. Chastened, he looked at his lap. "You're right," he said. "We're not in control of anything. But my emotions haven't caught up with what I've been thinking. I'm still raw. I just can't be expected to process this and then turn around and . . ."

"No one here is asking you to do that. But we need to expedite the healing. For Rosie. She needs us now, not a year from now. Sometime in the future, she may have a need to know who Rob is. We hope you can get to a place where that is okay," Dina said.

"I know. I know."

Julia knew it was easier for John to hear this from Dina.

The Convention of Wives

"Rosie may want to get to know our whole family a bit better. She suddenly has three half siblings," Rob added. "Siblings who share something else, unfortunately. The possibility that they are carriers of this illness. We've had all of ours tested, and we're still waiting for the results. We presume that you've had yours tested, as well?" Rob asked.

"We've been so busy taking care of Rosie we haven't even talked to them about getting tested. I don't know if they've done that on their own. John, have they talked to you about this?" Julia asked.

"About this? No. They'll barely pick up the phone. Somehow, I've become the bad guy here. You've seen to that. I haven't spoken to them much since the separation. It's killing me," John said flatly.

They all sat, sipping their coffee. Rob cut a piece of the jelly donut with surgical precision and put it on his plate, eating it with his knife and fork. The waitress came over and re-filled their cups.

"We need to move forward—you're right, Dina—all of us together as far as Rosie is concerned. I'll take care of making sure our kids are all tested. Julia, we'll talk to them . . . this week . . . together. It'll be easier in person since I'm up here already. They don't know how complicated life can become. I'll make sure they understand you weren't the only one responsible here."

Julia saw Rob stop chewing and look up at John.

"I'm talking about me," John said to Rob's unasked question. "Julia, when Rosie asks about getting to know Rob better, it'll just have to be all right with me. I'll work on getting there. Is everyone okay with that?"

The others nodded.

Rob reached for the check, but John grabbed it first. "I've got this."

Chapter Forty-One

Dina

Newark, New Jersey, November 2001

After all these years of not practicing nursing, Dina was amazed at how the smells and sights of a hospital came back to her. The combined odors of disinfectant, urine, and sweat; the fluorescent bulbs tricking patients and staff into feeling like they were living in endless daylight. Time seemed to stand still, wreaking havoc on sleep cycles and hormone levels. How had the experience left such an imprint on the circuitry of her brain?

It was three o'clock in the middle of the night and one of the few times Dina was thankful for Rob's MD plates as they pulled into the one remaining doctor's space in the ER parking lot. Rob had awakened and quickly taken the phone call when it came, his years of residency and on call kicking into gear. Dina had stirred but, having honed the complementary talent for falling back to sleep once Rob grabbed the beeper or his phone, began to lightly doze. She heard him say "my mother" and "I'll be right there."

"What are you doing?"

"Dina, go back to sleep. It's my mother."

"What's going on?" she said, then added, "I'm coming with you," before he had a chance to answer.

It stunned her how quickly the two of them were out the door.

The Convention of Wives

...

Rob walked up to the desk, introduced himself as Dr. Wasserman to the woman with bad highlights and claw-like nails, and explained that his mother had been admitted.

"Cubicle five, back through the doors that—"

"I know the fucking way," he shouted at the clerk, who recoiled as if physically struck. Rob stormed off.

"Rob!" Dina admonished, turning and mouthing *sorry* to the woman who shrugged and went back to her computer screen. She must get abused like this all the time, Dina thought sadly.

"I'm sorry," he said, pressing the large metal plate that opened the automatic doors. "It's just that with everything she's been through in her life, she's never been taken to the hospital like this. She calls me about everything, but not about a medical emergency? Shit."

Dina saw how concerned he was and squeezed his arm to comfort him as they reached cubicle five. They pulled back the pastel print curtain and entered.

Elsa seemed to be sleeping, her breathing labored. She was hooked up to an IV, and multiple wires led to a monitor measuring her pulse, heartrate, and oxygen level. Tears wetted Dina's eyes. For all the angst between Elsa and herself over the years, seeing her mother-in-law like this, so vulnerable, was heartbreaking.

"Jesus, I'm going to get the attending." Rob left the cubicle so quickly, he startled Fran, Elsa's neighbor, who had been dozing on a chair beside Elsa's gurney.

"Oh, Dina, I'm so glad you're here. She insisted I not call you; she was concerned about waking Rob up. Something about him never getting a good night's sleep, always being on call."

Always worried about Rob.

"And then she insisted on coming here to the Beth. Things

happened so quickly. Anyway, once we were here, I knew I needed to reach you. I'm so sorry."

"Please, there's no need to apologize, Fran. Thank you so much for getting her here. She hasn't been feeling well all week. I was planning on taking her to the doctor tomorrow. She's so stubborn sometimes, I . . . well, you know."

"I know your mother-in-law pretty well. She still thinks of Rob, and you, as children."

"I'm not sure she's ever thought of me as one of her children," Dina mumbled. And then, seeing the look on Fran's face, continued, "You know, Fran, now that Rob and I are here, I think you really should go home. We'll update you tomorrow. Let's get you a cab."

"Oh, no, I have my car parked right outside. They don't let people ride in the ambulance. I'll head home, but please call me. Tell Rob I'm hoping for the best."

"Of course, of course," Dina answered, not sure whether to worry more about Fran's safety driving late at night or anyone on the road who might cross her path.

"And, Dina, you're wrong. She's all bluster, that one. You've given her three beautiful grandchildren, and you've made her son happy. What more could she ask for?"

Dina hugged Fran and helped her gather her pocketbook, coat, gloves, and hat. She left a moment before Rob returned.

"She's stable, but it's definitely pneumonia again. I don't know how they got a film done so quickly. I don't understand how I didn't see it. My own mother. How could I have let her get this bad?"

"Rob, this is not your fault. You're her son, not her physician. You can't always feel like her medical status is your responsibility. We've seen her twice this week. It seemed like a bad cold to both of us. I was taking her to the doctor tomorrow."

"I know, but I should have picked up on it." He pulled the chair closer to Elsa, reached out, and held her hand.

The Convention of Wives

As if kissed by a prince, Elsa opened her eyes.

"Mom, you're going to be just fine. We're at the hospital with you. You need to be on some IV antibiotics, but you'll be as good as new in a few days. Dina's here, too."

Elsa glanced over at Dina, turned back to Rob, and nodded her head up and down, signaling her understanding. Coughing violently, she struggled to pull herself upward to a seated position. Rob helped his mother adjust herself in the bed, while Dina held tissues to Elsa's mouth and gathered the ugly green phlegm. Elsa stopped coughing and sat back.

"I need to tell you both something. I need—" The coughing began again, and Rob once more helped Elsa to sit, supporting her.

"Mom, shh, stop trying to talk. You need to rest. Please."

Elsa would have none of it.

"Water, I need some water," she demanded.

Dina poured some of the water from the pink plastic pitcher and handed it to Elsa, who sipped slowly.

"It is all my fault. I've thought about this for months now. I didn't know how to tell you both. But it makes so much sense."

"Mom, you really need to rest."

"Rob, don't tell me to be quiet. I have to say this. I know how this goes. I'm sick; at my age, I might die. I need to tell you both something now, before—"

"You're not going to die, Mom," Dina said, dismissively, tired of Elsa's exaggeration. "Anything you have to tell us can wait. Rob's right, just get some rest."

"You know, Dina, not everything in this world works out the way you planned. You of all people should know that by now," Elsa said, staring at her.

Even in bed, sick with pneumonia, Elsa hadn't lost her ability to wound Dina.

"Sorry. I know you think I'm being difficult. But there is

something you have to know. It's my fault, too. Rosie, that young girl, her illness. It's all my fault." Elsa began to cry, then cough.

After the fit had subsided, Rob insisted that Elsa not speak. And, finally, she listened. She put her head back on the pillow and was soon dozing.

Dina and Rob stepped outside the cubicle.

"What the hell was she talking about?" Dina asked.

"I have no idea. It's not unusual for someone her age, in this condition, to get a bit delusional. I don't think she knows what she's saying. I'm going to go and get some coffee. There's a vending machine in the waiting room. It's going to be a long night. Can I get you anything?"

"No, not now. I'm okay. I'm going to get her another blanket, and I'll just stay here with her."

Dina got a blanket from one of the aides, went back inside, and tucked in her mother-in-law, who didn't stir. Dina stared at the rise and fall of Elsa's chest, making sure she was still breathing. She knew the monitor nearby would alert her loudly with any precipitous change in her mother-in-law's condition, but she couldn't stop watching the movement of the blanket lying over Elsa's thin rib cage.

Rob returned about ten minutes later with coffee. Perhaps it was the smell that woke Elsa. She looked at both of them.

"Sit me up," she demanded.

"Mom, please."

"I said, sit me up."

Rob raised the head of the bed to an even higher angle and Dina propped Elsa's pillows to better support her.

"You need to listen to me, both of you. Years ago, in Barbados, when we came from Italy, before we got to the United States, something happened. Rob, you were too young to remember. Your cousin Ronnie's father—Ronnie who passed away? His father, Rolph. It was after the war. Rolph came to stay with us for a while, to help us move to the United States. Your father was so ill. It was a difficult time. We had a young maid helping us. She took care of you. You really took to her. I was so busy with your father. I ignored something I knew was happening in my own house. What was I thinking?"

Elsa breathed heavily.

"Mom, you're confused. Can't we hear this when you feel better?" Rob grabbed both of Elsa's hands.

"No, you have to hear this now. I'm not confused. The maid, the maid . . . her name was Rosie."

AFTER

Dina

New York, NY, June 2004

Dina was mesmerized by the light dancing off the large chandelier, its multicolored crystals hanging from metal spikes. In an attempt to diminish her sudden dizziness, she brought her gaze downward, but instead of the dull surface she craved, she was assailed by the sight of mint green marble, its veins pulsating on the floor and matching staircase. She'd barely regained her footing when the young event planner prompted her toward the flight of steps, where black-and-white photographs of punk rock musicians were hung on mica-embedded grass-cloth wallpaper, making the entryway a dazzling jewel box of reflected light.

"There's an elevator for anyone who's elderly or handicapped. The rest of the party walked up already. Are you sure you're comfortable walking? Can I help with your things?" the girl asked.

Dina's shoes were killing her, and she could feel the sweat under her arms. "I'm fine," she lied, holding tight to the railing.

The kids had insisted on this event space. They liked the "vibe." And, now, as she looked down through the Plexiglas at the crowd gathered in the ballroom below, she saw family and friends, a sea of swirling colors, strangers who would soon become inextricably linked by the festivities to come. Dottie and her mother sat next to each other in the bride's section, along with Dina's mother-in-law, Elsa. She couldn't believe they were actually going to be experiencing this moment, especially after the tumult of the last several years. It was time for some happiness . . . for all of them. Life was a constant revelation.

Dina headed downstairs, leaving Rob and the kids to finish dressing. She entered the gilded dining room and looked over at the table next to the buffet. There sat the items she and Rob had had delivered at the groom's request, as a surprise for his bride, to represent the melding of their family histories—the oversized challah from Tom the baker and the Shabbat candlesticks from both Rob and Dina's families. For all the years they'd fought about whose family history was more profound, suddenly it didn't matter; the candlesticks signified to both of them the passing of tradition between generations. And it was a time for traditions, as many as they could celebrate.

Rob appeared in the ballroom as she saw the Kinsellas sitting nearby. Dina noticed the dresses she and Julia wore were different versions of mother-of-the-bride, beige and attractive without being overly bejeweled. She wondered if Julia had given as much thought as she to the careful balance of pretty and invisible, knowing full well that any thought of drawing attention away from the bride at their stage of life was delusional. Dina still wasn't sure what she and Julia meant to each other, if anything. She wondered if they'd ever get together again, just the two of them. She also wondered who the guy with the ponytail was seated next to Julia. It certainly wasn't John, who sat a few chairs away looking anywhere but at his ex-wife.

As the processional began, Dina looked at her family, making a motherly inventory of sorts. Some things never changed. The kids had all cleaned up nicely. Zoe looked beautiful in a lilac concoction that accented her coloring. Daniel was so handsome in his dark suit. And finally, Allie, walking down the aisle with Aiden, the two so right on each other's arms.

The quartet began playing the song "At Last," and they all stood as the bride entered.

Rosie walked slowly up the aisle alone, her gown white Irish brocade. Her dark hair was pulled back in a loose chignon, and a veil made of a lace handkerchief was attached at the nape of her neck. Her hennaed hands held a bouquet of hydrangeas, tied with a ribbon of Scottish tartan. She halted halfway up the aisle.

Raj came toward her from underneath the canopy of yellow roses, stopping briefly to receive an embrace from his parents. He'd explained that the canopy would serve as neither a *chuppah* nor *mandap,* but something in between. Everything about this wedding was in between. His father kissed both of his cheeks before Raj continued to meet Rosie and escort her up the aisle.

They were married in a ceremony of their own creation, combining Hindu, Christian, and Jewish traditions.

Raj led Rosie around in a circle twice, and then they reversed with Rosie leading, all the while family members reading blessings aloud.

"With the first turn, we pray for happiness in the union of the couple."

"With the second turn, we pray for a long life filled with contentment, love, and companionship."

"With the third turn, we pray for the healthy life of the couple."

"With the fourth turn. Ho! Let the mountains of the world dance! Let the gates of cities ring with the sounds of joy, song, merriment, and delight—the voice of the groom and the voice of the bride, the happy shouts of their friends and companions."

The couple's vows were heartfelt and personal, Rosie promising Raj to always be his best friend, to be there with a hug when he needed it, to share in the joy they would create together. Raj promised pancakes on Sunday morning, to be a true partner in all they experienced, and to remind her to put socks on at night so that he might avoid her freezing feet. Dina felt sure she saw Raj's parents shift in their seats at that one.

The couple exchanged rings as Daniel and Brody, who had become legal officiants for the occasion, pronounced them husband and wife. Daniel then explained the significance of the breaking of the glass: first, its traditional interpretation as a reminder of the destruction of the temple in Jerusalem; second, as a symbol of the fragility of life and human relationships, advising the couple to enjoy every day as if it were their last together; and, finally, as a symbol of the breaking down of barriers between people of different cultures and faiths.

Raj broke the ceremonial glass and grabbed Rosie, and they kissed for what seemed like minutes. The crowd rose, shouted "Mazel Tov!" and applauded the couple. But, Dina thought, what they were all really applauding individually was the hope, the wish, and the dream of being in love. With all its imperfections . . . being in love.

Dina scanned the room of happy people, looking from Rob to Julia to John, then back at the couple now surrounded by friends and family. Tears streamed uncontrollably down her face as she felt her father's absence. All the effort and work raising and loving these children, parenting, and grandparenting them. To not see this, to never witness this moment of sheer joy, the promise of the next generation, was heartbreaking. Then she looked over at Julia, whose eyes met hers, similarly glassy. Julia's father, no . . . fathers, were missing too, along with her mother, Rosie's namesake. Dina wondered what the woman would have thought of this pairing, the need to accept with love the partners our children choose. Surely, she would have given her blessing.

Author's Note

Ten years ago, I found myself one of fifty or so "convention wives" propped up on pool lounges reading novels. It hasn't been that long since most of the spouses at these conferences were women. Who were they and what choices had they made along the way? Did they stay at home raising children, work outside the home, or had they figured out the magic balance between the two? If only I'd had the nerve to walk over to draw several into a sharing circle to garner some wisdom. Instead, I had an internal conversation, resulting in the outline of this novel.

The book was written in fits and starts depending on the pull of work, mothering, wifedom, and being a daughter to aging parents. I consider myself a true bagel of the sandwich generation, the hole representing the part of myself lost and now found along the way. I hope my children lead lives in which they can find fulfillment through work and creativity while meeting the needs of their loved ones. And when they struggle to find balance, which they inevitably will, may they rely on the support of family and friends.

I continuously marvel at the fortitude of women to live within the confines of the expectations and limitations imposed by the time and circumstances into which we are born. Regardless of how we maneuver through this maze, we are the glue. We drive history in ways that have often not made it into textbooks. The relationships we establish, the actions we take to improve the lives of our loved ones and society in general, in small steps and large, to sweeping effect, continue to astound me.

Acknowledgments

Profound thanks to my publisher Brooke Warner, project manager Samantha Strom, and copyeditor Jennifer Caven at She Writes Press, who kept this debut author marching along, and to Julie Metz and her talented team for the beautiful cover. My editor Brenda Copeland (The Editor's Shop) made a year of what could have been a slog a joy. My teacher at The Writer's Circle in Summit, New Jersey, Michelle Cameron, and classmate, now friend, Elizabeth Schlossberg provided constructive criticism that challenged and encouraged me.

Beta readers Laura Brass, Diane Bakst, Barbara Mitchell, Laura Queller, and Rebecca Rosenheck, and book club buddies Kathy Appel, Marcy Lazar, Debbie Livingston, Susan Schlisserman, Barb Simon, Lori Skoller, and Ellen Tripp supplied invaluable feedback (*who knew the singular of kreplach is krepl?*); and Westfield Shut Up and Write members (founders Stephanie Karp and Betsy Glavin Laskaris) were a warm and wonderful source of support. Jill Gorelick Miller and Elizabeth Schlossberg, friends who are graphic designers, provided informed input about cover design, and Jill designed the family trees. Thanks also to Susan Klugman, MD, Manisha Balwani, MD, and Lauren Siegel, RN who generously agreed to discuss Jewish genetic diseases with me when the novel was in early draft.

To my husband David, my soul mate who has patiently witnessed my numerous attempts at reinvention—were this a hundred years ago in some shtetl in Poland or on the streets of Berlin, I am convinced you would have been my match, my *shi- tach*. Thank you for seeing in me something I wasn't sure was truly there.

To our children Samantha, Zachary, and Jessica, who I love beyond measure, may you always have a sense of where you are going and, just as important, from whence you came.

About the Author

Debra Green has always been drawn to good storytelling, especially historical novels and Broadway musicals. While motherhood, hospital administration, and community volunteering were all rewarding, none fulfilled her creative longings. A graduate of Rutgers University and Columbia University's Mailman School of Public Health, she lives with her husband, David, in Scotch Plains, New Jersey where they raised their three children. When not writing, reading, or traveling, Debra can be found working in her ever-expanding vegetable garden. *The Convention of Wives* is her first novel.

Book Club Questions

Please note: To provide reading groups with the most informed and thought-provoking questions possible, it is necessary to reveal important aspects of the plot of this novel—as well as the ending. If you have not finished reading *The Convention of Wives*, we respectfully suggest that you may want to wait before reviewing this guide.

1. Dina and Julia both lose their sense of self while hoisting the banner of motherhood and wifedom. Have you experienced this sort of loss in your own life or witnessed someone do so? Did you or they mourn and move on or reinvent yourself or themselves? If so, how?

2. Both Dina and Julia's parents limited their educational and professional pursuits. How have expectations of and opportunities for women changed since the 1970s, just fifty short years ago? Why do you think Dina and Julia, who both had professional skills, become full-time stay-at-home moms?

3. Dina and Julia think their role as wives of physicians is more demanding than other married women. How are medical marriages similar to or different from other marriages in which a spouse has a consuming career (consider police and fire fighters)? Does the fact that medicine is a more lucrative profession make you think Dina and Julia are simply privileged whiners or are their struggles and frustrations justified?

The Convention of Wives

4. Was Miriam's ability to keep going after the pogrom, despite her significant losses (a child, her parents, her home), related at all to the period and circumstances in which she lived? If so, how? Do you think those of us living in comfortable situations in contemporary times have "gotten soft"?

5. Did you root for Miriam and Judah to wind up together? Are you or the women in your life still more attracted to men who can "take care" of them, or are women looking for equal partners both emotionally and otherwise?

6. How do you think Katherine felt when she landed in Barbados? How would you have felt if you were Katherine? Would you go halfway round the world, risking your life and the life of your child, to reunite with a husband?

7. Dina and Rob meet at work. How has the idea of meeting at work changed, especially considering the #MeToo movement?

8. Families keep secrets for lots of reasons. Has your family kept a secret? Has it been—or is it yet to be—revealed?

9. When Rob leaves Dina suddenly after going out to dinner at their favorite local restaurant, Dina starts her own small rebellion by drinking one of Rob's expensive wines. How would you deal with your spouse exiting with little explanation? Would you involve your adult children in the discord?

10. Are friendships like Allie and Raj's, between women and men, typical? Have you ever had a friendship like theirs, and if it ended, why?

11. Dina is proud of her daughter Allie's accomplishments as a doctor yet feels "left behind" by her daughter's success. Is there room within the concept of mothering for both feelings to occur simultaneously? Have you ever experienced these feelings?

12. Elsa and Michael meet under less than romantic circumstances. How can heightened emotions, positive and negative, lead to love? If so, why? Do you have examples within your own family history of such couplings? If so, what are they?

13. Was Dina justified in her feelings about Rob's mother Elsa moving in with them? Why does Elsa's background as a Holocaust survivor in part excuse or explain her behavior towards Rob and Dina?

14. What did Julia and Rob share in their backgrounds that brought them closer?

15. Why do you think Elsa waited to tell Rob and Dina about (Julia's mother) Rosie and (Rob's cousin) Rolph's relationship until Elsa was so ill in the hospital?

16. Rosie and Rolph fall in love at a time when a relationship like theirs— a Christian and a Jew—would not have been accepted by either of their families. How have things changed since that time? How have they remained the same?

17. How sympathetic are you to the characters of Dina and Julia at the beginning of the book, and have your feelings changed by the end? Who would you have chosen as a friend?

Resources

National Gaucher Foundation (NGF) serves US patients with Gaucher disease and their families through financial support, educational programming, patient services, and collaboration with medical professionals.

www.gaucherdisease.org

National Tay-Sachs & Allied Diseases Association (NTSAD) fights to treat and cure Tay-Sachs, Canavan, GM1, and Sandhoff diseases by driving research, forging collaboration, and fostering community.

https://ntsad.org

Jewish Genetic Disease Consortium (JGDC) unites genetic disease organizations to jointly strengthen public education and awareness about appropriate carrier screening.

www.jewishgeneticdiseases.org

JScreen is an at-home education and carrier screening program for Jewish genetic diseases.

www.jscreen.org

23andMe offers DNA testing with comprehensive ancestry breakdown, personalized health insights, and more.

www.23andMe.com

The Convention of Wives

Organizations that care for patients with genetic disorders, conduct research, and train experts in the field

The Center for Jewish Genetic Diseases at the Mount Sinai Health System
www.mountsinai.org/care/genetics

Montefiore Medical Center's Division of Reproductive Health
www.montefiore.org/womens-health-services-preconceptual-genetics-and-prenatal-genetic-testing

NYU Langone's Clinical Genetic Services
https://nyulangone.org/locations/clinical-genetic-services

Medical Genetics Institute at Cedars-Sinai
www.cedars-sinai.org/programs/medical-genetics.html

SELECTED TITLES FROM SHE WRITES PRESS

She Writes Press is an independent publishing company
founded to serve women writers everywhere.
Visit us at www.shewritespress.com.

Guesthouse for Ganesha by Judith Teitelman. $16.95, 978-1-63152-521-6. In 1923, seventeen-year-old Esther Grünspan arrives in Köln with a hardened heart as her sole luggage. Thus she begins a twenty-two-year journey, woven against the backdrops of the European Holocaust and the Hindu Kali Yuga (the "Age of Darkness" when human civilization degenerates spiritually), in search of a place of sanctuary.

All the Light There Was by Nancy Kricorian. $16.95, 978-1-63152-905-4. A lyrical, finely wrought tale of loyalty, love, and the many faces of resistance, told from the perspective of an Armenian girl living in Paris during the Nazi occupation of the 1940s.

Bess and Frima by Alice Rosenthal. $16.95, 978-1-63152-439-4. Bess and Frima, best friends from the Bronx, find romance at their summer jobs at Jewish vacation hotels in the Catskills—and as love mixes with war, politics, creative ambitions, and the mysteries of personality, they leave girlhood behind them.

Portrait of a Woman in White by Susan Winkler. $16.95, 978-1-93831-483-4. When the Nazis steal a Matisse portrait from the eccentric, art-loving Rosenswigs, the Parisian family is thrust into the tumult of war and separation, their fates intertwined with that of their beloved portrait.

Split-Level by Sande Boritz Berger. $16.95, 978-1-63152-555-1. For twenty-nine-year-old wife and mother Alex Pearl, the post-Nixon 1970s offer suburban pot parties, tie-dyed fashions, and the lure of the open marriage her husband wants for the two of them. Yearning for greater adventure and intimacy, yet fearful of losing it all, Alex must determine the truth of love and fidelity—at a pivotal point in an American marriage.

An Address in Amsterdam by Mary Dingee Fillmore. $16.95, 978-1-63152-133-1. After facing relentless danger and escalating raids for 18 months, Rachel Klein—a well-behaved young Jewish woman who transformed herself into a courier for the underground when the Nazis invaded her country—persuades her parents to hide with her in a dank basement, where much is revealed.